# Walter

## ✠ and the ✠

# Resurrection of G

A mysterious & dramatic novel in which the
medieval world confronts our own

✠

THE COMPLETE WORKS OF G

Volume I

# Walter ✠ and the ✠ Resurrection of G

A mysterious & dramatic novel in which the
medieval world confronts our own

✠

THE COMPLETE WORKS OF G

Volume I

**IGNSIA**
CIRENCESTER

## IGNSIA BOOKS

1A The Wool Market Dyer Street Cirencester Gloucestershire GL7 2PR
An imprint of Memoirs Publishing www.mereobooks.com

WALTER AND THE RESURRECTION OF G: 978-1-86151-539-1

First published in Great Britain in 1995 by Headline Book Publishing

The address for Memoirs Publishing Group Limited can be found at
www.memoirspublishing.com

The Memoirs Publishing Group Ltd Reg. No. 7834348

The Memoirs Publishing Group supports both The Forest Stewardship Council® (FSC®) and the
PEFC® leading international forest-certification organisations. Our books carrying both the FSC
label and the PEFC® and are printed on FSC®-certified paper. FSC® is the only
forest-certification scheme supported by the leading environmental organisations including
Greenpeace. Our paper procurement policy can be found at
www.memoirspublishing.com/environment

Typeset in 10.5/13pt Bembo
by Wiltshire Associates Publisher Services Ltd. Printed and bound in Great Britain by
Printondemand-Worldwide, Peterborough PE2 6XD

# FOREWORD
# BY IAN MOTHING

✛

All my attempts at writing an introduction have failed. There are so many doubts about the following text that it seems best just to let it speak for itself. If G did write it, I am not sure when or how. It would probably have been in his younger days, maybe when he was working on his much-praised *Phenomenologies of the Middle Ages*. The dream passages could be seen in terms of an extension of the work he was doing at that time. But this is something readers will have to judge for themselves.

In Appendix 1, I explain the circumstances in which the text came to light. Appendix 2 consists of a series of poems, more probably G's, which are related to the text.

# Walter

## INTRODUCTION

✠

## The Fool

*De plusurs choses a remembrer li prist...*[*]
(Song of Roland I.2377)

Since I met you in the harbour at Kyrenia, Philippos, when you asked me if I knew the art of transforming matter, and if you could share in my learning, I have taught you many things – about music and singing, true arithmetic, the writings of the ancients and their philosophy. I have even explained enough of the secret charts for you to be able to work out the rest for yourself, especially in the context of what you are about to read. Since I am old, and it will probably not be long before I leave this world, and since you yourself asked me about how I came to be here, I wish to set down another lesson for you, based on writings I made in my youth.

You do not know how much I am still haunted by my distant past, by the days before I came here. Over and over I relive scenes, some I witnessed first-hand, others at which I was not present. Just

*[*]He began to remember many things...*

1

now for example I closed my eyes and saw a horse wandering through the Lonzer forest, near my home town in Germany. The horse was dragging a dead man whose foot was caught in the stirrup. The ground had scratched the dead man's face featureless.

They said it looked like a lump of meat. Then again I smell the burning of human flesh beneath drizzle. Or else it is as though I am no longer here, but with Hildegunde once more, that autumn day at the castle at Frankenburc.

If I am to make sense of it all for you, I must start at the beginning.

I was born in Nurenberc, in the year of our Lord 1171. I close my eyes again and I see the linden tree, spreading its branches; I see its leaves, which sprouted year after year; I see its blossoms, which were blown away summer after summer; I see its branches stripped bare each autumn by the harsh wind and rain, yet still brooding, like a familiar spirit, arching over the wooden house where I was brought up.

It is night-time. A nightingale is singing in the old tree's branches. Its leaves shine gold as Venus descends. Mars shines red in the blue-black sky, low amidst the town-tops, and a silvery crescent moon rises through Sagittarius somewhere behind the distant church spire. The stars seem to spin in the silence.

In my dream my father's face mutates in the fires of my memory, becoming the face of old Uqhart, wizened, uncannily yellow, flamelit, superimposed over my childhood memories of Nurenberc. I hear the old man's voice. 'Sulphur and Quicksilver. Solve et Coagule.' I see every detail of the streets, the wooden houses, the churches, the castle and towers of the city, huddled in the deep blue of the night.

Then the nightingale falls silent and a scream pierces the stillness. I am in my parents' reed-strewn house. The mother I never knew, her ghostly angel's face streamed with tears, half smiles as she weeps for the joy and pain of childbirth. My father looks on, helpless, responsible. Silvery shadows fall on the blood-spattered baby.

The umbilical cord is cut. Umbilical cord - umbilical chord. The cutting of the harmony of the music of Eternity before birth. The first dissonance. In turn, my mother and father rock me, the baby, in their arms, and my mother puts me to her breast.

Then I see old Uqhart the Jew, my father's friend, and a priest, from the Benedictine Abbey, wearing his black habit, entering my parents' room. Uqhart brings herbs. The priest is carrying the unctions of the last rites, in case baby or mother die.

My father points to me. He smiles. I am healthy. So is my mother. Thus far. The priest nods and crosses himself. Uqhart leaves an earthenware jug on the table. It contains an infusion of Saint John's wort, oak leaves, fern seed and mistleberry mixed with warm, fresh milk. This is for my mother to drink.

Then there are the rituals which follow birth. While the men look on, the midwife, my mother's friend, takes me. I am washed in a tub of warm water. My fingers and limbs are worked to drive off evil humours. Then I am laid on a bed of rose-leaves mashed with salt. My palate and gums are wiped by the midwife's honey-soaked finger. Then the priest intones the words of the exorcism before I am wound in swaddling clothes.

I have often wondered if he failed to perform this office correctly, and if this is what led to all my troubles.

Next in my mind's eye I see a light, glowing brilliantly, almost burning. It is the light of the spring dawn. All the birds are singing. My father is no longer able to sleep. He leaves his bed, walking on tiptoe, drifting, a ghost of himself as he smiles at the mother and child who are fast asleep. Silently, he leaves the wooden house just as the dawn light is turning from pink to gold. He makes his way over the hard, red, dewy earth of the streets, through the cool of the morning air.

There are the familiar sights of my childhood: trees, leaves, pebbles, the slit windows of the crooked timber and wattle houses, every blade of grass. Sparrows and finches dart from treetop to treetop and blossom gleams brilliant and white against the pink and golden puffs of cloud.

Then there is darkness – the Lady Chapel – my father kneeling in prayer. The vaulted arches are still haunted by ghosts and shadows of night-time, remembered pain. Only a narrow, golden shaft of sunlight illumines the sad face of the wooden Madonna. The sun rises. Slowly the chapel is filled with light, shadows are dispelled and the air throngs with hosts of saintly faces, bodiless powers of heaven, angels hovering, almost visible. Even the solemn Madonna smiles at the birth of the cartwright's son.

The bodiless powers of heaven? Perhaps it is through them that I dream these things. Perhaps the same angels are present here angels who are outside time, for whom the past is eternally present. Perhaps their knowledge is being shared with me.

My father enters the house of Uqhart the Jew, the herbalist; unearthly symbols, crescent moons, circles, crosses, charts, parchments, crucibles, bottles, herb pots, rich scents, dust, timber, the bronze bell on the oak table, all the things I was one day to grow to love. Before they burnt him.

Uqhart is waiting. My papa offers him silver, fear in the air, fear of the old man, fear of knowledge. Uqhart speaks: 'Silver, a strange price for God's herbs. Then may your son, like the moon, reflect the light of God.'

I know the words of this blessing by heart, though my father told them to me only once.

My father told me the story of what happened next, though it is as if I were there. When he returned from Uqhart's house he heard shouting.

'Lickspiggot, Priest of Satan, Whoreswhelp! Give me my money back or I'll report you to the church authorities.' A brawl between two workmen: Josephus, a priest defrocked for his association with a heretical sect, and Wolfgar, a peasant who, my father said, loved to work with his hands in the workshops and was too proud ever to return to the land. But he was given to drink. He was the one who was yelling, and there was no doubt that he had started the brawl.

My father shouted at them to get out of the yard. My father was a tall, strong man. Everyone who knew him respected him. In a rage he was fearsome. It is extraordinary that he should have died the way he did, by his own hand. But that was later, and first I must deal with this mystery.

The peasant and the ex-priest Josephus rushed out into the street. But the peasant picked up an iron rod from the ground and pursued Josephus with it. Josephus picked up a hammer. The peasant took a swing at the ex-priest. But Josephus ducked and then, as he rose, brought the hammer round in an arc towards the peasant's head. Maybe he was expecting him to get out of the way. Probably he just wanted to frighten him.

But the peasant did nothing to avert the blow.

I saw his large, ox-like face staring wildly, bewildered, forgetting to duck, as if the death-blow were inevitable, fated. It is a look I have seen countless times in brawls and battles. It is as if the victims will their own death. There was a moment of stillness and silence, then blood, screaming, and the peasant was lying on the ground, motionless.

My father started the hue and cry. The ex-priest did not run. He allowed himself to be taken by the men who came. Then he went calmly with them to the castle.

I wonder how my father must have felt as he returned home - excited, on edge, maybe anxious to see his son, to talk with his wife, to tell her of this adventure, the fight and the killing. Yet something more horrible than the murder he had seen was to greet him.

The priest was waiting for my father. He was holding me in his arms.

My mother had died an hour previously.

I see a deathly white face, the face of a dead angel, and then I see the grotesque image of a child suckling a corpse's nipple, cold, acrid with the stench of death and of this world, mingling with the taste of filth and fever in my own mouth.

# I

## The Magus

✠

Whenever I think of Heaven, of Eternity, and wonder what it must be like, I see myself as a small child in a forest. It is a real forest, and it is a forest of symbols. There is a great sense of security, the light is always a rich, golden green. Yet how I came to be there is a mystery, the result of an event which, like so much else, marks my life off from the normal lives of most people.

It happened during a day late in the spring of the year of Lord 1176, a year before I was to go to school, when my father taking me to the guildhouse. I was staring up at the faces, the blue sky above them. I remember the potent smells of the town. Then suddenly, there was shouting, jostling and panic as a rider on a large black horse, a man who had a wild beard and wore strange clothes, forced his way through the crowds. Massive hands reached down, gripped me, and pulled me up on to the horse. My father shouted, but it was too late. We were galloping off at full speed, out of the central square in front of the church, round the back of the guildhouse, through the narrow streets, knocking people out of our way, through the town gates before anyone had a chance to stop us, then out through the peasants' fields and into the woods beyond, through villages, forests and fields, further away than I had ever been in my life.

Then there was the smoky log cabin, summer forest smells, the birds, the fear.

The first few days I just wept. I suppose I must have called out for my father. I refused food. Yet at night I slept long and well in the straw bed. My captors, the man with the long beard who had taken me on his horse and the young woman who was his wife or concubine, both spoke kindly to me.

There were two rooms in the hut, or rather there was one room with a rough divide between them. The small area on the far side of the partition was where I slept. The main room was where we were to eat, and where the couple bedded down for the night. There was no furniture apart from the simple bed.

Throughout the time I was there I remember that there were strange men coming and going all hours of the day and night, men with knives, bows slung over their shoulders, axes. I had heard the story of Saint Nicholas and the three orphans. At first I was sure that I would be chopped up into tiny pieces, burned alive, or cooked in a pie. Yet the people were kind to me. Somehow I knew that I could trust them. Perhaps children are better than adults at telling malice from kindness. I drank a little milk, nibbled at the stale crusts and the cheese placed before me. I even ate some pieces of meat. My mood became calmer. Something inside me began to see that this was an adventure, and this made it more bearable.

At last, one evening when the sun was setting behind the silhouetted trees, I remember the woman putting her arm round me and asking, 'Are you happy, here in the forest?'

I summoned up the courage to say what was on my mind. 'I am. But who are you? Where is my daddy?'

'Your daddy is safe and well. No need to worry.'

'But who are you?'

'Oh, you ought to know. We cannot go into the town. We are *vogelfrei*, free as birds.'

I did not know then that this expression meant outlaw. Instead, perhaps because of the cloaks which the man and the woman both wore, I thought that they must be bird people. I thought that perhaps I had been captured by strange spirits of the woods which I had heard people speak about.

I turned to the young woman for comfort. I had never had a mother of my own. I still remember the softness and the special smell of her. She seemed kinder and more understanding than ever my father or any of my nannies had been. I was still scared of them really, but my confidence grew. I came to trust them more and more and to feel that perhaps, after all, I would come to no harm.

At last I asked one day, 'Are you going to chop me up and cook me or bury me alive?'

This seemed to amuse the man, though the woman was horrified. She said, 'You will be safe. We love you. We'll look after you.'

The bearded man stayed out most of the day, but the young woman was there all the time, preparing food, sewing, or sitting outside watching me as I played. I remember a song she used to sing, which also made me think they were bird people:

*Ich zoch mir einen valken mere danne ein jar.*
*do ich in gezamete als ich in wolte han*
*und ich im sin gevidere mit golde wol bewant*
*er huop sich uf vil hohe und fluog in anderiu lant.★*

Sometimes I went for long walks, hand in hand with the woman. There were also days when I would ride out with the man on his horse. I came to enjoy the speed, the trees of the forest rushing by me. He and his friends taught me how to climb trees and shoot arrows, throw small spears. Sometimes they even took me hunting and trapping. The man taught me the names of the birds and the trees, and the flowers of the forest. I am sure it was because of this that I developed a taste for physical adventure, for sports and the things of war.

---

*★I kept and trained a falcon for more than a year.*
*When I had tamed him fully to eat out of my hand*
*All decked out all his plumage with the best golden gear*
*He rose up high above me and flew to another land.*

The adventure ended as suddenly and as inexplicably as it had begun. One summer morning, just as the sun was rising, the bearded man came in. He was smiling in a sad, different way, and I felt that he was nervous, unsure. After hesitating for a while, he told me that he was going to take me home. I remember the young woman kissing me, and I remember that there were tears in her eyes as she begged the man to take care.

We rode throughout the morning. Every now and again I looked up at the man. His face was very still. He said nothing. So I looked straight ahead and enjoyed the rhythmic plodding of the horse. We rode more slowly than usual, almost at a walking pace. The yellow corn was ripe for harvest in the fields beyond the forests. The sky was a bright, shimmering blue and the September sun was rich and yellow. I remember the smell of trees, forests, wayside flowers, wheat, animals.

As we rode on, the man's mood seemed to lighten. He talked in the way that I was used to hearing him talk. 'Look,' he said, 'there is the church of Saint Barnabas. Do you see that church there? They are building it out of stone. There must be some rich men in that village. Do you know what that plant is? That's right, foxglove.'

Everything he told me about - villages, houses, plants, animals - I repeated back to him, almost religiously. Did I sense it would be for the last time? I looked around me and then down at the rough, gnarled and hairy hand which held me firmly about my middle. I remember thinking that this was the hand of a Saint Nicholas and not the hand of a butcher.

We rode all day long, stopping now and again to eat some of the crusts and the game which the young woman had prepared for us, and to drink from the flagon or to refill it when we saw a stream where the water was good. The man sang to me, a sad song about the trees and the forests. I can remember neither the words nor the melody. It must have been a folk-song from his own village in the East. I can remember the atmosphere and the sound of the man's voice, however. I always hoped that one day, by chance, I might hear someone singing this song, that I would recognise it straight away, and that I would learn it for myself.

Just as the sun set, the towers and rooftops of Nurenberc came into sight, silhouetted on the distant horizon, jagged and foreboding against the gold and deep green-blue of the evening sky.

'Do you know where we are?' asked the man. 'Look over there, that town, Nurenberc, the end of our journey.'

We stopped in a copse not far from the city gates, but well out of sight of the guards or any travellers who might be passing through. There we sat together and ate the last of our food. The man explained that he wanted to wait until it was completely dark before entering the city.

Slowly the last traces of daylight faded. Darkness fell. There was only a half moon, but the stars were bright and it was possible to see. As soon as he thought that all the people of Nurenberc, apart from the watchmen, would be asleep, the man lifted me up high in the air, staring at me for a moment, smiling, putting me back down and then kissing me on the cheek. Then his face set in determination. He lifted me on to the horse and we galloped at breakneck speed over to the earth road that led to the city gates, into the town and past the watchman, who shouted something as we flew through the eerie, deserted streets. It was too late for them to stop us. I remember the familiar town smells as we galloped past the guildhouse, the churches and the sleeping houses. I was almost flung down outside the door of my house, and left there.

I shouted, panic-stricken, confused, not knowing what would become of me. But the man had already gone, leaving me alone to cry in the dark outside my father's house.

At last I heard movement and a face appeared from inside. It was my father. At first he did not recognise me and only snarled. In a gruff voice he told me to go away. He said he did not want any filthy beggars round his house at this time of night. For a terrifying moment I thought that he would just leave me there. I wept. Then he rushed down the stairs, embracing me and taking me inside.

In spite of my father's impatient questioning, I did not want to talk about where I had been and what I had been doing. This would have been a betrayal.

Soldiers came the next day. They quizzed me about the man, what he looked like. But I said nothing. I was frightened. One of them threatened to hit me if I did not speak, but that made me even more determined. Eventually they gave up and left the house.

When they went my father persisted in quizzing me, but I hated him for it. For a few days I became sullen, withdrawn, refused my food. I felt as though I was torn between two worlds, the world of the forest and the world of my home. I wanted to be true to both, but I knew that this would not be possible. Silence was my only refuge.

A week or so later my father led me to the high road, just outside the town, where the gallows were. A large crowd had gathered; rough people pushed and shouted horrible words, 'Murderer, child thief, priest of damnation!' And I saw the bearded man led out to the tree by the soldiers. At the sight of him the crowd grew quieter. There was a dignity in the way he bore himself. I thought for a brief moment that I caught his eye. I tried to look away. I thought that I would not be able to bear the sight, but something made me stare. Under the tree the man knelt and seemed to pray. I saw his lips move. He did not seem to have been hurt, so I can believe what I was told later, that they treated him well. I have seen men and women so tortured, broken and destroyed before being hanged that to hang them seemed a waste of time and rope. Moreover, he was not mocked and taunted as many are in the moments before their deaths. There was something about this man's presence that made everyone respect him.

There was silence as the noose was put round his neck. As the rope was pulled and he rose upwards, towards the branch of the tree, for a few seconds his legs, which were not tied, beat frantically in a running movement, as if in death he were running towards some kind of freedom, back to the forest maybe. There was a crack as his neck broke. His tongue hung out and his eyes stared wildly at the crowd, as if he were gloating over us because of some secret knowledge he possessed.

After all that has happened since, I can only conclude that he did possess secret knowledge, and that was why he had to die. But what was it? Was it about me? Later there was that meeting with Stefanus. He knew. He must have known. Was it something to do with the Brotherhood?

Not long after this, my father remarried. I hated his new wife, Erna. She was fat, lazy and sulky. Perhaps I was just jealous. Yet Papa seemed to tire of her and to pay more attention to me. Every evening, he used to teach me how to read the letters in the prayer book that my mother had used at the convent when she was a girl, and which she had taken with her when she ran away. We would read the same prayer over and over together, and then he would help me copy it on to the wax tablet he had made for me.

I remember that day when I was lying in bed with a mild fever. My father called for Uqhart, who arrived with his rosehip and camomile. In the past I had been frightened of the old man's white hair, bright, fiery eyes and Old Testament prophet's beard. Yet today I had my slate and stylus with me. I wanted to show off.

Uqhart asked me if I had learnt to read and write. I took the slate and wrote the word *scribo*, 'I am writing'. Smiling, he in turn took the slate and wrote *scripsisti*, 'you have written'. I was spellbound. Then Uqhart told me how he had come from a place near the edge of the world, called Toledo, where many people read and wrote all day long.

We carried on talking. I recited fragments of the psalms and prayers that my father had taught me. I listened entranced to Uqhart's stories of the far-off, foreign town, where there were big houses called libraries, filled with books and parchments in many different languages. He told me he knew Greek, Latin, Hebrew, Aramaic, Chaldean and Arabic, and that he had studied the arts of medicine and herbalism, and other subjects that were sealed as secrets.

After an hour or two, Papa returned from the workshops, fearing that the fever must have taken a turn for the worse since Uqhart had not yet reported back to him. Yet he found me recovered, talking with animation, brandishing the stylus and the tablet. Uqhart praised me, saying that such learning in one so young was very rare.

I have often heard it said that writing has magical properties, that it can cure afflictions. I have also seen illustrations of the sword of the Grail that deliberately made the sword look like a stylus. Certainly, for some of us, writing is the only way we can be ourselves. I have also noticed that, whenever I dream certain dreams of my mother, she appears surrounded by letters and symbols. At one time I used to think that reading and writing brought us closer to God and that was why it had healing qualities.

I remember standing, guiltily, behind the door when Uqhart talked to my father.

'Your son is gifted,' the old man said. 'I will happily teach him, if you will allow me. Learning would not be wasted on him.'

My father hesitated.

'I do not mean for profit,' Uqhart said. 'I would ask no money in return.'

'Why would you want to do such a thing then?' my father asked. He was suspicious of the Jew, but polite enough to do his best to hide it.

Uqhart hesitated for just too long, long enough to make me suspicious too. Eventually his reply came. 'For the love of learning,' he said.

For years I wondered whether Uqhart made this gesture out of the goodness of his heart, because he was fond of me, or whether there was some other reason.

I am sure that Papa had much respect for him. I think that Papa was the sort of man who could recognise the particular quality present in those who can read and write. Perhaps he saw in Uqhart the same light of learning that he had seen in my mother, and this is what drew him to the old man. Yet Uqhart was a Jew. And for his eldest son to be taught by a Jew would have been too shameful.

I never remember my father lying, other than that one day. I suppose he lied to spare the old man's feelings. 'I welcome your offer,' he said. 'But in fact I have already spoken to one of the monks from the Benedictine Abbey and hired a young monk to teach my son.'

Uqhart said he understood. When the herbalist left, I asked Papa when the monk would be coming. Papa said nothing. He strode away. He was a man of his word and would be true to it.

Two days later a brother Aloysius came to the house. He wore the black habit of the Benedictines, tied at the front with a new, white cord. He was not a tall man. His hair was closely shaven, his chin was narrow and jutted out so that it seemed odd in contrast with the top part of his head, which was large and round. His complexion was pure, his skin glowing with a fresh, pinkish colour.

After our conversation Papa had gone directly to the Benedictine Abbey in the centre of the town. He had offered the Abbot money if one of the brothers would undertake to come and teach me reading, writing and Latin. The Abbot recommended brother Aloysius. He told my father that the novice was very learned, but excessive in his devotions. He told my father that a tutoring Job would help plant the brother's feet more firmly on the ground. Papa told me all about this at a later time, when I was studying at Babenberch.

I took to brother Aloysius from the moment I saw him. What I remember most was his stillness. He had a smile that betrayed a knowledge of the Higher World, the world of God and the angels I saw in my visions, or so I thought at the time.

He came three times a week to teach me prayers and psalms, first by rote, then, once I could recite them, he would explain their grammatical structures, why words had such and such an ending, and so on. When I had learnt and understood a text thoroughly, so that I could read it both aloud and silently, without moving my lips, it was time for the lesson I loved most. Aloysius would take his wax tablet and write out the neumes of the chant that went with the text. Then we would spend a morning learning the music together, sometimes indoors, but when the weather was fine, out in the yard beneath the linden tree. During these lessons a special stillness and warmth fell around us. It was the same stillness I had felt when I prayed, the stillness I thought I had seen in my mother's face.

I came to love this stillness and thought it must come from the power of the music, expressed in the shapes of the neumes, which in turn must proceed from the angels and from God Himself.

Aloysius explained to me that the world is just six thousand years old. He said wise men were of the opinion that the world would soon end, the Last Emperor would come, then the Antichrist, and then the Last Judgement. The Psalmist said that a thousand years to God is like a day, and since the work of Creation is to last seven days, surely the Last Age, the Age of the Sabbath, was about to dawn. The thought terrified me. I was haunted and tormented by passages like those at the end of the Book of Isaiah, which talked of the flames of hell consuming the souls of the damned, whose worms never die.

One day I saw a vision of hell that still terrifies me, for it is a recurring vision. I see the souls of the damned all red and stripped of skin, tender, naked, parched and helpless. I feel the pain caused by the searing flames of the Lake of Fire. And all the while they are suffering, the poor people can never sleep, never forget where they are and why. All their sins are constantly before them, yet it is too late for them to repent, and they know they will be there for ever. Even if they try to weep, the pain merely increases. They can see their fellows but cannot talk to them. There is no comfort for them, nor will there ever be. If I were God I would save, save, save even the worst offenders from such torment. How could anyone feel joy in heaven knowing others were in such agony?

As for the Devil himself, I feared that he might appear any moment. I used to imagine him sometimes as a vile creature with horns, cloven hooves and a tail, grinning and mocking like a man but smelling like the foulest beast, like I had seen on the column of the church of Saint Margaret in Nurenberc. Then sometimes I would see the devil as a person of great beauty, set on seducing me from the true path.

In another vision I saw Saint John. He had a long, flowing, dark brown beard and piercing eyes like amethysts. He told me that I must become a priest of the Most High. This too has haunted me and caused me suffering. I could easily have become a priest. I could have settled anywhere and learnt from a parish priest as an apprentice. I could have persisted in the monastic life. Yet something always stood in my way – ambition, pride, circumstances. There is no point in my trying to justify myself. I knew that I should have left the world and, naked, followed the naked Christ to the Cross.

The lessons with Aloysius went on for over a year. Soon I knew much more about reading and writing than Papa. Perhaps this made him sad. Sometimes when I recited to him he would become moody. Maybe he was jealous of me. Maybe he would have liked to study, but he was too busy with his work.

Then one day early in the summer of the year of our Lord 1179 – the year when Hildegard of Bingen died, the year when our Emperor exiled Henry the Lion to England – Aloysius arrived with a letter from his Abbot. In it the Abbot suggested that I should be sent to the cathedral school at Babenberch. He wrote that his monastery would be glad to pay the fees, for it was considered that I was a clever young man and that such an education would not be wasted on me.

At first Papa scoffed at the idea. How could a cartwright's son be admitted to the famous cathedral school of Babenberch, where the sons of the nobility and ministerials went to study, a school run by the Bishop Ebehard, who had moderated between Pope and Emperor on more than one occasion? What good would it do me anyway, to receive an education that was for those far above the station of the cartwright I was destined to become?

Aloysius took my father aside. He told him that it was not unprecedented for the talented son of a wealthy and respected man, such as my father, to go to the Babenberch school; besides, my father should think of the prestige, of the future, of the respect that his son would command as a man of learning, the fine renown it would bring to his firm.

It is possible that Aloysius was under the sway of the Brotherhood, but I rather think that he was secretly hoping to make a monk and a mystic of me. Of course he mentioned nothing of his spiritual project to my father. My father was a man of religion. He had the greatest reverence for the saints of our Lord. Yet he was at one with his station as a tradesman and proud that he was free, bound to no one, to no Lord but God.

In spite of all this he allowed himself to be won round by Aloysius' arguments. When he talked to my stepmother about the matter, her eyes lit up. She was probably pleased at the thought of being rid of me. Eventually he went to talk to the Abbot. Soon the matter was settled and my departure arranged.

Just three months later I took my leave of the house, the work yard, the linden tree, my stepmother and my baby halfbrother Marcus, who I felt was usurping my place in the family. My father and I set off together in a fine new wagon. At last, after five long days' travelling, through forests, fields and tiny hamlets, over plains, through vineyards, up and down rolling hills, my education at Babenberch Cathedral School was to begin.

The atmospheres and the textures of my first day at school are a tangible presence in my mind: cloisters, towers and bells, other boys, huddled in their cloaks, newly arrived like me, holding fathers' hands, walking endlessly, on and on over the courtyard, kicking their feet through the russet brown autumn leaves while autumn clouds raced low over the treetops and roofs. I looked up at the patch of gold in the sky where the sun was trying in vain to break through. I held on tight to my father's hand for fear of being lost in the crowd, and bowed my head into the wind and drizzle.

I remember walking along a narrow lane leading out into the square. Papa was chatting with one of the other fathers, a wool merchant from Babenberch. Suddenly, breathtakingly, as we turned the corner into the market square, there loomed before us the largest and most magnificent building I had ever seen. I squeezed my father's hand and pointed. He explained that this was the cathedral, and that it was here I was to live and study.

I was filled with awe. We drifted slowly on and on with the crowd towards the great door that led into the cathedral and the darkness.

Once inside the cathedral I could just make out, in the soft yellow candlelight shining from the choir and the altar, strange but lovely wall-paintings, flowers and saints and angels, disembodied and seeming to hover in the incensed air. Every now and again I would see the faces of ugly demons, sculpted into the walls and arches, to show what evil spiritual presences were banished from this place. I remembered the words of the psalm: '*Terribilis est locus iste. Vere est aula Dei et porta coeli.*'★

[★'This is a place fills all with awe. Truly it is the house of God and the door to Heaven.']

The cathedral made me think of a mighty ship, sailing through the waters of mystery, with Christ as its Captain, its huge walls and windows pointing up towards the heavens. Then it made me think of a great forest, with its own scents and light and shade. The rose-window was like the sun that would shine in the New Jerusalem. I looked up at my father's face, solemn and prayerful, as if glowing in the candlelight.

After the office, I remember waiting in line in the Great Hall for a monk to write my name in the massive book of admissions. I stared at the flames and smoke of the log fire down at the other end of the hall. Papa wrote in the book: *Adam Ouwe inscribes his son Walter-1179.* Then this was countersigned with the word '*matriculat*' by the attending monk.

We were shown round. First came the library; I had never seen so many books and papers. Then there were the schoolrooms, cold, airless and bleak in the dull light of the late-autumn afternoon. I looked with fear at the rows of hard benches where boys in the past had sat hour after hour, day after day. Then we went to the dormitories. Endless flights of rickety stairs had to be climbed, till we reached the long, bleak, raftered attics, where there were some hard wooden beds, benches built into the walls, and acres of floor strewn with rough mattresses of stale straw. The few proper beds were reserved for the older boys. The brother showed me my place, in the corner under a draughty window. My father and I were silent, though we smiled and nodded politely.

We went back down the stairs to the courtyard, and the time came for us to part. I remember, after my father kissed me, watching him as he strolled off, sadly, hands clasped firmly behind his back. I stood silent, trying to choke back tears, until an older monk came along, told me to dry my eyes, to be brave. He put a hand on my shoulder and led me off to the refectory, to the old oak benches and tables where the vegetable soup and crusts were waiting. I did not say a word to the other boys, who were just as frightened as I was. Then I followed the crowd to compline, and at last to the dormitories, where I tried to sleep on the uneven, prickly straw mattress.

That night a vision came.

The other boys were asleep. Beyond the narrow window, the sky was an eerie, silvery dark blue because of the full moon. I alone lay awake, unable to sleep. I tried to pray, to God and the saints and angels, to ask for protection. Then there was a gold glimmering in the air. I thought of the others who were spending their first night here. I thought of those who had slept their first night here in the past and those who would do so in the future: those who were asleep now, who had slept, who would sleep. I could sense something of them, the boys from the past and from the future. It was as if I could see their faces without seeing them, as if I could talk to them, though some were as yet unborn, some were grown, some nowhere now, dead. Even in those who were dead I was aware of a stillness that had nothing to do with the heaven I wanted to believe in or the hell I so much feared.

Instead, it was as if we were all in a great forest, in a great procession moving slowly towards a light that was glowing, like a fountain of many colours, somewhere beyond the horizon. There was a strange scent in the air, a mixture of a damp woody smell and of incense. The trees all had a human presence, as if their branches were arms and their boughs were faces. There was music, which came from the fountain yet which was part of the trees and the forest also. We could not actually see the fountain, which we knew to be greater than the tallest building, like a cloud reaching up to heaven, yet we could sense it, and all of us knew where it was and that we were moving towards it.

I told this dream, but the monks said that dreams should be ignored, since it is very hard to tell whether they are of God or of the devil.

After that first day, individual memories blur into a swirl of days ruled by bells, lessons, the rounds of prayer - matins, lauds, vespers and compline - masses on Sundays and feast-days, and long lessons with the black-hooded monks: followed by endless hours of study, learning by heart Latin texts and grammar rules, studying Guido of Arrezzo's musical notation, and prayer texts; moments of play with new friends in the cloisters; the meatless meals twice a day in the old refectory (since meat was permitted only on certain feast days), the one log fire burning summer and winter, smoke from it curling upwards between the cauldrons of soup and vegetable stews; the long nights half asleep, half awake on the straw, dreaming of my studies, candles and incense, grammar and music, saints, angels and devils, hell and heaven, and of home.

The prayers and chants I had learnt with brother Aloysius were to be relearnt here. The monks would sing melodies over and over until finally the boys remembered the tune. This was laborious for the monks, especially if they were working with boys who were not musical or who did not understand Guido's music-writing system. So the fact that I knew many chants already and picked up new ones quickly impressed the monks who taught me. Also, my voice was stronger than most of the other boys'. Soon I could sing both by sight from the neumes as well as from memory, and had mastered the mnemonic techniques of associating different musical notes with different parts of the hand. Also I had little difficulty with the grammar or the texts we had to study. It was not long before my reputation was established as one of the brighter young pupils. I was taken aside, encouraged and shown many favours by some of my masters. This was a source of great pride to me.

One day I was summoned by the Abbot Wilfridus. There was another man in the room with him. Even then there was something uncanny about the way he studied me, the way he remained completely silent throughout the interview. Now I am certain that it was the Abbot Quintus from Frankenburc, who was later to play such an important role in my life. Anyhow, this is what Wilfridus said to me: 'If you continue to work and to understand as you have done so far, one day you will have to make a hard choice between serving God and serving men. Which will you choose?'

'I don't know,' I answered. 'Is it not possible to do both, to serve God by serving man, and to serve man by serving God?' I was speaking to impress, yet as I spoke the vision of Saint John returned to my mind, as if to rebuke me.

'You answer like a scholastic from Paris,' he said. 'If you speak like that there is no doubt that you will appear to do both extremely well. Yet you have obviously not understood the question, you are too young.' I remember it hurting me that he said this. But he went on, 'I have called you to let you know that the elementary stage of your education is over, and it is time for you to go on to the study of the liberal arts. You will begin directly after the autumn vacation. Be diligent and you will do well.'

I liked Wilfridus. He was a kind old man, who had such natural dignity that he never needed to shout or lose his temper like some of the monks. We were all sad when we learnt of his death, just a week or so after we returned from the harvest holidays.

During that harvest holiday back at Nurenberc something happened to me, something I shall never forget. As was customary for town boys, I had gone off with a group to join in with the work of the peasants as they harvested their fields. It had been a hard day's work, yet I was growing strong and I enjoyed the physical exertion. I was dragging my feet with tiredness, staring at the sun setting over Nurenberc, which was silhouetted on the horizon, singing to myself some of the chants I had learnt at school. I was walking along the edge of a field by the side of a wood. Somehow I had become separated from the other town boys. I began singing aloud, quietly at first, but then louder and louder.

A sense of peace settled over me. It was a familiar feeling, which I associated with being in church and with singing sacred music, and with dreams of my dead mother. As I went further, however, the peace gradually changed into a wild elation, ecstasy. I was no longer just walking towards the sunset, because the sunset was all there was in the universe, and this sunset was somehow part of what I was singing. I felt that my whole face was burning and I noticed also that I was no longer singing in Latin, or even in German, but in some other language. I tried to analyse the words I was mouthing to myself, but I was unable to. All I could do was enjoy the sound of them.

For a few moments I lost myself completely. The thought occurred to me that maybe I was in heaven, or that I was being given a glimpse of what life in heaven would be like. Yet the moment I questioned what was happening, the feeling left me.

I tried again to analyse the words coming out of my mouth. What was I saying? Was it all childhood gibberish or was there more to it? I had read in Paul about the gift of tongues, of what it was to talk in the tongues of angels. Were angels speaking, singing through me? If so, why did I not understand what the angels were saying?

Or was this a sign that devils possessed me?

A chill ran through me. If it was the Holy Ghost speaking, how could I be so depraved as not to know this? Surely I was damned. Or if they were devils, how could I be so depraved as to think it might be the Holy Ghost? What was happening to me? How could I not know? Was I to be damned? Was this the sin against the Holy Ghost, not to know what the sin against the Holy Ghost was? Or was I being given a vision of heaven so that, when I reached my preordained place in hell, the pain of being there would be the greater?

As I walked further my mood veered from elation to despair. I began shaking. Then I looked round, fearing that I might be seen in this state. No one was there, but all the same I turned off the main path into the shelter of some woods. There, I threw myself down on my knees and asked forgiveness. Immediately, tears poured from my eyes and down my cheeks. I rubbed my eyes, but some grit on my hands got into them and caused them to hurt. I blinked away the pain. Then I tried to make the same singing sounds I had done earlier.

The sounds came, the strange language, the songs and rhythms. But this time there was no ecstasy about producing them. Rather, there was emptiness, a bitter emptiness. I got up, and it was almost as though nothing had happened, only I could still sing the nonsense songs and I was confused as to how this should be.

I resolved to try to put the matter to the back of my mind until I had asked someone at the school about it. One of the priests or brothers would surely advise me. In the meantime I would just have to wait.

I never received a satisfactory answer at school. I never really managed to ask about my experience in a way that would have made sense.

Many of the boys were unhappy at school. The lazy and insolent were often beaten for the slightest offence with leather straps or with sticks. The monks would never beat us with their hands, however, for they said that would be to insult our dignity.

I never became involved in anything like this. I was only beaten for insolence once, in an astronomy lesson when I calculated the date of Easter for the year 934 BC. Yet this was exceptional; most of the time my behaviour was exemplary. I was devout. In retrospect, I must have been devout in a way that was inappropriate for my years.

To me it was all a glory. The trivium: Grammar, when I first learnt the works of Virgil and Ovid; Rhetoric, when we were taught how to construct speeches and letters, record-keeping and law; Logic, when I discovered the works of Cassiodorus, Bede, Isidor, Alkuin, Hrabanus.

Then the quadrivium. Arithmetic taught me about the essence of numbers: one is the sign of unity, the Creator; two is for harmony, balance; three for the Trinity, creativity, redemption; four, the first squared number, harmony, completeness, the four elements, thus the four Gospels, and so on; five for the five senses, the pentagram and its dangers; six for the days of Creation, the union of fire and water, and therefore the human soul; seven for all that is good, the seven heavenly orders - Seraphim, Cherubim, Thrones, Dominions, Virtues, Principalities and Powers - the seven gifts of the spirit; and so on, and so on.

In Astronomy we learnt the calculation of dates and were shown how to use the cathedral's sundials, water-clocks and astrolabes. We learnt the division of time into its parts: centuries, *lustra*, which last five years, weeks, days, quadrants, minutes, moments, the time it takes to discern that time has moved on, the *ostentum*, the time needed to take in something with the eyes, and the *atomus*, the smallest possible division of time. Though for all our powers to measure time, there is nothing we can ever do to recover it, not even the smallest atom.

In Geometry we were taught how the universe is a system of concentric spheres, and how each of the seven heavens contains, in ascending order, the air, the ether, Olympus, the fiery space: the firmament of the stars, the heaven of the angels, and finally the heaven of the Trinity. We learnt too of far-off lands. One of the monks who taught us had actually been to Jerusalem on a pilgrimage. He told us how he had stood on the spot that is at the very centre of the world, just thirteen feet to the west of where our Lord was crucified.

Yet my greatest love was Music. I sang in all the services at the cathedral from a month or so after my arrival at the school. It is to this that I owe my facility with singing and writing music. Most of all I wanted to understand the source of music. At times music seemed so powerful, I thought that to understand it would be to understand all things. At other times its fleetingness, its fragility, made me wonder if the contemplation of music was not the same as the contemplation of death. And I was still bewildered by my experience of ecstatic singing that day after the harvest.

I took time to learn the arts of versification also. I pondered on the relationship between the numbers in stress and syllable counts in versification and music and their effect in songs and poetry. This in turn appeared to be linked with spiritual disciplines we learnt, such as counting breaths while exhaling prayers, and using rhythms that reflected the symmetry and proportions of the cathedral in which we prayed.

During the year of our Lord 1184 I remember hearing of the festivities in Mainz, where our Emperor's son Henry and Frederich of Swabia were both knighted. During that year too I first saw the mystery play called 'The Play of the Antichrist', which depicted how the Last Emperor, an Emperor of Germany, will come, how he will subdue the Greeks, Jerusalem and the rebellious king of France. Then he will be tricked by the Antichrist, whose terrible reign precedes the Last Judgement.

While I was at school I became obsessed with the idea that the worlds of learning and of prayer were the true worlds. Therefore I disdained the petty worldliness of some of my fellows and plunged into my studies and the monastic way of life, which I considered to be the doorway to a truth superior to theirs.

The key to understanding the meaning of the whole of the universe seemed to lie in the concept of number. I reflected for hours on the idea that God was One, yet expressed himself in terms of the Trinity. So much seemed linked with this. I had read that the three paths of knowledge corresponded to the three persons of the Trinity: memory with the Father, reason with the Son and love with the Holy Spirit. I had read too that the Seven Liberal Arts were the inspiration of the Holy Spirit, and that they corresponded with the seven gifts of the spirit. I knew that there were Seven Archangels.

Throughout my studies I found these number correspondences everywhere. I heard of the Jewish tradition of analysing the Old Testament in terms of numbers represented by the letters of the

Hebrew alphabet. I read Boethius' theories of music and experimented with proportions on the monochord, and I learnt how simple number relationships lay at the heart of the understanding of all music: the octave is based on a one-two relationship and the fifth on a three-two relationship. And was it not said that worldly music is a reflection of the divine music? So I came to believe that to understand number was not only the key to understanding the divine but also a means of entering directly into the mind of God. This was the timeless world – the world of number and music, the world of the essences of things and loves.

My time at school was brought to an abrupt end, not by the discovery of the Light of Truth but by the Fires of Destruction. I was fourteen at the time; it was the year of our Lord 1185. We were in the cathedral singing compline when we smelt burning. At first we paid no attention, but soon the smell was overpowering. Smoke was billowing in from the south door.

Panic broke out and we rushed for the open air. I went via the scriptorium in order to save the Virgil and the Ovid I was so fond of, stuffed them down the front of my shirt and ran as fast as I could.

I remember seeing flames, hearing the cracking of wood, running for fear of losing my life, hearing boys screaming, seeing some monks remain calm and trying to organise an orderly escape, and others rushing, pushing their fellows aside, thinking only to save their own skins.

The fire had already engulfed most of the kitchens and the school buildings by the time I got outside. Most of the houses in the town were wooden: I knew well enough that there would be no guarantee of safety there. It was night-time, but everywhere was lit by the flames. Now even the stones of the cathedral seemed to be burning. I could feel the heat and I could hear the great stones crashing to the ground.

I did not stop running until I was on the plain below the hill on which the town was built. I turned round and stared long and hard at the flames licking round the cathedral and large parts of the town. I was far enough away that it all seemed silent, unreal. Only every now and again I would hear a great crash as giant timbers or whole stone structures fell to the ground. Then there would be the crackling and hissing of burning, shouts and screams. Then silence again.

A group of peasants stood close by, watching the spectacle in silence. It was not until dawn broke that the fire burnt itself out. I have no idea how many people died or were burnt. I remember trying to make myself pray for them as I stood there, but I was in too much turmoil, too exhausted.

I was taken in by a peasant family. The place stank of pigs. I had no choice but to be grateful.

I woke with a start a few hours after dawn. The peasants were already out working in their fields. I remembered what lessons I should have been attending that day. There was no point. There would be no more lessons. I felt for my Virgil and Ovid. They were still there. I was glad to have saved them.

I returned to Babenberch and eventually, after picking my way through the ruins, some of which were still smouldering, I found the Abbot. He put on a brave face, though I could tell he had been weeping. He said it would be best for me to return home to Nurenberc.

I set these things down here for this reason: many years later I was accused of starting the fire at Babenberch. I swear that I was in the chapel, singing compline, at the time that it started. Besides, anyone who knows how much I loved that school, and how much I loved learning, would never dream of thinking me capable of such a crime.

## II

# The Papess

✠

After the fire I returned to Nurenberc, where my father and Erna persuaded me to give up learning and the Church. I trained as an apprentice and then as a journeyman cartwright in my father's firm. I was not happy, for I missed my books and the company of those who were able to stimulate my mind. But everything went smoothly and uneventfully for three or four years - until that Sunday when I first glimpsed Katrin through the incense smoke and the crowds in church. It was the sixth of April in the year our Emperor Barbarossa set out on the Crusade during which he was to die.

I remember that day I first saw Katrin as if it were yesterday.

It had been a bitterly cold winter, yet at last a southerly wind blew. That morning I woke very early. Dawn was just breaking and I saw, through the window in the wall of the part of the house where I slept, the tiny buds on the branches of the linden tree. I stood up and looked out. I could see the moon still shining through the linden tree's branches, pale and weird in the morning light. The sun rose, burning deep red on the horizon. There were golden shafts shooting through the rose-pink clouds as I set off to church with my father.

I can see her now, just as she was that first day, amongst the crowds, through the candlelight and incense smoke in the church. She was the most beautiful creature I had ever seen, with pink cheeks, a red mouth, long auburn hair, a pale complexion, and brown eyes that sparkled with life and what I mistook for joy. Her face reminded me, and still does remind me, of certain pictures of angels in the illustrated books I had seen in the scriptorium at Babenberch. Ever since, that face has haunted me; perhaps it will haunt me beyond death, for I sinned with her.

That Sunday she was wearing a tight-fitting grey woollen dress. Her shape was perfect. For all my monkish education I could not stop looking at her. In the crowds on the way out of church I could not resist greeting her and asking her where she was from. She told me her family had just moved from Thuringen. She looked me in the eye, haughtily. She looked down to my feet and then up to my eyes again. Before I could say anything more she blushed and walked away. All that week I could not stop thinking about her, the way she looked, the sound of her voice. I made a mess of the work I was supposed to be doing for my father.

The next Sunday, as we were leaving the church, though shy, I was drawn to her like a magnet. I became separated from my father and soon found myself standing next to her. I remember that some of the townswomen had placed dried sunflowers all round the threshold of the church because of the belief that no adulterer would be able to leave a church guarded by sunflowers.

I broke the uneasy silence and asked, 'You are new here, aren't you?'

'Yes.' Her gaze at once defied and devoured me. 'Do you like it in Nurenberc?' I asked, forcing a smile.

She nodded.

'Could we meet?' I blurted.

To my surprise, she nodded. I had been sure that she would reject me. My heart was pounding. 'We could go to the old mill,' she said. 'I often go there when I have time.'

'When?'

'How about next Thursday after Nones?' I was surprised she used the monastic expression for time. It was her way of telling me that she was not just an ordinary miller's daughter, that there was more to her. Fortunately, we were separated by the crowds before I said anything silly.

I ran all the way home. I ate little, avoided talking to Erna and Marcus, my new halfbrother, and spent the rest of the day reading from the Ovid and Virgil that I had saved from the fire at Babenberch.

From then on my thoughts were full of yearnings and lechery. I imagined what Katrin's breasts would feel like to the touch, how they would taste if I kissed them, what she would look like naked. I knew such thoughts were evil, of the flesh. I knew lust was one of the seven deadly sins. Yet, as my eyes closed and the sun shone upon them, that did not matter. Besides, however hard I tried to banish these desires, I could not.

The three days of work between Sunday and Thursday were endless. All the time I was speaking to Katrin in my head. All my thoughts and actions were for her. I wanted to tell her everything about myself. My moods veered from dreaminess to nervous despair at the slowness of the passing of time.

At last Thursday came. I arrived early. I sat on a large stone by the old mill. Sunlight fell yellow and gold through the forest leaves. A squirrel scampered up a tree, birds darted from treetop to treetop and a light breeze blew. A zephyr. I remember the green of the grass and moss on the woodland floor and the tiny yellow, white and blue flowers.

There was a stream running next to the mill. It was said that since the mill was first built, some fifty years before, the waters of the stream had ceased to flow with sufficient force to turn the great wheel. That was why the mill had slipped into disrepair. The stream's clear water splashed over the stones. There was no one around. I waited. Then there was the sound of footsteps, the cracking of twigs underfoot. Katrin. She was beautiful.

She sat down next to me on the stone. I remember the scent of her, her perspiration mingled with herbs. She was out of breath from running. It would have been easy to take her there and then. The mill was deep in a glade, and no one ever came there, no one except the birds and a few deer. I was strong enough to take her. But that would have been wrong.

I do not remember in detail what we talked about. That was not important. She explained that her family were weavers and that they had moved from Thuringen in the north in the hope of finding more work. She said she had a brother whose ambition was to become a cloth merchant.

All the time my senses were lost by those red lips, her slim body, her fragrance. I rested a hand on her knee. She did not object.

She asked me about myself. I explained that I was a journeyman cartwright but that I had been to school in Babenberch. She said I must be very clever. She too had been to a convent school, and knew how to read and write, and loved singing, though she had had to leave at a young age because her father and mother needed her at home. I was so excited that she could read and write, that we would be able to talk about the things that interested me. She sighed and said that it was hard to love learning and music but to have no time to pursue them. I felt a deep affinity, and put my arm round her shoulders. Again she did not object.

Next I remember her singing to me. It was the old song everyone knows, in which a girl talks about her lover, who has ridden off and left her:

*Gruonet der walt allenthalben:*
*wa ist min geselle also lange?*
*der ist geriten hinnen*
*owi, wer sol mich minnen?*\*

I had never heard it sung so beautifully, nor have I since. Her voice had a quality that made what she sang more subtle and expressive than the most magnificent plainchant or any court singer I have heard. She sang more slowly than most, with a sad, lilting voice.

\* *All the forest is sprouting green: / Where is my love? Where has he been? / He has ridden far away / Alas, who will love me, say?*

Whenever I think of that song, I see the rich green forest, the sunlight pouring through the trees and the flowing of the water. It is the style I made my own when I sang at court, yet I owe it all to her.

I kissed her for the first time that Thursday. I remember the sweetness of the taste of her lips. We did not make love until our next meeting.

We walked for an hour or two. Deep in the forest, where the trees grew so tall that it was as if we were in a massive, living cathedral, and the light shining through the treetops was like light shining through green stained glass, we found a massive oak tree that had been struck by lightning. Its trunk was hollow and it looked like a small house. I told Katrin the story of Baucis and Philemon from Ovid. I remember we stood inside the trunk for a while, in silence, wondering what it would be like to be lovers in the forest for ever, turned into trees by some generous god.

If Katrin taught me how to feel, it was Uqhart who taught me how to doubt. That first meeting with Katrin took place the very same week that I began studying with Uqhart the Jew.

I had been sent to him by my father to fetch the herbs used by my stepmother when she became unwell from drinking too much. Uqhart lived by supplying herbal remedies. My father was fond of the old man and had used his cures for as long as I could remember.

Not everyone liked him. He was a stranger in Nurenberc, because he was a Jew and because he spoke German with a stranger's accent. There was some bad feeling towards Jews at that time because of the Crusade. Many of them had fled Mainz the previous year when they heard that the Crusade was starting.

It was said that the Jews were responsible for the death of our Lord, yet I knew from my studies at Babenberch that many of them were masters of great learning, as were the Saracens. I had made a point of finding out more about Toledo during my school-days. The Jews and some Saracens there had made fine translations from the Greek and the Hebrew. I longed to go to Toledo myself; yet what hope was there for me, the son of a cartwright, unless I gave up everything?

I did not know Pauli very well in those days, though he had lived with Uqhart ever since he was a small lad. I knew him, of course, and had seen him on a number of occasions. He was about a year younger than me. Some said that he was Uqhart's son, and that his mother died during the course of the long and arduous journey from Toledo. Others whispered that Pauli was a Frankish, Christian boy who had been stolen from his parents by the Jew's black arts. Yet in those days no one had ever challenged Uqhart in public.

In order to reach Uqhart's house I had to walk through a part of town where I knew few people, though it was not far from my home. It was the district where newcomers lived: tradesmen, peasants seeking work in town, nobles who had fallen on hard times. Some of the houses were very tiny, very poor, yet others were surprisingly large. The lanes were less narrow than where I lived. I remember that day the sun was beating down, and a wild dog followed me through the deserted streets. It was black and had a vicious yellow glint in its eyes.

Uqhart's was a wooden house, like ours, but it was larger, and inside it was divided into more rooms than normal. The front room was small and served as a shop. What went on in the rooms behind, no one knew for certain, for few had ever been there. I was to find out.

Pauli was mixing herbs at the front of the shop that day. I told him my business and he went to fetch Uqhart. I asked him for the herbs and looked round at the various charts, crucibles and tools he kept, as well as the bundles of dried herbs. Uqhart smiled at me in silence and began preparing the herbal mixture. I still remember Uqhart's kind, wizened face, his grey white hair, his dark, piercing eyes.

I was determined to strike up some sort of serious conversation with him. I was aware that he had been responsible for my schooling. I was keen to discuss the fruits of my learning with him.

At the same time I was nervous of giving the impression that I believed the rumours about his practising the black arts.

When he came back with the herbs I asked him, 'Is it true that there are those who know how to turn lead into gold?' I had read some things about the art of alchemy during my school-days, though I knew little enough about it.

He did not reply directly but said, 'I hear you know Latin and that you have studied the liberal arts at Babenberch. That is rare for the son of a cartwright, is it not?'

'I hear you know other languages, Greek and Hebrew, and that you have studied secret arts,' I said, this time in Latin. Pauli's ears pricked up. He sensed I was throwing out a challenge.

'If you want to learn from me,' said Uqhart, 'you are welcome. You may come on Fridays, between the end of your work and the setting of the sun.' He was speaking Latin too, in a mock-serious tone I found amusing, for it reminded me of how we had sometimes spoken to one another to mock the masters at Babenberch. So I took up the invitation.

My first lesson with the old man must have been the Friday after my first meeting with Katrin.

I was keen to find out more about herbs and flowers and alchemy. I welcomed the opportunity to break the routine of work. Also, I was secretly glad to have something to take my mind off Katrin.

So, on that Friday, I went to see Uqhart. When I arrived he offered me a herbal infusion in an earthenware drinking-cup. It was delicious, very refreshing after a difficult day's work. Then he led me through the room at the front of the house, past the oak table, and through a smaller room lined with shelves all loaded with bottles and herbs, crucibles, tools of various kinds, and books and stacks of papers in such quantities as I had never seen since the scriptorium at Babenberch.

I remember the faint red rays of the setting sun shining in through the slit windows, shedding just enough light for me to be able to see. I remember too the scents of timber and herbs, then a burning, sulphurous smell as we passed through the middle room into another, larger room. In the centre of it I saw the source of the smells: there was a fire, which had burnt down, and over it there was a retort containing some substance that glowed with many different colours. Also, on one of the tables, there were several beautiful books, some open, some lying in piles. On the wall were charts of some sort, bearing strange symbols of moons, crosses and circles. Some of the writing I recognised as Hebrew, since I had seen Hebrew manuscripts at the scriptorium in Babenberch, though in those days I could not understand it.

I had no time to collect myself, or ask any questions, before Uqhart took my hand and rubbed chrism into my fingernail.

'See. What is that?' he said.

'A finger.'

'Look, it is an angel.'

For a moment I wondered if he had gone mad, but when I looked down at my fingernail, sure enough, I saw in it the face of an angel. She looked half like Katrin and half like visions I had seen of my dead mother. I said nothing. Uqhart smiled. I started to tremble. My body perspired, a sweet feeling ran in my back and up and down my spine, and bright, cascading lights exploded in my head. I could not speak.

'What is this?' Uqhart said, and he took my left hand, rubbed more chrism into the fingernail of the fore-finger, and pointed again.

'Angel,' I said as if in a trance.

'No, it is a devil.'

What had been like rays of light in my back now chilled to ice, my trembling became the trembling of fear, and in my fingernail I saw the face of an ageing slut, like Katrin, old, with boils and a hag's painted face. Then the face changed to that of a jackal. It was hideous. My trembling became convulsive.

I shook myself from the trance and looked at my nails again. They were quite normal.

I looked over towards Pauli, who was smiling noncommittally.

'It is enough,' said Uqhart. I looked at the old man questioningly. 'Tell no one of what you have seen and felt, for the sake of your own honour; no one will believe you. One day you will understand. Now go!'

The last words were spoken with such definitiveness that I went straight out without saying a word.

I felt calm and collected but strangely torn, as if perhaps some vital door within me had been ripped open. Outside the house I felt worse, as something of the feeling from when I had seen the devil on my nail returned. I was terrified that I had come into contact with forces – spiritual forces – that the Christian religion forbids us from meddling with.

Impulsively, I sprinted to the Lady Church, knelt and prayed for my soul. Now the angel feeling returned, the warmth and closeness of what I took to be the Divine, and I thought of my long dead mother, of her grave wet with dew in the night-time, silent, cold even in spring, and then of my own feelings, confusions, futilities. I forced myself to stare at the crucifix over the altar and, just as I had been taught at school, breathed in deeply and exhaled the words '*kyrie eleison, kyrie eleison,*' about me. This brought some peace. The face of old Uqhart formed before my eyes just for a moment, and then mutated to that of Katrin. Katrin, Katrin. I longed for her silently, painfully. Then I remembered where I was and tried to sing the evening hymn, '*Te ante lucis terminum*'.

I left the church and ran home. There, my father greeted me. I sat down with him at the old oak table, in the part of the house we used as a kitchen and where we took our meals. The light was fading outside. The calm ordinariness of the house was a comfort and relief greater than I could ever have thought possible. My father commented on how well I looked and offered me some ale. I accepted, allowed a small conversation about business to develop, and then went to bed.

During the next few days my torments were doubled. I became

obsessed with the notion of an eternity spent wrapped in the closeness of the oak tree we had found, Katrin and I, like Baucis and Philemon. Yet the stillness of this idyll was interspersed with urges to touch Katrin, to see her naked. I became intensely curious about the act of copulation, which of course I had never experienced before.

Then my thoughts would turn to the alchemist, to his angel and devil. It was as though I no longer knew myself. Doors had been opened within me to a strange orgy of powers and images that were sublime, demoniac, Bacchanalian, angelic, yet at odds with the grace of the Christian religion. All the same, I kept my word and mentioned nothing of Uqhart's angel and devil to anyone.

Katrin and I met again that Sunday afternoon. The weather was cloudy and drizzly. My spirits were downcast. I could not help wondering what would happen if Katrin no longer liked me, how I should feel if she failed to turn up. Also, in my imagination I had entertained so many lustful and sinful thoughts about her that I felt embarrassed about seeing her again. I feared that she might possess the sight, that she might read my mind, that she might know how depraved I was and what acts I had contemplated performing with her.

I still remember the rich smells of the forest and the textures of the light – golden, green and brown – as I walked out of the town, heart racing with anticipation, through the rain, which by now had made great puddles on the muddy ground, beneath the dripping wet leaves of the trees, and I remember looking up every now and again at the threatening, overcast skies.

By the time I reached the old mill I was soaked to the skin, yet I did not care, for the exertion of getting there had warmed me. As I approached, I heard a strange sound coming from inside the mill itself, the sound of music, a long, lovely melody being played on a flute. At first I hesitated, wondering if the music had some supernatural source. Then I remembered that Katrin had told me she played the flute.

It was hard to find a way in because the mill was so overgrown. Eventually I managed to find a gap where what had been the back door was wedged half open.

There I saw Katrin sitting, legs outstretched, back leant against the dusty wooden wall. Her long auburn hair hung loose about the flute that she held pressed to her mouth.

I listened, then I sat with her. The sight and scent of her mixed with the scent of the rain had an intoxicating freshness about it. It was as if she was the spirit of the rain and the forest, and the music she was playing was that spirit's voice. I could not stop myself from staring at her. She did not seem to mind.

I talked about the song she was singing. She tried to teach it to me. When I learnt the song we decided that I should learn the flute.

My first attempts were not very successful. We laughed at the noises I made. I can still remember her freshness, her spontaneity. If only I could find that now in this ageing world. Yet I was the one who destroyed all that about her. Or maybe it was she who wanted to destroy it, and I only helped her.

The rain was beating down on the roof again now. Soon we were kissing. She put up no resistance when I touched her; she touched me in return.

Soon we were making love. I remember that, as we did so, lightning was striking in the distance, shining brilliantly in the gap in the roof. When the thunder came I took it as an omen that I was doing wrong. A part of me wanted to run away from the house and the forest that very moment. Then I looked down at her; she was all but naked, lying there, on the dusty wooden floor of the mill, mine. Soon the lightning was almost directly overhead. I could see that the storm was making her nervous too, but by then I could no longer stop myself. We were lost in one another, pressed close, ribcage almost touching ribcage, lip pressed upon lip.

A part of me sensed, as I lost myself in the lovely herb-like scent of Katrin, in the act of love, as the storm raged about us, a third presence - someone, something, incorporeal yet familiar, looking on. I did not try to visualize this until afterwards, when it was too late. It seemed like the presence of an old man, like myself perhaps but older, looking back from some time in the future.

I told Katrin about this while we were dressing. Katrin believed in ghosts and spirits. She thought it was the spirit of one of our ancestors. She said that if she were to die she would come back to me as a spirit and look after me. I remembered reading in Tertullian that women were more susceptible to magic and intuition than men, so I thought carefully about what she said.

As I walked home that evening I felt a mixture of satisfaction, sadness and self-disgust. Had I used Katrin or had she used me? Did I love her? What did that mean? I certainly missed her already. I certainly wanted to be with her all the time.

The rain had stopped but the leaves were still dripping, and clouds blew, yellow and grey, fleeting before the setting sun, over the rooftops.

I thought of marrying her. But what would my father say? I had plans to become a monk. Would I now have to take my father's business more seriously? Another question formed. She had given herself easily; was I the first? Surely not. Did that matter? It did matter. Or at least it seemed to, though I did not know why.

I ate nothing that evening but went to bed as soon as I returned home. I tried to pray but could not. It would be a whole week before I saw her again.

# III

## The Empress

✠

That Friday Uqhart greeted me with enthusiasm and friendship. He led me once more through the door and back into the workshop, strewn with charts, books and herbs, with the stove and the retort in the very middle. We sat at a table in front of the altar-like oven or kiln.

Uqhart said, 'You have done well not to speak of your last lesson.' How he knew this I am not sure; maybe he could tell from the look on my face. He went on: 'It is best never to talk of devils and angels, at least not of the experience of them, which is fraught with deceit, for they are only harbingers. Today I shall teach you the signs of alchemy, which are the signs of the planets. *Solve et coagule, solve et coagule* – remember this.'

I remembered these words for a long time afterwards, and wondered if my feeling for Katrin was a harbinger, but if so was it an angel or a devil?

The lesson continued. First Uqhart drew a circle with a cross below and a cup-shape on top. Then to the right a cross with a half moon below. Then a half moon with no cross.

'This is the lesser work,' he said. 'Mercury, the messenger of the gods, flies from Saturn to Jupiter and the moon. Thus lead is changed to zinc and thence to silver.'

Secondly, he drew a circle with a cross below, then a circle with a cross above, finally a circle with a dot in the middle, and he said,

'This is the greater work; thus zinc is turned to copper, which is turned to gold. Mercury flies from Mars to Venus, and finally to the sun. Now, the circle is the sun, the crescent moon receives the light of the sun, and the cross is the earth, where your Christ was crucified. Therefore it has been written that quicksilver is led like a lamb to the slaughter and sweats blood to free mankind from poverty and distress. Yet the circle is the symbol of perfection. Go home, think on this, and tell me, on Friday, what it means. Tell no man what has passed between us.'

Again I left on command without speaking a single world. I had seen some of the signs before; they were taken from astronomy, which I had studied a little at school. But I had never before seen the signs linked with the metals.

The next Friday Uqhart was impressed by the observations I made based on my knowledge of astrology. From then on I was to see Uqhart every Friday. During those lessons I learnt much concerning the Hebrew language, Hebraic beliefs, the systems of Platonic thought used by the Jews and Saracens to describe the workings of the cosmos, and how these might be used actually to change lead into gold. Meanwhile I noticed that inside the egg-shaped retort, the substance that had been all the colours of the rainbow when I first saw it had now turned foul and putrid.

I still remember the old man's books, which he let me study during the course of these lessons – ancient manuscripts, some in strange languages, Greek, Hebrew and Arabic, with symbols and pictures: the Dragon, the World Serpent eating its tail, sages of old holding serpent-wrapped staffs, the two-headed hermaphrodite embraced by an eagle, wild wolves eating the sun and the moon, eagles and eggs, devils, dragons, and kings and queens lying naked together. Slowly, patterns emerged that I understood a little. I learnt some of the Greek and Hebrew words and began to get a grasp of the grammars of these languages.

There was no more mention of the devil or the angel, but plenty of talk of the presence of different spirits. I remember Uqhart saying that we all try to climb Jacob's ladder, but the knowledge we acquire as we climb higher never helps us, for the weight of our flesh causes us to fall back.

To think that they burnt all his books too.

I continued to meet Katrin most Sundays and feast-days, whenever she could get away. It was quite easy for me to see her because at that stage of my journeymanship I was frequently walking or riding out on business for my father, visiting the houses of landowners, ministerials, monastics, lords and knights who wished to buy wagons or wheels from my father's workshops, or have broken wagons repaired.

When I saw Katrin, it was always secretly, in the forest or in the mill. We nearly always talked about music. We played and sang together. I learnt much from her and her singing. Also, whenever I sang to her, particularly new songs which I had composed myself, I saw that her eyes would glaze over and she would listen intensely, as though my singing had a capacity to charm. It was through her that I became aware of the power of my own voice and music.

There were days, though, when she would sulk, when she seemed to resent me and everything about me. Then we would not make love and I would leave in a terrible state of guilt and worry, wondering what I might have done to offend her, if perhaps she had met someone new, if I, because of my inexperience, was not good enough for her. Then my jealousy would return and sometimes possess me so fully that I wanted never to see her again. At times I thought I might be bewitched, or going mad.

Then, at the next meeting, she would be her old self again, smiling, enthusiastic, kind and full of love. She would never say why she had behaved differently on the previous occasion, and I would wonder if perhaps she had done it on purpose, to tease me, to have me at her feet, to enjoy the power she had over me. In any case, I was besotted with her.

I remember so much that was wonderful. On Saint John's day we climbed to the top of a hill and watched the sun set together, and made love. I remember the strange orange and purple light in

the sky. Just after sunset we saw a spark float across the sky where
the sun had been. I wondered if it was an angel descending from
heaven.

We ran back home together, hand in hand. I remember the tiny
flowers on the woodland floor looked like reflections of stars in the
night sky and seemed to swirl in front of our eyes.

Why did I not marry her? I am sure that was what she wanted.
I can only attribute to myself the basest motives. I was ashamed of
what I had done with her and did not dare talk about it to my
father, though now, looking back, I am sure that he would have
understood. He often talked about finding me a wife through his
connections at the guild, but I would have had to wait a long time,
until I was in my late twenties, probably thirties. In some ways I
was still hanging on to what I thought was my vocation to be a
priest, which would of course have meant renouncing her and my
feelings for her as sinful. Perhaps I nurtured an ambition to marry
someone richer, who would provide a dowry of some sort. Maybe.
Even then I was dazzled by the glimpses I had seen of life at court
and wanted to join the knightly classes – an ambition which, alas, I
was to fulfil.

Uqhart taught me many of the differing theories of medicine and
I enjoyed the mocking way he explained them, pointing out the
strangeness in some, for example the belief that when culling herbs
one should avoid sexual intercourse and refrain from using an iron
implement.

So I learnt how beech leaves would cure rheumatism, how
blackberries cured gout, how bay and peony, Apollo's flowers, were
excellent if used for divination, how elder, hemlock, nightshade and
parsley were of the devil's garden, how saffron and wormwood kept
away fleas and cured their bites, how blackthorn was used to foretell
death, and how fern and hawthorn warded off thunder and
lightning. I also learnt how popular ivy, myrtle and poppy were for
barren women, how dill, clover and nettles kept witches from
curdling milk, and how Saint John's wort and hempseed, bay and

marigold would, if picked at the right time, cause a virgin to dream of her husband-to-be.

By midsummer I could not stop thinking about whether or not Katrin had been a virgin when we first met. My monkish education had left me with a number of ideals, and one of them was purity. I remembered the passages in the Book of Leviticus that forbade the Levites from marrying women who were not pure. A fallen woman was something to be disdained, feared. Also, it seemed that there were two Katrins, and I could not be sure which was the real one. One was young, innocent, pure, full of love and life. The other was sullen, sulky, possessive, grasping, always trying to persuade me to make some permanent commitment, to stay with her forever.

Dark thoughts and jealousy crowded in on the time I attempted to devote to prayer. Again visions of hell and the Apocalypse troubled me, only now I would see the demons of hell performing filthy acts. I could not confess my sins to a priest for shame. I fell that I was stifling in a nightmare of angels' wings, beating all around me, whilst demons' talons were constantly clasping at my heels. At the same time I needed Katrin, I wanted to be with her and thought of her and missed her every moment we were apart. Yet I sensed that she was already joined to another.

Uqhart taught me many different ways of anatomising man. He talked of the *evestrum*, our dark double, which knows the future because it comes from the *turba magna*, which we must seek to know with our rational minds. He talked of man consisting also of the elementary body, made of sulphur, quicksilver and salt, given life by the *archaeus*, the vital force. He said we also possess a sideral body, through which we are influenced by the stars, an animal body, the seat of our lusts and desires, and a rational soul, by means of which we attempt yet fail to understand, to unify the diverse elements of ourselves. We fail because this synthesis can only be achieved by the spiritual soul, which, if we allow it, will encompass the unity of the true self.

Uqhart talked of the elementals – the spirits of the four elements

- and how they affect the being of man, together with metals, which correspond to the stars and thus influence man's astral body. He said that we must purify our astral body through the process of alchemy, so that we can return to the *Yliaster*, the primeval and original cause of all existence.

He explained how ghosts are no more than the astral corpses of the dead, elementaries who cannot think for themselves but only seem to, until they are dissolved into the ether by the alkahest of time.

All this was very well, yet I still remembered the angel and the devil. I wondered if Uqhart really was performing only alchemical magic, or whether perhaps he was interested in *goetia*, necromancy, the summoning of spirits. I also wondered if the act of sex joined the sideral bodies of men and women, or their *evestra*, in a way we do not understand and cannot directly perceive, and if it was this joining that made illicit sexuality a sin.

Fits of jealousy about whom Katrin might have loved before me became increasingly intense. The fear it inspired certainly had something to do with Uqhart's anatomies, though to this day it is hard for me to understand why I should have suffered so much as a result of this.

One evening I returned home after making love to Katrin in the forest. I walked in through the front door of our wooden townhouse full of warmth and love in my heart for Katrin. Yet when I stepped inside, I noticed a change in the atmosphere, a feeling of tension and cold, a presence that shook me to the core.

There, sitting with my father, was a tall man, with fiery, tawny eyes, a man with long, flowing white hair and a white dyed woollen monastic tunic. I remember the look on his face. He smiled at me. Perhaps he meant well at the time, yet those eyes of his burnt right into me. If there are flames in Hell, I thought, then I was sure they would burn with exactly the same light as those eyes of his. I felt straight away that he was a man of spiritual power, perhaps a visionary. I had known men who projected such an atmosphere during my time at Babenberch. They were usually the monks who did not teach but led lives of silent prayer or devotion.

The man left without saying a single word to me.

'Have you seen that man before?' my father asked.

'No. Who is he?'

'He says he is from the north. He is a hermit but a man of noble birth. He says he knows you, and that he has your interests at heart.'

'But I've never set eyes on him.'

'He says there is a Brotherhood of Watchers who are interested in you, Walter.'

That was the first time I ever heard of the Brotherhood.

'What does he want of me?'

'He says you are seeing a girl. Is that true?'

'Yes.'

'He says you must break with her immediately.'

'But, Father…'

'I did not say that, he did. I was young once, Walter. I know how it is. Who is she?'

'Katrin. The auburn-haired girl from church.'

'I thought so. She's attractive. Quite easy, I should imagine?'

To hear my father talk like this shocked and angered me, not least because, in that word 'easy', he had expressed my own darkest feelings about Katrin; she was 'easy', whilst the love I aspired to was… well… then I did not know what it was; only later was I to recognise it in Hildegunde.

My father looked at me. 'You're not serious about her, are you, Walter? I mean about marrying her. You know she is well below us. She is probably just after our money.'

To hear him say that outraged me. How could he know what there was between us? What did he know of music, of the spiritual union it promised? All he could think about was wheels, carts, money, material things. That was how I thought at the time; now I am not sure whether he was right or not. Probably I shall never know.

My father continued. 'He knows too that you study with Uqhart. He says you should break off that relationship also.'

'But why?'

'He did not give a reason. He said that if you searched your own heart you would know. Walter, what have you done? How did you come to have such people interested in you? Was it something that happened in Babenberch when you were at school?'

'I don't know, Father, I really don't know. What should I do?'

'You have no choice. Our position in the world is fragile. If people of our station come to the notice of the Church authorities or of the nobles, and if we go against them, you know as well as I do that they have the power to sweep us away like flies.'

I could not think what to say, my feelings were in such turmoil. This noble priest, this unwanted visitor from the north, seemed an embodiment of my own conscience, the conscience I was trying so hard to fight. Yet the thought of losing both Katrin and Uqhart was more than I could bear.

I met Katrin again two days after Tremgistus' visit. My intention was to tell her that I would not see her any more. In order to do so I suppose I had conjured in my mind a dark image of her: Katrin the temptress, the seducer, the woman of easy virtue. But when I saw her I fell for her all over again. Being with her was worth more than anything a noble or visionary might say or do. Being with her was more valuable even than heaven itself, for heaven was always uncertain, yet Katrin was there in the here and now.

The time was drawing near for the Feast of Fools, the annual trade fair and procession. This meant a lot to Katrin. She tried to persuade me that we should go and be seen together.

I was making progress learning how to play Katrin's flute. That day she had yet another song to teach me. I mentioned nothing of the priest, or of my father, to her. But, in my mind, I resolved that I would continue to see her, no matter what it cost.

One of Uqhart's lessons was on the anatomy of God and man. He explained that the Divine presence was like a flash of lightning, that it zigzagged between passive and active poles. All was brought into being by the Divine Will. Its active manifestations, on the right of the zigzag of lightning, were Wisdom, Mercy and Eternity. On the left, the passive side, were Understanding, Judgement and the Reverberation of the Splendour of Eternity. These polarities were balanced by Knowledge, Beauty and by the Foundation of the lower world. So this lower world could also be represented as the trunk of a tree, the central, balancing forces pushing up from it, and the active and passive polarities on either side were like the branches. Seen this way the lightning was like the tree of life. I have always been intrigued by the notion that Beauty exists in the field of tension between Eternity and the Reverberation of Eternity, and between Mercy and Judgement.

Uqhart went on to explain how the shape of the tree was present in the World of Matter, the World of Thought, the World of the Spirit and the World of the Divine, and that in turn each of these was present in Man. I took this to be an echo of the teaching I had learnt at Babenberch: 'As above, so below.' This meant little enough to me at the time, though.

Uqhart explained that these four Worlds were reflected also in the concept of the four Elements, rising from Earth to Air, and then on into heaven, like Jacob's ladder, and how these four worlds were implied too in the divine names, YHWH, IHUH, JSHS and AGLA (*Atah Gibor Leolam Adonai*).

There was much more that I learnt from Uqhart, but more important than anything he said was the way he said it. He expounded system after system, connection after connection. Yet always there was a sense of doubt, of questioning in the way he set things out for us, as if he wished to make clear that if we, if anyone, including himself, was ever going to learn the truth, then we must continue to keep an open mind, to doubt, to question.

That fateful evening before the fair, Katrin and I had arranged to meet at the old mill. It was raining, just like the first time we made love. I arrived earlier than the time we had set. The rain poured down. I waited and waited.

The mill was a bleak, barren place without her, almost ghostly. Tangles of creepers wound their way in and out of the planks, and looked to me like the deformed limbs of the dead. The rain was relentless, and it seemed that all our poor little world might soon be washed away. Words from Matthew's Gospel went round and round in my mind: 'Whoever causes one of these little ones to stumble, it were better for him that a millstone were tied round his neck and...'

What sort of person did these words refer to? To Katrin? To me? Then I began to think about the sin against the Holy Spirit that could not be forgiven. Had I committed it by loving her? Or would it be a worse sin to abandon her? Then there was another saying of Uqhart's that I kept thinking about, and from which I tried to draw some consolation: 'How can you expect me to be perfect, when I am so full of contradictions?' A bell chiming in the distance through the rain told me that Katrin was more than an hour late. This was the first time she had ever failed to arrive on time. I was tormented by the visit my father had received from the old priest. Could it be that he had already moved to stop us from seeing one another?

At last I heard the sound of someone coming through the forest. I listened carefully. I thought it must be Katrin, but then I realised there was not one person but two. I could hear a girl sobbing and every now and again the rough, angry voice of a man.

I peered through a gap in the timbers. My feet and the side of my shirt were getting wet through. At last the two figures came into view. Both were soaked. Katrin looked very small, very upset. Next to her was the tall, burly figure of a young man, her brother. He had been treating her roughly and I resented him for that.

I looked round the mill and found a piece of wood of a decent length, light enough to manipulate but heavy enough to do damage if needed. I stood out of sight as they made their way towards the mill.

At the last minute Katrin made a dash for it. Her brother started shouting and running after her, but she was too quick for him. Her lightness was an advantage on the slippery ground. She ran round towards the back entrance of the mill, calling my name as soon as she was sure she was clear of him. I rushed to meet her and she fell, exhausted, into my arms. Her face was pale and tear-stained. There were cuts and bruises.

As soon as she caught her breath Katrin said, 'He knows about us. I don't know how. He's threatening to tell everyone, my parents, your father, the priests, everyone.'

If I had thought more quickly I could easily have barred her brother's entrance, but by the time I had taken in what Katrin was saying he was already half inside. He was a tall, strong creature, with broad shoulders and a puffy, spotty face. His eyes squinted; they were stupid, cold and cruel...

He said, 'So you are the fine young man she does it with, Walter von der Ouwe? I would have thought that someone with your education would have had more taste than to do it with a bastard and a slut.'

I remained silent.

'I'm telling the truth,' he went on in the sneering, whining voice that was hardly compatible with his size. 'She's my father's daughter, but not my mother's. She is a bastard all right. And the number of men she's had! Don't think you're the first.'

'Don't listen to him!' Katrin screamed.

'What do you want?' I asked, trying to keep calm.

'If you want her, you pay me a silver penny a time: a Nurenberc penny. You can give her the penny to give to us. You're not having her free. She's ours and she's got a price. Otherwise you can marry her. But I don't reckon that fine father of yours would be very pleased if he knew more about her.'

'Stop it!' Katrin said. She clutched at me as if she was hanging on to life itself. 'Don't listen to him, Walter. He's always been like this. He always wants to ruin everything.'

'And you can pay your first penny now, or she comes back with me.' He strode over towards us, grabbed Katrin by the arm and started pulling her.

'Don't lay a finger on her,' I said.

'Give us your money then.'

'Get out!' I shouted, and brandished the stick, to threaten him and show him that I meant business.

He hesitated for a moment. 'Have it your way,' he shrugged, and backed out of the mill. 'But I wouldn't want to be you going home tonight. Your father will be the first to know. And there's another man I'll be talking – to some priest, you probably know him. Father Tremgistus he calls himself. Long white hair, yes, you've heard of him. Very generous he is. Seems to have taken quite a liking to you, Walter. I shall have to have words with him. Sure you don't want to change your mind?'

'Get out!' was all I could bring myself to say, even though I feared the consequences.

As soon as we were alone, Katrin pressed herself close to me and whispered, 'Walter, you will never leave me, will you?'

'No.'

I do not know if she sensed the lack of conviction in my voice. In any case, she half smiled and wrapped her arms round me, like a child. It was probably the first time that there was no sexual desire in our embrace. It was the physical communion of despair.

We sat down in silence, huddled against the cold, the damp and the drizzle. There was only the sound of rain and our breathing. Katrin, who had normally been so full of life, now seemed lost, somehow not made for this world.

'I cannot go home,' she said. 'What is to become of me?'

'Will your brother really do what he says?'

'Yes. You can only trust the wickedness in him.'

I told her I would stay with her in the mill that night. I swore to her that I would never leave her, though I knew that each moment it was becoming easier for me to do so.

'Tomorrow is the fair,' I said. 'We'll dance in front of the lot of them, without a care in the world, and then I shall talk to my father, ask his forgiveness, and we will get married.'

'What if he says no?'

'He won't.'

I can't remember what we talked about then – possibly my father's first marriage, how he met my mother by the roadside when she had just left the convent in which she had spent her girlhood, when he was a journeyman cartwright like I was. In any case, we continued to talk until at last we fell asleep.

I remember something Uqhart said, that prayer is answered because of the mere fact that one part and the other of all that exists are connected, like a musical string which, plucked at one end, vibrates at the other. Yet what if prayers are not answered? What if an apparent connection, like that between Katrin, and myself turns out to be nothing of the sort? Like on the terrible day that was to follow.

We did not wake up till well after the dawn light had spread, bloody and red, over the sky. I woke first. It was bitterly cold. As I looked down at Katrin, my first feeling was one of resentment. To think that I was considering the sacrifice of everything I had for that creature lying there. What claim could she have on me? I almost left her there and then. But then I suffered a violent change of mood and was filled with compassion for the sleeping girl. All I wanted then was to be with her forever, to look after and care for her. Then again I thought of the life I had left at Babenberch, the life of study and prayer I had aspired to. If I were to stay with her, I would be turning my back on that. My mind was paralysed by contradictory feelings and desires.

When she woke up, a sense of adventure once more overtook us. It occurred to me that I could make a good living like Uqhart, selling herbs and medicines, or, failing that, the two of us could sing and play music together. I had heard of wandering singers and players who lived well enough. I mentioned this idea to Katrin. She was full of enthusiasm and we talked until at last the world seemed more full of hope for us, and we were overcome once more with desire for one another.

The sun rose further. Having nothing better to do than to slake our lusts, we made love once more and then slept, entwined. By the time we woke again it was midday. By that time the fair would have started, so we got up, dressed and walked out, arm in arm, into the light, ready to face the world.

Only when Nurenberc came into sight did we start to feel nervous again. I thought of the work I was neglecting. I was supposed to be helping my father with his preparations for the fair.

As we walked, we said little. The light was September yellow now rather than summer white, and a few fluffy clouds sailed overhead. High above, a lark was chirping merrily to itself, oblivious to our adventure.

Looking back, when I think of the depths to which I sank thereafter, the number of women I have had, none of whom I loved except Hildegunde, I am surprised that I still have any sense of the way I felt then, so green and over-sensitive. Debauchery is the lie, and lies are quickly forgotten. It is the first guilt that contains the truth.

I remember Katrin pointing up to the lark and saying, 'Haven't you noticed? That lark always sings when we meet here.' I had not noticed, but I remembered something I heard someone say about birds being the spies of heaven.

It was not long before the town was in sight. We could already hear the shouting and the music. There was the beating of drums and the sound of pipes and flutes, salesmen shouting, animals mooing, bleating, crying.

We entered the town by a route that avoided both our parents' houses. There was beer being served at every corner, and music everywhere in the late summer air; the smells of food cooking, spices, perfumes, cattle, dung; men drunk, already shouting and fighting, tradesmen, peasants and good-for-nothings, girls dressed to attract the men and older women who knew better.

We joined in the throng. It must have been the same as every year, but to me it seemed different, for I could not feel part of it. Even so, there was a sense of security in the crowds. We held on tight to one another, fearing most of all that we might be parted. Some familiar faces smiled, others scowled at us.

I bought beer for us both. We drank and danced together amongst the poor folk, slowly and shyly at first, then more and more vigorously, till everything - faces, colours, crowds and blue skies - whirled above and about us and we were tired and happy in the animal-like warmth of the swarms of people.

Eventually we realised that we were hungry. We went to a stall and bought bread and cheese and more ale. We sat on a bench and ate as the crowds pushed and shoved about us. There were banners and bright colours everywhere. Pigs and cattle were being herded through the streets. There were bear-baiters, musicians, wandering preachers warning of the Judgement to come. Every garden and orchard was full of people. The music grew louder and louder as each group of musicians tried to outdo the others.

Inevitably, amongst the crowd that gathered in front of the town hall, I glimpsed the face of my father, standing stonily next to one of his newest carts, which he had brought to display.

Meanwhile Katrin was saying, 'Look, over there, how pretty!'

I took it into my head that I wanted to buy something for her from the brown-skinned man who was sitting on a paving-stone. On a rug spread out before him were all sorts of jewellery, bracelets, rings and necklaces. He must have travelled from hundreds of miles away in the East to trade. Maybe his home was even further to the East than Jerusalem, near to the Earthly Paradise.

Katrin decided she wanted a cheap brass ring with a rose-like pattern engraved in the place where a more expensive ring would have had a stone. I remember it clearly because it was identical to a pattern I had seen engraved in one of Uqhart's books. Katrin insisted that I should put the ring on her finger - on the finger that the aristocrats use to signify betrothal, the finger from which it is said that a nerve runs directly to the heart.

Then, somehow, my father was standing next to us. He saw us with the ring.

'Father, Father, this is Katrin.'

'I know all about you...'

'Father, forgive me. I would have told you, but...'

'I would have arranged a marriage for you. Now you are no longer a son of mine. Don't let me...'

'Father...'

I suppose I understand now how he must have felt, to see his son throw himself away on a girl from a low family, who had nothing to offer, who was, as far as he could tell, cheap. He probably feared the disgrace in front of his fellows. Yet I felt then that I would never be able to forgive him for what he did next. He spat at Katrin's feet. Then he threw a purse at me. It struck my face and caused tears to well in my eyes.

'You are no longer my son...' he said. Turning to Katrin, he gritted his teeth and hissed, 'You liar, slut, whore...' He turned and disappeared into the crowd. For a while I was too stunned to move. The pain in my face was nothing to the pain of losing my father. I loved him. I had always loved him and now he was rejecting me. How could I ever be happy now?

Katrin must have understood what was going on in my mind, but she was thinking only of herself. She cried, 'Walter, don't hate me, please don't hate me.'

I felt lost, too hurt to speak, now hating my father, now hating the girl who had driven me from him.

During the afternoon we returned to the forest, loved and slept once more. We tried to make plans for the future, but by then I was close to despair. Katrin was quiet, sulky. I did not know how to read her. Was she being selfish, wilful? Or was she also struck to the quick, torn between love, hope and terror at what the future might hold?

In spite of everything, Katrin wanted to dance. So, in the evening, we returned to the town and went to the streets where only the poor people remained; grander folk had gone to the castle. We danced out on the streets for all we were worth, which was not much. We danced as if to drive away our sorrows, or at least the truth. As it grew dark the more respectable townsfolk drifted away and only the travellers and vagrants remained.

The beer we were drinking was strong; it had gone to my head.

Part of me was in love with Katrin and with freedom. Part of me felt out of place amongst all these homeless people. I looked up to them, admired them almost, yet felt afraid of them.

'The new musicians are coming,' somebody shouted. Soon they appeared, dressed in once fine clothes, court cast-offs: a singer with black hair, tunic and breeches, a drum player dressed as a knight, a lady lutenist dressed like a noblewoman and a flautist with long, blond, curly hair and bright blue eyes, wearing an open shirt and knee-length breeches made of leather.

At first Katrin was intrigued, but when she caught a glimpse of them she became pale and asked to leave. I insisted that we should sit down in the corner of the street and have one more drink before we returned to the forest. Besides, I wanted to hear these musicians that everyone was making such a fuss over.

The first song they sang was a sad one, about a man whose lover left him. It was almost completely dark now, but torches had been lit and were flickering about us, shining down on the makeshift stage where the musicians were playing and singing. They sang well. The singer produced his voice the same way as Katrin.

I was entranced by the music. I recognised the second song. 'Katrin, do you hear'?' I said. 'The song you sang me.'

Katrin had been staring down at the ground, uneasily, her hand resting on my arm. She started, as if from a dream.

'They play excellently,' I said. My enthusiasm was genuine. To enter the world of music once more was a solace to me.

Katrin looked up at the stage. It was not just the light - she had turned a ghastly white.

'What's wrong?'

'Nothing,' she said.

The singer with black hair was pointing at Katrin, waving and laughing. She hid her face in her hands. Then they began a new song, a lewd song, describing the act of love. I looked at Katrin. She was shaken, though I still could not fathom why. Now the singer was pointing at her, making faces at her. Everyone was staring at her, laughing at the way she hid herself.

'Do you know him?' I asked.

Katrin said nothing.

The singer jumped down from the stage, clasping his codpiece in both hands, moving towards Katrin, making yet more obscene gestures. Now he was singing out of tune, in a rough, growling voice.

'What are you doing here? Stop it! Stop it!' screamed Katrin.

The man laughed. 'Come back with me, I can still love you.'

I stood and confronted the man. In my rage I must have challenged him to fight.

Sobbing hysterically, Katrin shouted, 'No, no, Walter, don't get hurt! Don't let him hurt you! It is all true!' Soon she was weeping so much that she could no longer speak.

I rushed to help her. The musician put his hand on my shoulder and said, 'Pure and virgin as the autumn dung. She is my mistress. I left her briefly for another. But she screws well, as you no doubt know. She looks good. She can come back and be mine.'

The man returned to the stage and they continued singing.

I helped Katrin to get away from the crowds. She was shaking. She said, 'You won't leave me, will you, Walter?'

'No, of course not. Were you his lover?'

'Yes.'

'Was he the only one?'

'No. Don't be stupid. There were many others. Since I was young. My stepfather, my stepbrothers, anyone who wanted to. I had no choice.'

'So it's true what he said, your stepbrother I mean.'

'Walter, you are the only one who has ever been kind to me. Don't leave me.'

I felt something inside me melt, fall to pieces. I wanted to cry, but could not.

'I'll get us both a drink,' I said. I kissed her on the forehead. It was to be for the last time.

As if in a trance I made my way to the table where beer was being served. The musicians were playing another song I had learnt from Katrin. I realised that it must have been the black-haired singer who taught her all the songs she had taught me. I recognised the lilting singing style, though in fact Katrin's voice was the more beautiful of the two. I was already thinking of them as a couple, him on top of her, loving her as I had done... She was his. He was hers. I, if I had married her, would have been cuckolded before my own wedding. These were the thoughts raging in my head as I made my way slowly through the crowds. I could not justify them to myself. I still cannot.

I got two cups of beer and slowly made my way back to where I had left Katrin. She was not there.

I drank my cup and waited. The musicians were still playing. I waited longer. Still no sign of Katrin.

The tall girl came and sat next to me. She offered herself to me for a silver penny. I told her to go away. I was growing angry by now, angry and desperate. I drank Katrin's beer and got up to fetch another.

When I returned, Katrin was still nowhere to be seen. There was no room to sit. I thought that maybe she had gone back to the mill. I drained the cups of beer and looked round the crowds in the hope of catching a glimpse of her. No sign of her at all. The singer was still singing, but he seemed to have forgotten the incident that had so affected me.

So I made off through the streets. Normally I would have been afraid of walking through the woods alone at night, but, driven by drink and by rage, I gave no thought to any dangers I might encounter, nor to the nettles and brambles that stung and tore at my skin and ripped my clothes.

There was no one at the mill.

I threw myself down in the corner where we had slept and loved. No one came. All night long I stared through a crack in the roof at the stars. Maybe I slept, maybe I did not. All I remember is lying there, my mind awash with images of the day, twisting and writhing with alternate loathing and longing for Katrin.

When morning came and she still had not arrived, I got up. I can remember little of what followed. I must have just walked and walked, without purpose, numbly, unless in some dark corner of my awareness I was expecting to see Katrin's face behind every tree, in every clearing. I do not know what drove me. It was the first time it happened to me, this frantic walking, mind blank, just driving myself on and on.

I must have wandered for nearly two weeks, from village to village, not even trying to work out where I was in relation to my home. I spent my father's coins on food and ale, sometimes going for a day or two without food, wandering through the forests and harvest fields, heedless of the autumn rain, with only blurred thoughts rushing through my mind like the dark, rushing autumn clouds. Other days I would spend sitting at some inn or other drinking ale, eating my fill, wondering why I was so alone, so cut off from the world. Then I would stride out into the world again, past barns and houses, thatched and timbered, sometimes in ruins, farmers, serfs, women wearing brightly coloured head-scarfs slaving over the autumn crops, rain-blown, windswept churches, some humble and some brightly painted.

Each time I tried to do something about myself, three giant ghosts – Damnation, Jealousy and Self-loathing – would stand before me, opening their arms wide to take me into their sickly embrace, and my mind would grow numb and I would continue to walk onward, aimlessly.

Then, one day I had the intuition that perhaps, after all, what had happened between us was part of nature, part of what God had intended. But this feeling lasted only for a second; immediately the darkness returned, the despair and the self-loathing. Only now I was able to cope with it. That was when I knew I was healed, and I saw the face of Christ, crucified, and risen, in the forest.

I returned home. My father forgave me. He did not exactly slay a fatted calf; that was not his way. He said he understood, that he had been sad rather than angry, but that he could not have coped with seeing me unhappy and the family's good name compromised. He made it clear that he wanted our life to return to normal.

After a day or so I went to Katrin's house to try to find her. It was deserted. The neighbours said that the whole family had moved out suddenly, just after the Feast of Fools had begun. They had given no reason for their departure nor any indication of where they would be moving to.

I asked everyone I thought might know where they had gone to. They had disappeared without trace, as if they had never been there. I tried to puzzle out what must have happened. I guessed that it must have been something to do with the priest who had visited my father. He must have pressurised them into leaving. But why? Something to do with my relationship with Katrin. I could not see why he should be so interested in us.

Eventually I gave up my search. I gave up any hope of ever meeting Katrin again. I carried on working as normally as I could.

# IV

## The Emperor

✠

My life settled into a routine. I worked hard for my father yet there was nothing to replace Katrin, and I felt empty.

Now, I fail to understand why I paid so little attention to my father. I suppose his prosperity made me take him for granted – and his stillness. I am sure now that he must have yearned for my mother. Perhaps he saw in her the perfected soul the Cathars talk of. I have heard that it is not uncommon for Cathars to commit the sin of suicide to rid themselves of the awfulness of this world. Who can blame them?

During that time after Katrin's disappearance, my one consolation was my lessons with Uqhart, which I continued in spite of the warnings from the priest who had visited us and the fears of my father. I studied more Greek and Hebrew, as well as the lore concerning the correspondence between that which is above and that which is below, how the movements of the constellations and stars are reflected in the human world and in the worlds of the animals and metals.

I was no longer alone in my studies: Pauli joined in with me. He had lived with Uqhart all his life and assimilated Uqhart's way of thinking so that it was all second nature to him. He had a good knowledge of Hebrew, which he sometimes spoke with Uqhart. His Latin was good for reading though he could not speak with the same fluency as myself. In Greek he was way beyond me.

Pauli was small and thin, with black, wiry hair and brown eyes that darted nervously, waspishly. I remember him clearly during those lessons, reeling off lists of alchemical processes, herbs, symbols, tenses and declensions of ancient languages, hunched and nervous yet full of humour, trying to catch my eye, always ready to share a joke, especially if, for any reason, Uqhart was not with us. Pauli had a wild intelligence and could assimilate new material quickly when he was inclined to, yet there were days when he would stare vaguely into space and sulk.

The contrast between the two of us was clearest in our different attitudes to music. For me, music was always, and is still, something solemn, something sacred. Pauli, on the other hand, loved bawdy songs, which he collected and composed. Whenever we were alone he would sing them to me and study my reaction.

Many were so funny that I had to laugh. It was from Pauli that I first heard the old Provençal song about the *cons gardatz*. The song says there is nothing worse than a *cons gardatz*, not even a fishing-hole without fish, and it says that the *cons* is the one thing in the world that increases the more one steals from it. There is more besides, but I should not set that down here.

It was through music that we became friends and through music that we were to embark on the adventure that was to lead to his death. Music - how can music be so linked to the Ideal yet lead to such consequences? Or is it inevitable that drawing close to the Ideal should lead to death?

With the first money my father paid me for my work in the firm I purchased a lute from Uqhart. I had seen it in his shop. He had it from Saracen traders in Spain – they said it had magical properties. Whether or not this was the case, it became my constant companion, and I still have it. Most singers accompany themselves on the fiddle, but this rarer, more exotic instrument suited me well, or so I thought. In those days, during leisure hours, I used it to compose songs of my own – though it was almost as if my lute were teaching them to me. Some of these were in the folk tradition, but most of them imitated masters like von Kürenberc, von Aist and a new singer called von Sevelingen.

Pauli was a great mimic. He could sing back my songs to me after just one hearing. If he liked the song, his rendition would be flattering; but if he disliked either the song or my singing of it, his rendition would be cruelly mocking, but always funny. He did hurt my feelings at times, but through this experience I learnt invaluable lessons. I owe him a great deal. He was the first singer with whom I ever practised the art of the *tenzone*. When we alternated verses, which we made up as we went along, the result could sometimes be very funny, and sometimes intoxicatingly beautiful.

There was an uncanny side to Pauli also. When he thought he was alone, I would sometimes find him beating out strange, irregular rhythms on a table or whatever was to hand, and singing - or rather chanting weird - melodies with words in a language unknown to me. At first I thought it was Hebrew, but he denied this. He said it was his own language and that he was charming spirits. I remembered my own experiences of singing in strange tongues. Yet this language of his had no warmth or kindness in it. It frightened me. When Pauli was in this state he would stare blankly, as if he were seeing visions in a darker, occult world. On several occasions after I had seen him like that, he was surly and moody for some time.

My time as a journeyman was drawing to a close. I was to be accepted as a full member of the guild and as a full partner in my father's firm.

I should have been overjoyed, but I was in a state of utter turmoil. The feeling of hurt resulting from my parting from Katrin persisted. I missed being able to devote myself to study as I had done at school. I was tormented by the thought that perhaps I had a priestly vocation. I burned with the desire to see more of the world.

I was finding out more and more about those who lived from singing. One day my father sent me on a commission to one of the

Bishop's attendants at the castle at Nurenberc. When I was there I saw a courtly singer. He was visiting Nurenberc from Eschenbach, from where he had ridden on business. As to his outward appearance, I was filled with envy of him. He was dressed in fine clothes and rode a beautiful horse. He moved very graciously. As soon as I realised he was a singer, I did what I could to prolong my stay at the court. I managed to catch some of his singing in the great hall.

I remember standing there, peeping round the corner at the Bishop, the fat little toad of a man stretched out on his folding chair, surrounded by his hangers-on, smiling smugly at the flattery the singer dished out to them. The sight filled me with disdain as well as envy. I was half surprised, half heartened that his singing was nothing special. Pauli and I were just as good. If this man could live by flattering the Bishop and his like, then so could we.

The next time we met I told Pauli what I had seen at court. We hatched a plan to set out into the world to see if we could live as wandering singers. Our idea was to make the trip under the guise of a pilgrimage. At first we thought of going to Santiago de Compostela, but that was too distant. Jerusalem was too dangerous now it had fallen into the hands of the Saracen, and Rome was unsafe for Germans because of the wars between our Emperor and the Pope. In those days many people were talking about Chartres, and how they were building a magnificent new cathedral there. That was where we finally decided to go.

Pauli told Uqhart of our plan. To our surprise, he was full of enthusiasm. He too had heard about the new cathedral. There were rumours that it was being built using patterns of sacred geometry. He said we were to inquire amongst the masons and master builders after the significance of the number one hundred and fifty three. He also said they were building a new college there, where we might be able to study.

My father's intuitions about the journey were sounder than Uqhart's. He was unhappy about it. He said he was growing old and in need of more help in the firm. Yet his saying that just made me all the more determined to go. My father understood well enough how much the trip meant to me, though I did not tell him the whole truth about what we intended. As a man of religion, he was sensitive to the spiritual benefits of a pilgrimage. He knew of people who had been to the shrine of Saint James at Santiago and had received remission of sins. Many of these people led long, prosperous and happy lives as a result.

Eventually he gave in. I continued to work hard for him throughout the winter, yet all the time I was yearning for spring, and the day of our departure.

At last spring did come. It was the year of our Lord 1191. The siege of Acre would have been at its height, the siege that would culminate in Richard the Lionheart of England having over three thousand of the town's inhabitants massacred in full view of the Saracen army.

In spite of his misgivings about our journey, my father had given me money and bought me the best horse he could afford. This was the horse that would soon be dragging Pauli's dead body through the forest.

I remember the excitement I felt on the day of our departure, and the sadness in my father's eyes. I remember hugging him, something I had not done for a long while. Did he have any sense of foreboding about what the immediate future held in store? Perhaps it is just as well we cannot see into the future, for if we could the present would be unbearable.

Pauli and I set off, heading northwest towards Fürth, then north towards Eltersdorf and the larger town of Erlangen. We took it in turns leading and riding the horse. Sometimes we would sleep rough; more often we spent the night in cheap taverns.

As we rode through the forests, which were green and airy in the spring light, Pauli's conversation grew darker, wilder. Once, as we were walking through a forest path, he said, 'Have you ever slept with two girls at once?'

'No. Should I have?' There followed an uneasy pause.

'You know when you were with Katrin, did you ever see anything?'

'What do you mean?'

'Did you ever see any ghosts or spirits?'

'I don't know what you are talking about,' I said abruptly to shut him up. But I was lying. The moment he spoke the memory shot into my mind of that time in the mill when I sensed the presence of an old man, though I could not see him. But I did not want to talk of such things to Pauli.

'You know what I think?' he went on. 'Sex is not just doing things with your body. There is more to it than that. It is a means of summoning spirits. I shall experiment during our journey. If I get the chance.'

I felt not only shocked at this, but afraid.

Another day, late at night when we were sharing a room in an inn – I remember the straw was particularly foul, though we were the only people there – he said, 'You believe in God, don't you?'

'Yes, of course,' I answered.

'I've been thinking,' he said. 'Maybe there is no God and no devil. Maybe there is no beginning and no end. Maybe the whole universe just carries on like this for ever.'

I tried to interrupt him. 'You should not say things like that.'

'Tell me how you can know that anything exists outside what you can perceive through your senses.'

I was going to say faith, but I knew he would just say that faith belonged to the category of belief, not of knowledge, that it was a state of mind, not a faculty. So I kept quiet and allowed him to believe that he had got the better of me.

Such conversations were only disturbing interludes in a life which, at first, promised to be idyllic. Cool spring breezes blew as we walked on and on through the forests, beneath the sunshine and the blossoms, the horse crushing underfoot the young grass and the spring flowers.

The sense of freedom was intoxicating. Sometimes we would join with other travellers, but more often we were on our own.

Whenever we felt like it we would stop and play music together, in towns and villages, inns and fairs, sometimes just by the roadside – wherever we happened to be resting. Often we would attract groups of admirers, who would listen to our songs, then join us in singing the songs they knew.

The first and last place we ever played in public for money was an inn at Erlangen. Erlangen is a small town and the inn was the centre of any life the place had. There were all sorts there: girls looking for men, travellers, drunks, a couple of monks who had not found anywhere better to stay, some peasants, even a knight and his servant, whose great horse we noticed tied outside.

The inn itself was in the town centre. It consisted of three large wooden houses that had been knocked together. The central house had a big downstairs room with a few tables and lanterns. The floor was strewn with rushes from the river that passed nearby under an old stone bridge. This room was where food and drink were served and where we were to play. In former times, guests would have had to sleep here also, but since the landlord's family had purchased the two adjoining houses, these were used to accommodate guests.

Pauli told the landlord that we would like to sing for our board and lodging. The landlord said we could stay for free as long as our singing was good enough to attract custom; otherwise we would have to pay like anyone else. As soon as this was agreed, we were plied with questions by other people at the inn, about where we came from, what we did and where we were going. The girls paid particular attention to us.

That evening, we began with some of my more serious songs about courtly love. These were mocked. I felt disappointment that the nobility of my aspirations had not conveyed itself to the audience. Part of me disdained them for not understanding. At the same time I grudgingly sympathised with them. Maybe my songs were too artificial, too convoluted for this sort of audience.

Pauli's bawdy songs went down much better. He played his flute and sang, with me strumming an accompaniment on the lute. The people laughed and stamped their feet, and it was not long before the whole company was singing and dancing. When they were tired I sang a couple of slower songs, which this time were appreciated.

At the end of the evening a number of people gave us money, enough to be able to stay at the inn for a week. We became convinced that we would be able to live, maybe even grow rich, from singing.

That night one of Pauli's ambitions was fulfilled. Two of the younger women who were hanging around at the inn offered themselves to us. I declined, but Pauli took them with him to his room. He told me the next day that he had possessed them both. I was upset by this, though I was not sure why. He stayed in bed late with the girls every day from then on. I rose early and tried to say matins, but I found that feelings of homesickness, guilt and nostalgia were creeping over me.

We stayed at the inn for nearly a week, on the invitation of the innkeeper, singing and playing every night. We drew quite a crowd.

We left Erlangen with our pockets full of money, and with some new songs. Pauli's whores turned out to be the inspiration for a number of choice lyrics.

For Pauli there was nothing complicated about his relationships with the girls. He enjoyed the physical pleasures they brought, and that was the end of it. I have done my share of whoring, but I have always suffered appallingly from my conscience. Pauli was not troubled by this.

When we left the inn we had trouble shaking Pauli's two girls off our trail. We left early on the Monday morning, leading our horse through the busy market-place. The girls must have heard that we were leaving and insisted on coming with us to the edge of the town. Then they made to follow us into the forest. The last thing Pauli and I wanted was for them to attach themselves to us, so as one man we both mounted the horse, tossed the girls some money, and rode off into the forest away from them as fast as we could, until at last they gave up the chase. Poor things!

That day we tried to push on towards Frankenburc. My aim was to avoid Babenberch because of the associations it had for me. I did not want to meet anyone from my schooldays. This was to be a fresh start.

The morning went well, but by Sext we realised that we were lost. We pressed on as clouds gathered. The forest was dark and oppressive. We had provisions for the rest of the day but began to despair of finding anywhere to stay the night.

Towards evening it rained again. This made progress even harder. We grew miserable. There was no village in sight and no one to ask the way.

We travelled non-stop the whole of the evening and well into the night. The only shelter we found was a hollow, tucked under some rocks on a steep hillside; though even here it was bitterly cold, and we were not well protected from the wind and rain.

Pauli slept deeply. This was probably his undoing. I remember lying awake bitterly cold, watching the clouds race across the sky, dimly lit by the moon. Every now and then the rain would stop, the clouds would grow thin and the moon would shine through, misty, silver and ghostly. Then it would cloud over again and the rain would fall. The night seemed to last for an eternity and the horse would neigh and champ and pull at his lead, hungry and unable to rest. Dark thoughts and forebodings troubled me all that night. I thought of hell, of Katrin, of wood demons, and wondered what the powers were that drove the winds and the storm.

If Pauli had not been sleeping so soundly I would have woken him and suggested that we should press on for the sake of keeping warm. But I wanted to let him sleep; I did not want him to think I had woken him just because I was scared.

The next morning we were both frozen. We walked in silence. As the sun rose higher in the sky we began to dry out slowly. The weather was a little better, but it still threatened to rain at any moment.

We were exhausted and spoke little as we trudged through the forest. We were still lost. It was not until mid-morning that we came across a peasant who told us how to find a road that would lead eventually to Kitzingen.

Pauli was pale and silent. Even then I was worried about him. It was as if all the energy had been drained out of him. Eventually we found an inn in a small town called Forchheim. We sat round the fire, dried ourselves out and managed to get something to eat.

I felt fine. Pauli said he felt well, but he still looked very poorly to me. His face was pale and his eyes bloodshot. There was a grim sallowness about his cheeks. He looked hunched, old, haunted.

We offered to sing that evening and did so. But there were not many people in the inn and our efforts were greeted at first with indifference, and then with hostility. Pauli had all but lost his voice and was barely able to get through the songs, let alone create any excitement as he had done at Erlangen. In those days I had not yet learnt to respond to the mood of an audience, so I was not much help.

We resigned ourselves to having to pay our way and went to bed early. Again Pauli did not go alone; a girl who had been hanging round him all evening followed him to his room. I was uneasy. I could not rid myself of the thought that the rain was punishment for the sinful ways we had fallen into the preceding week.

The next morning at breakfast I asked Pauli if he thought that God was angry with us. Pauli chortled with laughter and blurted out that God sends his rain on the just and the unjust. But his laughter soon turned into a coughing fit. Outside it was still raining and in the distance I heard a roll of thunder.

Pauli admitted that he was not well enough to travel, and we decided to stay another day.

Pauli grew weaker as the day wore on, yet he insisted on sleeping with the girl again that night. He woke next morning to find that she had gone, and that she had taken his money bag. No one in the inn knew who she was or where she had come from. Fortunately, the only money in the bag was his share of what we had earned in Erlangen.

Perhaps if Pauli had been fitter we would have pursued the girl; but his health had taken yet another turn for the worse. He was coughing much of the time and his forehead was hot to the touch. We decided to leave it another day. If he continued to get worse we planned to go back to Nurenberc together.

The next day came. He was no better but no worse either.

It was that morning, over breakfast, that we made the decision which was to cause his death and to change the course of my life. We decided to divide the money we had in two parts and that, for the sake of speed, Pauli was to ride my horse back to Nurenberc alone, while I continued on to Chartres.

Our parting that morning was hurried. The weather was fine, but there were clouds and both of us feared that the storms might return.

I remember Pauli setting off into the forest, hunched and small-looking on the horse. He was coughing even then. How was I to know that I would never see him again?

I imagine him riding through the forests, coughing all the time, growing weaker and weaker, too ill perhaps to realise the danger he was in. Nurenberc was less than a day away if one made reasonable progress. He must have driven himself too hard.

I imagine him fainting from weakness, being carried a little further, unconscious, swaying uneasily on the horse, then the horse giving a jolt, Pauli falling, perhaps, for a terrifying moment, realising what was happening, but it being too late as he struck his head on a sharp stone on the ground, his foot becoming entangled in the stirrup. Then I see him being dragged hither and thither by the horse, the flesh and skin of his face being scratched away by the hardness of the forest floor.

They said his face, the whole of his head, looked like dead meat. To think that in so short a time my dear friend had become a faceless corpse, a ghoulish apparition striking terror in the peasants and woodmen who first saw him. By the time the Bishop ordered soldiers to recover the body rumours had already spread, that a monster had been seen strapped to a horse, a ghost, a harbinger. Then, when it became clear that the horse was dragging a human corpse, there were those who said that the victim had been slain by spirits of the forest, by the elf people, by witchcraft, or that he had sold his soul to the devil.

To this day I am still troubled by the thought that perhaps Pauli did not die because of an accident, as I described it. Perhaps presences from another realm were involved. Yet I am convinced that, even if this was the case, Uqhart was not to blame.

I can imagine the old man howling when the horse and the corpse turned up in Nurenberc. They said then that his howling proved that he was possessed by the spirits of evil. Yet surely it was grief and horror at what he saw. Surely this would have been enough to unhinge anyone.

The authorities accused Uqhart of sending demons to attack Pauli and me, of ritually sacrificing us to the Evil One. They denied that Pauli was Uqhart's son, maintaining that Uqhart had kept him as a slave all those years and that Uqhart's aim had only ever been to sacrifice him. Nobody who knew Uqhart or understood anything of his learning could possibly accuse him of practising magic of that nature. Yet I was the only one who could vouch for this, and I was far away at the time.

If only I had had the generosity of spirit or the foresight to return with Pauli to Nurenberc. As it was, I continued, unaware of his fate. I headed west. At first I missed Pauli, but soon I came to relish the greater freedom I had as a result of being on my own. I continued through the rolling countryside of Franconia, through the forests and vineyards, alongside brooks, passing through village after village, staying in this town and that, singing in this inn and that, making sufficient money to live off, to drink, to eat, to sleep, to do whatever I wanted. I felt proud to be independent, free, able to support myself. And I was pursuing my ideal, the ideal I suppose I was eventually to find embodied in Hildegunde, the ideal of freedom, music, harmony, grace, purity.

Yet, as ever, I was oblivious of the cost. I was as oblivious to Pauli's death as I was to the massacre of the three thousand at Acre.

# V

## The Hierophant

✠

I continued on my pilgrimage. But the days were drawing in, and the excitement of travelling alone was wearing off. I had lost my way a couple of times and had not enjoyed sleeping rough.

I was not in the best of spirits that morning when I caught sight of the man I came to know as Father Jonathan, walking along the forest path. He was dressed in the white and black robes of the Cistercians and would have looked like a great magpie had it not been for the glowing pink of his bald head.

I greeted him, asked him where he had come from, where he was going. He was the kind of man one immediately trusts and tells everything about one's life. I told him all about my education at Babenberch, my pilgrimage, how I was living as a singer, and so on. He had food and drink with him, which he offered to share. Soon we were deep in conversation.

'You have heard the old Welf has died?' he asked.

I had heard no such thing.

'These are troubled times,' he went on. 'There been rumours that our Emperor, Henry, died of fever in Italy on his way back from the victory in Sicily. And there are those who maintain that he plotted the murder of one of the candidates for the bishopric of Trier.'

I had heard this rumour and asked him if he thought there was any truth in it.

'The only truth is,' he said, 'that there are those who want to foment civil war, and they will put about any rumour that suits their purpose. Still, that is the way the world is and how it probably always will be, before this age of sin is done with. So,' he pointed at my lute, 'music is important to you.'

'It is my chief love,' I replied.

'Then you must come to the monastery. I have friends there who maintain that music is the first and foremost amongst God's gifts. There are brothers who have copies of the collection of Latin and German songs from the monastery of Benediktbeuern. Perhaps you would care to come to the monastery with me?'

'How far is it?'

'Just a few miles. We shall be there before Nones.'

I accepted the invitation enthusiastically. Until then I had only ever had dealings with Benedictines, followers of the Augustinian rule. Yet I was aware of the spread of influence of the Cistercians and the rule of Bernard de Cîteaux. These white-robed monks had a reputation for the cult of learning and purity of life, which led them to build their monasteries out in the countryside, away from towns. Also, during my travels, at various inns and taverns, I had already heard of Graf Friedrich's court at Frankenburc and how many Provençal fashions and courtly manners had been adopted there. Of course, at the time, I had no notion that I would ever find employment at the court. None the less, the reputation of the court was part of what drew me to the monastery, since I assumed, rightly as it happened, that there would be links between the two.

I remember how happy I felt as we approached the monastery. This was partly because of the good humour of Father Jonathan, who seemed to grow more light-hearted as he recounted anecdotes about this or that brother or this or that adventure. Also, the closer we got to the monastery, the more peaceful the atmosphere became. The birdsong grew brighter, more harmonious, and the breezes blowing through the forest began to taste more sweet. It was almost as if the monastery were generating and spreading round itself an atmosphere of peace that touched not only men but also the things of nature.

An hour or so later we stopped in a glade, and Father Jonathan shared his lunch with me. After that, the forest path we had been following went uphill. To the right there was a steep drop, and every now and again it was possible to look through the trees and glimpse the rolling plain stretching out far below us. At last, we emerged from the forest to find ourselves on a chalky ridge, high above the rest of the surrounding countryside. Then, suddenly, deep in the valley before us, we saw the monastery, brightly lit by the afternoon sun, silent and still.

The monastery was a new building. The style was simple and harmonious, the stones close fitting. There was no church tower, only a ridge turret. On the hills I could make out a few peasant huts. The land rose more gently on the other side of the river. Beyond the orchards was rich land belonging to the monastery, where corn was growing. Father Jonathan told me that all the land belonged to the monastery. Apart from the breeze, the muffled sound of a bell and the mooing of cows, all that could be heard was the occasional creaking of the great mill-wheel, which was driven by the river.

I felt instantly that there was something spiritual about this place, that it might be a holy city, an antechamber of paradise. The bell rang for Nones as we walked down the hill towards the monastery, and I could easily have believed that the bell had the power to banish evil from wherever it sounded, and created a direct link between this world and the next. However, when I think of what was going on that very day at Nurenberc - the discovery of Pauli's body, the arrest of Uqhart, the spreading of rumours and vicious talk, which I alone could have put a stop to - then I can only marvel how it is that God, the Angels, the Powers can allow one to experience such peace, such a sense of holiness, whilst veiling the truth about what is happening to loved ones. I call to mind what Uqhart said about angels being only harbingers, not the truth.

In front of the entrance to the monastery was an expanse of close cut emerald-green grass such as I had never seen before. Two other monks, like Father Jonathan wearing the white, woollen habits of the Cistercians, came to greet us. They were old men, yet to my mind there was something youthful about their appearance, a curious light shining in their faces, which I remembered seeing in the faces of certain monks at Babenberch. They greeted Jonathan with warmth and affection. Each of them hugged me in turn, though they did not know me, or at least I presumed they knew nothing of me. I was overwhelmed by the feeling of peace.

Then I remember lights flashing in the sky, and the earth seemed to heave a great sigh and open as if to swallow me. I remember the feeling as I collapsed. It was as if I had lost control of my body and the grass was rushing up towards my face. There was blackness as my face struck the ground and I passed out.

It was already night when I woke up. A kindly face looked down over me lit by the light of a tallow candle. I was lying on a low mattress in a cell, wrapped in warm woollen blankets. 'Welcome,' the old man said softly. 'I am the physician of the monastery. How do you feel now?'

'I feel tired,' I replied. In fact I barely had the strength to drink the bowl of soup he offered me.

My strength returned very slowly. On the first day, against orders, I attempted to walk to the chapel, but my muscles simply gave way beneath me and I fell, crumpled, on to the cold, dewy earth. Father Jonathan found me flat on my back amongst the tufts of green grass, staring up at the blue sky, at the wisps of white cloud. I could not move. It was a week before I was well enough again to greet the summer sunshine outside the cell allotted to me.

As I lay in the physician's cell over the next few days, I forced myself to admit that I was ill, that I had suffered a breakdown, phtisia, call it what you will, and that I was in no fit state to resume my travels.

In any case, after a week of rest I was well enough to join the monks at their offices. Father Jonathan was a regular visitor, and I talked to him a great deal about my education and aspirations. Apart from the usual round of tasks - cooking, farming, cleaning and devotions - the monks also spent much of their time between offices copying manuscripts. There was no disguising my enthusiasm for this.

As soon as I was able, Father Jonathan took me on a tour of the scriptorium. It was a long, narrow room, with a low wooden ceiling supported by huge beams. Shelves were stacked with ancient and modern manuscripts of great splendour, many bound in precious leather binding. The glory was that the low shelves made the whole stock immediately accessible to everyone. Shafts of sunlight shone through narrow windows in the roof, illuminating the work tables running along the centre of the room. There was an atmosphere of still, dusty, golden irreality. It took my breath away, and my first feeling was that I would gladly have spent the rest of my days there.

Such treasures were there, in some ways even greater than those I had seen at Babenberch. In addition to the beautifully decorated books of psalms, Gospels and prayer-books, bright, colourful and perfect enough to rival any of the work done at Regensburc, there was also a great wealth of books by the ancients. Father Jonathan told me that the monks here followed the practice of scratching one ear whilst ordering books by pagans, to remind themselves that the pagans were no better than animals; though the glory of much of their writing was such that there were times when this was hard to believe.

There were also bound collections of Latin and German songs, composed by authors either still alive or not long dead. These were about nature, flowers, the glories of spring and the wonders of love. Amongst them there were some German songs that I already knew. I was shown the manuscript copied from Benediktbeuern. Some of these songs were intoxicating. I sang some to the other monks. They looked from one to the other as I sang, then asked me to sing more. I could tell that my singing was to their taste, and this brought me great joy. They even encouraged me to sing songs of love.

To me the strangest books in the library were the collections of sibylline oracles, prophecies of the last things written in Latin, in the forms of verse used by the pagans, yet speaking of the Last Days, the Last Emperor and the millennium. These words spoke to me, stirred my heart in a way I would understand only much later.

There were about fifty monks in the monastery. There were no oblates, so I was the only man who was not a priest. They treated me with great kindness and consideration. Many of them were of high birth but had become monks out of religious conviction, or because some infirmity had made it impossible for them to lead an active life. Father Werner and Father Ulrich for example were both hunchbacks. These men were amongst the most kind and holy I have ever met, a far cry from the sons of the devil, or monsters conceived on the night of the sabbath, which the ignorant and superstitious hold hunchbacks to be.

On feast-days and at times when we were allowed to mix together freely, I spent many a splendid hour exchanging secular songs with the brothers who were interested in music, and they would help me to learn more of the new religious music, which involved experimenting with part-singing. To my mind nothing could be more appropriate for praising God, for surely the harmony of music is the same as the harmony of the spheres. Yet there was a hot debate at the monastery with some of the older monks who felt strongly that music used to worship the One God should have one line only.

I stayed on throughout the autumn. Whenever I suggested that it was time for me to be going either Father Jonathan or the Abbot himself would find another excuse to keep me there. After a few weeks I became certain that I had found my heaven on earth. What more could I want? The life was hard and simple in some ways, but then there was the sense of peace, the music, the chance to study, the time to reflect. I was fully prepared to accept that the Cistercians, whose aim was to return to the original spirit of the Benedictine rule, were the authentic heirs to the primitive Church, and that they were playing a role vital to the salvation of mankind.

I saw little of the Abbot, whom they called Quintus. There was something about him that was larger than life. He was tall, broad but with an athletic build for his age. His jaws were strong and firm, so that his head looked square rather than round. His expression could change from the utmost joviality to the most complete seriousness within seconds. I realised immediately that there was something familiar about him, but it took me a long while to remember where I had seen him before: he had been present in the room with the Abbot Wilfridus of Babenberch when Wilfridus had announced that I would be continuing my studies of the liberal arts.

I remember the day after mass in the morning when he approached me, face beaming, and said, 'The time has come for me to put an important question to you, my son. You have no idea how much we value your presence here. Will you accept my offer of a habit? You will still maintain the status of a novice, of course. Yet this will show that you are a full member of our community, and show that you are committed to staying with us. You will make me so glad if you accept.'

I agreed without hesitation. I felt that he was doing me a great honour.

'Come with me and confess then,' he said. I remember still the penetrating look in his deep blue eyes as he spoke. 'This will be the first stage of your preparation to join us fully.'

It was my first confession since leaving home. I broke down in tears as I told him about my relationship with Katrin. For whatever reason he was very kind to me. He reminded me of the story of Christ and Mary Magdalen and of the words of our Lord to the woman who was caught in adultery. He reminded me also of the story of Tristan and Iseult, adding that the passions of love are intimations of heaven, but can only truly be satisfied there. He said that the sin was to mistake earthly love for the true love of the saints, which is present on earth only truly in the cloister, for here we were wedded to the Divine.

All these words were, of course, partly aimed at encouraging me to stay. Moreover, the penance he prescribed involved extra hours of copying and studying in the scriptorium, a penance that was hardly burdensome to someone like me, since I loved its atmosphere of timeless learning.

At the festival of Saint Nicholas that year I received the novice's habit. It was agreed that after a further year I should take my vows to become a lay brother, and then consider training to become a priest.

My life as a monk began in earnest. We rose at midnight for matins and stayed in the chapel until lauds. To begin with I found it hard to stay awake, for the Rule demanded we sleep less than I was used to sleeping. I remember the practice was that if one of the monks fell asleep during matins he would be given the lantern to hold. Only if another brother fell asleep was that brother allowed to wake him and pass the lantern on to him. I realised that, in this state of being half awake and half asleep, prayer and devotions came more easily, and at times I was sure I could perceive the forms of saints and angels moving through the chapel. It was at this time that I became convinced I could sense the presence of different angels. To me, they are not the small, fluttery beings I have sometimes seen in illustrations, though I am sure that such beings exist. Rather they are large, powerful, spiritual beings, capable of filling a whole room, a whole chapel with their presence.

Those who have spent little time in silent prayer and contemplation mistake such presences for God himself, because they are of God. Yet anyone who learns to distinguish between spiritual presences comes to recognise angels as distinct.

I read about the Jewish doctrine that each of us has at each moment a good and bad angel whispering to us and telling us what to do. They are attached to us and are with us throughout our lives. I remembered with unease the day Uqhart had made the angel and devil visible to me on my own fingernails. I wondered if what he had shown me were my own angels and devils, not beings alien to me. This would explain the point of his demonstration, if not how he performed it.

Also at this time of day ideas would come to me, which I would attempt to follow up in the time of private prayer that followed, which I would spend either in the chapel or the scriptorium. My favourite object of contemplation was the Platonic idea of the orders of the universe, structured like a giant pyramid, with God as One at the very top, then the Trinity, then the orders of angels, then the heavenly bodies, then man, then the orders of beasts, plants and minerals. I would see in human society an extension of these orders into those who pray, who were closest to God, those who fight, and those who work. In my arrogance I assumed that it had been granted to me to live the life of one who prayed.

At other times I would contemplate arguments about the nature of the existence of God, like Anselm's idea that since it is better to exist than not to exist, and since God is the greatest, the best thing of which we can conceive, then it is impossible to conceive of him not existing. I would turn such arguments round and round in my mind, trying to see all their different permutations and implications.

Another problem that exercised my mind was the reality of things. Is it possible for us to see the created world as anything more than a forest of symbols, thoughts in the mind of God? Or does matter have an independent reality, separate from the Idea of the Divine?

After such mental and spiritual exercises came lauds, when we were to reflect on our past failings and ask for forgiveness in preparation for low mass, which was spoken rather than sung. By this time, other than in mid-winter, the sun would be beginning to rise and I would look up at the morning sky, through the high chapel windows, and dream of the worlds of the spheres up there, just out of our reach.

Then followed the hours of reading and copying, or other physical work. In the middle of the morning came high mass, which was celebratory except in Lent. For this service we would reserve the richest chants and the most noble incense. At the consecration we would ring out all the bells at once. It must be the closest sound to heaven that there is on earth. This was my favourite part of the day. When the office was over I was often so involved in the music and in my devotions that I would find it hard to get up from my knees and had to be reminded to leave the chapel and get on with the next task of the day. It came to me once that perhaps I was more in love with beauty than with God.

A period of instruction came straight after mass, when various older priests took it in turn to explain to me ways of meditating on the Scriptures and to demonstrate the best techniques for breathing during silent prayer. Then Sext was said, and I divided the rest of the day between copying manuscripts, private prayer, cleaning, serving in the special guest-house for the wealthy, working with the mill and the hydraulic machinery, which was Brother Jacob's pride and joy, and helping out in the yard where the monastery's wagons were kept. Other monks supervised the work in the fields, looked after the animals or saw to the bees. The beehives were not far from the chapel. When I saw them I thought of the words of Gerard, that if only the human race could desist from the filthy act of copulation, then God would let us multiply in purity like the bees.

It was only on feast-days that I was allowed to write music and to sing for the other brothers, though I have to admit that I spent much of the time I should have devoted to prayer in thinking up rhymes and melodies.

The day's work was broken by Nones, then by the one and only meal of the day, after which we could talk freely about subjects other than work and devotion, play chess, practise music for the services, read, write or copy. Then would come vespers and a time of silent devotion and study, before compline and sleep.

We would rise again at midnight to say matins, and so the cycle of the day would be repeated, and the cycle of the weeks would repeat themselves, so that in the course of the week each of the psalms would be said or sung at least once and a large proportion of the Gospels and the Old Testament would be read.

I once heard it said that different souls associate with different aspects of the life of Christ - sanguine temperaments with the Incarnation, ethereal temperaments with the Resurrection, and melancholics with the Crucifixion. There were many times, when I was alone in silent prayer and my mind turned to the suffering of my fellow man, that I was sure I could actually feel the pains and the agonies suffered by the crucified Christ, in my own hands, feet and side, and that, melancholic as I am, I almost foresaw the life of stupidity and sin that I was to lead, though not clearly enough to do anything about it. I began, then, to understand that we are all crucified by time, pulled one way by the past, and the other way by the future, leaving the fragile body of the present painfully awaiting resurrection.

In my memory those days have blurred into one. I might well have spent the rest of my life there had it not been for the fact that my conscience became troubled by thoughts of my father.

I should have gone to see him sooner. I knew I should have done. Yet I consoled myself with the thought that he believed me to be on a pilgrimage. And I was on a pilgrimage, though it had changed from an outer one to an inner one. I suppose what held me back from visiting him sooner was fear that I would be unable to bear his disappointment if I told him I would not be returning to work with him in the business.

Amongst other things, he would have argued that my becoming a monk, particularly a Cistercian monk, was inappropriate for someone of my station. It was true that many of the brothers were from noble or knightly backgrounds, often younger sons with little hope of an inheritance, yet nobles all the same. How was I to know that I was being encouraged to stay because of something to do with my birth, which was only to become clear much later? I really thought then that it was purely because of my talents that I had been accepted so readily into the community.

Early in the new year, round about the time we all heard that Richard of England had been recognised at an inn near Vienna and captured by Leopold of Austria, I received a visit from the Abbot Quintus. He came to my cell to ask me to accompany him to the court at Frankenburc. He said that I should take my lute and be prepared to sing some of my songs to the Graf and Graefin of Frankenburc and the assembled court.

The next day, at first light of dawn, we made our way up the chalky hill that rose above the valley where the monastery was secluded, then down again into the next valley, where we followed the river, glittering serenely golden in the early morning sun, over the new stone bridge built by our order, and then into the first narrow streets of the town and up the sharp incline leading to the magnificent castle of Friedrich of Frankenburc.

During the walk I did everything I could to impress the Abbot. I engaged him in conversation about my own experience of the Platonic tradition via Uqhart the Jew, whose ideas were by no means dissimilar to those of Quintus, though Uqhart of course did not allow the same dominant role in his cosmology for the person of Christ. The Abbot listened attentively and praised me for the wide range of learning I had acquired at my young age (I was twenty-one years old at the time).

'This Uqhart,' he said, 'where does he come from?'

'From Toledo, where there are great libraries.'

'I know all about that. But why did he come to Germany?'

To my shame I did not know the answer. Rather than lie, I told him, 'He never said. Perhaps the Jews were persecuted there.'

'Nonsense. There is no more liberal town in the world. There Jews, Christians and Saracen all live together. They even organise great public debates to air their views. I tell you, in that town religion is a public pastime rather than a matter of belief.'

'Surely we should all learn from one another,' I ventured.

'There are subtle but great dangers in Jewish doctrine, and I caution you to be wary.'

'Is there not a doctrine,' I pressed on, 'that at the Last Judgement the Jews will share in the Resurrection of the Righteous.'

'That's as may be,' he said. 'But what matter is that to you, since you are a Christian?' He stared at me and added, 'Are you not?'

I nodded and changed the subject to the passages of Virgil I had been studying recently. Years later I wondered if that innocent conversation had perhaps been one of the links in the chain of events leading to Uqhart's burning.

At last we reached the great castle walls, where we had to wait until the guard was certain that we were to be allowed in. The Graf had even had a wooden bridge built over the moat, which could be raised with ropes if ever there was an attack.

There were considerable crowds near the keep, and I allowed myself to be carried along into the lower hall, where I was lost in the sea of men-at-arms, retainers, peasants and tradesmen. The Graf was sitting on his folding chair in the middle of the hall, receiving visits from other nobles, ministerials, priests and peasants, all of whom had requests to make, or cases to be judged, or business to settle.

This was my first view of the man who was later to be my master. He was stern-looking, very tall, in his late forties, but slim and warrior-like in his appearance. He moved with ease and obviously still possessed considerable strength. He spoke in a manner that gave little of himself away, without feeling, almost mechanically, as he dealt with the business of the day: the purchase of the land of an heirless serf, a request for funds to extend a church, marriage licences to sign, and a judgement required in a case of witchcraft. The Graf dismissed the latter without even hearing the evidence.

My memory of the room that day was that it was dark and very cold, in spite of the fire that was burning. The light was poor because it was a dull day. It was only thanks to the light of the fire and the torches that I could make out the tapestries that were later to become so familiar to me.

On either side of the Graf were two scribes, one a priest and the other presumably a lower-ranking ministerial.

When he had completed his business, the Abbot presented me to the Graf and asked if I might sing. It was decided that I should wait till after the meal, when the ladies would be present, and it was requested that I should sing songs in praise of them. This, at last, was the true setting for my songs. I would be able to sing for an audience who would appreciate courtly music. My heart raced with excitement.

There followed an endless wait while the trestle-tables were set up and the food and drink was brought in from the kitchens. The Graf remained seated the whole time on the folding chair, which was symbolic of his office.

Then the ladies came in. I had never seen such beautiful creatures. They bore themselves in such a courtly manner and wore the most exquisite clothes in the latest fashion. I felt my body stir at the sight of their red mouths and as I imagined their slim, white bodies beneath their clothing; and my spirit stirred as I reflected on their wisdom, dignity and purity. I was too nervous to attempt to distinguish who was who amongst the ladies. The Graefin sat on a seat next to the Graf and the other ladies sat in twos and threes on cushions and on the seats beneath the windows.

I picked at the bread, and at the venison from a recent hunt, but the prospect of singing before such noble company took away my appetite.

At last the time came. I was introduced by the Abbot, who praised both my learning and my singing. The ladies all looked at me. In the light of their beauty I felt strongly my own unworthiness.

I bowed as courteously as I knew how and took up my lute.

Some of the ladies were laughing at me. I remember one of them looking at another and whispering that she was surprised I had been let in at all. Far from putting me off, this actually angered me and gave me the courage to put up a fight. My heart raced even faster and my hands were drenched in perspiration, but I was determined to see through the task I had set myself.

Throughout my first song, a popular song of battle, everyone listened attentively. I finished and there was silence. Next came a love song of my own. A number of the ladies stared at me, stony-faced, while others started to chat amongst themselves, though whether this was to approve or disapprove I could not tell.

I sang two more songs, and by the time I had finished it was as if I were no longer there. Everyone was talking, paying no attention whatever. I finished and hung my head. I felt defeated. Yet the Graf ordered silence, praised my singing, though formally and without warmth, and asked me, most courteously, to sing one more song. In desperation, I sang the saddest love song I knew, for myself alone, paying no heed to the silent crowd, not caring whether I touched anyone's heart or not. When I had finished, there was silence. The Graf threw me money, which in my pride I disdained to pick up. Fortunately the Abbot picked it up for me so as not to cause offence. Then he led me out of the hall as the court continued about its business.

'They enjoyed your singing,' said the Abbot on the way back, as soon as we found ourselves once more out in the fields beneath the open sky. That was the first word we exchanged; I had been sulking until then because my singing had not been as well received as I had hoped and expected.

'It does not matter,' I said. My experience of the haughtiness of the court was leading me to decide that the monastic life was the life that would suit me best.

'You did not see them as I saw them, Walter,' the Abbot insisted. 'They were very taken with you, particularly the Graefin, and she is the one who counts.'

In spite of the Abbot's words, I felt that I had failed, that my songs had been greeted with indifference, and that there was no future for me as a singer. Until that point there were days when I still thought that I might continue my pilgrimage to Chartres, or that I might resume my attempts to live as a courtly singer. I had still not committed myself with finality to becoming a monk. Now I had nothing better to do. I had, or imagined I had, renounced all desires to marry as a result of what had happened between myself and Katrin. I had spent some time travelling and living rough and this had dulled my appetite for life on the road. At the monastery I was surrounded by people who were kind to me; I could continue to study and to play music. Moreover, I was excited by the prospect of an inner journey, an inner pilgrimage.

Three days after we returned I went to see the Abbot to tell him of my decision. He expressed pleasure at what I told him. I asked leave to visit my father to inform him of what I had decided, but the Abbot persuaded me that the time was not yet right for me to leave the monastery and run the risk of falling to temptation. Instead, he prescribed for me increasingly strict spiritual disciplines and daily regimes, all of which I accepted with enthusiasm.

It was not long before my day was organised in such a way that every moment was spent either in devotions, work or study. I ate only once a day and learnt more and more techniques of prayer involving breathing and the exercise of the imagination in order, through contemplation, to think beyond the symbols of religion and to perceive the true essence of the Divine of which our worldly symbols are mere reflections. I came to believe and understand that many things of which we talk symbolically, like the Seven Cardinal Sins and the Seven Cardinal Virtues, are not descriptions of human behaviour but actual spiritual realities, set against one another like chess pieces or warriors in a spiritual battle that is more real than the material world we see about us.

In the meantime I had asked the Abbot three times for permission to go home. Each time he would remind me of my vocation, my love of religion, music and study. He would say that, since I had already turned my back on the world, I owed the world no explanation. He threatened me with the spiritual dangers I would encounter outside the monastery; the temptation to return to the life of a cartwright, the temptation of women, and so on.

It is true that there were moments of darkness in my perceptions of the monastery. For example, I knew that the floor of the parlatory was made out of millstones that had belonged to poor peasants, millstones they had possessed without the permission of our founding monastery, and which the monks there had taken from them and smashed as a punishment, in order to protect their revenues. Also, I had read about the way our founder, Bernard of Cîteaux, had treated the great French scholar Abelard. But I put such thoughts to the back of my mind, for at the time I had faith in the Order and in my destiny – or rather I was unable to distinguish between faith and gullibility.

I suppose I could have just walked out. Fear of compromising my future stopped me from doing so. Also, I was convinced that the vow of obedience was to be taken seriously.

Eventually I made an appointment with the Abbot himself. By this time I was rather nervous of him. The appointment was directly after matins. It was still dark outside when I arrived at his cell. I was shaking both with the cold and the fear I felt.

'Come in, Walter,' he said formally and impatiently. He was sitting on a large wooden chair behind his desk. A single candle burnt, illuminating the papers he was dealing with and lighting his face in a way that made his square face look oddly angular, unreal. 'What do you want?' he half snarled.

'Father Abbot, I have come to ask your permission to return home to my father. I wish to convey to him my joy at having found my true vocation at last.'

'You want to go and ease your tradesman's conscience, or waste time with that Jew, more like. Don't you know how many terrible temptations will lie in wait for you if you venture into the world? Women, the company of devils who will try to lead you from the true path, those who will do everything in their power to shake your vocation.'

'Yet I cannot be at peace until I have seen him. I should never be able to take my vows sincerely.'

'It is written that, if you wish to follow Christ, you should leave the dead to bury the dead.'

'Father,' I said, 'I beg you on bended knee.'

'Very well then,' he said, 'but I assure you that no good will come of it. I shall expect you back within a fortnight, or else your place here might be called into question.'

I was shocked to be dismissed in such a summary fashion. I had the freedom I craved, yet there was a bitter taste in my mouth.

Just one hour later, as the sun was rising – a faint, eerie red – over the forest, Father Jonathan came to me in the refectory.

'Are you sure you wish to go?' he said. 'You know the Abbot thinks it is dangerous for you to leave now.'

'And I suppose you do too.'

'I have seen much in my time, Walter, much that you would scarcely believe.'

'Please,' I said, 'I must go.'

He did not stand in my way but gave me provisions for the journey and led me to the great wooden gate leading out of the monastery enclosure.

As I set off into the forest I remember the light was dull and the chill of the night still hung in the air. I tried to put the foreboding, grey atmosphere out of my mind. I was impatient to see my father. And it was true: I was looking forward to seeing Uqhart again. I thought of all the new learning I had acquired, which I wanted to discuss with Uqhart. I was arrogant enough to think that with my newly found grace and wisdom I was going to be able to convert Uqhart to Christianity, to convince him that the one missing element in his cosmology was the Person of Christ.

On my way I passed through Babenberch, which I reached after two days' walking. It was the first time I had returned since the great fire had destroyed the cathedral and the school in the year of our Lord 1185 and brought my own schooldays to an end. The place was still a ruin, though reconstruction had begun. It was almost as if the memory of those flames should have been a warning about those that were being prepared in Nurenberc. I stood for a long while among the ruins, the debris and the foundations of the new buildings.

Two days later I stayed in the same inn where I had first sung with Pauli. There was a hushed atmosphere and I noticed that people were looking askance at me as I entered. I realised that this was because I was wearing a Cistercian habit. Eventually I was accepted into the company of a group of travelling merchants who were sitting round the fire. We drank beer together. They told me that there was to be a burning at the market square in Nurenberc in two days' time. I did not pay much attention.

Two days later, just before midday, I arrived, finally, at Nurenberc. I had never seen the town so full other than at the time of the Fair of the Feast of Fools. Everyone was out on the streets. Yet it was not like the Fair. There were stalls selling ale and food, but people were silent or talking only in low murmurs, motionless, all gazing in the same direction, towards the scaffolding in the main square. The air was humid and clouds hung low in the sky. It had not rained, but it promised to at any moment. There were odd, gold-brown streaks across the clouds where the sun was trying to shine. The atmosphere accentuated the stench in the air, the stench of burnt human flesh.

I pushed my way forward to see. Flames were still licking up from the pile of wood, though the fire was burning down. There was a golden, tawny redness in the flames that was identical to the colour in the sky. I could just make out, in the flames, the blackened figure of something that had been human. As I stared, the ropes binding the corpse must finally have burnt through. I saw the teeth, open as if to shout, in the blackened and eyeless head, as the body lurched defiantly forward towards the crowd. It collapsed to the ground, showering sparks over those standing close by, sending a pillar of flame towards the skies, and dissolving to nothing in the blackness of the ashes.

Just then it began to drizzle.

The crowd had fallen silent. People's faces were ashen with hatred. Some were grinning with satisfaction at seeing what they considered to be justice done; some were lost in the horror of the spectacle; others were growing bored and wondering what to do next. I turned to the people next to me and asked them who had been burnt and why. I heard what they said, but my mind rejected it.

I gleaned first of all that the man had been a heretic - not only a heretic but a magician who cast evil spells, who had sacrificed a young Christian man to Satan. He had cut off the young man's face and tied him to a horse. It was only through the direct intervention of Saint Sebald, they said, that the horse had been led back to Nurenberc, still dragging the young man's poor, torn body. Under torture the magician admitted that he had sacrificed another young man in this way, and that he had cursed that man's father, causing him to take his own life, tormenting him by means of the evil spirits he had conjured. Someone else said that the magician had resisted torture for weeks before he finally admitted to his crimes, to practising the black arts, keeping devilish substances, worshipping the devil and conspiring against our Lord. His insensitivity to pain showed that he was of the devil.

It was only after I had grasped the essence of the story that I heard someone say the name Uqhart. As I began to understand, I trembled and felt like vomiting. Then I think I must have fallen to my knees. I remember the crowd looming above me. I must have shouted out his name as I realised what had happened.

Then someone screamed, 'Stop him, stop him. He is calling on his spirit!'

The horror of what had happened was just beginning to sink in. I realised that Pauli must have been the young man who was supposed to have been sacrificed, and that I was the other man. I just had the presence of mind to pull myself together before I was recognised, before the crowd lynched me or tore me limb from limb.

I stood up and said, 'What are you saying? Look at me. I am a Cistercian brother. I am praying, for you all and for this town of evil.' Then I pulled my hood low over my face and set off to my father's house.

When I got there, it was deserted. All was silence. There were no workmen laughing and shouting, no sound of the cutting of wood or the beating of steel. My stepmother and halfbrother were nowhere to be seen. The linden tree was still there; otherwise it was like the house of a stranger, a ghost-house.

I looked closer. All the tools had been removed from the workshops and from the yard. I looked inside the house: all the furniture had gone. I stood outside, trying to think. The rain was beginning to pour down now, and the town seemed bathed in an uncanny yellow-grey light. I feared talking to the neighbours. I did not want to be recognised. I did not want to have to give account to anyone for who I was and what had become of me.

Back out on the street I saw a stranger, a woman whose back

was hunched with age. 'I am trying to find Adam von der Ouwe, the cartwright,' I said.

'Well, you won't find him here, not in the land of the living. He drowned himself. Over a month ago. Everyone here knows that.' I stared. She went on. 'Some say it was because his wife ran off with that lover of hers from Fürth. But others say he was cursed by that magician they burnt today. I can well believe that. They say he killed his own stepson...'

My next memory is that somehow I made my way to the graveyard. It was already dusk. What I had done in the intervening hour or so I do not know. But I remember the gravedigger. I remember his face. There was a gigantic swelling on his jaw; he would be joining the dead soon. He was showing me where my father's grave was. I remember his voice: he hissed and gurgled as he spoke, like a devil sneering from the pit. He was pointing to a fresh plot.

'Should have been buried at the crossroads, that's what I think,' he said, 'him being a suicide. This is holy ground. No place for suicides here. Suicide is a sin, an unforgivable sin, even if he was driven to it by that Jew. There's been no sweeter smell in Nurenberc than the smell of his flesh burning today. That Jew's stepson is buried there,' he said, pointing to another, slightly older grave, this one marked with a cross. I thought of poor Pauli, remembered his voice, his songs. 'He had that poor Christian boy work as his slave till for his pains they found him being dragged through the forest by a ghostly horse, and all his face was a pulp of beaten meat, poor lad. No one would have recognised him but for Uqhart's howling when he saw him. The demon's got him, and not even the torture at the castle would make him repent.'

I remember falling. It was as if the graves, the dark, underground world of the graves was pulling me. Then I remember the man's face bent over me, grinning a toothless grin. I think there were other people there. I remember standing up and lashing out at them. I don't know if I hurt them. I certainly knocked the big gravedigger over for long enough to get away.

The next thing I remember it was night-time and I was in the forest, not far from where Katrin and I used to meet. The forest was a grey, misty shadow. Night was drawing in. All around me I thought I heard neighing, the neighing of the horse dragging Pauli. All the time there was the smell of burning in my nose. I wanted to return to the monastery. But I knew that it was through my staying at the monastery that the disaster had come about.

I remember throwing myself on the ground, as thoughts throbbing with anger and remorse crowded in on me and tortured me. The realization that the time I had spent at the monastery was a deceit was too much for me. Each new thought that came, each new realization, was like a blade being thrust into my head. I twisted and writhed on the cold forest floor as the mists rolled about the trees. By then it was almost dark. I was sure I could hear spirits, ghosts, goblins, spiteful things of night, everywhere, laughing at me. If only they had been more real, more present than the truth of what had happened.

Then I was standing on one of the bridges over the Main, upstream from the centre of the town. Everything would have been pitch-black had it not been for the pale light of the half moon peering occasionally from between the clouds and reflected in the dark waters. I knew it was the bridge from which my father had jumped. I wanted to jump too, into the blackness, the void, to be with him. There was a close, oppressive, leaden silence over all the world. The wind was cold, bitterly cold and loveless. All my loves - Katrin, my home, my school and the monastery - all were empty now, and gone.

As I stared at the water I remember my despair turning to an icy bitterness and defiance. Death, then, would have been too easy. I wanted to suffer more, on this earth. Most of all, I wanted to know. I had to know why everything had turned out like this.

I trembled with hatred for myself as I stood there and saw a hallucinated, distorted reflection of my face in the water, gigantic, round and grinning, hairless and white with a mocking, toothless grin. As if driven by wild, demoniac forces, I ran off, back into the forest, where I walked aimlessly for days and nights, drinking from streams, eating nothing, praying only for death.

Somehow, I ended up at Fürth, where I was nursed by a kind priest, Father Ludovicus, who had found me lying in the market square, quite unconscious.

I have odd, disjointed memories of him. I remember him trying to feed me with sweet-smelling soups, and offering herbal infusions to help me sleep. I remember trying to tell my life story to him. And I remember moments when the insanity would return and I would start flailing and writhing on the floor, howling self-recriminations.

He listened patiently to me, and helped me regain my equanimity. I shall always be grateful to him.

As soon as I could, I set off again for Nurenberc, to the castle. I wanted to talk to the Bishop. He was a loathsome creature, but if anyone knew the truth about Uqhart's death, it would be him.

It poured with rain as I dragged myself through the forests that lie between Fürth and Nurenberc. I was still exhausted. Yet what had been a bitter inability to reconcile myself to the changes in my life had now become an oppressive, leaden certainty. My only aim was to lighten the load by discovering more facts.

On my way through the wooden gates that stood at the south of the city, I noticed a number of the Bishop's men, bearing arms, standing round, chatting. I thought they were there because of the rumours of revolt amongst the peasants.

As I was passing, I heard one of the guards shout, 'It's him!'

At first I paid no attention, but then I sensed a surge of movement towards me. It was me they were after.

Stupidly, I started to run, but the ground was muddy. My feet kept slipping and the puddles slowed me down. I cannot have run far before I felt a hard thump on the back of my head. I fell face forward into the mud and blacked out.

I woke in a dungeon. I was quite alone. The back of my head throbbed mercilessly. I was thirsty and cold. Eventually a jailer came with water. It stank of urine. I asked for food, and got nothing but one or two stale crusts a day.

I became feverish. My attempts at devotions were beset with vile hallucinations. I remember once imagining that the dungeon was infested with black, crawling insects with skeletal jaws, and that the jailer was a giant black eagle with vicious talons and sick, yellow eyes. Outside I heard the crashing and clattering sounds of war machines, which were like giant insects with metal snouts, hanging in the air above Nurenberc and spitting fire and evil all over the town. I had the sense of travelling, uncontrollably, forward in time, perhaps to the days of Armageddon.

It must have been four or five days before I was dragged to a larger cell. The light shining through the slit window high up in the room hurt my eyes. Behind the table, in all his glory, sat the Bishop himself. There were guards on either side of him, each armed with a pike.

The Bishop was a mean little man, bald, fat, with a face that would have been oafish had it not so radiated selfish ill-will and hardness of heart.

'Who are you?' he croaked.

'Walter von der Ouwe, the son of Adam von der Ouwe.'

'But he is dead.'

'My father is dead, I know.'

'No, no. Walter von der Ouwe is dead. He was killed by the magician Uqhart. You are either an impostor, or an evil spirit impersonating him.'

In my shock, I tried to stand up, but the guards pushed me down again. The Bishop took the crucifix from round his neck and held it out towards me as if I really were some demon.

'No,' I said, 'listen...'

I tried to tell him my story – how I had returned, how I had seen the burning. I managed to stop myself from weeping or shouting; this man would have taken it as proof that I was an evil spirit, or that I was possessed by one.

'Why do you think Uqhart killed me?' I asked.

'He confessed to it, here in this very dungeon.'

Clarity of mind was fuelled by anger as I realised that it was here, in this very place, that Uqhart was tortured. It was here that they would have branded him, beaten him, humiliated him. I realised that I was fighting for my own survival.

'There has been a mistake,' I said. 'For the last six months I have been living as a monk with the Cistercian brothers at Frankenburc. I beg you to send word to Abbot Quintus. He will vouch for me.'

Suddenly, a worried look darkened his pug-like face. The Cistercians are a powerful force and it is in the interest of no ruler, temporal or ecclesiastical, to get on the wrong side of them.

'Take him back to his cell,' he said.

From then on, things changed. I was moved to a better cell. There was enough room to stretch, and there was a desk, a table and some light from a small slit window, which looked out over the river.

A new jailer was assigned to me who brought me very good food, ale and even books, a candle to read by, and, finally, my lute. I felt my strength returning. This new jailer's name was Brother Andreas. He was in his early twenties, thin, blond, nervous but well versed in the arts of conversation and disputation. He chatted to me about the events leading up to my imprisonment. We also talked about philosophy and religion. This went on for a week or so.

One day he slipped into my hands a piece of paper on which he had written: 'Walter, friend, we are overheard. All will be well. Soon I am to take you to the Bishop. Promise him anything he asks. You have protection.'

I tried to catch his eye, but the look on his face made it clear that I was not to show that I had seen the note. Instead of remaining seated as usual, Brother Andreas stood up, told me to take my lute and papers and follow him.

I hardly dared hope that I was leaving my cell for the last time. As we made our way up the spiral staircase, my blood was chilled by the sobs, shouts, and screams of those who were being tortured. I wondered what lay in store for me.

I was led to a private room on the second floor of the castle, an antechamber to the main upper reception hall where feasts were held for the most noble guests. The scents in the room, compared with the stench of the dungeons, were heavenly. There was the smell of beautifully prepared food – game with rare fruits and vegetables – and this mingled with the scent of incense. There were beautiful tapestries, woven red and gold, hanging from the walls all round us. The chairs were wooden and beautifully carved, with faces of lions on the arms. I would have thought I was dreaming, or in heaven, had I not been so nervous and suspicious.

I was welcomed by the Bishop. He was sitting on a folding chair, wearing fine robes. On the table in front of him was a bottle of wine and three goblets, and the most magnificent spread of game, hams, sweetmeats, rare fruits and cheeses. He offered me a goblet of wine, which I accepted.

Unlike the first time we met, the Bishop did everything he could to exude goodwill towards me. The faces he pulled were jovial enough, though his eyes remained as hard, grey and unfeeling as I remembered them from before.

'It is obvious,' he pronounced pompously, 'that a mistake was made in the trial of the magician Uqhart - but only with regard to your person. And you only have yourself to blame, since you were away for so long, without sending word. It was genuinely believed that you were dead.'

I remembered Andreas' note and resisted any temptation to contradict him.

'None the less,' he went on - it was significant that he used Latin, so that the servants would not be able to overhear us – 'as Bishop of Nurenberc, I am your superior and your master in all matters temporal and spiritual. Therefore I am able to command you, and I shall do so. Uqhart was guilty of casting spells which led to the death of his stepson, and thereby to the death of your father. The man had many marks of the devil, one of which was the fact that he was quite insensitive to pain. Do you understand? My point is this: the common people must not be led to doubt the veracity of the findings of Uqhart's trial. Therefore I am commanding you that you should not speak to any individual about what has passed between us, neither should you voice any suspicions regarding Uqhart's trial.'

I understood that he was frightened of somebody or something. I also knew that frightened men are dangerous.

'I have total faith in the judgement of my superiors,' I said. 'Therefore the virtue of obedience is important to me. It is for this reason also that I have chosen the Cistercian way of life.'

At the word Cistercian I noticed that he winced slightly.

'Good, then we need discuss the matter no further. I have made arrangements for you to travel immediately back to the monastery at Frankenburc, where the Abbot will take charge of your future. Now, I understand you have a fine voice and great poetic gifts. When we have eaten, perhaps you will sing to me.'

I thanked the Bishop again. We ate, though it is curious how food, no matter how good, sticks in the throat when one is in the company of a person one despises as much as I despised the Bishop.

# VI

## The Lovers

✝

I spun out my journey, living wild in the forest for three or four weeks before I decided that I would, after all, return to the monastery at Frankenburc - not because I wanted to live as a monk, but because I wanted to know why the Abbot had delayed my departure. The more I thought about it, the more I became convinced that he was to blame for Uqhart's death, and my father's.

I entered the great gate to the monastery and announced my arrival to the brother on duty. He told me to wait and sent for Father Jonathan, who came within minutes. Father Jonathan was clearly nervous but welcomed me with as much warmth as he could muster. I was pleased to see him. He led me directly to the Abbot. By now I suspected the Abbot of keeping me at the monastery under false pretences and I felt sure that he knew all along what was happening to my father, but I could not be sure. The very sight of the Abbot angered me as he stood there, beaming his spiritually superior smile at me.

He neglected to ask me how I was, what I had been doing; he knew already. This added to my suspicion. I greeted him carefully and courteously. He must have sensed my coolness, especially the way I recoiled when he embraced me.

My plan was to ease my way back into life at the monastery, where I knew at least that I would be lodged and fed, and then look for ways to find out more about the events in Nurenberc.

However, I was not to spend so much as one night there. The Abbot Quintus had foreseen my resentment. He suggested that I should go to the washrooms and clean myself up. There was a mirror there. It was true that I looked a sight, with long, knotted hair and a gaunt face burnt brown by sun and wind and stained with dirt, despite the fact that I had often bathed in lakes and streams.

Then I was invited to the Abbot's cell, where I was offered a meal of game, fruit, vegetables and wine. There he told me, bluntly, that I had been invited to serve and sing at court in Frankenburc. Apparently the ladies remembered me from my first visit and the Graefin still talked about one of my love songs in particular. The Graf and Graefin were willing to offer me employment, to sing, write and help with the education of the pages. I would have the opportunity to learn the courtly arts of horsemanship, weaponry, falconry and so on. If I worked and served well, eventually I should have the opportunity to become a knight.

I ought to have been overjoyed. Instead, I felt numb. I was being told what to do. There was no choice. Because of what I knew, my presence at the monastery could no longer be tolerated, yet I was being sent to a place where it would be possible to keep an eye on me. After the meal I asked to spend time on my own, to think matters over. I went to the abbey church and tried to pray, but I could not recapture the way I felt in former days.

I returned to the Abbot's room. The Abbot was alone. I fell on my knees and implored him, 'Please, your grace. I know there is something you are not telling me. I must know what it is.'

All he said was, 'You are very tired, Walter. You have a terrible ordeal behind you. Come, I will take you to somewhere you can rest.'

'I must know,' I shouted once more.

Then he said, more sternly, 'Walter, you must not be arrogant, or entertain thoughts and ideas above your present station in life. You have many friends. We are your best friends. All we want is for your own good.'

I stood up, grabbed my lute. I asked curtly if I might go to Frankenburc straight away.

The Abbot nodded. I left without saying another word.

So, for this, my second arrival at Frankenburc, I was alone. Apart from my clothes, all I possessed was my small purse of money and my lute. I reflected that I would be singing to those who held in their possession vast tracts of land, stretching distances greater than I had travelled in my whole life.

It was late in the afternoon when I arrived at the town. I walked in through the gates and visited the site where the new church was being built. The town was small, but clean and prosperous, with rows of recently built houses. Some of the houses were of stone rather than wood; they looked very fine indeed. I remember the fresh smell from a bakery I passed. It was a clear day, but the light was hazy, and a mist swirled lazily, almost serenely over the slow waters of the Main in the valley below.

The castle enclosure stood at the far end of the town, majestic, daunting, on the top of a steep hill overlooking the town. I felt hope, ambition, the taste of new freedom, stir in me as I climbed the winding pathway leading to the gates at the top of the hill.

I remember the feeling of trepidation as I presented myself to the gateman, a doddery old fellow with a bald head and pot belly. The castle was smaller than the one at Nurenberc, but it was newer, and built of a magnificent, greyish-white stone that shone in the sunlight. There was an outer wall before one reached the castle compound proper. In the space between the inner and outer walls were some houses, an area where animals were kept, including stables, and another area which was kept clear for weapon practice. Then there was an inner wall, into which defensive towers were built. At the very centre was the main fortress, strong and square, but I noticed that some of its arches had splendid zigzag decorations, just like the noblest of churches, and befitting the high birth and gracious life of those it housed. Or so I thought at the time.

Behind the castle the land stretched away to a plateau, higher than the plain from which I had climbed via the town. The plateau was forested, apart from an area immediately behind the castle, which had been cleared. This was the place where one day I would fight Johannes of Ulm in the tournament.

I had to wait for about half an hour at the gates. The old man tottered off and did not return. All I had for company were two surly-looking soldiers who guarded the entrance and made it plain from their bearing that I should proceed no further.

Through a grille fixed over the narrow window facing into the courtyard I glimpsed a noble lady stepping out from a door on the opposite side of the courtyard. She was young, beautiful - breathtakingly beautiful - with long, flowing gold-blond hair. Her face was girlish. She was wearing a blue dyed dress. She moved with such grace. I fully expected her to disappear from view at any moment, to re-enter the main building of the castle through a different door. Yet, to my surprise, she continued to walk in my direction. My heart leapt when I realised that she was coming to talk to me.

She welcomed me to the castle, using noble, courtly figures of speech, and then asked after my journey and well-being. When I had replied appropriately, she led me in silence across the courtyard to the lower hall.

This was Hildegunde. Even at that first meeting I was attracted to her. Yet, since she could be sent on errands like greeting lowly singers, I assumed that she was not of high birth, perhaps too girlish to be worthy of the noble love of which I had learnt to sing during my studies and my short time of wandering with Pauli.

I remembered the lower hall from my first visit. This time everything was much quieter. The Graf Friedrich was sitting on his folding chair in front of the fire discussing business with four knights and three ladies - one of the ladies I recognised as the Graefin. As before, I was struck by how tall and powerfully built the Graf was. This was discernable even though he was sitting rather than standing. He was truly a giant of a man and, though his fighting days were probably over, given his age and status, one would still have had to be a brave man to cross him.

I was entranced too by the nobility of the appearance and

bearing of his wife, the Graefin. She stood behind the Graf, her hand on his left shoulder.

Hildegunde joined the group, sitting next to the Graefin. Rich tapestries hung from the stone wall behind the group of nobles and on the walls to the right of them. The floor was strewn with grass, flowers and newly gathered rushes, creating a pleasing, fresh odour. Beautifully embroidered cushions were strewn over the window-seats and the stones that jutted out beneath the pillars. On the wall that had no tapestries I saw displayed a number of shields. Of course pride of place was given to the one bearing the Graf's own coat of arms, a giant black eagle on a white cross against a golden field. I noticed that another of the shields was painted red and was decorated with diagonal stripes and the sign of the crescent moon. No doubt it had been captured from the Saracen. I gazed at it in amazement.

In retrospect I imagine that the Graf must have been bored with the business in hand. I entered the hall timidly, but I was greeted warmly enough. The Graf introduced me to the others and asked me a few courteous questions about myself, to which I knew how to reply appropriately. Then he asked me to play and to sing. The Graefin said that she was very keen to hear a composition on the subject of noble love.

I was tired from walking, but I did as best I could. I sang one song praising the virtues of courtly life, another on the subject of the ideal lady, and then a crusading song, which was a favourite of Barbarossa's and I thought might please this audience. Frankenburc was a Hohenstaufen fief.

The Graefin stared at me wide-eyed while I sang, as if to devour not only every word and every note but my person also. Hildegunde remained in the hall, but she kept her eyes averted; she left as soon as I had finished. The men and other ladies listened quietly. As I sang I felt the power of the music issuing from my voice and from my lute. I reflected on how powerful these people were, how they could destroy me at whim. I remembered the story of Orpheus, of how he tamed the beasts. I should have reflected more deeply on that legend.

The Graf Friedrich thanked me for my singing and confirmed that I was welcome to stay at the court for as long as I wished. In return for my keep I was to sing at mealtimes and banquets when required. Also, I was to play a part, under the guidance of the courtier Theodor, in looking after the education and training of the pages, the younger members of the court. I was to teach them such skills as horsemanship, armed combat, music, dancing, backgammon, chess, how to carve meat and how to present wine properly, while kneeling. I agreed readily, though amongst these skills were many I myself had not yet mastered.

Theodor was a shortish man, about forty years old, with curly, greying hair, a thin face and a wiry physique. He was full of nervous energy. Amongst other duties, he was in charge of the domestic arrangements at the court. First of all he led me to the place where I was to sleep. In order to get there we had to go through the rear courtyard, pick our way amongst the ducks and chickens that were kept in the far corner, then climb two flights of stairs, and finally a ladder, to a small storage room-cum-loft, which was tucked just under the very top of one of the towers. The main function of this room was defensive, since there was a trapdoor leading out on to the roof. There was a slit window, which offered a view over Frankenburc but which promised to be horribly draughty in the wintertime.

The room was being used to store hay. Theodor suggested I could use this to make a bed for myself. It occurred to me that in the winter I would be able to use the hay to stop up the windows. This was to be my home throughout the time I spent at the court.

Next he led me to the women's quarters, on the other side of the courtyard, to be measured for clothes. This was where the young women of the court spent their days, when not with the men, either reading, singing, studying, sewing or weaving.

The sight of me made some of them giggle. I presumed this was because of the unfashionable, tattered clothes I was wearing. Hildegunde was amongst them and she played a leading role in what followed. I was measured and fitted out with one set of clothes for everyday use - a strong woollen jacket, a shirt, boots and riding breeches - and also a clean jerkin, dyed dark red, and matching breeches, which I was to wear when singing in front of the nobles.

Then Theodor took me on a tour of the castle. I was shown the quarters of the pages, for whom I would be in part responsible, the kitchens, the new baths that had been built, the quarters of the noblemen, the stables for the hunting horses, the wooden houses for the married people, which were built outside the keep but within the wall, the stables where the warhorses and dogs were kept. Then he showed me the aviary for the falcons, the massive armoury in the vaults beneath the castle and then the means of access to the roofs and ramparts.

Finally Theodor led me back through the lower hall, where now there were people milling round - retainers, men-at-arms, clerks, servants, grooms, equerries, pages - past the place where they stored the trestles, which were used as tables for banquets and beds for important guests, past the great chests where the carved wooden drinking-goblets were kept, and then up the wooden stairs to the private chambers, which were used by the Graf and Graefin for private relaxation, for intimate times together with those who were close to them, or for receiving in private those to whom they owed allegiance. The Emperor Barbarossa himself had been there on a number of occasions, as well as Philip of Swabia and envoys of popes.

I stood there, proudly sporting my new clothes, lost in admiration for the room, for it was also the place where the treasures were kept. I had never been anywhere more like I imagined heaven must be. There were the most colourful and artfully woven tapestries, with pictures of strange creatures and scenes of hunting and battle, intricately carved cupboards, another Saracen shield, and richly decorated golden and silver chalices, plates and trinkets spread for show over the carved wooden table at the end of the room.

Theodor was just telling me that there were other rooms, which were to have been for the Graf's heirs but sadly he had none as yet, so they were standing empty – when the Graefin came in. She was calm, tall and slender. Now, at closer quarters, I could tell that her face had lost its freshness and was beginning to wrinkle with age. Her hair was brown but beginning to turn grey. It was knotted into a plait, which hung long down her back. She wore a simple, long, deep-red dyed woollen dress, which made her look even more striking, since it emphasised the straightness of her bearing and the power in her face. In her youth she must have been very beautiful, and she had not lost the habit of thinking herself so. Her eyes were indomitably proud, and this was the chief source of the grace she possessed. She was a woman used to commanding not only obedience but also love and admiration.

She asked me to sing again. She told me that she admired my voice and my songs. Then she went on to quiz me about my abilities as a horseman, whether I knew how to shoot an arrow, whether I knew how to hunt, play chess and backgammon, train falcons. She asked me, too, with an almost vicious look in her eye, what I knew about armed combat on horseback.

I answered all these questions truthfully, making no attempt to disguise what I did not know. The Graefin appeared pleased with the account I gave of myself.

She asked me which books I knew. She had read many of the courtly romances. I was able to recite to her excerpts from Tristan and from King Arthur. She said that if I worked hard I would certainly manage to cultivate the ways of the court, and acquire the appropriate graces, correct manners and so on. Above all she said that she wanted me to learn love and respect for the ladies, the art of *minne*. As she said this she smiled seductively and I felt myself blush.

Then I was dismissed. I went to my room, or rather my attic in the tower. I was delighted to have this space to myself and tried to compose a song that would sum up my feelings, but I was exhausted and fell asleep before the song was complete.

The next time I saw her was at the second meal the following day.

At the castle we ate twice, once in the middle of the morning and once in the early evening. It was this latter meal that the nobles would extend into a banquet if important guests were present. This suited me far better than eating just once a day, as we had done in the monastery. Also, I loved the spices that were used in the food – peppers, gingers and saffron – which had been brought back specially from the Holy Land.

I recognised Hildegunde immediately because of her long, golden hair. She came and sat next to me.

We did not speak at first. Then she addressed me. Her manner was dignified, lively, utterly natural and yet controlled. She asked me my name, where I came from, and so on. I answered briefly, then asked her similar questions.

'My name is Hildegunde. I am seventeen,' she said, 'and I am the ward of the Ritter of Ochsenfurt, the orphan of his younger brother who was killed on the Crusade.'

'What is your role here?' I asked her.

There was a charming pride in the way she spoke. She took herself seriously but without boasting.

'I am one of the chief ladies-in-waiting to the Graefin von Frankenburc. I presume that this is what I shall remain until they find a nobleman for me to marry.'

Even then I felt a pang of exclusion, of envy. I was not noble and I knew that I would never be allowed to enter into a legitimate relationship with a girl like this.

After a silence I asked, 'Are you interested in music?'

'Yes,' she said. 'That is why I wanted to talk to you. I remember the songs you played the last time you were here. I liked them very much. I play the fiddle and the psaltery. I can sing passably. In fact the Graefin and I often sing together.'

I was taken aback. I was beginning to realise that I was speaking to no ordinary girl. 'Where did you learn all this?' I asked.

'At the convent school in Rupertsberc, where I lived until I was fifteen.'

'Then you must have studied Latin too.'

It turned out that, like me, she had whole passages of Virgil by heart, and some Ovid too. I could hardly believe my ears - or my eyes, for the more I looked at her the more her beauty impressed itself upon me.

Now I shall never forget it.

If it had not been for the fact that the time had come for me to go and sing to the Graefin, I think I could have stayed with her there, talking all night long. From that first meeting it was her face, and not Katrin's, that came to mind when I sang of *minne*, of love. That night also, when I slept, I noticed that I was continuing mentally the dialogue I had begun with her that evening. From that moment it seemed that all I had ever learnt and done had been for the sake of relating it to her, that somehow I had always known her, and that all the thoughts I had ever thought were one side of a dialogue, only I had not known who my partner in the conversation was going to be...

> *Si ist mir liep und liebet mir fur elliu wip,*
> *si ist mir iemer lieber dan min selbes lip,*
> *si ist lieb ane zal, daz spriche ich offenbar,*
> *si ist min liehtiu rose rot und ouch min spilnder sunne klar.* *

As I came to know more people about the court, so my daily life became more full. My main responsibilities lay in the direction of music and singing. There were others with good voices and with talent too, yet I was favoured. Some of my time was spent organising music with others, and also training the younger pages and wards in the arts of reading, writing and music. I worked under the direction of Theodor.

Theodor encouraged me to cultivate knightly virtues, and he

---

* *She is dear to me and gives me more joy than any other women, / She is more dear to me than my own life / She is infinitely dear to me, and I confess this openly / She is my fair red rose and my shining bright sun.* (Reinmar von Brennenburg)

held out the hope that perhaps one day I might be dubbed a knight, which was not without precedent for a young man of my status, provided he possessed the requisite devotion, talent and military skills. To this end, in addition to my musical and educational duties, the Graf arranged for me to take part in and learn other activities, to fight my tendency towards melancholy by leading an active life, shunning sloth, and learning gymnastics, riding, swimming, hunting, falconry, fencing, in addition to archery, chess, music and versification, which I had already mastered. There were many musical instruments at the court, some of which I had never even set eyes on before. There were fiddles and lutes made with much finer craftsmanship than mine, rebecks, lyres, a very fine harp, flutes, sackbuts and horns of various kinds. There was even a hurdy-gurdy, which it required two men to play. I came to master each of these instruments in turn.

I began to spend more time with the young nobles training to become knights. There were many fine young men among them, and one or two fools. At first, because of my low birth, the nobles did not accept me. It was only when I showed that my talents lay not only in singing, but in such pastimes as dancing, archery, swordsmanship, hunting and the competitions to see who was best at jumping on to a horse when fully armed, that they began to treat me as one of their number, and eventually, as it happened, to look up to me. The time I spent in the forest as a young boy came in useful, for at that time I had learnt how to make long bows cut from yew. I could shoot very accurately with these. Many knights said that they would themselves disdain to use such a weapon, for it was contrary to the rules of battle for a knight to kill a man or a horse at a distance. Yet they were interested to see how the bow worked and to learn how deadly a weapon it could be in the hands of one who knew how to shoot it well.

I had long discussions with Theodor and also with the Graefin about the courtly and knightly virtues that we heard were being practised in Aquitaine and in other courts in the German Empire: honour, fidelity, moderation, right-living.

Yet the most important influence for me was Hildegunde. Since that first meal we had always tended to sit next to each other at supper, and we talked together about our reading, about my songs, or about what we had done during the day. Whenever I saw her I took the image with me and thought about her until the next time we happened to meet. Because of this, and because I took the opportunity of talking to her at mealtimes and whenever else I could, I soon got a good idea of what she did during the course of a day.

Every morning she would attend chapel with the other women. As a sign of favour the Graefin would often let her stand next to her. They would talk together on the way out of chapel. Then Hildegunde would spend time with the women, helping with the weaving and sewing. But she did not have to put in as many hours as most of the others since she was a particular favourite of the Graefin's, and the Graefin would often ask Hildegunde to read to her for an hour or so before lunch. Hildegunde had a sweet reading voice and was very learned for her age. There was nothing one could not talk to her about. Hildegunde had many interesting ideas of her own, but she knew when to speak, when to listen, and when to reflect back the ideas and views expected of her, embroidering them perhaps but not appropriating them.

In the afternoons the women would rest for an hour or so. During that period Hildegunde would often spend time with the Graefin and practise singing. Hildegunde was learning the harp. She could already play the psaltery well and the fiddle passably. Then, for an hour or so before Nones and supper, she would instruct the younger girls in the arts of dancing, singing and the correct presentation of food, as well as dressmaking and reading.

The court had quite a good library, situated in the vaults of an older part of the castle. It contained nowhere near the number of manuscripts as the one at the monastery, but it did have a good selection of secular literature, courtly romances, songs and the like. Hildegunde and the Graefin spent a lot of time organising the younger girls in the copying of manuscripts, and in persuading priests and passing knights with a taste for learning to look out for more manuscripts for the court to purchase, before they fell into the hands of the monasteries. Like me, Hildegunde was in the habit of going to the library after supper and staying up late in order to read. If ever we were there together, I would find it hard not to stare at her. But we were not able to speak then, for the library was designated a place of silence and one of the older women was always on guard.

Hildegunde led a busy life, but a rich and harmonious one, filled with learning, music and the fine pursuits of the court. I never heard her complain, and she always smiled at me in the most graceful way whenever she saw me. I suppose that in many ways her role at court amongst the women was parallel to mine amongst the men. For that reason perhaps, it was not frowned upon when we talked together about music, poetry and court business that affected us both.

The main difference between us was one of birth: she was noble. Her father was dead; he died on Crusade with Barbarossa, and his property had fallen into the hands of his brother, the Ritter of Ochsenfurt, who had sent Hildegunde to Frankenburc. Even in those days I could tell from the way she talked of him that there was something about her uncle that she did not like.

I thought about her constantly. To me, she embodied all the courtly virtues. Everything I did – all my striving to master the ways of the court, to put into practice the ideal of courtly life, to master the arts of war, to perfect my singing and writing, to strengthen my body and take an interest in political questions – all this was to please Hildegunde.

I remembered my experiences with Katrin: how could I forget? A part of me, the basest part, would have given anything to repeat them with Hildegunde. Yet the better part urged me to respect her purity. Did she not go to chapel first thing every morning? Did she not pray with the Graefin and the other ladies every evening? Did she not follow a programme of private devotions. And when I watched her praying in chapel during the main services, could I not see the light of purity in her face? When the Virgin Mary was a girl, surely she could not have been more beautiful and graceful than Hildegunde. I saw her as the pure soul the Abbess of Bingen describes: '*O felix Anima, et o dulcis creatura dei, que edificata es in profunda altitudine sapientie dei...*' ★

Hildegunde used to tell me what the Graefin would say to the women about their role at the court; how it was the duty of a true lady to think of her God and her Lord and to keep herself always pure. She should bear children, of course (she said this despite the fact that she had no children of her own). The willingness to bear children made her equal to a man in bravery, for in childbirth she risked her life just as a man risked his life in battle. Yet, also, a lady should be sure to remain modest, yet beautiful; generous, yet aware of her rank. She should cultivate the arts of music, reading, writing, poetry, dancing, even riding and falconry if she wished, and indeed all pleasant things fitting to her station.

I heard all these things, but I also knew that there were women in the court who were willing to give themselves to any young man who took their fancy, provided that the young man was in favour with the Graf. They were not whores, for they did not take money, but they were of easy virtue. I heard too that even a married woman would sometimes take a younger man, if he pleased her. I had read of such things in the courtly romances, which were often about adulterous loves. Yet I dismissed such thoughts with regard to my own person – fool that I was.

Like Hildegunde, I was fired with enthusiasm for the nobility of courtly ideals. I would work them into my songs, which I made as clever and witty as I could, yet full of yearning and desire both for the beauty of the ladies and for the ordered life they inspired. I was to surmise later, from the manner in which I ended up having to leave the court, that the Graefin thought the love and yearning

★ *O, happy soul, sweet creature of God, formed in the great height of divine wisdom.*

I used my art to express were those of a young servant, a grateful vassal, and that they were directed exclusively towards her and her person. Yet nothing could have been further from the truth. The object of all my admiration was Hildegunde. Everywhere in the castle reminded me of her. There was the place she walked in the mornings with the Graefin; there was the place where I had chatted with her one morning, where I often returned in the hope of seeing her again. There was the room in which she and the other young women sewed, there was the bathing-room where I had once glimpsed her undressed... Even the shapes of the arches and the curves in the patterns in the paintings and tapestries seemed to echo shapes and forms in her face and body.

Before we became lovers, it seemed there was always a golden light playing about her features, the same light I used to see in Uqhart's eyes. Was it some light from an invisible world, the light of which the Abbess of Bingen wrote: *Verbum dei clarescit in forma hominis et ideo fulgemus cum illo edificantes membra sui pulchri corporis . ..* ★

Or was it a light that came from another world, which is neither divine nor diabolical, but separated from ours, the world of ideal love and beauty...?

> *ir sueze sur, ir liebez leit,*
> *ir herzeliep, ir senede not,*
> *ir liebez leben, ir leiden tot,*
> *ir lieben tot, ir leidez leben...* ★

I had only been at the court for a few months when she was as I remembered her just now. It was the year of our Lord 1193, the

★ *The Word of God shines forth in human form / and therefore we shine forth with it / forming the members of His beautiful body . ..*

★*[it mingles] sweet bitterness with love's suffering / the heart's joy with its yearning, / the life of its love with bitter death, / the lover's death with its bitter life...* (Gottfried von Strassburg, Tristan und Isolt).

year Saladin died, the year Richard of England was handed over to our Emperor Henry and charged with the murder of Conrad of Montferrat. It was the year too when Dandalo first became Doge of Venice, and was married to the sea, which once seemed to me to have lent him such appalling powers of destruction.

There is one afternoon I remember down to the tiniest detail. It was the middle of autumn. I was getting used to my round of duties. It was dark and cold, but not unbearably so. The smell of the smoke from the fires was in every corner of the castle, and for much of the day we had to burn tallow candles in order to see what we were doing.

It was a time of year I loved. The harvest was gathered, most of the tithes were in, and I had done with riding round the estates collecting dues. Many of the animals had already been slaughtered and salted. The time for battles was long past, but it was not yet so cold that all the sweetness was driven out of life. There was little enough to do, so I had a lot of time to myself and for my music.

Most afternoons I engineered an opportunity to meet Hildegunde during the meal in the great kitchen under the main hall. On this afternoon, Hildegunde and I were talking about books, as usual. I loved these moments when Hildegunde would look dreamily about her, searching her mind for details of texts. I was thankful that earlier in my life I had taken time to learn so much by heart. I still wonder if perhaps my happiest moments were spent reciting to Hildegunde, allowing myself to become intoxicated both by the words and by the sight of her. It was as if my mind and my soul were talking directly to hers, and as if all the nobility of her spirit was somehow laid open to me...

I was talking about the idea that God is the absolute point of perfection and how, descending from Him, there are orders, starting with various ranks of angels – firstly the archangels and then the cherubim and thrones and principalities – how the next order consists of the stars and heavenly bodies, then there is man, then animals, plants and various metals and stones, and finally dull earth. Each of these orders represented a step away from the Divine in a descent towards the chaos of matter, though the Divine is present still in the basest material things, even if this is harder to perceive. I was saying that perhaps the presence of the essence of the Divine made possible the transformation and redemption of Creation, and that this was the quintessence which turned lead into gold.

All the while Hildegunde sat quietly, her eyes sparkling with grace and enthusiasm, her hair fine pure gold in the light of the fire and candles, seeming to glow with its own light like an angel's.

I said that human beings were the most perfect reflection of the quintessence, since our bodies contain all the elements, yet we are spiritual too. And this is why we hold a privileged position in the cosmos, both below and above the angels, for we are able to perceive the order of this macrocosm from within it. This is not given to the angels, who are purely spiritual. It is because of this perception that it is said that we are made in the image of God, since each of us has a microcosm within.

I mentioned the writings of the mystic Hildegard of Bingen.

Hildegunde interrupted me, saying something that quite took my breath away. 'I was at the convent school at Rupertsberc before I came here,' she said.

'Did you know the Abbess?' I asked foolishly.

'How old do you think I am?' she laughed. 'But I know many people who knew her.'

I was dumbfounded. I should have guessed that there was a connection there, a thread leading from Hildegard to Hildegunde, because of the light I perceived shining forth from her.

'You knew people who knew her?' I repeated, feeling embarrassed at the lecture I had just delivered, I who had these ideas merely from reading.

'Yes, the Graefin for example.'

'What!' I was so excited. I could not believe my luck!

'The Graefin used to correspond with the Abbess until the Abbess died in 1179.' She looked at me playfully askance to make sure I took in the significance. 'I was only three then,' she said. 'The Graefin enjoys discussing with me Hildegard's idea that a worldly court should, like a monastery or convent, embody the order of the Divine. The Abbess believed that the presence of music, art and worship at a worldly court were vital.'

Hildegunde laughed that special laugh of hers again. These were ideas I had not come across. 'Go on,' I said.

'It is through music and art, you see,' she said, raising an eyebrow at me, 'that rough-living men like you might just be charmed and enthralled by higher things, and their hearts made sensitive to the movements and subtle presences of the spiritual. Then men of violence and war might gradually be led to do the will of God, rather than acting merely for their own gratification. This is why she is determined that here in Frankenburc art, beauty, moderation, loyalty, right-living and respect for the ladies should be cultivated, so that our court should become a heavenly Jerusalem.'

I pretended to look hurt at her jibe about rough-living men. Truth to tell, I had always seen myself first and foremost as a singer, and I worried that my recent devotion to the arts of war might have changed my personality. At the same time, the way she spoke to me, so familiar, so direct, stirred something within.

'Seriously, Walter. That is why she wants you here. It is for your music that she values you more than anything else.'

There is only one word to describe my reaction to her words. Joy.

Of course I was thrilled by the nobility of these thoughts, for it seemed to me that perhaps here at court I would be able to fulfil the aspirations and ideals I had come to cherish at Babenberch, during my conversations with Uqhart, at the monastery and through my singing. Most of all, though, I knew I loved Hildegunde, as a sister, a soul mate, as the most lovely soul I had ever dreamt of encountering.

That same evening I had to go directly to the upper hall of the castle, to sing to the Graefin. After my first song, I talked to her about Hildegard of Bingen. I began by quoting what Hildegard had written about Adam having been the perfect musician and how the Devil had decided to tempt him because he was jealous of his powers. The Graefin asked me what I knew of Hildegard, and I told her which works of hers I had read. I had some of the melodies from the *Ordo Virtutum* by heart and was able to sing them to her.

She became animated. She told me how much she loved the work of Hildegard, and the Provençal poets, and how she longed for her court at Frankenburc to be full of music and courtly love, which would in turn reflect the divine love. I could scarcely control my enthusiasm.

From then on she began to treat me with what I took to be an extra degree of respect, even favour. The immediate upshot was that I was given more responsibility regarding the education of the younger members of the court. Indeed, some of the older servants were made responsible to me. Of course I was proud but not for myself. All my thoughts were for Hildegunde. It seemed to me at the time I was gaining promotion that perhaps the court could be seen as a reflection of the hierarchies of Creation, and that I had taken a step towards perfection. Yet of course all I had really done was to take a step towards my own downfall.

In spite of all my feelings of inner turmoil, physically I grew strong and healthy pursuing my life at court.

Winter came and went and, the following year as the days grew longer, I spent more of my time outdoors. I learnt all the arts of war, how to handle horses and dogs, the arts of hunting, falconry. Theodor was my guide and my kind and assiduous teacher. I in turn passed on all I knew to the younger men who were in my charge. I became a good horseman and skilled with weapons, everything from the sword and the mace to the pike and the lance. I spent long hours with the young men, charging about the fields and courtyards, dreaming up battles, battle strategies and battle games.

Also, as the year went on, more young knights, and those aspiring to be knights, would pass through the court, mostly younger sons in search of a dowry. Some were arrogant and rude, but many were pleasant to spend time with, practising weaponry, singing, gaming, cultivating the high spirits and joy which are supposed to be the essence of a young man's life at court. Some of them were such good fellows and so friendly towards me that I almost forgot the inferiority of my birth. But they would all move on sooner or later, for, as the song says, 'to dally too long is a disgrace for a gentleman'. Such a life was not for me, for I was bound to the one court.

All the same I ate well, grew broad in the shoulders and developed a healthy complexion. I understand now that there were many ladies at the court who must have found me attractive, yet this was the last thought to enter my head. The only lady I thought of was Hildegunde. It never really occurred to me, at that time, to imagine that she might reciprocate my feelings, certainly not in a carnal way.

I remember a dream I had in those days, which I put into a song. I dreamt of the most lovely May weather, everything sunny, green and golden. I was dancing in a meadow with other young men and women. One of the young women was very beautiful, and I gave her a crown of flowers to wear. I would have liked to give her jewels, but all I had were the flowers. Then I was alone with her, and the two of us were gathering flowers in a far off wood, breaking them together, to make them into another crown, a special one. I was very happy. When I woke I knew that the young woman I had dreamt of would always be part of me. She was Hildegunde.

Most men are not like I was. My fellows at court would play the game of courtly graces when they were in front of the ladies, yet the moment they were alone they would make crude comments and innuendoes. Moreover, they would boast of their prowess, how many women they had known, noble and peasant alike, even other men's wives, and would give details of where, when and how. Not only were they oblivious to the mortal sin of adultery, but they had no worries as to whether the women they were sleeping with might be related to them, in which case they ran the extra risk of committing the sin of incest and begetting monsters hideous to behold. To me, at the time, adultery seemed a shameful thing, and I could not understand those who glorified it in their speech and deeds, though I suppose many of my songs have implied adulterous loves.

I could easily have been drawn into debauchery then, as of course I was later: yet in those early days I disdained those for whom love was nothing but carnal pleasure. Maybe it was something to do with my monkish upbringing. Maybe it was something to do with the turmoil and sorrow caused by my relationship with Katrin. In any case, in my mind there was a clear distinction between high love and low love. Even in my songs I praised the former at the expense of the latter.

Maybe there was more to it than that. I was not a virgin, yet I wanted to be pure. I wanted to purify myself. I saw Hildegunde almost as someone divine, who should not be sullied even mentally by carnal thoughts, which I had almost come to fear. In many of my songs I moralised about moderation, but of course that is one quality I never fully possessed in those days.

On my journeys I saw many beautiful buildings to the glory of God, such as the world has never seen before, not since the Temple of Solomon. I think of the sweeping curves of the arches, I am intoxicated by the bright colours of the wall-paintings lit by the sunlight, or glimmering in the candlelight in the early evening, or glimpsed through the incense during a church service, when the smoke curls towards the ceiling echoing the shapes of the interior. Could anything be more bright or more lovely?

Yes, to me, only one thing. The memory of Hildegunde, as she was then. In those new buildings, in those arches and stained-glass windows, in the geometric shapes of the pillars and towers, in the glowing, smoky and brilliant light, it is her lines, her form that I see. The shapes of her body and the movement of her mind, its divine essence, are reflected in the architectural shapes.

By the spring I had become a good rider and was well able to defend myself, so I was often asked to deliver messages to other courts. These were often secret, and it was a sign of the great esteem and confidence in which I was held in those days that I was entrusted with such tasks. I enjoyed very much finding out how different courts functioned, and what was going on in the political world. It was thus that I was amongst the first to know when Henry took Sicily, the terms of Richard of England's release from prison, the details of the Emperor's peace with Henry the Lion. I even got wind, long before anyone else, of the secret information that it was the Old Man of the Mountains, not Richard of England, who had killed Conrad of Montferrat, and that the assassins had entertained Henry of Champagne, and apologised for the murder.

As the pattern of things unfurled, it was hard for me to believe how naïve I had been for so long. I had always thought that the world of princes and the nobility was fixed and unchanging, a world where everything was decided by consent and goodwill. I knew that wars occurred, and that they were necessary; yet I thought that wars were always fought by us Christian knights and soldiers against the powers of evil and darkness. I had heard many stories about the Crusades, and when I was practising arms it was always a Saracen enemy that I imagined myself fighting, or at least an army of those who had turned away from God.

Hildegunde and I grew closer; there was so much that we had in common. For example, she had read the Sibylline prophecies of Lactantius, Tibertius and many others. We talked of the Last Days, and the subject filled us both with dread. I remember even then a haunting yet indistinct feeling that the two of us were somehow bound up in these mysteries.

The thoughts about my father and Uqhart continued to weigh upon me, and eventually, one evening, when the spring sun was shining brilliantly, just when we had done with rehearsing music together, I told Hildegunde about these things – about my friendships with Uqhart and with Pauli. Pauli's death, Uqhart's burning, my father's suicide. This was during the spring of the year after I first set eyes on her.

I was a fool, for I knew that I have the power to touch people's emotions; why else should I have gained employment at the court chiefly as a singer? Hildegunde was young, no doubt easily impressed. And I was so transfixed by my impression of her as an embodiment of perfection that it never occurred to me that her perfection might encompass those qualities of sympathy, tenderness and generosity which we singers claim to seek in ladies, yet set out never to find. Until then Hildegunde and I had often talked of our ideals our thoughts and observations. We had even talked about love, but only with regard to Andreas Capellanus' book on love. We never talked of how we felt, certainly not about how we felt towards one another. Yet that day, as I told Hildegunde of the evil things that had befallen me, I saw, by the light of the fire, that there were tears in her eyes. I asked her what the matter was.

She took my hand and leant her head briefly against my shoulder. She said, 'You know, Walter, there are some of us who are destined never to be happy, never to be at home in this world.'

From the way she spoke I sensed that, just maybe, she could be mine.

The next day I was to ride to the court of Zertheim to deliver a message and discuss an urgent matter on behalf of the Graf of Frankenburc. On the road, in a deserted spot, I knew of a massive old linden tree, which had impressed me by the perfection of its form, its age and dignity. I had once said to Hildegunde that if there were such a thing as an embodiment of the idea of a tree, then surely this must be it. She had said that one day she would love to see it. So, I suggested we meet there the following evening.

Hildegunde agreed readily. She said she would slip away m the afternoon. The tree would be easy to find, since it was off one of the main roads west towards Zertheim. It stood on its own near common land in a secluded valley. The plan was that I would arrive later and that there we would be able to talk alone in a way not possible at the court. I suppose we were both aware of our real intentions, but we did not admit them to ourselves, or to one another.

*Flos campi, cadet in vento, pluvia spargit eum.*
*Virginitas, tu permanens in symphoniis supernorum civium:*
*Unde es suavis flos qui numquam aresces...* *

In the towns and villages the boys had been out gathering flowers for the girls they wished to marry. It was beautiful May weather, and the light was of a texture and clarity more radiant than anything I have ever seen, before or since. The temperature was perfect, neither warm nor cool. Little gusts of wind caressed our skins. Zephyrs perhaps. There were myriads of tiny flowers on the forest floor. Nowadays such weather has lost the power to make me happy, for it always reminds me of her.

I remember that I arrived early and tortured myself wondering if she would come, if she really did love me. I took flowers and blades of grass, and plucked them, like a little girl, counting, 'She loves me, she loves me not.' It always seemed to work out that she did love me; yet the more that happened, the less I believed it.

That evening Hildegunde gave herself to me, there, beneath the linden tree, as the sun was setting and the moon rising in a crystal blue sky. Where we lay together, on a bank of moss and grass, the earth was still warm from the heat of the day. Until that evening she had been a virgin. When we had finished loving, as we lay close together, as the first chill of evening caused us to draw even closer for warmth, as the translucent sky turned purple and then dark, as the stars lit, one by one, like candle-lights of heaven, I swear it is true, there was a nightingale, singing, in the linden tree above our bed. We lay on our backs and looked up towards it. Everything was so still that I remember thinking perhaps this is how it feels to be dead, one's own body lying next to the body of one's wife or lover, the person with whom one has shared life on earth.

* *The flower of the field falls in the wind and the rain splashes it. / O virginity, you dwell in the symphony of the inhabitants of the supernal city: / Where you are the beautiful flower which never withers...* (Hildegard of Bingen)

I imagined there must have been angels, invisible powers of heaven, flying low in the scented air above us. I seemed to hear a voice saying, 'Loves turn to crystal there, and die'. It was not Hildegunde speaking. Maybe it was a spirit, or just my imagination, for I was always having to think up new lines for my songs. I was not sure what these words were supposed to mean.

I thought of what Aristotle wrote about the crystal spheres in the heavens. I wondered if maybe the crystal spheres were made of past earthly loves, so that, even if the lovers themselves had died, at least the loves themselves still existed somewhere.

I tried to explain this to Hildegunde; it was the sort of thought she usually relished. But I could see from the way her eyes were staring in the twilight that her mind was really on something else. I asked her what the matter was.

She asked me if I had ever loved before.

The air was growing chill, yet I was lost in thought. There was a feeling of peace, stillness and security. It was as if Hildegunde and I were really one, already one, and that as I talked to her I was in a way talking to myself.

So, like a fool, I told her about Katrin. Maybe too I was driven by some need for absolution, for confession. I had already made my confession to God, but I felt a need also to make some confession to a woman. I told her the whole story, sparing no details, convinced that she would understand me.

When I had finished, I turned towards her. Her face was pained, ashen grey in the fading light. Tears were streaming.

I looked down upon her, touched her shoulder, shook her gently, asked her what the matter was.

At first she just continued to stare and to weep. Then, her face distorted in a way that made her look almost ugly. She said, 'Poor Hildegunde is torn apart.'

Her words went through my heart like a dart of sorrow. Now, nothing would ever be the same. For all our closeness, there was between us a darkness, an evil.

That evening, we made love again, beneath the stars, thought that second time our loving was more animal, more desperate. Then she stole back to the castle at Frankenburc whilst I rode on westward to Zertheim.

I rode beneath the great, arching trees, over the rolling hills with their vineyards, copses and grazing sheep, past the small groups of peasant houses with their smell of pigs and human excrement, through the great, lonely expanses of high hill country, whilst moon and the stars shone brilliantly from a pure, cloudless sky.

As I rode, my whole being seemed to have divided into two separate entities. Firstly there was the Walter who was ecstatically in love with his Hildegunde. This Walter felt all the joys of new love: the racing heart, seeing Hildegunde's eyes everywhere I looked, still trying to catch the smell of her on my clothes, on my hands, reliving every moment we had ever spent together, and tracing the miraculous course of events that had led to the moment of our lovemaking. The other Walter was detached, an onlooker who somehow knew that the whole relationship was doomed, that the love we had was spoilt and would lead to a catastrophe. I thought of the words of Hildegard of Bingen, of the way she describes the sorrow of the pure soul fallen to earth:

> *O gravis labor, et o durum pondus*
> *quod habeo in veste huius vitae,*
> *quia nimis grave michi est*
> *contra carnem pugnare**

It was such a fall that I caused Hildegunde, who was the purest being I had hitherto ever met. So, there were two parts to me now: there was the part that was ecstatically in love with Hildegunde, and there was the part that was detached yet sensed the occurrence of some spiritual wounding. All that bound the two Walters together was a shared knowledge of what had happened that evening.

*\* I am weighed down by the labour and heavy weight / which the vestment of this life has brought me, / for it is always so hard for me / to fight against the flesh.*

I made a resolution. It was a vague resolution at first, yet it was to become the guiding light of anything that has since been honourable in my life: whatever else happened, I would attempt to protect Hildegunde from harm, and try to live in a way that would be worthy of her. I have failed in this. Nevertheless, as an ideal it has always been with me.

Then there was the song. I needed to think of a new song for the Graefin on my return, and my mind was always casting round for ideas. I wished to write in a style that was becoming popular, as if from the point of view of a woman, who sings of her passion for her lover. In fact these songs are not far removed from certain wanton songs I have heard peasant women sing about their menfolk – only for the courts, of course, the carnal element has to be made more genteel, implied rather than stated.

A melody was forming in my mind. I was already humming it to the accompaniment of the horse's hooves as I rode through the night. The words formed too without trouble:

*Under der linden an der heide, dâ unser zweier bette was,*
*dâ muget ir vinden schône beide*
*gebrochen bluomen unde gras.*
*Vor dem walde in einem tal,*
*tandaradei,*
*schône sanc diu nahtegal.*

The song is famous now, so I need say no more about it. Walter von der Vogelweide, that self-righteous prig of a fellow, even he sings it. I do not care. I know about that evening with Hildegunde, and I know about what followed.

\* *Under the linden by the heathland, / Where there was one bed for the two of us, / There you may find, both so lovely, / Broken flowers and crushed grass / Before the forest in a valley / Tandaradei / Sweetly sang the nightingale...* (Walter von der Vogelweide)

Whether or not anyone remembers that song, which was to bring me so much sorrow, that evening always will have happened, and it always will have been mine.

# VII

## The Chariot

✠

I remained obsessed by questions about my past. Whenever I went travelling on behalf of Graf Friedrich, or whenever I was in the company of someone well-connected and sympathetic at court, I would attempt to elicit information. I would mention the white-haired man who had driven Katrin from me; I would mention too that I had known Uqhart and that I had studied at Babenberch. I would do so as innocently as possible, of course, just in case I witnessed an eyelid flicker with embarrassment, or a too-rapid change of subject.

I would also tell the story of when I was kidnapped as a child. My excuse was that I was often asked why I should have developed a taste for courtly life, and for outside, physical pursuits, given that my education was bookish and monkish. This gave me the opportunity of telling the story, and studying the reactions of my audience.

This plan bore fruit in an unexpected way. It was an evening, just a week or so after I first made love to Hildegunde, in the main hall of the castle after the evening meal. I had just finished entertaining the guests with my singing and found myself telling my story to a small group, including a knight and his lady from Hüttenheim and two or three ministerials from Nurenberc and Babenberch. The story went down well, as ever, and I thought no more about it.

Later in the evening, when it was dark and most of the other guests were about to bed down, Rudolfus, one of the ministerials took me aside.

'Let's go for a walk,' he said. 'I have something to tell you.'

We left the great hall and went out into the moonlit courtyard of the castle.

'Your story interests me,' he said. 'You see, it is my job to file and catalogue the records of the Bishop's court in Nurenberc. It so happens that I have seen the records of the proceedings against the ex-priest Josephus.'

The night was clear and the sky was full of lovely stars. *At last*, I thought, *I am to find out the truth...* 'Do the records not correspond with my version of the story?'

'No. It is all more complicated. The case stuck in my mind because of its irregularity.'

'Are the records always accurate?'

'Just about always. Since they are kept secret from all but the likes of me, there is little point in falsifying them.'

'What were the irregularities you just mentioned?' I asked.

'Firstly, there was nothing in the files about Josephus making any confession. Normally a confession document is the most important record in a trial, to ensure there can be no dispute about the defendant's guilt. Yet the trial was held in private.'

'Why do you think that was?'

'During the course of the trial it was put to Josephus that he should remain silent about his "connections". If he did so he would be hanged with dignity and his mistress would be allowed to go free. If he spoke out, his mistress would be taken and the two of them publicly tortured before being executed.'

I thought of the lovely woman who had cared for me in the forest.

'What were the connections they talked about?' I asked.

'That's precisely it. I don't know. It's interesting though, isn't it? I don't suppose you have any ideas?'

'None.' I looked up at the castle battlements in the moonlight.

They were dark, like the secrets that seemed to hem in my life. 'Is there anyone who might know?' I asked.

He hesitated. 'There is one of the chief ministerials at the Bishop's court at Nurenberc. His name is Stefanus. When you next come to Nurenberc, I could arrange for you to meet him.'

I loathed the Bishop and his court because of the time I had spent in prison there; for that reason I had avoided returning to the city. Yet there were interests of the Graf I could use as a pretext for going to Nurenberc.

'Rudolfus,' I said, 'I shall never be able to thank you enough. I hope we shall be able to meet soon in Nurenberc.'

As I led him back to the hall before going off to my garret to sleep, I sensed a nervousness in him. I wondered if I had been too enthusiastic, if I had gone too far.

For weeks I burnt with curiosity about what I might discover from Stefanus. At that time I was becoming well known for my singing and would often be asked to ride out to deliver messages to other courts, where I would stay and literally sing for my supper, yet it seemed an eternity before a chance arose to go to Nurenberc. At last I was asked, or rather volunteered, to take to the Bishop of Babenberch the Graf of Frankenburc's invitation to the tournament he was holding later that spring.

When the day arrived, I felt more apprehension and fear than anything else. I set off along the familiar roads, where I had wandered with Pauli, where I had made love with Katrin. I stayed at some of the inns where Pauli and I had played, and where I had stayed as a Cistercian monk.

After three days I arrived at Nurenberc. I made my way through the town gates and the familiar streets to where my father's house had stood. The town was so full of sadness and terrible memories for me that, as I walked through the streets, I half expected to smell once more the burning of flesh.

Yet all was peaceful. At the place where I had spent my childhood the linden tree was still standing, but the house and the yard where I had played and grown up, where anvils had rung out, where labourers had sung and sworn, where I had first learnt how to talk, how to walk and run, where I had first dreamt of love – all that was now nothing more than ashes. The authorities must have ordered its burning to drive out any evil spirits that remained. Yet the linden tree was still there. I stood and gazed at it. Its trunk was charred, but somehow it had survived.

I tried to remember happier times from my childhood, but all I could think about was that day when I returned from the monastery to find crowds gathered in the main square, Uqhart's blackened body falling forward, his teeth wide open in a deathly laugh. Round and round in my mind went the sequence of events leading to my discovery of my father's suicide, and I felt once more the sensation of blades being thrust into the back of my head, like when I first found out what had happened and ran into the woods.

Now I had overcome all that. I was in control, or at least I thought I was. I allowed these images to play in front of my mind. I confronted them. And the old feelings of anger and despair subsided into a quiet yearning for the times before these events took place.

I led my horse back through the town centre and up the hill to the castle.

I announced my arrival at the gates and was led straight to the Bishop, who treated me with great courtesy, offered me wine and invited me to sing that evening. He made no mention of our previous meetings; on the contrary, he seemed keen that the matter should not be raised but rather that we should be as formal and courteous as possible.

I asked if in the meantime I might have an interview with Stefanus. The reason I gave for wanting to see him was that he was a scholarly man and that he had studied Plato and the Ancients. Rudolfus was assigned to take me to his room, which was up a set of stairs and situated just beneath the west battlements.

Stefanus had just taken a bath and I spent some time chatting idly with Rudolfus, who in turn seemed anxious to avoid any mention of the reasons why I was there. Stefanus finally appeared, wearing only a towel.

I was impressed by Stefanus. He was in his late forties, very self-assured. His head and face, like the rest of his frame, were broad and square. He gave an impression of immense strength, both in the determination that shone in his eyes and in the energy with which he moved. He was very friendly towards me, warm and kind, yet at the same time asserting the superiority conferred by his age and status.

He dressed quickly. After that it was not long before Rudolfus left us and I explained why I was there. I told him, briefly, the story of my kidnapping and of what I understood to have been the fate of my kidnapper. I told him too that Rudolfus had given me reason to believe that there was more to the story, and I asked him if he could tell me any more.

Immediately his manner changed. He remained friendly, kindly, but became thoughtful, as if to imply that it was out of place for me to be asking such things. Yet this reaction was an answer in itself: and he was intelligent enough to understand that I would realise this.

'Perhaps we should go for a walk,' he said. So we left the castle by a back gate and began picking our way over rocks and then strolling over the grassy slopes overlooking the busy town. The weather was still bleak. It was a cold day. There was no rain, but dark clouds were scudding low over the town and there was a chill wind. Stefanus, despite his age, and despite the fact that he had only just emerged from the bath, did not seem to mind the cold. On the contrary, the direction our walk took seemed to be such as to guarantee not only that no one should be able to overhear us but also that the wind would immediately blow away all our words, so it would be as if they had never been spoken.

Stefanus looped his arm round mine, and on one occasion put his arm round my shoulder as he spoke quietly, conspiratorially, to me. His manner was like that of an old schoolmaster, or an uncle who has just been reunited with a long lost nephew. Sometimes there seemed something feminine in his manner; but at others treated me as though I were some great lord and he my vassal.

He avoided my question. 'Are you happy at the court at Frankenburc?' he asked.

'Yes, very.' He looked at me quizzically as if to communicate his surprise that I was not content to leave well alone.

'Your singing and music,' he said next, 'you have an appreciative audience?'

'I have been very fortunate. My new songs are often welcomed very warmly.'

'I know,' he said, 'for there are many who learn your songs to sing at other courts. I know more of your music than you would probably imagine.'

'It is very kind of you to pay me such a compliment, sir, and I hope to have the opportunity to sing for you myself. But I am anxious to know more of how the ex-priest Josephus came to die. I know you have access to the papers. You will probably feel that this is just an idle whim of mine...'

'I shall tell you what I know. I was a junior clerk at the time. The ex-priest Josephus gave himself up to a night-watchman at the city gates. He was taken to the castle, where he confessed that he had kidnapped you out of vengeance. He had been in your father's employ before he fell into outlawry. He confessed also that he still belonged to a heretical sect, the evil Cathars, and asked for absolution in order to avoid public torture. It was taken that his confession was genuine. Also, there is always a danger of revolt amongst crowds when there is a public torturing. So it was decided to hang him without further ado.'

'Was the trial held in public?'

'No, it wasn't.'

'Are you sure there was not more to it? I have been given to believe that the man might have had connections about which he was supposed to be silent.' I asked the question in all innocence, not knowing what dangerous ground I was treading on.

Instead of affirming or denying this, Stefanus stopped, put his hands on my shoulders, looked me in the eyes and said, 'Walter, you see visions. We know that you see visions. You have heard some things also. I do not know how much you know already, how much you have discovered, how much you might have been told. All I can say is that there are things which, for the sake of others, as well as for your sake and mine, I cannot tell you. I can assure you that no harm will come to you and that there are many people who wish you well, very well. I am most certainly one of them.'

'I don't understand.'

'Just wait, Walter, be still and wait. All will become clear sooner or later, if it is not clear already.'

On impulse I said, 'What about my father and Uqhart the Jew? Is what happened to them something I must not know about?' I said this without thinking seriously that Stefanus would even know what I was talking about. Yet he was visibly shaken by the question. In fact his reaction disturbed me more than what he said eventually, when he had regained his composure. I was surprised that he knew so much about me. Given the difference in our status it would have been quite understandable if he just kicked me out, there and then. But this is what he said:

'As far as I understand it, your father drowned himself either because he was cursed by the Jew, or because he himself was involved with the black arts of the Cathars. And the Jew was burnt because it was well known that he practised the black arts and because he had even sacrificed the Christian boy he had kept with him since he was a small child. Yet we must speak no more of these things. It is time to return to the castle.'

I remember glimpsing our reflections in the troubled waters of the moat as we walked back. I had learnt more than I dared hope from him. I had not realised that my father was under suspicion of involvement with the Cathar heresy. Also, I was confused and embarrassed that Stefanus knew that I saw visions. For all his kindness, there was a certain menace in his voice, which made me feel that I should not ask any more questions. Besides, the very mention of the Cathars in certain circles is likely to bring forth a hysterical reaction, and unless one chooses one's words very carefully there is always the danger of incriminating oneself.

From then on we talked about nothing more of any consequence; we merely exchanged small talk as it is customary to do at court. The rest of my stay in Nurenberc passed without incident.

What Stefanus had hinted about my father and the Cathars made sense in some ways. There was always something detached, something brooding about my father, as if he genuinely despised this world. (Unlike me. I have often pretended to myself that I hate it, yet the thought of leaving it now fills me with sorrow and dread.)

Until his death, my father had been for me both a still point and a symbol of inevitable triumph over adversity, though there was always a sadness, a resignation about him. He was always there, working in the workshops, directing the hired labourers, producing cart after cart, wagon after wagon, slowly increasing his wealth, no doubt with the patient aim of handing it all over to me, his son, so that I could carry on his name and role in Nurenberc. Even so, although there were periods when I worked hard for him and despite the fact that I loved and respected him, I never really appreciated him. It was his very stillness that made it so easy for me to take him for granted. Now that he was dead, I reflected more and more on what sort of a person he had been.

In spite of all his success, there remained something deeply pessimistic about him. He was often withdrawn and sullen, and I remember him frequently fingering my mother's old prayer-book. I have heard that it is not uncommon for Cathars to commit the sin of suicide to rid themselves of the awfulness of this world. Who can blame them?

Stefanus was killed by robbers just three weeks after our meeting. I was struck to the core. Had he been murdered? Was his death the result of our meeting that day?

# VIII

## Justice

✝

Preparations began for the Graf's tournament. I had been hoping to use the occasion to make more inquiries about Stefanus' death, and the fate of my father and Uqhart. But the turn of events turned out to be much more dramatic than I would ever have imagined.

It was the first festival that the Graf of Frankenburc had held at his castle. For the sake of his prestige it was important that the occasion should be a success. The Graf did not want the same excesses that we had heard of from Toulouse, for example, where it was said that one lord had used thousands of choice wax candles just for cooking, where another had driven seventy-two teams of oxen to sow fields with thirty thousand silver shillings, and yet another had burnt thirty horses, all to show how wealthy they were. Even so, it was to be a massive gathering, and tents would have to be set up outside the castle walls to sleep everyone. There would be great banquets, dancing, singing and a mêlée on the Monday, since the truce of God was effective at that time, before the civil war, from Thursday until Sunday, and on those days there could be no fighting.

The tournament was to take place during Pentecost of the year of our Lord 1194. Everywhere there was hope that at last we would be able to enjoy a period of peace and prosperity. The harvests had been good and Saladin was dead. Richard the Lionheart of England had just been released for a ransom of one hundred and fifty thousand silver marks, and had become the Emperor's vassal. So now Henry was much more secure as Emperor, Richard having been one of those who had stirred up the Welfs to oppose him.

At court we were all working extremely hard. My main tasks were to compose songs for the banquets, to train the other young knights for a display of arms, and to help with the logistics of the feeding, accommodation and entertainment of all the guests. Also, I had to train hard on my own behalf since the Graf had graciously asked me to lead the opening mêlée. I was to take on the captain of the opposition in a one-to-one joust before the rest of the fighting started.

I continued to see Hildegunde daily, though it was hard for us to find time to be alone. I loved her passionately; but since that evening when we first became lovers, it seemed that we had lost more than we had gained. Sometimes she would run up to me, smiling and friendly like a favourite sister. At other times she would be haughty, as if she hated me. Maybe this was just for show, or maybe she did resent me for taking her innocence. Her nature was such that she would do anything to avoid gossip. Before we became lovers our everyday meetings had been full of spontaneity. Now there was a degree of artificiality about everything we did. Our friendship was over, and in its place there was a difficult love.

On the evening of my return from Zertheim I had my private audience with the Graefin. She always wanted to be the first to hear any new song I had written; of course it flattered me to oblige. Like a fool, I played and sang for her my *'under der linden'* song. The Graefin was in raptures. She made me sing it over and over again. Her eyes stared fixedly at me, as if she wanted to devour me. Then she talked about my riding in the mêlée *for her* and called me her 'brave knight'. This was foolish of her, for she knew as well as I did what my social rank was. Even in a fighting army I would have been lucky to be granted the rank of sergeant. All the equipment I had was borrowed from the Graf.

It occurred to me for the first time that even a noblewoman like her might have carnal desires for a young man like myself. I resolved that in future I would watch my step.

She made me promise to play the song to nobody but her until the first evening of the feast, when all the guests would be gathered for the mêlée the following day. She said that she wanted all the company to be impressed by the high standards of music and artistry at her court and did not want to run the risk of the song being heard anywhere else before the tournament. Of course I burned to play it, or at least to sing it, to Hildegunde. Yet, stupidly, I allowed myself to be ruled by the Graefin, thinking that it would be a great pleasure, a great compliment for Hildegunde to hear me sing of her as my lady in front of all the nobles of the region, in a way that only the two of us would understand.

The preparations for the tournament were long and arduous. The Graf was meticulous over every tiny detail. I knew that he had been successful as a military commander during the wars in Italy; now I was beginning to understand why.

About two weeks before the tournament he told me that my opponent in the joust was to be Johannes of Ulm. Everyone knew Johannes of Ulm by reputation. He was a fearsome giant of a man who had distinguished himself in countless battles. He was known for his great loyalty to whomever he served, yet also for his readiness to pick a quarrel with anyone he considered a rival. He was so sturdy on horseback and his lance packed such a forceful blow that in previous tournaments he had unseated several of his opponents at the first pass. Two had died from their wounds.

By that time I was strong, and I was a good horseman. Even so, I was worried about the mêlée. After all, it would be my first tournament in public. The stakes would be high (though I did not realise just how high). But I would not allow myself to show the fear I felt.

I told Hildegunde who my rival was to be. I was surprised at her reaction, for she blanched and begged me not to take part. From then on - this was about ten days before the tournament - her behaviour towards me changed once more. Now she was never haughty or distant. On the contrary, she did everything she could to be with me, and would stare at me, with big, sad eyes, and used any opportunity she could for us to be alone, to make love.

There was a watchman called Ulrich, an old soldier with a kind heart, who was loyal to us. Hildegunde would come up to my attic room in the dead of night, and we would love until just before dawn, when he would warn us that it was time for her to leave. I remember Hildegunde's body, brighter than any dawn, whiter than snow by first light, to my eyes at least, and I remember her hair wet with tears, pressed against my face, as we huddled together, dreading the moment of our parting. I sang:

*Owe, si kuste ane zal*
*in deme slafe mich,*
*do vielen hin ze tal*
*ir trene niderisch,*
*iedoch getroste ich si,*
*daz si ir weinen lie*
*und mich al umbevie.*
*do taget es.* ★

Five days before the tournament we were to meet in the forest, just three arrow-shots from the castle. It was a lovely, moonlit night and I was yearning to see her. I remember that she arrived late, pale, out of breath and trembling. On her way she had been seen by the Graefin. The Graefin had said nothing, but stared after her. Hildegunde said that it was too late for her to turn back, so she carried on, in order to warn me that the Graefin would be sure to find out that I was missing.

I do not to this day know why Hildegunde took that risk when she could easily have made some excuse and returned. It was as if she had a foreboding that things would not turn out well, as if she

★*Alas, she kissed me countless times in my sleep / and her tears fell down and down / yet I consoled her, / so that she stopped weeping, / and took me in her arms / then day broke.* (Heinrich of Morungen)

wanted to spend as much time as possible with me before it was too late. She sought me out everywhere. Even when I was training on the tournament field, or practising arms in the courtyard with the younger men, she would come to watch me. It is hard for me to imagine now, and I certainly did not understand then, just how much distress I must have caused Hildegunde. For me, she was, and is, an ideal. It was hard for me then to understand how an ideal might suffer.

In any case, now I was the one who worried about being indiscreet. There could have been few people at the court who did not know about us. I worried, but I did little to avoid seeing her. I suppose we both knew that things could not go on much longer as they were. The one thought that never occurred to me throughout all this was what the Graefin's reaction might be. It was precisely this that would turn out to be crucial.

Our assignations were wonderful. Hildegunde would always ask me to sing to her. I realised that she already had most of my songs by heart. It was as if she were storing them in her mind in case anything should happen to me, so that a part of me would live on in her, even if we could not be together. We would make love and talk about everything in heaven and on earth. And she was so beautiful; to love her was ecstasy. All I wanted was for her to be mine forever, that our union should be blessed by the Church. Yet whenever we talked of this we both fell silent, sad.

Just before the guests started to arrive, Hildegunde's behaviour changed again. I became aware that she was avoiding me. She was even absent from supper. She was not at any of the places where I normally saw her. At last I caught sight of her walking across the courtyard. I ran after her and called her name. When she saw me, she made at first as if to move towards me, then burst into tears and ran off into the women's quarters.

Then one day when we were in the dining-hall together she said, 'Why didn't you tell me about them? Why are you using me? Don't you care? How can you be so careless with your soul? They told me why we can never be together.' Then she burst into tears. At the time I thought she just meant the Graefin and her uncle.

Later I came to suspect that perhaps there was more to it than that. Maybe the reason for her subsequent actions had something to do with those same forces that stood between myself and Katrin. That evening Hildegunde ran away from me when she saw me in the courtyard, just as the guests first started to arrive.

Then, my evening meeting with the Graefin was cancelled. The Graefin's pretext was that she too was busy with the preparations and that I already knew of my instructions for the tournament. As it happened, I was never to talk to her alone again.

There were so very many guests, and so many of them were illustrious, that I would not know where to begin listing all their names. Even princes and princesses of royal blood were there. I noted the different fashions, particularly amongst the men. The knights from the Rhineland wore their hair in artificial ringlets, which they made by twisting their hair with metal tongs, whilst the fashion in Thuringen was to grow one's hair very long at the front, yet to have it cut short at the back.

I enjoyed talking to the many men and ladies from different lands. I remember a very scholarly man called Lambert d'Andres, a squat fellow with blond-grey curly hair and smiling eyes, who had come with his master all the way from Macon. He told me that he had been writing a history of the family he served, and that he had discovered they were descended from the noble knight Sifridus, who had lived at the time of Charlemagne. He said that all noble Franks were descended originally from the Trojans, who had been driven out of their city when it was sacked by the Greeks, centuries before the birth of Christ.

I enjoyed numerous such conversations. Many of the guests, including some of the Graf's closest relations, treated me with great courtesy and paid much attention to me. The ladies showed a particular interest, I could not understand why though. I was, after all, a mere vassal at the court. I had no property of my own and none of the status that this would have conferred. I presumed that my fame as a singer must have spread. There was also the great honour the Graf was doing me by allowing me to represent him personally in the tournament.

At that time I was full of enthusiasm. In my innocence, I was hoping for much from the tournament. I was ambitious, thinking that perhaps, if I were to distinguish myself, I might be offered a higher position, maybe at a different court, and that this would make it possible for me to marry Hildegunde. I thought that I might be made a ministerial at one of the imperial courts, and be given a small fief somewhere, a manor to which I could retire with Hildegunde and from which I might still serve a noble lord. I would fantasize about becoming a full vassal of the Graf. I imagined the occasion, placing my hands, joined together, between those of my lord, who would then close his hands over mine, as I said 'Sir, I become your man', upon which he would kiss me on the mouth and give me the token or charts by which I would come into possession of land from him. It was possible too that I might be dubbed a knight. I dreamt of taking part in the ceremony: the ritual bath, the vigil of arms, the giving of gifts and the banquet that would follow. My birth would not have prohibited my becoming a knight, since I was the son neither of a peasant nor a priest, but a free craftsman.

The first banquet was held on the afternoon and evening before the tournament, which had to take place just before Pentecost, when the Truce of God would come into force and when some of the Graf's younger relatives were to be knighted. The feast began in the tents outside the castle. As the evening drew on, we moved into the castle itself. During this banquet I was encouraged to mingle freely with the guests and was able to speak with many of the noble ladies and their lords. Fine though many of the ladies were, none of them compared in beauty or nobility of spirit to my lovely Hildegunde.

Hildegunde's guardian, the Ritter of Ochsenfurt, was one of the guests. He was an old, bald man, hunched and wizened. The majority of noble lords, whether they had come to watch the spectacle of the mêlée or to join in it, treated me, as I said, with great courtesy. Yet he paid no attention to me. Indeed, it seemed to me that he deliberately attempted to snub me.

At last, in the evening, we were all assembled in the great hall. A magnificent fire was burning, and the banquet served to the guests by the young women of the court was a wonder to behold. There were all sorts of meat and sweetmeats, fish and even fruit from distant lands. Many spices were used, which came from the far ends of the earth. There were candles everywhere, and the hall was decked out with flowers, which were even brighter than the tapestries. There was the rich scent of foods, the perfumes worn by the ladies, the sound of their talking, the sea of faces. The courses were interspersed with dancing, gaming and entertainments, including a juggler and a bear-tamer. I was to play before the very last course. I relished the privilege of being able to move in such illustrious company. So many of them, men and women, wore beautiful jewels and clothes made of wonderful material – thick wool from Flanders, scarlet from Brussels, striped from Gent, or fine wool from Florence made in the Calimala style, silk from Cyprus and brightly coloured linen from Reims – not to mention all the furs, vair, ermine, lamb and sable.

I met Johannes of Ulm. That afternoon, during the feast, he seemed a pleasant enough fellow. He was strong as an oak, a great bull of a man, quite old, probably in his late thirties. He had a great black beard, which was greying round the edges, and dark, twinkling brown eyes. When he realised who I was, he came over and slapped me on the shoulders, knocking the wind out of me. I reflected that Nimrod must have been a man such as this.

He said that I found him in good spirits for, after all his years of soldiering and whoring, someone had found him a wife, a young virgin who would bear him many sons so that his name would live on. The Graefin of Frankenburc had found the girl for him, and he was grateful, for she was a fine-looking girl. What could I do but congratulate him? Though my immediate reaction was to feel pity for any poor girl who was to be married to such a brute, friendly though he might seem in such surroundings as a banquet.

He was quite tipsy. When I congratulated him, his face beamed with pleasure, and he told me again not to worry about the tournament the next day. He said that he would enjoy a good fight with me, but that he would be sure not to do me any real harm since I was a vassal of the Graefin - and besides, I was too pleasant and feminine a youth to end my days impaled on his lance, not yet having experienced a true battle, where real slaughter was done. Then again he slapped me on the back, though this time I braced myself and was not winded.

At first I thought this was the Graefin's way of helping me, of doing me a favour. I asked him who the lucky girl was. All he would do was to raise an eyebrow and put a finger to his lips.

Throughout the meal I became increasingly nervous. Never before had I played before such noble company, and not since I had first played at Frankenburc in the company of the Abbot Quintus had so much hinged on my playing. My instinct was to still my nerves with wine, yet I knew from experience that could ruin my concentration and spoil my singing.

There was to be one dance before I sang. I played the fiddle and watched the ladies dance in rows opposite the men, joining hands with them, bowing, and dancing in circles in a most courtly fashion. Then the other musicians went to eat and drink, leaving me alone to sing. The plan was that I should first sing three songs. I would begin with a fast one, then sing my new song and end with a song I had written some time ago, about the qualities and virtues of a chivalrous knight and how he should present himself before ladies. So, as the meal was drawing to a close, I took my lute and plucked out some well-known melodies. The ladies gathered round to listen, the men standing mostly further back, propped up against the walls.

My first song was a song of battle, praising those who had gone to the Holy Land to save Jerusalem from the Saracen. I saw that everyone's eyes lit up, especially the ladies'. I felt that things were going well for me.

Next was the new song, '*under der linden*'. I started singing as slowly as I could. The women were entranced. I looked at each of them, one after the other. The younger ones were blushing and the older ones seemed lost in memories they would never dare speak of. Only a few looked on sternly. I imagined these either could never have known love, or had been hurt or deserted, or that something had happened to them in their lives so that now love meant little or nothing to them. I shot a glance at the Graefin and noticed, to my surprise, that she was staring stonily.

Then I sought Hildegunde's eyes. In my naivety I had imagined that she would be flattered yet keep her composure, perhaps allow a flicker of acknowledgement to pass across her lips. Instead she looked lost, drawn, hurt. Her eyes seemed to be lifeless yet at the same time to shine out of their sockets with despair. Her cheeks were flushed, but not with the healthy flush of youth. The red was an unnatural dull colour, and the rest of her face seemed an appalling waxen white. I remembered how she had looked on that evening after we had first loved, under the linden tree. Was that what she was remembering? Was she angry with me for some reason?

I realised that I had looked at her for just a little too long, and turned my eyes back to the Graefin. She was smiling now, yet I sensed that her smile was false. It was the mask of someone who wills evil and cannot hide this, no matter how they might distort their features.

My song was nearing its close:

*daz er bî mir laege, wessez iemen*
*(nu enwelle got!) so schamt ich mich.*
*Wes er mit mir pflaege, niemer niemen*
*bevinde daz wan er und ich...* *

It was then that the silence of the audience in the hall was broken. Someone, a woman, was sobbing convulsively, then calling out, with

* *If anyone were to know that we lay together / (Heaven forfend!) then I would be ashamed. / What he did with me / May no one ever know but he and I... / (Walter von der Vogelweide)*

a desperate voice. It was my name that she was calling. 'Walter... Walter!' I heard a dull thud as she fainted and fell. It was Hildegunde.

I stopped singing immediately and stood up to see what had happened. Already, other ladies were moving to help her. They got her to her feet and led her from the hall.

I started towards her too, but I was stopped by the Graefin. 'Do not worry yourself over such a small matter, Walter,' she said. I had never heard her speak to me in that tone. 'She is to be married next week. You know what virgins are. The thought of it and the emotion in your song must have been too much for her.'

'Married,' I said, trying desperately to maintain my composure, 'Married to whom?'

There was venom, hatred, jealousy in the way she half spoke, half hissed her words at me. 'My dear boy,' said the Graefin, 'you must be the last person in all the court to know. She has been given to Johannes of Ulm.'

I looked across the smoky hall. There was Johannes of Ulm, staring at me, his eyes ablaze, but this time not with soldierly comradeship but with anger, hatred. Perhaps he was not a courtly man, or a cultivated or well-read man, but he was certainly not so stupid that he failed to realise what had passed between Hildegunde and myself.

He fixed me with his gaze. I admit that I was terrified. At the same time, I knew I had to stand my ground. He started towards me. My instinct was to run, but I am proud to say that I did not do so. I stared back. All my thoughts now were for Hildegunde. Cost what it may, I would make sure that, even if she were never to be mine, at least she would not be given against her will to this brute.

Johannes of Ulm was striding towards me. Only just in time did three or four other knights intervene to stop him. He offered no resistance.

'So,' he half said, half spat, 'you dare sing your filthy songs to my wife-to-be. If I find you have so much as laid a finger on her, you are a dead man.'

'Sir,' I said, 'I shall not disguise the fact that I love Hildegunde, nor that she has loved me.'

Johannes of Ulm was already trying to draw his sword, and was only just held back from doing so by the men standing on either side of him. Fortunately, my master, the Graf of Frankenburc, stepped forward and raised his hand.

'Gentlemen,' he said, 'I can see good reason for both parties to desire satisfaction here. As the fates would have it, there will be an opportunity for them to meet, but not until tomorrow, in the field.'

Until the Graf spoke, everyone had been silent. Now there were general murmurs of approval from those gathered round.

A broad smile spread slowly over von Ulm's face. 'My honoured host is right. Young Walter can have the pleasure of spending the rest of the night looking forward to his death. For tomorrow I shall show no mercy. With the Graf's permission we shall dispense with mock weapons and use battle arms – or perhaps Walter will not have the courage to face this. Tomorrow evening there will be nothing left of him but a rotting carcass fit only for the dung heap. Yet I shall take my time. You are right, sir. We will meet tomorrow, and settle our differences then.'

He strode out, followed by the servants and knights who had accompanied him.

At first, no one spoke to me. Simon, Wolfi, Herbert and Kaspar, the young men who were due to fight on my side in the mêlée, came up to me and pledged their support. I tried to find words to thank and reassure them. I told them that the matter was between Ulm and myself, that they were to let me ride out alone, and that it was not right for them to risk getting hurt.

A number of ladies from different courts came up to me to whisper that they would be praying for me that night. They stared at me as though I were some sort of sacrificial victim. They were enjoying themselves. Only the Graefin was nowhere to be seen.

At last, when most of the other guests had dispersed, the Graf of Frankenburc himself came up to me and took me to one side.

'You are a fool,' he said. His tone was not unkind, and I took heart. 'You have taken a young lady of the court without my permission. And now you have won for yourself one of the fiercest warriors in the Empire as an enemy. What are you going to do about it?'

The truth of the matter was that he too was in his element. Besides, he had nothing to lose – or so it seemed to me at the time. My death would cost him nothing. I could easily be passed off as a scoundrel who had abused his kindness and got what he deserved. The story of my death would gain prestige for his court throughout the land; it would be the talk in courtly circles for months to come. If, on the other hand, by some miracle, I were to persevere and stand up against Johannes of Ulm, then the glory of his court would be the greater.

'Sir, are you angry about myself and Hildegunde?'

'I was young once.'

'Will you let this marriage between her and Ulm go through?'

'It is the will of the Graefin. As for the rest, it is up to you. Do you wish to leave the court now, to take flight, accept shame and probable outlawry? You can if you wish; I will not stand in your way. Though of course it will mean leaving Hildegunde to him.

'I cannot.'

'Then you will stay and fight?'

'I must.'

'Good. Then listen.'

I had never known the Graf of Frankenburc more animated and enthusiastic than he became that evening. He spent over an hour explaining tricks of battle to me: ways of controlling a horse in the fray, how to make dummy moves that will unsettle an opponent and upset his balance, how to deal with a man heavier than oneself, the weak points in his armour and the best points of leverage for unseating him. The Graf spoke with years of experience. I learnt much and I must say that I enjoyed this masculine talk of war and the things of war – or at least I would have done had I not been so pessimistic about my chances.

At the end of it all he patted me on the shoulder and wished me luck and God's blessing for the morning, though I was sure that he did so more out of desire to see a good fight than because he cared much for my cause. How could I have guessed what was really going on in his mind?

I returned to my room in order to prepare myself for the tournament. I knelt at my bed and said what I could by way of a confession. I slept fitfully. All night I relived over and over again the events of the evening: mingling with the guests, drinking, eating, chatting to the fine ladies, singing, then... then everything changing, as if a chasm were opening: Hildegunde fainting, von Ulm's threats, Frankenburc giving me advice about the mêlée. The Graefin. I thought she was my friend, fool that I was. Why had she arranged the marriage between Hildegunde and von Ulm? What had possessed her? Was she jealous that I had slept with Hildegunde, jealous of the spirituality of our love? Or was there more to it? Perhaps she had sensed the hurt, the darkness that our lovemaking had caused, or perhaps it was through her that was being judged.

Then my mind would turn to the next day. I would see myself riding out against Johannes of Ulm imagine various courses the mêlée might take. Each time I would fall or be killed in a different way, and I would tense with fear as I suffered the different pains – of being knocked off the horse, clubbed over the head, run through by Johannes' lance, or slowly, agonisingly stabbed to death with his sword. Lines describing the battle scenes in the Song of Roland would come to mind, how some were killed with lances and others had their heads split open, so that their brains spilt upon the ground. Then I would let my mind dwell on what the last moments of pain and fear would be like before the leaden coldness of death took me, how it would be to lose for ever the power to see and hear the things of this world. As I lay there, it would be as though this were actually happening, and then I would wake suddenly, in a cold sweat, shivering with fear, looking out the window at the moon, trying to calculate how long it would be till the morning came.

I shuddered as I remembered the rules of the Church, which

were enforced in some places, that anyone killed in a tournament was denied the right of burial in consecrated ground. I remembered having read, as a monk, that each of the seven deadly sins was present at a tournament: pride in the desire for honours; anger in combat and the desire for revenge; despair when defeats were inflicted; envy and greed at the thought of booty; gluttony during the feasting; and lust because of the way the women were expected to behave. I also remembered stories of demons seen flying through the air above tournaments, holding tournaments of their own, uttering spine-chilling cries of joy as they waited to snatch the souls of those who fell. I remembered too the stories of those who had fallen in mêlées coming alive for a few moments to tell the living of the terrible torments they were suffering in the afterworld as a punishment for having taken part in the contest.

I would try to banish such thoughts and try again to say my confession, in case there was anything I had left out, a sin I had forgotten that would bar me from eternal life. So then, as now, my past spun round and round in my head, and I tried to make some sense of it, to see some pattern, some redeeming feature, some reason to hope that I might, after all, escape the fires of hell.

Once, I fell into a fitful sleep and dreamt of the legendary knight whose lady had asked him to ride into a tournament wearing no armour, but only her shift. He obeyed her and was mortally wounded during the battle. That evening the lady came to the banquet wearing her shift drenched in his lifeblood.

How pitilessly slowly the time passed until the hour before dawn when, at last, Simon came to my room. He was to be my groom and follow me into the mêlée after I had done single combat with Johannes of Ulm. Simon was a tall, thin but strong lad of about eighteen. He was the second son of a noble family that had fallen on hard times. I was glad to see him, glad of the company, since he had been a good friend to me, glad that at last something was happening, that at last the waiting was over.

Simon said little. I supposed that it was hard for him to find appropriate words. Together we made our way to the lower hall, where the fire was already burning brightly and where our battle clothes and equipment had been laid out for us. I put on the armour the Graf had leant me. The hauberk was not too heavy. I preferred agility. For that reason I dispensed with the heavy leg plates that had recently become fashionable and made do with simple shin and thigh guards. I prepared the sword and lance that I would carry with me into the fight, and tried on the helmet. I had heard that there are some who like to keep the helmet on for a few hours before doing battle in order to get used to its weight, but I preferred to carry it until mass was over.

Soon I was joined in the lower hall by the other youths, Wolf, Herbert and Kaspar. We ate together a breakfast of meat, bread and fruit, which had been laid out for us by the kitchen women. We talked a little about the tactics we had agreed, but we had been through the plans so many times before that there was not much to say, so the conversation went in fits and starts. The sun had just begun to rise when we went to the stables to prepare the two destriers we were to have at our disposal.

The plan for the tournament had been that I should ride out to begin with and fight alone against Johannes of Ulm. Only when the outcome of our fight seemed predictable would the signal be given for the other four men on each side, one mounted and three on foot, to continue the combat. I presumed now that there would be a considerable wait before that signal was given: they would not wait until the outcome of the fight was predictable, but until one of us lay dead or dying.

It was a drizzly day and rather cold. In spite of this, by the time we emerged from the stables, wearing our armour and leading out the two horses, there were already some ladies about, all of them staring after us. The tent of Johannes of Ulm and his followers were outside the battlements. I was grateful that I would not have to set eyes on him again until the open-air mass was celebrated on the tournament field.

More ladies appeared, dressed in all their finery. The drizzle made the clothes of the younger ones stick close to the forms of their bodies. They did not seem to mind the men staring after them.

Many smiled flirtatiously at us as we led our horses through the great gates in order to make our way to the open-air mass. I remember that as I left the castle and walked across the fields there was a lark singing, high above us.

In the distance, far back within the castle, I was sure I heard someone, a lady, singing the refrain from my '*under der linden*' song. It was not the Graefin's voice. I looked back towards the castle and noticed how all the battlements had been decorated with banners for the occasion. They were all hanging sadly in the drizzle.

There was no sign of the Graf or the Graefin. I reflected on how different things would have been if I had not known Hildegunde. Perhaps then the Graf and the Graefin would have walked to mass with me in order to make public their support for me. Yet the thought of not having known Hildegunde was almost sacrilegious. To have known her, even if she could never be mine, was worth more than any support from the great ones.

At last we were all assembled beneath the grey skies, and mass began. I was to stand to the front and left with my fellows. Johannes of Ulm was to the right, and I noticed that the Graf and Graefin were at the rear of the congregation. Everyone was there but one person. Hildegunde.

It was only after the mass had started that I saw her making her way alone through the gates of the castle to join the congregation. She too was wearing a fine dress, blue with gold trimming. But her hair was uncombed and her face streaked with tear-stains. Her complexion was red and blotchy.

As mass was being said I kept looking round at her. I yearned to be beside her, to put my arm round her, comfort her, or perhaps be comforted by her. Then I reflected on the fact that all I had here at the court was borrowed: it was not mine, but only granted to me on sufferance. Without the court I was nothing. Hildegunde was all in this world I could lay claim to. Yet there she was, in a state of anguish, and there was I, on the verge of what amounted to a ritual slaying. This was all I had in my power to offer her.

I was not unduly nervous. I was in control now. I had passed through the terrors of the night and I had accepted that I would probably die. In the meantime, however, there was much to think about. I wanted to be able to look at Hildegunde for as long as possible. I needed to concentrate on my fighting tactics, to reassure my horse and my companions, and at the same time I wished to participate fully in the mass so that If I were to die I should meet my Creator in a state of grace. Above all, I did not want to lose face. I thought of another line from the Song of Roland: *Male chancun n'en deit estre cantee...*★

I kept meeting the gaze of Johannes of Ulm, whose eyes were fixed on me, staring and sneering. He was standing just a matter of yards away, with the knights and young men who were to fight on his side in the mêlée. I was well aware that if I somehow managed to survive the initial onslaught of Johannes himself, I would also have to defend myself against these men, who would no doubt have been instructed to give priority to killing me.

I looked round at the group of men who would be fighting on my side: Simon, Wolfi, Herbert, Kaspar. All good youths. I smiled to each of them in turn. None of them had anything to fear, save an accident; the opposition would have no interest in killing any of them. Yet they, like me, were young, as yet untried in battle, and I did not know how much I could rely on any of them to fight for me if the worst came to the worst.

There was another group of men, standing by the ramparts, nearly, but not quite, out of sight. I recognised some of them, but not all. The Graf had left the congregation and was talking to them. One of them was the Abbot Quintus. Another was tall and had a long beard. His eyes seemed large for their sockets and his hair was long, like an Old Testament prophet's. They were all quite old men, in their late forties at the very least. One of them, a shorter man with a fine, bald head and carrying a stick, also wore ecclesiastical dress of some kind. I was sure he was blind; he had to be led by the others. Another was of medium height, with curly grey hair, and wore the clothes of a nobleman...

(★*No dishonourable song should be sung about it.*)

They had certainly not been at the castle the previous evening. I felt resentment at their presence, though I was not sure why I was so suspicious of them. In fact I became quite anxious about them, and had to remind myself that there was no point in worrying since in an hour or two I would probably be lying dead or dying in the field.

I tried to turn my thoughts to my immortal soul, to make myself concentrate on the chanting of the priests, whose voices were borne towards us by the wind, as was their incense. I tried to pray for forgiveness for my many sins. Above all, I prayed for Hildegunde, since it was the fault of no one but myself that she had been brought to her present state of unhappiness.

The mass was over and it was time for the joust to commence. After the blessing of the congregation, both fighting parties in turn were presented to the priests for blessing.

We made our way to the end of the field that had been assigned to us. At first, my party was silent. It was as if, in some way, they had already disowned me, maybe because of Hildegunde, or maybe because they felt that I already belonged to Death. Or maybe they were so overwhelmed by the situation that they could not think of anything to say.

I chatted to them to raise their spirits, as if there was nothing to fear. I recalled a couple of incidents that had amused them during our training. Simon and Herbert smiled big, almost tearful smiles; Wolfi and Kaspar began offering me advice as I continued my preparations. I mounted the Graf's horse. Now that the moment of parting before the battle had come, they smiled at me and wished me God's blessing. It really was as if they expected never to see me alive again.

At last I was mounted and the joust was about to begin. I remember feeling exhilarated, acutely aware of everything that surrounded me; my clothing, my companions, the sky, the crowds in front of the castle, the freshness of the air, the low scudding clouds, the movements of the horse beneath me, everything down to the tiniest blade of grass seemed brilliantly present to me.

Although I had every reason to believe that I was about to die, it was almost as though, having nothing left to lose, I was more fully alive than I had ever been before.

I could see at the other end of the field that Johannes von Ulm's horse was ready also. I prepared my weapons – the lance, the shield – and strapped the sword for ground fighting in my belt. Then I waited for the Graf to give the sign for us to ride out.

Any unease had now left me. I felt a sense of harmony, of oneness with everything around me. Ironically, I remember feeling a deep sense of gratitude towards the Graf for all he had given me. I looked towards the crowds, where I knew that Hildegunde was. I felt my love for her bloom within me, sweeping through me like a pure spiritual presence. I looked towards Johannes of Ulm. He was a noble and worthy opponent. If he hated me, it did not matter. As I looked at him, mounted and fully armed on the opposite side of the field, I felt that the fight which was to ensue was part of some greater harmony. If, when I look at Johannes of Ulm, I am looking at my death, I thought, let it be so; at least my death will have been a noble one.

When the signal was given and we both charged, the feeling was indescribable. There was the coolness of the morning air on my face as it filled the inside of my helmet. There was the rhythm of the horse's hooves on the soft, dewy earth. There was the sound of a lark singing somewhere overhead. I was aware of the castle to my left, the forest to my right, the drizzly grey sky, and the crowds of people, totally silent as they looked on. All the time, though, the focus of my attention was the magnificent figure of Johannes of Ulm, charging towards me, distant at first, then growing larger and larger.

The first pass was deliberately taken wide by both of us. The risk of contact at a gallop is too high, the results of a thrust with even the best horsemanship too unpredictable, whether one is at the receiving end of the lance or holding it. Even so, I had suspected that Johannes might try to take me by surprise. These fears turned out to have been in vain.

Only after the pass did I realise what his plan was. He had allowed the first pass to go wide so as to be able to catch me off guard. Only ten yards after the pass he turned his horse round, much sooner than one would normally do in a courtly fight.

One of the tips the Graf had repeated over and over to me was to look at my opponent at all times, and if I could not look round then at least to use my power of hearing to the utmost. All the same, I only just had time to turn the horse round in order to be able to face him. It required all my horsemanship to manage the manoeuvre. If I had still been sideways on to him as he charged, nothing I could have done would have been able to stop him from dismounting me and probably running me through there and then. As he charged, I saw that his lance was aimed right at my head, and I could see that he was grinning, not expecting, me to be able to perform any evasive action.

Now, to aim for the head is a risky business; for if the lance can be avoided, and if it goes over the opponent's shoulder, one is vulnerable for the rest of the pass. By spurring the horse to move one way and then ducking low, I was able to avoid his blow. Then, righting myself as quickly as I could, I swung my own lance round as he continued on past, catching him a blow on the back of his head.

The blow was not of sufficient force to do anything other than shake him and rile him. Yet that was what I wanted, since it increased the chance of his making mistakes.

I turned my horse and rode behind him. It is very dangerous for a rider to be pursued because of the difficulty of turning one's own horse round. As I chased him across the field I heard a cheer from the onlookers. Even if he was going to kill me, at least I had humiliated him for this moment.

He rode well, though, and there was no way I could catch him. Also, I was loath to unseat him from the rear since that would have been uncourtly. So I slowed down in order to rest my horse and to give him the chance to face me for a new charge.

As soon as he realised that I was no longer close behind him, he turned round and charged straight at me again from close quarters. I should have had time to defend myself, but I was too much taken by surprise. Also, given the unconventional nature of the charge, it was hard to judge what to do.

As it was, he managed to deflect my lance with his shield, while his lance, which he deliberately aimed low, with little or no thought for the welfare or value of the horse, caught my leg, cutting into the flesh. The point continued into the flesh of the horse, whilst the shaft of the lance levered me away from the saddle as the horse whinnied with the pain and reared up on its hind legs.

I had no choice but to dismount. The horse would be unreliable from then on.

If it had been a normal contest, that would have marked the end of the riding and the beginning of the mêlée. I would have had to pledge the horse to Johannes and offer a ransom for myself. Yet from the way he laughed at me as he rode past, I knew that there were to be no negotiations. He had drawn blood and blood was what he wanted.

He rode away leisurely and turned slowly. Still laughing, he taunted me with the lance, pointing it, now at my head, now at my chest, as if deciding the means by which he would dispatch me.

The pain in my leg shot through me. In a way I was grateful for it, since it helped my concentration. I struggled to my feet and began to remove my armour – first the breastplate, then the leg protectors, and finally the helmet. The hauberk was all I kept on.

Johannes of Ulm laughed at me all the more, but there was sense in what I was doing. Armour would not protect me against a knight on horseback. My only hope was mobility, provided, of course, that my leg held out. It moved to order, but it hurt and I could feel the warm, wet trickle of blood on my knee. I drew my sword and waited.

Slowly at first, then with increasing speed, Ulm rode towards me. Since I was disadvantaged, for the first time I felt it legitimate to use some deceit. I limped on my leg as if I were more badly injured than I was. I held my sword limply in one hand rather than two. I wished to let it be known that I would continue the fight. I also wanted to give the impression that there was no strength in me.

I saw from the vicious glint in my opponent's eyes that, if I had thrown myself down on my knees there and then and begged for mercy, I would have received none, but that he would have enjoyed killing me slowly, inflicting as much pain as possible.

I continued my deceit until the last moment. Then, when the lance was only about a yard from my body, and Johannes of Ulm was charging at full speed, I sidestepped his thrust and managed, as I had planned, to catch the lance between my left arm and my body. I held on tight.

My aim was either to unseat my opponent or at least wrest the lance from his grasp. I realised in the split second as I began to get a grip on his lance between my body and my arm that he would be too strong for this. He had too firm a hold on the lance.

Some inner voice told me that my only hope was to break the lance with my sword. I still had a firm hold with my left arm, yet the lance was being forced out at an angle and at the same time my grip was being forced further up towards the shaft, to a point at which I would be vulnerable to blows on the head from my opponent's gloved hand. So, with all the strength of my right arm, I swung my broadsword in a great arc over my head, and down to where I knew the shaft of the lance would be.

There was a sickening cracking sound. Immediately, the lance dropped to the ground, and I with it.

My whole body was jarred by the fall, and it was only the desperate fear that I would be done for there and then if I did not get up that gave me the impetus to struggle to my feet.

Von Ulm was turning his horse and trying to reach for his own sword. I could tell that something was amiss from the slowness and awkwardness of his movements.

He turned his horse, still trying to grasp his sword. There was a look of anger and agony in his eyes.

Then I realised why. He was unable to grasp his sword, to grasp anything, for out of the end of his sleeve there poured a stream of hot, steaming blood. There was no hand there - only tatters of severed flesh.

I looked down to where the lance had dropped and saw that his gauntleted hand was still grasping it. It was severed at the wrist.

Yet the fight was not over.

Johannes spurred his horse to charge me down. If I had dodged one second later I would have been trampled.

I did not have time to wield my sword again, but I did have time to make a grab at his foot. I hung on, despite being dragged along for a number of yards, until I felt, with satisfaction, that his massive weight was becoming dislodged from the saddle. I feared being crushed if he landed on top of me, so, the moment I felt sure he was about to fall, I let go, falling awkwardly myself, yet hearing, from three or four yards further on, the satisfying thud of his great armoured body falling to the earth.

I stood up slowly, not knowing what to expect. By now my leg had seized up badly and I could hardly move.

I thought my opponent must surely be finished now, but to my horror, like some crazed, lumbering bear, or some ghost of himself, Johannes of Ulm slowly raised himself from the ground and strode towards me.

He was unarmed and his wrist was still dripping blood. His eyes were wild, inhuman. Of the convivial companion of the night before nothing remained. This was a hurt beast, an unthinking killer.

As he lumbered towards me, I held the sword to his chest. He pushed it to one side. I did not want to run through an unarmed and injured man, so, foolishly, I hesitated.

Before I had a chance to decide what to do, he was upon me, and to my horror he had me grasped in a great bear-hug, squeezing me with all his might, breathing his poisonous, vile breath into my face in desperate, rapid puffs, staring at me with mad eyes, all but breaking my ribs against his breastplate.

Slowly, I managed to free my arms and press the flats of my hands against his chin, forcing his head back as far as I could to relieve the pressure. I was able to breathe, but only just.

At last his strength gave and, with a great cry, he fell backwards.

To stop myself from falling I had to place a foot on his massive barrel of a chest. The onlookers must have taken this as a sign of my triumphing, for a great cheer rose up from the castle walls.

I looked round and saw that the others who were to fight in the mêlée were coming towards us. I took it that the fight was to continue and drew my sword to face the opposition, knowing that I would not be able to hold out much longer. I only prayed that my side would arrive in time.

Yet the signal had already been given that the fight was over. Enough in the way of feats of arms had been seen for one day. Enough had been done for honour, and there was no point in risking any further injury or damage for the sake of the tournament.

I was congratulated by all the knights and carried in triumph back to the waiting crowd. By this time, however, the wound to my leg was causing me a great deal of pain, and I passed out.

The rest of this day, which should have been my day of glory, was spent drifting in and out of consciousness. I was in so much pain whenever I woke that I could not think, talk or enjoy my victory in any way.

# IX

## The Hermit

✠

I have often wondered how the soul acts on the body. I once read that it was by means of light, since light is found in both the spiritual and the material worlds. That would explain how at times we can sense a person's spiritual state by means of a light seeming to shine forth from them. And it is such light, not pain, that I remember as I lay there after the fight. For Hildegunde was next to me, nursing me, and I bathed in her presence.

They set up a bed for me in a small room on the ground floor, not far from the kitchens. By the evening my wound had been staunched and treated with herbs to stop it rotting. For the rest of the night and the following day I drifted in and out of consciousness. Despite the pain, it seemed to me that I was in heaven since Hildegunde was permanently at my side. Every time I opened my eyes, the first thing that I would see was her face, and when I closed my eyes I could sense the presence of her soul. Perhaps it was then that I experienced her love most perfectly. It has often been written that pain quells carnal desire yet leaves intact the essence of love.

On the second day, as soon as I had the strength to talk, I asked after Johannes of Ulm. She shuddered when I mentioned his name.

'Yes,' she said. 'You and he are all the talk of the court. He has lost much blood, and he is unconscious much of the time.'

'Is there no hope for him?'

'The dirt got into the stub of his wrist when he fell. They had to wash the wound constantly to stop it from becoming infected. But this caused him much pain, and poisons spread whatever they did.'

I thought that I would never have wished such an end on anyone; yet it had not come about through any wish of mine.

I was still convinced that I had covered myself in glory. As I slept and dreamt and held her hand, it seemed to me that I was already at the end of all my longing and all my seeking. Was I not a hero? Had I not proved myself worthy of Hildegunde in battle, in song? Had not the Graf of Frankenburc in the last few months and during that evening before the tournament demonstrated his love and affection for me, thereby announcing his patronage? There was always the Graefin of course, but what was her will compared with his? She was mere decoration as far as the court was concerned. His was the iron will by means of which it was controlled.

In my feverish state I allowed myself to believe that he would raise my status to that of a knight and that I should live in the castle with greater responsibilities; or even that he would grant me a small fief, which I would administer for him whilst continuing at court. Also I dreamt of marriage to Hildegunde.

Within a day or two I had recovered sufficiently to be able to receive people. Everything that happened encouraged my belief that as a result of my performance in the joust I was regarded as something of a hero. First to come were knights and pages from the castle. Theodor was beside himself with enthusiasm for the joust. In fact it was through him that I was able to reconstruct the exact sequence of events during the fight, for at the time everything had happened so quickly. Then ladies came, those who were based at the court, relations of the Graf, and many from courts miles away who had come to see the tournament. All of them praised my bravery and commended my singing and gallantry, expressing their wish that I should recover soon. Many more important people came. Even the Abbot Quintus of the Cistercian monastery of Frankenburc came to visit me, in order to express his desire that the two of us should be reconciled. I received no visit from the Graf or the Graefin. I suppose that I should have been suspicious of this, but I was not.

My thoughts kept returning to Johannes of Ulm. I did not hate him. I would not have him die, only give up his claim to Hildegunde. If he loved Hildegunde, how could I despise him for that? To my mind Hildegunde was the most adorable of all ladies, and the worst I could feel for those to whom she had not pledged her heart was pity.

My visitors told me that no one had been able to cleanse his wound because of its rottenness. The wound was still bleeding persistently in spite of all the tourniquets and bandaging applied to it. Because of the processes of cleansing the wound, he had been in much pain, and now he lay there exhausted, unconscious most of the time. It was thought that he would not live for long. I heard that when he woke he was able to talk, but they told me he had changed. He was pale and drawn. He spoke of nothing but the shame of his defeat, yet insisted that his shame was well deserved. He repeated over and over that it had been sinful of him to allow himself to grow angry with me and to hate me. He said that now he had lost his right hand, which as a soldier was all his life to him, all he wanted was to die.

Such talk from a man of renowned valour was upsetting for many at court. Consequently, he was receiving fewer and fewer visitors. I heard that even the knights with whom he had travelled visited only rarely now. It was more than they could bear to see their once fierce fighting and drinking companion turn into a wreck whose only conversation consisted of self-reproach.

I learnt that Johannes now had a priest in constant attendance, that he had left all his goods to the Church and that, whenever he woke, he spent his time in prayer and confession, weeping and calling on our Lady and all the saints to pray for his forgiveness. The more I heard of this, the more I pitied him. After two more days I was well enough to sit up and to concentrate for reasonable periods. I dictated via Hildegunde a message to be taken to

Johannes. In it I wished him well and said that I bore him no malice, only that I wished to know whether or not he still laid claim to Hildegunde. As soon as I had sent this note I regretted doing so, thinking that it would be seen either as too offensive, too weak or too niggardly.

Within hours of sending it, I received a note from him, dictated to the priest who was attending him. I could hardly believe what I read. He addressed me as his beloved brother in Christ. He asked for my forgiveness for the great wrongs he had done me and said that he not only forgave me but thanked me for the injury he had received from me. At first I wondered if perhaps I was reading the ramblings of a madman. He went on to say that through his wound he had come to know Christ, and that he renounced both Hildegunde and life itself. He begged me to come and visit him as soon as I was well enough.

I could not tell, nor shall I probably ever know, whether he had found peace or whether the shock of his injury had been so great as to unhinge his mind and destroy his spirit.

At first I was nervous of paying him a visit, not least because I feared a trap. I discussed the matter with Hildegunde. She said that from all she had heard it was true that Johannes was too weak to do anyone any harm. Also, the knights who had ridden with him were preparing to depart. She said that they would not dare carry out any act of revenge against me, since they would be sure to be punished by the Graf; also they were neither kinsmen nor vassals of Johannes, so they would have no motive for any attack against me, particularly in view of Johannes' weakness and present state of mind.

Since the fourth day, Hildegunde, for the sake of propriety, no longer stayed with me the whole time, and when she was present she always brought another lady. Now that the time of being with her alone had come to an end, I was keen to take the first steps in my new life so as to be able to prove myself still worthy of her.

I made arrangements to visit Johannes of Ulm on the sixth day after the joust. I found that my leg was strong enough to walk on if I used a stick to help me, and with practice I found that I could get around the room in which I had been laid up without too much trouble. I arranged to visit Johannes in the company of Simon and Wolfi. I trusted these young noblemen more than anyone in the world.

They supported me as I made my way down the steps, across the courtyard, and eventually to the room near the chapel where Johannes was being cared for. As I hobbled my way across the courtyard, a number of people gathered round to get a view of me. I enjoyed the fame, thinking little about where it would lead.

I looked into the little cell-like room. A candle was burning. There, on a low bed, stretched the enormous form of Johannes of Ulm, and next to him sat the priest. There was no one else. As I approached I caught the smell of Johannes' wound. It was the smell of rotting, one I have ever since associated with death and the battlefield. He was lying on his back. His wounded arm was bare from shoulder to elbow. The stub was tightly bandaged, though I could see the blood and filth seeping through at the end where his hand had been.

His massive, bearded head was turned towards me, though his eyes were closed. His complexion was sallow, lifeless in the candlelight. His whole bulk was deathly still, and for a moment I wondered if I had come too late.

The priest looked up at me with sad, hollow eyes. He was an oldish man, the pitiful thinness of his frame and the fragility in the way he held his wax-like bald head contrasting strangely with Johannes, who looked like a felled giant next to him. The poor man was no doubt exhausted by the time he had spent waking with Johannes. There was no possible danger for me here. I dismissed Simon and Wolfi and sat next to Johannes. I tried to pray.

The priest touched Johannes' head gently, stroking his hair as a mother would stroke a sick child's, Johannes' eyes opened slowly. I saw him wince with pain for a moment, but then, as his eyes focused on me, he smiled in a way I shall never forget, peaceful, otherworldly.

I asked him how he was feeling and wished him a speedy

recovery. He seemed to ignore my words, yet his gaze reached right through me, to the very depth of my being.

'You fought well,' he said. 'You are a brave man. I congratulate you.'

I tried to interrupt, to say something suitably courtly to congratulate him on his own skills as a soldier, but he raised his left hand to silence me.

'I have not long,' he said. 'I have heard. You are the One. Forgive me that I opposed you. It was in ignorance. Beware the Graf and his wife. They are willful. They wish to use you, to manipulate you. Beware too the Abbot Quintus.'

The priest shushed him. I was surprised, and looked round to see a look of alarm and fear on the priest's face.

Johannes showed something of his old fierceness and strength of will, enough anyway to silence the priest. Raising himself slightly, he said, 'I am a dead man now. No one can silence a dead man when he chooses to speak.'

Then Johannes' speech became rambling and incoherent. I could barely distinguish one word from another. He talked of soothsayers and predictions, of Charlemagne and a Brotherhood of prayer. It was only later that I began to understand what he was trying to explain to me.

Then his great eyes opened and he turned towards me, and he seemed to see me afresh. 'Take Hildegunde and love her, if they will let you. She was never for me. But be careful of them. I have lived long and well...'

His eyes closed. I sat with him a while longer and stared at him, trying to pray, before I was finally ushered out of the room.

With the help of Simon and Wolfi, I returned to my own room across the courtyard. I fully expected to find Hildegunde there, but there was no sign of her.

Johannes died later that night. He never regained consciousness after our meeting.

I continued to rest and recover. I was brought food from the kitchens. Another day passed and my only visitor was Theodor.

Hildegunde did not come that day. Nor the next. On the third day after my visit to Johannes of Ulm there was still no sign of Hildegunde. By then I had given up hope of a visit from the Graf or the Graefin. Theodor visited regularly. He was his usual cheerful self, but I felt that he was hiding something.

After two more nights, the other guests had all left. Simon and Wolfi called occasionally. Apart from Theodor they were my only visitors. Something must have gone wrong, though I could not imagine what.

By that third day I could take it no longer. I resolved to put my leg to the test and make my own way across the courtyard to the lower hall, where I expected to be able to find the Graf and the Graefin, and maybe even Hildegunde.

It took me a while to get up and dress on my own, but I managed. My leg was stiff, but the wound was healing well. I took my stick and set off across the courtyard. As I walked the stiffness became easier and I was making good speed.

I regretted having stayed in bed for so long. I saw Theodor coming towards me and waved cheerfully to him.

I thought Theodor would be pleased to see me up and about, but all of a sudden he became quite different from the cheerful visitor I had received just the previous day. On seeing me, he flew into a blind rage, calling me every name under the sun, cursing me for having got up without telling him, asking me what I thought I was doing and where I was going. I told him that I was well enough to continue my duties at court and apologised if this was causing him any offence.

For a long while he stared at me, as if lost for words. Then he said, 'You might think you are well enough, young man. But what do you think the court wants of you? You have upset the Graefin, and no amount of pleading will reconcile her to you. She and the Graf have left the court to visit relatives in Swabia. I must tell you now that the last thing they expect to find here when they return is you.'

At first I thought he must be joking. I simply could not believe it. 'Why? What have I done?' I asked.

'It is their will. How can we question them?'

'But Hildegunde? Where is she?'

'She has been sent away.'

'Sent where?'

'I am not at liberty to tell you.'

'What about the Graf and the Graefin? When did they leave?'

'About two hours ago. Be grateful that you did not run into them . . .'

Theodor continued to stare at me, first in anger, then in pity. He must have realised that his words were destroying the very fabric of my life, my hopes for the future and for everything I loved.

I looked away from Theodor's staring eyes and tried to take in the scene around me. It was true that the courtyard was less full than normal. Many people must have travelled with the Graf and Graefin, or maybe the Graf had given leave to the members of the court to visit their own relatives, as is the custom when great lords visit those who would not be able to support all their train. A chill wind was blowing through the few banners that had still not been taken down after the tournament. They whirred and made an empty, ghostly sound, as if even they wished to frighten and mock me.

Suddenly, I realised that the castle, which had been so much of my life, which I had invested with so much meaning, had become an empty shell. Now that the Graf and Graefin had disowned me, and now that Hildegunde had gone, the very walls seemed burdensome and foreboding. But I had to know where Hildegunde was.

'Theodor, you must tell me. Hildegunde. When did she leave? Surely you can tell me that.'

'About two hours ago.'

'With her uncle?'

Theodor was silent

'Where is she going? Please. You must tell me.'

He looked about nervously to make sure there was no one who could overhear us. I realised that if I pressed him he might give way. 'Please,' I repeated.

'Walter, you have been my best ever charge. I shall never forget the days I spent teaching you. If I tell you where Hildegunde is, you must realise that it is out of loyalty to you, and that I am disobeying others. I know this sounds cowardly, but …'

'Of course I shan't tell them. I shall never see them again, not if I can help it. In any case, why should I be disloyal to you, when you have been the architect of all that was good and pleasant in my life here?'

Something happened then which I never thought would be possible. Theodor stepped forward and embraced me, hugged me to him. He whispered, 'She has gone with her uncle to Ochsenfurt. He will either marry her off or she will go to a convent, I don't know which.'

He stepped back suddenly, regaining his composure. I smiled at him, thanked him, turned and made to return to my room. Theodor called after me, 'Don't go after her, Walter. It will only bring pain to both of you.'

I turned round to face him. 'I have to go,' I said. 'There are plenty of courtly singers who sing empty songs about love. For me it is what I truly feel.'

Theodor was silent, and I continued on my way to my room, where I gathered together my few possessions. They did not amount to much: a bag containing a few coins, the Virgil and Ovid I had saved from the fire at Babenberch. I had one change of clothes, which Hildegunde had measured me for, and of course there was my lute and a few manuscripts containing notes of my own songs.

As soon as I had assembled these things, I made my way back out to the courtyard. Theodor was still there. So were Simon and Wolfi. Wolfi had with him a fine, fresh young horse from the stables, one of the noblest I had ever seen. At first I feared they might try to stop me from leaving. I walked over to the small group to say goodbye to them.

Theodor pressed a purse of money into my hands. Wolfi made it clear that the horse was for me.

I tried to find the words to thank them, but I am sure I only managed to mumble incoherently.

I think that even then I imagined that all would work out for the best, that it would only be a short time before I sorted out the misunderstandings and I would be able to return the horse and the money. My main thought was that I was just two hours behind Hildegunde. I was determined to catch up with her and her uncle before they reached Ochsenfurt. I mounted the horse and rode out of the gates after her.

I rode all the rest of that day, despite the fact that my leg caused me such pain that at times I thought I was going to faint. By nightfall I had covered most of the way to Ochsenfurt, through the forests and over the rolling hills of Franconia, through the villages along the Main and the valleys where the vineyards were ripening.

There was no sign of Hildegunde or of her uncle. Only when I dismounted in the evening did I realise just how much damage I had done to my leg: the pain was almost as bad as the day after the injury had first been inflicted.

I spent the night at a small inn in a little town called Breitmarkt. When I was alone, I counted the money that Theodor had given me. I had assumed that the purse he gave me would contain silver coins, but in fact more than half of them were gold. I wondered how he had come about so much money. I hoped that it was not his personal savings; I also hoped that the money was not stolen. In any case, it would be enough for me to be able to live independently for a long while. There would be no need for me to sing for my supper unless I wanted to.

I ate a small meal. By the time I got myself into bed, my leg had stiffened up. It was throbbing and pulsing with pain. I undid the dressing and saw that, if I had gone on any further, the wound would have opened. It was weeping once more.

By the next morning I had slept little and the pain was even worse, though the wound itself looked like it had continued to heal during the night. I had no choice but to stay put. There was no way I would be able to ride any further that day.

I comforted myself with the thought that Ochsenfurt, the next place I would go to seek Hildegunde, was only two or three miles away. Perhaps she was there, in which case I was closer to her now than I would have been had I stayed at the castle. I had to rest to be in a fit state to confront Hildegunde's uncle.

I remember the desolation I experienced when I woke that morning. I had been dreaming of the time just after the joust, when I could open my eyes whenever I chose, look up and see Hildegunde's face. Now I realised just how much everything had changed since then. I was attached to no court. I had no trade and no future. I had no connections, no property, nothing to offer her except a few songs. I had exchanged a bright future at one of the best courts in Franconia for the musty straw of a dingy inn and a hopeless chase after a lovely girl I would not be able to provide for, even if I were to marry her.

Then the many other darknesses of my life crowded in on me: the deaths of my father and Uqhart, the ghost of Katrin, which still haunted me, my frustrated ambitions as a scholar and as a mystic. Everything had happened so quickly. To think that it was just over a week since the mêlée. Then, I had been surrounded by well-wishers, the centre of attention at a great court: yet now, I was quite alone, an anonymous, rootless man with an injured leg in a cheap tavern.

It was three days before I was well enough to set out, and even then my leg still caused me considerable pain.

I rode to Ochsenfurt and made inquiries about where I should find the knight Alberich, Hildegunde's uncle. His manor was just outside the town. The land was hilly but rich. There were many fields of wheat, and there was much pasture for animals as well as a good many vineyards. The house itself was built partly in the remains of an old stone structure, which I was told by the local innkeeper had once been a monastery. Those parts of it that had fallen down were replaced by timber, so the house was of unusual appearance, being half stone and half wooden.

When I reached the manor, I stood before the gates and hammered and shouted as loudly as I could. I kept this up, on and off, for nearly an hour. I was not willing to believe the place was totally empty. Then I walked round the fence to try to find the lowest point. This would have been hard enough to climb, even if my leg had been in a good state. As it was, I did not dare risk it.

Instead, I rode over to a peasant who was working in a field nearby. The poor fellow was frightened of me. He seemed half starved. He was dirty, his hair thin and his head bent forward as if he was expecting me to strike him at any moment. His dark eyes darted suspiciously, hungrily. Something about him made me think of a weasel or a ferret. I wondered if the knight Alberich of Ochsenfurt was one of those who ruled their peasants by ill-treating and starving them.

I asked him if he had seen a beautiful young woman at the manor, with long golden hair. At first he refused to answer. I threw him a silver coin. The poor man dived for it as if he had never seen so much money in his life - which probably he had not. In any case, his manner changed from one of surly defiance to grovelling subservience. He said that yes, everyone had noticed the lady with the long, golden hair. Everyone was talking of her on account of her beauty. She had arrived two days ago, but she and the Ritter of Ochsenfurt had ridden out that morning. It was not known when they would return.

I gave the man one more coin and told him that he would receive another provided he kept his mouth shut about my presence in Ochsenfurt and provided too that he would come and fetch me from the inn the moment he saw the lady return. He blessed me as if I were a saint.

I returned to the inn. My leg was hurting badly, and I needed rest.

Two whole days passed. I was beginning to give up hope. Wild thoughts stormed through my mind. I imagined myself breaking into the manor, carrying out Hildegunde by force. I imagined myself setting fire to the place and running through the smoke and flames to rescue her, taking her away to be my own, forever. Then I would sink into bouts of despair, imagining her already married.

On the evening of the second day, just after supper, the peasant came. He was excited and out of breath from running. Firstly he reminded me nervously of my promise of more money; he asked me if I was prepared to keep it. Instantly I was filled with excitement and asked him if he had seen her. I showed him the coin that would be his. He smiled with greedy satisfaction and told me that he had seen his master and the lady with the golden hair. She had been sitting on a horse led by his master. They were just two or three miles away and would very shortly be coming down the road that passed the inn. I paid the man his money and promised him more if he would lead me to a secluded place where I could confront them.

We set out along the forest road as the sun was beginning to set. The man led my horse along the road running to the west away from Ochsenfurt and the manor. It was surrounded on either side by overarching trees. The road was hilly, but its straightness meant that from the top of each crest it was possible to see along it for a good distance.

We had walked over a mile and I wondered if perhaps the peasant had made a mistake, or if he was just lying. Yet he had the instincts of one who has always lived on the land, and whenever I suggested stopping and waiting he would insist on going further, telling me that I had chosen a bad spot or that it would mean too long a wait.

At last, when we reached the top of another hill, he stopped me. I could hear nothing and see nothing, but he seemed to be able to sense that someone was coming. He led the horse off the road and told me to look. How he could tell they were coming I shall never know. After a few minutes I glimpsed, just coming into sight over the crest of the next hill, through the trees whose leaves glowed emerald green, Hildegunde's long, golden hair, glinting in the evening sun. By the time she had reached the top of the hill I could see that she was riding and that her horse was being led by her uncle Alberich, the Ritter of Ochsenfurt.

I told the peasant that I wanted to surprise Ochsenfurt; but by now he was getting nervous and wanted to take no more part in my plans. I gave him another coin and he fled as fast as his legs could carry him.

The trees were quite dense on my side of the dip, so I was able to ride down into it without being recognised. When I reached the lowest point, I took cover just off the road. The advantage of being at the bottom of the dip was that I would be impossible for Ochsenfurt to do anything but face me.

So there I waited, still mounted, for the woman I most loved and the man I most hated to come within striking distance.

I left it until the last moment before spurring my horse and riding out to confront them. At the sight of me, they stopped dead in their tracks. Hildegunde looked deathly pale. Ochsenfurt's nasty, beady little eyes stared up at me from his wrinkled, apoplectic face. For a moment I thought his head might explode with rage.

'What do you want?' he snapped.

'I want to talk to Hildegunde.'

'Well you can't.' He made to continue on his way, ignoring me.

'Hildegunde!' I called to her directly. 'I said we must talk.'

She remained silent. I could not read the look on her face; was it surprise or distress?' I could not even tell if she wanted to see me. For a moment I feared that she too had turned against me.

'Leave us alone, cartwright,' sneered Ochsenfurt, 'you have nothing to offer Hildegunde. No money, no connections, no power. Get out of my way!'

'You can call me what you want, Ochsenfurt, but remember the fate Johannes of Ulm suffered through me. Perhaps it is a fate that you would wish to share.'

'Yes,' said Ochsenfurt, 'you look like the hanging sort. I suggest you leave this land quickly, oaf. A threat against my person is tantamount to murder, to treason. Start riding now, for there will soon be many good men on your trail.'

'Stop it!' Hildegunde screamed suddenly. 'Stop it! I will speak to Walter. I must. Follow me!'

In his rage, Ochsenfurt had let go of the reins of the horse he had been leading, so Hildegunde was able to turn the horse. She rode away, back up the path in the opposite direction.

Ochsenfurt stared up at me, his bald head growing redder and redder, and glistening with sweat. 'You'll pay for this,' he threatened. He turned to run after her, but was soon out of breath.

I rode past him, and followed Hildegunde.

The sun had almost set by the time I caught up with her. It was like a giant, orange orb in front of us, still casting long shadows over the path, though the bright green of the forest would soon be turning grey.

We rode next to each other in silence for a while. There I was, just feet away from her, no one else around for miles, yet still I felt a terrible emptiness. What if I were to take her in my arms and kiss her, would that make any difference? She continued to look straight in front of her, her eyes glazed. I did not dare try to touch her.

As soon as we had put a reasonable distance between ourselves and Ochsenfurt, I suggested that we dismount so we could talk.

I had never seen her like this before. She was absolutely rigid, whether with fear or resentment towards me, I could not tell. All I wanted was to touch her, but I did not dare because of the look on her face.

We led the horses deeper and deeper into the forest. It was all but dark, and I could see the horses' breath curling in front of their faces. Still Hildegunde did not speak.

'What has happened?' I asked.

'Don't you know?'

'I only found out three days ago that you had gone. Since then I have spent most of my time in an inn. My leg...Anyway, it's better now.'

She stopped walking. We had reached a clearing. I listened, but there was no sign of pursuit. Fortunately, it was not cold. The heat of the day would last well into the evening, though there were the first signs of dew forming on the grass and on the leaves of the trees.

Hildegunde was staring at me. In the poor light her face seemed grey and her eyes too big. I could not understand what had upset her.

'Who have you talked to, Walter?'

'No one. Only someone at court who told me you had gone.'

'Who?'

'One of the servants. They asked me not to say.'

'Not the Graf?' She grew paler and paler with every moment. I wondered if she was sick.

'No.'

'So you don't know…?'

'No.'

Slowly, as if time had ceased to flow at its usual speed, Hildegunde turned from me and covered her face with her hands. Then she doubled over, as if in pain. I tied the horses to a tree and went to comfort her. I tried to wrap my arm round her shoulders, but she pulled away.

She sobbed, 'Don't touch me.'

I stood to one side. I could not imagine what had happened to her. Hildegunde, who until so recently had always been completely sure of what she wanted, and so full of life, seemed to have lost herself. The life that had once been hers, the light that used to shine all about her, had faded. She was grey, a grey creature of the forest, as the last light of the day drained away.

'What happened?' I asked, as gently as I could.

'You know,' she turned round and stared at me now, her eyes red with weeping, angry. 'They must have told you.'

'There was hardly anyone left at court. In the last few days I received almost no visitors.'

'What about the Graf? Didn't he see you, to tell you? He said he would.'

'He never came at all. But what happened between you and him?'

'If you knew, you would not have followed me. You still think I am the same as I was... then, when I was just yours.' She broke down and sobbed uncontrollably once more.

'What happened?' I said. Now it was darker still, the shapes of the leaves and the trees were becoming more sharply defined. A full moon was just high enough to be able to shed silvery, web-like light into the forest through the gaps in the trees.

'He took me. The Graf.'

'What do you mean?'

'You heard. He took me. In the room in your tower. Your room, Walter. He made me lie with him. He possessed me. He made me do it. Over and over again. I thought it would never stop.'

'How?' I asked stupidly. It was all I could think to say.

'What do you mean? I am his property, he told me. He could do with me what he wanted, since I had been with you. No one would marry me now, he said, not now that I had lost my virginity. I could be anyone's. I tried to get away from him, but he was so much stronger than me – and then he made threats about what he would do to you. He said I did it well. He said he could see why you liked me so much. I screamed and cried, but he didn't care...'

I walked over to her, to try to comfort her. This time she threw herself into my arms. I held her close to me. To think that I had been lying there in the castle, dreaming of glory, only a week ago it must have been, yet then, just across the courtyard, Graf Friedrich of Frankenburc possessed her, raped her.

The images in my mind became obscene as I continued to imagine what had happened between them. I saw Hildegunde naked, the Graf likewise, bearing down upon her...

Hildegunde must have sensed what was going on in my mind. She pulled away from me.

'It doesn't matter, Hildegunde,' I said, yet no matter how I tried, my voice sounded lame. 'Just say what you want. If only we could be together.'

'It's no good, Walter. You know I would gladly have lived in the lowest hovel if only I could have been with you, as we were then.'

'But nothing has changed.'

'It has, Walter. My uncle is trying to keep what happened a secret. He still has ambitions to marry me off. That is why he will never forgive you, or the Graf, for what happened. He had his eyes on Johannes of Ulm's wealth. He thought that since Johannes was old, and given to fighting, if I married him it would not be long before his wealth came our way. He could not wait to get his greedy hands on it. Now Ulm has left it all to the Church. They are stronger than us, Walter. It is only a matter of time.'

'Hildegunde, what do you want me to do?'

Before she had a chance to answer, we heard the sound of men shouting and dogs barking. It came from a considerable distance, but it could only mean one thing: Ochsenfurt had sent his men after us. Perhaps the peasant had betrayed us.

We mounted immediately and rode as fast as we could, splashing through a stream that soaked our legs but which would at least have the virtue of putting the dogs off our track. By then the sun had set, but it was not completely dark in the forest because the moon was three-quarters full.

We rode on for another hour or so, by which time we were both exhausted. I was suffering badly from my leg, though I tried not to let Hildegunde see this. When we were confident that no one was on our trail, we slowed our horses to a walk.

The night was fine. All the stars were out. The trees arched over us like the vaults of a great cathedral. Owls hooted, and every now and then the foliage would rustle eerily as some tiny creature scurried away to avoid us. I remembered the first night we had loved. I remembered the song I had written about it. If we had sinned in what we did, then we were certainly being punished.

Neither of us spoke. We were both tired. I tried to think of something to say, some plan for the future that would make everything all right. But the truth was that there was no hope for me, for us.

I had judged that we were travelling north. It turned out that I was right, and that we would soon reach the Hohenfeld. The land rose up out of the forest. This meant that we would be more exposed if anyone was still pursuing us. But there was no sound; we must have thrown them off our track.

Eventually I started to talk to Hildegunde about happy times we had shared together. She would say only, 'Yes, yes.' She was right, of course; there was no need to talk about those days. They were present with us, all of them, unspoken, like an essence, a presence, a world one senses yet which is destined to remain for ever inaccessible.

What followed was like a dream, both sublime and horrible. High on the Hohenfeld hill there was a castle. I remembered that the nobleman who had lived there had left it to the Church some ten years previously and that it now housed a community of Carthusian sisters. The feeling of stillness I experienced as we rode towards it was like in the dream I had as a child, on my first day at school, when it seemed I was part of a vast community of invisible souls, moving inexorably towards an invisible source of light. As we emerged from the forest and climbed the hill, there was the building, high above us, shining silvery blue and grey, solemn, magnificent.

To think that it was my idea to request shelter for the night at that place. Was it Providence that led us there, Providence for Hildegunde? Was it chance? Or was it some darker force? There was so much I ought to have said to Hildegunde, so much that I did not manage to say. How many times I have wished that I had lifted her down from the horse, made a rough bed for us there and then in a hollow, and made her mine again. Yet it was not to be.

We did not exchange another word until we arrived at the gate and knocked. Hildegunde's face looked ghostly pale in the silver light, and her hair could have been that of an old woman. The door opened. An old lady, tall and thin but oddly attractive, allowed Hildegunde to enter the yard of the building. I was to wait outside.

After some time, Hildegunde and the woman reappeared. Hildegunde was to be allowed a bed inside.

By now the moon was high in the sky. The bright silvery light made me feel uneasy. It made everything unreal, like a dream in which one is not allowed to speak.

I was told that I could either sleep outside the walls or go to an inn that was a mile or so further to the north. The tall nun gave me directions and apologised for being inhospitable, but she said it was their rule that, other than in exceptional circumstances, no men, let alone young men, were allowed inside the precincts of the convent.

I suppose I was glad for Hildegunde to have somewhere proper to sleep. The door was closed on me. I went back to the forest, tied up my horse and bedded down for the night.

Immediately I thought myself a fool. Why had I let Hildegunde go inside? I could have had her, there. I could have been lying next to her, in the forest, like that first night we loved. If she had not been willing, I could always have forced her; if the Graf could, then why shouldn't I?

The moment I caught myself in the midst of these thoughts I realised how depraved they were, unworthy of myself and cruel with regard to Hildegunde. Then again, the thought of her and the Graf together filled my mind with obscene images. I wanted to castrate him, kill him. I wanted him dead so that he would no longer be part of Hildegunde. And I wanted her for myself, desperately, carnally.

Then I would look towards where she was, to the moonlit stillness of the convent. What was happening to me? What had become of the calm, aloof Walter and all his aspirations towards beauty, towards the spiritual and the pure? How had I managed to sink into such a state, so quickly?

Was Hildegunde right? Was there no way we could be together? I thought once more of Uqhart. Was it true that I needed more time, more refinement, to become worthy of her, in the same way that the substances in the athanor required purification?

Memories of Uqhart, Hildegunde, the Graf, all turned in my mind as I fell into a fitful sleep, regularly interrupted by the pulsing of the pain in my leg.

I woke early. The sun was already up and all the birds were

singing. I was soaked through with dew and my leg hurt. The air was chilly. As I stood, my leg felt very stiff. I checked the wound. It had not opened, but it was not getting any better.

I went to the gates of the old castle and rang the bell. A different nun answered this time, but she knew who I was and offered me bread and milk, which I was glad to accept. I offered her money; she refused.

This nun was younger than the first. I recognised immediately that stillness about her, which I had once sought for myself. I remembered Hildegunde as I had first known and loved her. It was as if this quality was something she had once possessed naturally, though I had deprived her of it.

I asked if Hildegunde was ready yet; I was told I must wait. The door was closed on me once more. I sat, leaning against the wall, facing the morning sun and waiting for it to dry me out. I looked at the skyline, the endless expanse of forest, as the sun rose ever higher. It was becoming warm. I grew impatient because I wanted us to be well on our way before the heat of the day made travel impossible. Of course, I had no clear plans about where we would be going.

At last the door opened and I was asked to go in. This time it was an older woman. She was short, quite plump, wearing a brown habit, with a large silver crucifix round her neck. She said that she was the Abbess. She asked me to come in. I remembered the nun saying the previous evening that young men were invited into the convent only under exceptional circumstances.

I was led to a small, vaulted room. The walls were bare, but in one corner there was a finely carved wooden screen. In front of it were two benches and a desk. Hildegunde was sitting on one of the benches; the nun I had seen the previous night was sitting next to her, on the other.

Hildegunde was no longer wearing the same clothes as the previous evening – they had been replaced by a habit the nuns had given her. Her long hair was tied back and her face looked severe, yet serenely beautiful. Something of the old light had returned, yet now it was suffused with a resignation, a sadness that made it all the more poignant.

'Are you coming?' I said, and leant forward to take her hand, still hoping against hope that what I sensed would not, after all, turn out to be true. Yet my intuition was correct.

'No, Walter,' she said. 'I wish to remain here. You know why.'

To this day I do not know whether she was talking just for herself or if she had been told something about the Tremgistus and Antonius. If I had pressed her, would she have been able to help me understand? But I was aware only of something inside me melting, as if I were weeping, though I was not. I was just standing there, motionless.

I listened to Hildegunde as she continued to speak. She told me that she had spent last night confessing to the Abbess. That morning she had taken Communion. She said that as she prayed she had been filled with the conviction that she must stay in this place, at least for the time being, and therefore wished to thank me, since she saw in me the instrument of Providence which had led her here. Also, she said that she would always love me, but that she knew she must say farewell, for we could never find happiness together on this earth.

I was torn between anger, sorrow, self-loathing, and at the same time a deep respect for her, which led me to believe that perhaps she was right in what she was saying. These conflicting thoughts and feelings paralysed me. I could think of nothing to do or say. Afterwards I berated myself for not having stood my ground and argued, pleaded with her to come with me. Yet I had nothing to offer her outside the walls of the convent, and I felt this all too acutely.

If only I had forced myself to stay longer. Having lost so much, though, it seemed almost too easy to lose something more. I felt totally defeated, resigned, so I stood up slowly, said that I understood, that I knew I was unworthy of her, yet if ever I became worthy of her, in whatever way, then I would return. I think I must have said that I would always love her, which was true, for I always have and always will; but as I spoke those words they sounded hollow.

She said something about always being with me in spirit, if not in body, which was kind of her - though such words could almost have been an insult.

As I left I mumbled something to the Abbess about Hildegunde's horse being tied up outside. I left, omitting to take a last look at Hildegunde, something else I have long since regretted.

I left her there. Outside, I mounted my horse and rode off, not caring where to. Was I a fool? Was I wronging her by leaving her? I do not know. I remember well how I felt as I rode away into that beautiful early morning, as the golden light of the sun shone on the spiders' webs. I felt empty, desolate, judged. I knew I had nothing to offer her. There was nothing I could do. And it was all my fault.

Later, when I was in prison in Aletus, I used to sing a song about those days and that parting:

*De moi doleros vos chant*
*Je fui nes en descroissant*
*Onques n'euc en mon vivant*
*Il bon jors.*
*J' ai a non mescheans d'amors…* ★

★ *I shall sing to you of my sorrow / I was born when the moon was waning / I have never had / Any good days in my life, / My name is 'Ill-starred in love'… (Anon)*

# X

# The Wheel Of Fortune

✛

*O nos peregrine sumus*
*Quid fecimus, ad peccata deviantes?*★

For the next few days I rode aimlessly. I was tempted to return to the convent at Hohenfeld to see if Hildegunde had changed her mind. I knew that the Carthusian life was hard. The nuns spend their time in silent contemplation, confined to their cells, eating little, meeting to talk together only once a week, unless there was some special matter to discuss. They do not live in communities but rather as groups of hermits. They even grow their own vegetables on little plots that they tend for themselves. When I was a monk at Frankenburc I heard that it was not uncommon for them to go mad, if they did not die early.

I was torn by the dual aspect of my love for her. On the one hand, there was the love that went back to when we first met. If that had been all, I would still have missed her, her grace, her wit, her learning, the way she could stimulate my mind and draw ideas from me. I might have been able to bear the thought of her living in the convent; I might well have seen her sacrifice as an adventure of the mind and the soul, as a legitimate attempt to find fulfilment and closeness to God.

★ *Oh, we are pilgrims / What are we doing, turning to sin? (Hildegard von Bingen)*

Yet there was more to us now. My flesh craved hers in a way that was carnal, yet which went beyond the carnal. I entertained the idea that sexual relationships bind souls and bodies in ways we cannot fathom, and that it is because of these connections that adultery and fornication are sinful.

This train of thought engendered dark terrors. I remember when I was falling asleep one day in the forest I saw the pure soul as delicate, pink, skinless, having the shape of man, stretched out on a cross-shaped stone, in a cave high above the world, guarded by angelic creatures pouring holy oil on the soft tissue of the soul, to soothe the pain of the tenderness of earthly existence. At the fall of the soul, occasioned by the body's losing its purity, brown mucus would grow on it; the angels would turn into satyrs, tear their clothes off and perform bestial acts, whilst the soul would try to pluck the mucus off itself, and then, despite the pain, rise up from the stone and plunge out of the cave into the sea below, to try to cleanse itself. This was the cleansing that I yearned for.

At times, in my jealousy, I would even hate Hildegunde for the part she played in giving herself to the Graf. Surely she could have resisted. Surely it would have been better to die, to suffer any pain. Then I would hate and curse Katrin for leading me on to sin with her, seeing my separation from Hildegunde as a punishment for that sin.

I was aware of the irrationality of these thoughts, yet they obsessed me. The only relief from them came with torture from a different source: the memory of Uqhart's death and my father's suicide.

Why had Uqhart been killed? There were enough people who hated Jews, but this was nearly always because of usury, the only trade they can practise legally; and Uqhart was not, as far as I knew, engaged in usury of any kind. On the contrary, he kept himself to himself, making what little money he needed from his work as an apothecary. There was little by way of an organised Jewish community in Nurenberc. Besides, having come from Toledo, he counted as an outsider amongst Nurenberc's Jews themselves.

Surely the Bishop's judges at Nurenberc, however viciously they administered justice, could not themselves have believed the story that they allowed the gullible and uneducated people to believe - namely, that Uqhart had caused Pauli's death by necromancy. They were far too well educated and well informed. So why had they acted as they did?

As I rode on through the forests I thought more deeply about details of my past to which I had paid little attention until then. There was my sudden release from prison at Nurenberc, which was linked in some way with the Abbot Quintus. Yet it was Quintus who had refused me leave to go to Nurenberc before Uqhart's burning. I could not see the connection, but I was sure there was one.

I remembered the group of old men talking to the Graf on the day of the tournament. I remembered the way I was separated from Katrin. Then there was my father's death, my sudden departure from the court at Frankenburc. How much were all these disasters my fault and how much were events being driven by a force beyond my control, which I did not yet understand?

I was so totally absorbed by these questions that I lost track of time and of where I was going. The thoughts went round and round in my mind, as if it were at the centre of a mighty wheel, a mill-wheel or treadmill driven by demons.

After three or four days, hunger drove me back into human company. I ran into a group of players on the road near Offenburc and they let me share their food. In return, I taught them some songs. I followed them that night into the city. We spent the afternoon singing and playing in the main square. In the evening we carried on playing in the largest inn in the town. We were well enough received and we drank ourselves into oblivion. The next morning they were gone and I was on my own again. I did not care. I felt that they had shown me the way I was to follow.

Thus began a life of drifting from town to town, from inn to inn, singing and playing to get money for food and drink. I attached myself to anyone who would have me in their company, and left them as soon as I could. My great pleasure was to study the play of emotion on the faces of those who listened to my music; how could I inspire feelings in others when I felt nothing myself, since all my feelings had been bound up with Hildegunde? And now I felt nothing. It was as though I was dead inside.

Sometimes I would ride past the castles of the great. I would be tempted to present myself as a singer and try my luck, but I resisted. I could not bear the thought that they might disdain me, laugh at me. Ironically, for all my numbness of feeling, I was still possessed by an embittered pride. And I was restless, too; I would not have tolerated being bound to a court.

In my inner turmoil one thought remained constant: I wished to join Hildegunde, not in body but in spirit. I had read stories of those who, like Gregorius the Pope, had inflicted on themselves long periods of abstinence and as a result had achieved states of grace during which miraculous events had occurred. It would be too much to expect miracles for someone like me, yet penance and reconciliation with God was something I was beginning to crave.

I was torn between heading back towards the familiar places of Frankenburc and Nurenberc, and pressing on into unknown territory to the west. I knew there were hermits who lived in woods and caves, and one of my ideas was to look for a place I might stay as a hermit, and seek salvation that way. At the same time, I was beginning to enjoy the life of the taverns. The money Theodor had given me was a reasonable sum, and if I wanted to I could still earn extra money by singing and playing.

I felt a relentless need to convince myself of my powers as a singer. So I played at fairs, inns, markets, wherever I could. The magic never seemed to fail me. Whenever I sang, crowds would gather, at first out of curiosity, then a kind of trance would descend upon them, even the roughest. Occasionally I was filled with a sense of warmth, as if the songs were the means of gathering together familiar spirits, a link, forged through time, with shades and textures of things I had felt, seen, experienced in the past - my days at school, days spent with Katrin, with Pauli, at court, with Hildegunde - and it seemed that, through the repetition of the words and melodies, something of the essence of who I really was could be glimpsed, at least in part. What was that essence? Something to do with autumn light, leaves and falling.

My music brought me into contact with many people. I got to know some lovely young women who were on the road like myself, trying to eke out a living by selling their bodies or their songs. I did not sleep with them, but I amused myself by acting as their gallant protector for a day or two. They must have thought me a strange fellow, but they were flattered by the courtly attentions I bestowed on them. I felt I was doing them a favour by showing them, just for once in their lives, what it might be to be loved, before whatever dark fate overtook them. Often I joined the company of soldiers of fortune. With them it was always the same: they would threaten me, thinking I could not stand up for myself, but as soon as they saw that I could fight like the best of them, we became excellent friends - for a day or two at least.

Then there were the inevitable monks, always running errands from one monastery to another. They would be quite happy for me to tag along with them. I knew the ways of the monasteries and could talk to them about learned matters, or church gossip. Even young nobles were glad to have me ride with them, since I knew much of courtly life. Some had even heard of my exploits at Frankenburc. But I was on my guard; I sensed that the time was not right for too many people of influence to know of my whereabouts.

I allowed myself to be driven hither and thither, drifting along with the various groups of travellers. Eventually I decided that I would make for Chartres, where I had originally intended to go with Pauli.

The first time I broke down, after my separation from Hildegunde, was when I confided my planned pilgrimage to Chartres to one Brother Alfredus, a fat and arrogant young Benedictine from the Rhineland. I thought he would be impressed by my resolve, since he was so proud of his own learning. Yet I remember his words: 'Haven't you heard?' he said. 'The cathedral they were building has been burnt to the ground.' We were leading our horses through a forest path at the time. I made an excuse to stop and encouraged him to go on, saying I would catch up with him later.

As soon as I was alone, some way from the path, I fell to my knees and allowed the tears to come. I wept bitterly for an hour or so, before pulling myself together. I remembered with shame the lie I had told my father, when I first set out to sing with Pauli, when I said that we were going on a pilgrimage. At that moment, in the forest clearing, I understood, for the first time, coolly and rationally, what it meant to have lost Hildegunde. My life was without substance, without meaning or direction. I must either give it purpose or find some way of bringing it to an end.

I realised there was still too much defiance in me for suicide. So where was I to start looking for meaning? The answer was obvious. I would return to the Frankenburc monastery and confront the Abbot.

Two weeks later I was there. The day I arrived was chilly and overcast. The greyness of the sky permeated everything. How different from that first day I arrived with Father Jonathan, when there was bright sunshine and everything seemed suffused with peace and serenity!

As I trod the familiar, chalky path to the great gates, I shivered with nervousness and pulled my cloak around me. I feared meeting anyone from court who might ask me to give account of myself, or ask me what had happened to Hildegunde.

I rang the bell at the gates that led into the cloister. I was admitted by a novice I did not know. I told him my name and said that I needed to see the Abbot Quintus urgently. The novice looked uneasy about my request.

Nonetheless, Quintus himself soon emerged from his office on the other side of the cloisters and greeted me warmly, like an old friend. He never ceased from plying me with questions until I had told him every detail of my recent life. As if that was not enough, he pressed me to confess myself to him, there and then, which I was pleased to do, thinking that this might be the first step on a road towards my reconciliation, not only with him and the monastery, but also with God and myself.

I have always been scrupulously honest in my confessions, and supposed that others were just as honest; I have always trusted the authority of the Church, even when I was at odds with it. Only in my darker moments have I suspected and feared the power that confession places in the hands of the confessor.

After confession, the Abbot led me to his private chapel, where he said mass just for the two of us. This was a great honour, and all the time I felt like the erring, prodigal son, returning at last to the fold. Then he invited me back to his rooms to share a simple lunch of bread, ham and raw onions. He did most of the talking and every now and then would throw out odd questions, which made little sense to me then. 'What do you know about Brotherhoods of prayer?' he asked me once, in that deceptively warm voice of his. Of course I had heard of such institutions; there were any number of them - brotherhoods set up to pray for the souls of the departed, kings, queens, nobles and high-ranking churchmen. Although my answer was evasive, he seemed satisfied enough.

At another point he turned to talking about the feats of arms performed by Charlemagne during his life. As it happened, I had read the histories of his life when I was at school, so nothing he told me surprised me. I was even able to correct him on one or two matters of detail.

'You are knowledgeable,' he said. 'I suppose you *read* all this, did you?'

'Of course.' At that time I was unable to perceive the purpose of his question.

He went on to talk about the glories of the Crusades, noble deeds of battle, the tragic and untimely death of Barbarossa, how a great emperor was needed once again to assure the recapture of

Jerusalem and thus herald the new age of the millennium. What could I do but agree? What could any Christian do but agree? Yet why was he labouring all this with someone like myself?

At last I worked up the courage to ask the question that was churning in my mind. 'I have nowhere to sleep,' I said. 'May I stay here for a while?'

His stare cut me short. 'With the Frankenburcs still furious with you? With the reputation you have gained amongst the monks for worldliness and deeds of arms? The Graf would hound you, and your presence in the monastery would be like a corrupting cancer.'

I felt wounded at this; but there was truth in what he said. Now that he had made his point, he smiled kindly, but remained silent.

'Why did the Graf and Graefin turn against me?' I asked. 'Surely I acquitted myself nobly in the mêlée. Surely my conduct at court was exemplary.'

'Either you are playing games with me,' he said, 'or your innocence of women is greater than if you had known none.'

'So, it was the Graefin then,' I hazarded.

'I have nothing more to say on the matter.'

His jaw was set, and I could see I was going to get no further. A creeping sense of despair invaded me.

'But what am I to do?' I blurted, allowing my head to fall forwards into my cupped hands.

My loss of dignity seemed to be the cue he was waiting for. He stood up, walked over to me and placed his hands on my shoulders.

'There is a prophet, a visionary,' he said kindly but deliberately, 'who lives by the Hammersbach River near the town of Zell in the Black Forest of Swabia, not far from the Schouwenberc castle. He has been blind for many years, yet he sees much that is hidden from the rest of us. If you want my opinion, this is the man you should visit. His name is Antonius.'

In a flash I remembered the blind man I had seen with Quintus on the day of the tournament; this must be Antonius. But why all this fuss and complication just for me?

'Come with me now,' he said.

Yet more surprises lay in store. He led me to the counting-house next to his office, where a single shaft of sunlight shone through the one narrow window, high in the wooden wall. A bag of coins lay on the table. 'This is for you,' he said. 'All silver. To compensate for our lack of hospitality.'

I was aghast. What had I done to deserve this? I felt that I was acting out a part in a play which he had rehearsed but I had not. I was struck dumb.

He led me to the gate and embraced me with what seemed like real affection. These were his parting words, which I was to ponder for months and years afterwards: 'Don't forget, Walter, all we are doing is for your sake and for the sake of the Kingdom. Who knows how events will turn out, the exact nature of the role you are to play?'

The first part of the journey, over the hills of West Franken, went comparatively quickly, but everywhere there was an atmosphere of gloom. Henry the Lion had died, and his death brought with it the threat of civil war. Moreover, the crops had failed the previous year and famine was just beginning to take hold in the land.

As I left Franken and entered Swabia the terrain became more difficult. In the mountains of Swabia the famine was severe. In some regions the peasants were already no more than bags of bones. Could God really have willed such misery on these people – punishment in this life for a sin that was not theirs, and eternal fires of damnation in the next?

I remember a vision I had on the eve of Saint John's day that year. I had not eaten for two days and I had not met anyone on my way. To pass the time I was reflecting on the seven arts and the knowledge and learning I had acquired throughout my life: I rested beneath a tree and drank some water, still pursuing my thoughts. Then, in the sky, just for one moment, I saw a shape, like a great cone made from threads of fine silk or cotton, suspended in the air, perfectly geometrical. It hovered there for a moment, though I knew at the time I was just imagining it, for what it represented was the system of all possible knowledge. Just for that moment it was completely clear to me how the system worked. I have often wondered since if this was just a foolish dream or if I glimpsed something of enormous value.

At last I reached Pfortzheim, and it was here that I first came close to falling for the temptation of low women. After all the travelling I had done I was filthy and wished to bathe myself in the public baths. As it happened, at that town the public bath was the place where the prostitutes did most of their soliciting. I noticed that some of them were young – sixteen, seventeen, eighteen – and very beautiful. Two of them came to talk to me while I was taking my bath. They offered me their services and began to undress. I made it clear that I was not interested. Even so, they were happy to stay and chat. Though I knew that their lives were sinful, I found them pleasant to talk to and pretty enough at that, so had it not been immoral to do so, I would certainly have wanted them.

One of them, Sophie, said she was religious. She said that she attended mass regularly and gave a portion of her earnings to the Church. I asked if their priest had warned them about the dangers of their way of life. I found out that on the contrary he encouraged them, and used their services for free as a price for absolution.

On my arrival at Pfortzheim I had been feeling so dejected that I could easily have contemplated joining my father and Uqhart in death; yet the company of these girls restored me to myself. I thought how wonderful it would be to live like them, sinning innocently, living as a creature entirely of the flesh. I wondered if perhaps, if I did lie with them, something of that innocence and spontaneity would rub off on me.

The road I had to follow to the Schouwenberc castle from Pfortzheim was horrendous. I had to make my way through difficult mountain passes and the most wretched terrain. There were no proper paths and the forests in the valleys were marshy underfoot from recent rains, and often so dense that I had to double back on myself – I ended up losing all sense of direction. Then the mountains, though they looked smooth and rounded from a distance, would thwart any route I planned with sudden ravines, sheer drops and impenetrable forests. I went for miles without seeing anyone and I often had to go without food, for there were so few people in certain regions that it was impossible to purchase anything to eat.

I arrived at the castle four weeks after setting out from Frankenburc. It was late afternoon when I reached the plain beneath the castle. It was a magnificent sight, high on the top of a hill. The Castle was built of a reddish sandstone that glowed against the evening sky as I looked up towards it. I climbed the hill to ask after Antonius.

When I reached the top, I realised its site was more compact than that of Frankenburc, which is built on a rounded hill. To compensate for the smallness of the site, the Zaehringen had built two tall towers of five or six storeys above the main halls. The last of the Zaehringen had died a while ago, and the region was now run by a ministerial family who had named themselves Schouwenberc after the castle.

I was received warmly by the Lord Heinrich and his Lady Mathilde. I was soon to discover that they led a truly courtly life, though they were not by any means as rich and powerful as the Frankenburcs. There were many fine people at the court who praised my songs and my singing. Had I been younger, had I not suffered as I did at the court of Frankenburc, and had I not met Hildegunde there, I am sure that I might have stayed on happily at the court of Schouwenberc for a very long time. Yet I could not face it. My temperament was much changed now from what it had been. I viewed everyone, every new situation, not with enthusiasm and hope, but with suspicion. Besides, it was already late August and I was anxious to be on my way before cold weather set in.

Nonetheless, this is how I see heaven on earth: to live as a lord of a castle just like Schouwenberc, high on a hill in a land where it is always spring, with Hildegunde as my lady. There we would be able to love at will, sing, dance and play, and all our courtiers would be our friends, people we knew and loved, whom we had chosen for the special qualities we recognised in them. Even the servants would be our friends. We would not order them in the haughty way most nobles do, for as friends we would know and agree who was to do what. The physical chores like cooking and serving, looking after the animals and growing corn and vegetables would be shared by all, and would be undertaken joyfully because the work would be light and would offer us the opportunity to be together. Much time would be spent in studying and in discussing learned things. All would live as couples, each man with his own wife and much time would be dedicated to the arts of love as well as the worship of God. Most importantly, music and poetry would be everywhere...

If only one could know that heaven was truly like that, how much easier it would be then to accept the bitterness of death.

The Schouwenbercs said that Antonius was held in awe by the townsfolk, who thought h prayed constantly for their town. For that reason they kept him in food and drink, and did everything they could to avoid offending him, lest some evil should befall them.

They sent me off in the right direction to find Antonius, but I was still looking for his hermitage for most of the following day, and it was only by asking at every inn on my way that eventually I found it. Indeed, I might still have missed the little hut where he lived had not an innkeeper who lived on the edge of the town of Zell sent his son to show me where it stood.

I was intrigued by the boy's reaction. He must have been ten or eleven, but he would only go so near to the hut where Antonius lived and no further. It was as if the place were surrounded by some aura, into which he dared not enter.

I remember that day was almost unbearably hot and the sunlight dazzlingly brilliant. Larks were singing overhead, and in the forests there reigned an atmosphere of profound peace, as though there had never been any discord in the world, nor would there ever be any. They sky was a deep amethyst blue.

My spirits lifted and I was full of excitement when I was shown the hermitage. It was huddled under a great oak tree by the river. From the outside the house was small – nothing to speak of. It leant to one side and looked as though it might fall over at any moment. If I had not known that it was a hermitage I might easily have walked straight past it without giving it another thought. They boy scampered off before I had a chance to thank him.

As I approached I could see that the inside walls were brightly painted with pictures of our Lord, our Lady and the saints. There was a table, which served the hermit as an altar, loosely decked with a white cloth, and two candles were burning. I saw Antonius kneeling in front of the altar, presumably in prayer.

He seemed to sense my arrival. As I drew closer to the hut, he turned round and looked in my direction. I say 'looked', but he could see nothing, at least nothing in this world. His eyes were completely white, lacking both iris and pupil. He was bald, small of stature, quite plump, though his movements were graceful. He wore a brown habit. Those blind eyes of his made his face both dignified and fearsome. Because he could see the light of this world, I feared he might see all the more clearly by the light of the spirit, and I dreaded what he might be able to read in me.

As I came closer still, his face changed. He closed his eyes and smiled in a way that was almost friendly.

'Welcome,' he said in German. 'What can I do for you?' His voice was kindly, but he intoned his words in a way which suggested to me either that he was a prophet and mystic as people claimed or that he was mad.

'I come to ask advice,' I began. I talked Latin to impress on him that, however lowly my station might be, at least I was a man of some learning. I asked him to confess me and knelt in front of him to tell him the story of my life. This was in the hut's first room, which served as a chapel.

To begin with he merely nodded and said 'Yes... yes', as if he had heard so many confessions in his time that it would scarcely be worth listening to one more, and that he would prefer to get it over and done with as soon as possible. A couple of times he even interrupted me with irrelevant comments and observations. For example, he asked me if I thought it strange that he had painted walls and burnt candles despite the fact that he could not see. He said that he personally had directed the painting of the walls, for the iconography reflected certain secrets of the mystical world, which he had seen.

There were indeed mysterious patterns I had not seen before.

Wound round all the pictures of saints and angels were curious motifs, including caterpillars and butterflies. On the left wall there was a great serpent whose tail was wrapped in a spiral. Also, on the right-hand wall, I noticed there was a sign of infinity divided into sections numbered nought to twenty-one. In each of these sections was a motif, and round the sign were strange pictures. In the very middle there was a picture of a wheel with animals like monkeys running over it. At another point there was a picture of a skeleton culling bones, there was a man hanging upside down, a chariot, a lion, and so on. The signs might well have been the same as those on the chart I gave to you, Philippos; but I cannot be certain of this. I do remember that the sun beat down so fiercely that the images seemed to detach themselves from the wall, to come alive.

I asked him what the signs meant. My curiosity was aroused, since I had not seen anything so strange or beautiful since Uqhart's books. I wondered if they represented some system of thought, some means of understanding the world and the Christian faith that I had not yet come across.

Antonius told me that such knowledge was for initiates only.

I continued my confession, still unsure whether I was dealing with a learned visionary or a madman. As he listened he appeared absent-minded, and I genuinely thought that he was paying no attention.

Then he began anticipating what I was going to tell him.

He knew before I told him about Uqhart being burnt, about the fate of my father, about the outcome of the tournament, even about my wanderings in the last few weeks. I could not believe what I was hearing.

Everything he said was pronounced in a benign sing-song tone of voice, in a way which suggested that it was of no consequence since it was so obvious. He nodded his head in the way of those whose habit in conversation is to repeat sentences one has said to them. Usually one takes this as a sign of stupidity; yet Antonius was not repeating, but anticipating.

It was uncanny. To reveal secrets about oneself requires a certain courage. There is always the fear of shocking the listener. Yet here was someone who was not only unshockable, but who knew me better than I knew myself. In fact his responses to me were so matter-of-fact, so full of foreknowledge that, as I knelt there outside the hut in the late afternoon sunshine, talking against the sound of the splashing of the water and the singing of birds overhead, I felt that this blind, bald man was not separate from me, but that he was a part of myself I had always known but not yet become fully aware of.

What happened next was stranger still. After I had confessed myself, he offered me absolution and led me to the innermost room. Here I could see the rough straw mattress on the floor, where he must have slept. I noticed also the earthenware water flagon and the plate that he used to eat from; on it there was still half a crust of bread and half an onion. From the smell, it was clear that he was not a man much given to washing.

Again I knelt in front of him. I was worried, having seen the strange images on the walls, and having borne witness to his powers of divination, that the form of absolution he used might contain some pagan or magical elements. I was nervous but complied. He offered that I should join him in saying mass. I did so and took the Eucharist. The form of words he used followed precisely the forms of Christian liturgy.

It was then, just as we finished saying mass together, as the words of the dismissal were finished, that he threw himself on the ground at my feet and covered them with kisses. He was breathing strangely and making small grunting noises. I was frightened at first, then I realised he was weeping. Since his eyes were glazed white and malformed, these animal-like sounds were the only form his weeping could take.

I was rigid with embarrassment that this holy man should honour me thus, and at the same time I feared that it was no honour but that he had completely taken leave of his senses. At last I was able to help him to his feet and ask him what was the matter.

What he said haunted me. For years afterwards I felt that I did not know myself, that my life has been in some way double.

'Do not take it badly,' he said, 'that you have been separated from Hildegunde, for, as you know, there is important work for you on this earth and Hildegunde would only stand in your way. You know too,' he continued, 'that it was only right for you to be removed from the spiritual dangers of Katrin and Uqhart...'

I was beginning to lose my temper. 'What role are you talking about?' I said impatiently, 'And what spiritual dangers?'

'The Last Days,' he said. 'Your role in the Last Days. That is why it is important that your soul should remain pure.'

I was too shocked to do more than beg him to explain.

'There are those,' he said, 'who can read charts that plot the courses of the heavens, and such men have taken an interest in your affairs ever since your birth; how else would a poor cartwright like you have gained access to an education at Babenberch? I, myself, have the gift of prophecy as a result of my life of devotions, I have seen visions that confirm the charts others have read...'

What he went on to tell me filled me with revulsion. He made me feel that my real self did not exist, that all I had ever felt and loved was just supernumerary to some appalling divine plan. My feeling of myself began to shift hopelessly. My mind raced as I remembered other conversations I had had about Brotherhoods of Prayer, my vision of Saint John, things I had heard about the Last Days, the Last Emperor, the new Charlemagne, and the Crusades. I remembered the tall priest who had visited my father when I was seeing Katrin. I remembered the secrecy surrounding the trial of Uqhart. I remembered the rambling words of Johannes of Ulm and I remembered the suddenness with which my fate at court had changed when my relationship with Hildegunde became known. Suddenly I realised that these people must all be linked, that there were forces interfering with the course of my life, controlling, manipulating. Yet I did not understand why or how.

I flew into a rage, and did something I was to regret for years afterwards. Instead of just playing along with Antonius, instead of allowing him to think what he wanted about me so that I would be able to find out more later, I pressed him angrily to tell me who else was involved in the conspiracy.

He did not answer. I tried to provoke him by accusing him of killing Uqhart and my father. All he did was turn to the altar, kneel and begin to pray once more. Strange words came from him as he prayed. It was the same language that had come to me on the way home from the harvest that day when I was a boy of eleven. It was the secret language I still resorted to in prayer during times of great anxiety or distress. I liked to think this was the language of the angels Saint Paul had written about. And this man was using it!

I was dumbfounded. At last, in an impotent rage, I strode away from the hut, flung myself on my horse and rode off at a mad pace into the green of the forest, away from that cloying, oppressive place, repeating to myself that Antonius was just a foolish old man who had happened by chance to pick up some information about me, and who had embroidered these facts into a lunatic fancy to suit the aberrations of his declining mind.

By evening I had reached Offenburc. It was then that, for the first time - in order to escape myself, in order to escape the thoughts that were turning round and round in my head - I took a whore.

The experience was depressing. She was good enough to look at; yet to commit the carnal act with her was a sad parody, a mockery of what it was to be with Hildegunde. I felt Hildegunde's presence the whole time. It was almost as if she were already dead and her spirit was there to warn and admonish me. There was no escape.

I stayed in the town with the girl for three days, until I could no longer stand the sight of the poor creature, and my curiosity about what Antonius had said had reached a fever pitch. Then, like a madman myself, I rode back to Zell to confront him, vowing to remain calm this time.

It was past midday when I got there, and a blazing hot sun was beating down on the land. I returned to the precise spot where I had seen Antonius. It was definitely the right place, where his hermitage had stood: I recognised the path, the great oak tree, everything, even the patterns of stones on the ground. Only now there was no Antonius, no hermitage, no house, nothing – just burnt earth and ashes where his hut had stood.

I was terrified. I wondered if I had gone mad, if I had imagined my meeting with him. I wondered what was meant by the remains of the fire. Had Antonius been attacked? Had he left of his own accord? Who had started the fire?

In a state of utter confusion I went into Zell and asked everyone I could find – the local priest, workmen, peasants at the market – what they thought might have happened to him. To my surprise, no one knew much or cared. Apparently he had often disappeared like that but always returned to the area, eventually.

Thereafter I fell into dissolution and debauchery. I had given up all hope of Hildegunde or of being able to pursue a life of learning, and slept with any girl who came my way. I took up drinking in whatever tavern I happened to come across, and made sure that my purse stayed full by singing whenever I had the opportunity.

I became like the goliards. I accepted that I was damned. I took nothing seriously. I laughed at myself and at the world. Consequently, I was popular with other dissolute and vagrant men. A learned man who makes light of his learning, a man who has been a monk yet can laugh at mystics, a man who can sing yet is not pompous about his art – I suppose that is how I seemed. Such men are always popular, and expendable.

I did not dare stay in one place too long. After my meeting with Antonius, I feared that those who had taken an interest in me in the past might catch up with me. Perhaps it was fear that what Antonius said might turn out to be true that made me want to waste myself, to prove myself ordinary, normal, incapable of any special role in the world. The thought of having been chosen by God or by destiny to play some vastly important role was appalling to me.

I tried to run away from the dark thoughts that continued to haunt me. I tried to convince myself that all I had learnt and said and done so far in my life were lies and deceit. I still wrote songs, but they were mocking, bawdy songs, like Pauli's.

For all my attempts to make light of religion, however, there were moments when I shuddered as I remembered my vision of Saint John. The vision returned to my mind over and over. Was it really Saint John who had appeared to me? Were the events of the Apocalypse really about to begin? I knew of Joachim of Fiore's preaching. The thought that I had a role to play seemed ridiculous. Surely all these visions were nothing more than my own crazed imaginings. Or maybe they were sent by devils to test me. How was I supposed to know whether or not they were true?

Throughout the autumn and winter I drifted from girl to girl, castle to castle, inn to inn. I drank and sang with many people, good folk, most of them, even the rogues and whores. I was fascinated by them, and I yearned, like them, to be able to live a life without a conscience. But I could not. Nor could I do anything to change the course of my life. I felt caught in the grinding of the great wheel of fate, but could see no meaning in its motion, no more than in the roll of dice.

# XI

## Fortitude

✠

By the year of our Lord 1196 famine was causing numerous deaths amongst the poor. Henry, our Emperor, was fighting to ensure that the crown would pass directly to his son, without need of election, so that the situation in the land might become more stable.

If only he had succeeded.

There were rumours that several people had seen a ghostly rider on a black horse. They had tried to run away, but he rode up to them and told them not to be afraid, for he was the old king Dietrich of Bern. Rather, they should fear for the future, because the Holy Roman Empire would soon suffer misery and catastrophes of many kinds.

One day in March that year I found myself at an inn. It was a dingy place, just a few tables, some bales of straw and a table from which wine and beer were served. There was quite good light from the candles, however, which is more than can be said for some inns.

There were a few other men there, among them one who looked like a degenerate noble, wiry and spotty, with wide, staring, yellowish eyes, wearing clothes that must once have been of high quality but which were now torn and stained. I overheard one of the guests ask what the town had by way of whores. The wiry, yellow-eyed man began praising the appearance and skills of a certain Katrin, a young woman who was distinguished by her long auburn hair and her musical abilities. He made gross innuendoes about how well she could play the flute (both by sucking and blowing). For once I did not join in the laughter. I felt the blood drain from my cheeks. Could this be my Katrin?

When the man heard he would have to travel to the other end of town to meet this girl, he decided not to bother, but decided instead to take his pleasure at the usual stews, just round the corner. I sat and drank some more, but eventually curiosity got the better of me and I asked the spotty noble for a further description of this Katrin.

The man insisted on taking me there himself. Maybe he had some financial arrangement worked out with the woman, or maybe he just wanted someone different to talk to.

He led me to the very poorest area of town, where most of the houses were little more than shacks. The one we stopped at was larger than most, and the door was secured with a number of bolts and latches. I was surprised at how fear and nervousness knotted my stomach as he knocked on the door and shouted that he had a customer.

At last the door opened and a face appeared. It was haggard, scarred in places, bruised, and with spots barely disguised by the white powder used as make-up. But it was Katrin's face all right. She had aged appallingly in so short a time.

At first she did not recognise me but smiled a tired, flirtatious smile. With the dark rings under her eyes and her reddened lips, her face was a parody of the one I had loved. As she opened the door I noticed that her figure was still attractive, though she was much thinner – maybe through illness. She wore a tight-fitting dark red woollen dress, but with an unusual mottled pattern painted on with a light green and yellow dye. There were bright red, blue, yellow and green patterns down the front. It created a sickly impression, not alluring at all, more like something an insane woman would choose to wear.

I greeted her. On hearing my voice, she recognised me.

'Walter. It's you.' Her voice had changed; it was croaky, sneering. 'Come in, Walter. You, go away,' she said to the man who had brought me to her.

There was a fire in the middle of the one room in her house. It lit her face eerily.

There was a long silence. I was beginning to regret having come. There was an unpleasant scent in the air, from the herbal perfumes some women use, but this was mixed with something else.

I was not sure that I could recognise what it was - urine perhaps, or some medicine. It turned my stomach. The glow of the fire was reddish. I sensed something evil, something foreboding. I had never been with a girl in a place like this. Those I sought out were usually happy, stupid creatures. This was different.

There was silence for a while, an uneasy, painful silence that she broke, sarcastically, sneeringly, by asking me what I wanted. She undid her dress and pulled me towards her. There were the first breasts I had ever caressed, now shrunken and withered - through age and illness, I supposed. At first I was tempted. Absurdly, I wondered if it would be impolite to refuse sex, given her profession. But I was far too shaken to want that. I freed myself from her and tried to ask her what had become of her.

She would say nothing at first, so I told her how I had been a monk, and a man of the court, how I had fought in a tournament, yet how my fortunes were now reversed.

Suddenly she flew into a rage. 'Why didn't you follow me?' she screamed at me. 'Why did you leave me to fall into this life? You said you loved me. I suppose it's your precious son you want now, is it? Well he's dead. He died of the fever when he was six months old.'

I did not react. I felt numb. Could she really have had a son by me? Or was she just saying it in order to make me suffer? The look on her face was sincere enough; no one could have feigned those accusing eyes. I tried to remember what I must have been doing in those fifteen months when she was carrying and caring for my son. I thought of my life with my father, then my abortive journey with Pauli. I thought of my pretensions to the life at the monastery, to the life at the court. All the time I had had a son, whom now I would never know.

A selfish, resentful thought occurred: why had this woman born my son, and not Hildegunde? But I only had myself to blame. It was my choice. I did not have to sleep with her, with either of them.

'What was he like?' I asked stupidly.

She did not answer but stared at me, with a look of sheer hatred. Her dress was still open. Those were the breasts my son must have suckled. She noticed that I was staring at her, and she did her dress up. My mind reflected dimly on the misery she must have suffered. It was like a tangible presence surrounding her, filling the room, threatening to engulf me if I did not keep it at bay.

She said, 'He had your face, Walter, your eyes, you pig, you liar...' She began shouting at me, calling me every name under the sun.

I did not react. I had to agree with her. I was only worried in case anyone outside heard her and there was a disturbance. I feared she might become violent. Eventually she ran out of energy. She threw herself on to the bed and sobbed.

I remembered what it had been like when we were together in the mill and when we used to walk through the forests near Nurenberc. I remembered that last evening I saw her, when she said that her stepfather and brother had given her to anyone who had wanted her, and how I was the only one who had ever been kind to her. At the time I had been merely disgusted by what she said. Any pity I might have felt for her was drowned by the pity I felt for myself and by my own precious sense of slighted purity. Now I thought of all the ill that had befallen me since I had known her. For the first time I wondered if perhaps I had deserved it, if perhaps it was fair punishment after what I had done to her.

I sat by her and nursed her, like a child, though it revolted me to touch her. I asked her to tell me what had happened that last evening we had spent together, at the fair of the Feast of Fools.

Eventually, through her sobs, she said that, when I had left her to get drinks, she had been approached by two men, who dragged her to her feet and led her to a side-street. At first she thought they just wanted to dance, which she did not mind, but they whispered that they would hurt her if she screamed. They said they had a message for her: she and her family were no longer welcome in Nurenberc. They all had to leave in the morning. On no account was she to see me any more. They said her family had received a visit also. To show that they meant business, they set about hurting her, pushing her between one another, groping her, threatening to rape her. Then, suddenly, they left.

She panicked, looked for me in the dance area but was unable to find me. In the meantime she was worried about her family. So she rushed home, where she found them already packing to leave. At first no one would speak to her. Then there was a terrible row as her stepfather and stepbrother accused her of destroying all they had.

During the previous day the family had been visited by two men. The first was a tall, bearded ecclesiastic with burning eyes. From her description I recognised immediately that it must have been the same man who had visited my father: Tremgistus. The other was a tall, strong-looking man, no longer young, about forty, who had ginger-coloured hair. He wore clothes of the nobility and had rings on his finger which – he told Katrin's family – bore royal insignia. He said that he had royal authority; of course this terrified Katrin's parents. He presented them with a letter containing orders banning them from Nurenberc and any area within forty miles of Nurenberc.

Katrin said that she was unable to find out any more detail because her father and stepbrother started beating her. Eventually her mother intervened to protect her, but she did so only by taking the blows herself, while Katrin escaped from the house. This was the last Katrin ever saw of her family.

She returned once more to the dance, still hoping to find me. By that time I must have been wandering madly round the forests of Nurenberc. At last, when I did not come, she managed to attach herself to the singer who had gestured to her so obscenely. She gave up hope of finding me again. For a while she travelled round with the singers, sleeping with her old lover again, since that was what he wanted. This lasted for four or five months, until it became clear that she was pregnant – and the singer sent her packing.

Then she had drifted from town to town, man to man, until at last she gave birth to my son. But she could not look after him properly – he had fallen ill with a fever and died after six months. After that she soon found herself living the life of a prostitute. At first she had had some luck; some wealthy nobles and townsmen had taken her regularly. But she grew ill, and they tired of her one by one. Now she had to take whatever came her way. Some of the men beat her. There was nothing she could do about it.

While she was talking, I looked at her. Every now and again I caught a glimpse of the girl I had once loved – a movement, a gesture, a speech mannerism. She asked me if I was going to take her with me. How could I? The one person I loved was Hildegunde. I could not face the humiliation of dragging round with a woman who had lived as a common whore. I could not face the attachment, the responsibility or the shame. I offered her money, to help, but I did not offer to take her away.

At the mention of money, the calm she had shown while she was telling her story deserted her. She flew into another rage, more fierce and desperate than the first. She shouted and screamed, and then she attacked me physically, scratching at my face with her nails, swearing at me, telling me I had ruined her. It was as if she had become completely mad, as if the sorrows she had been through and the telling of them had caused her to take leave of her senses. I was terrified. I had not thought her capable of such violence.

By then I had had enough. All I had wanted in the last few months was to escape my past, and here it was, in the flesh, screaming at me, accusing me, tearing at me. I wanted to forget all that. I wanted the peace that comes from indulgence of the flesh. So I fought free from her and pushed my way out the door.

I stopped briefly and looked back. She was out of breath now and had stopped shouting. She was ugly. I had never seen anyone look so ugly. She hissed at me to go and never to return.

That is my last memory of her. I never found out any more

about my child, though the thought of him haunts me, as does the thought that if I had behaved properly he might still be alive.

I continued to wander. In spite of the famine, or maybe because of it, people were still prepared to pay to hear a singer sing songs of love and tell tales of battle, so I was not short of money.

But I was in a wretched state. My clothes stank and hung in tatters about me. There were only three emotions I was capable of: sorrow at the loss of Hildegunde, hatred of everything that had controlled my life, and a yearning for oblivion, which I tried to achieve by drinking as much as I could, whenever I could.

This continued until the year of our Lord 1197. Everything seemed in a state of terrible decline. Jerusalem had still not been retaken from the Saracen. The Empire had been ravaged by famine for two whole years. Yet again the harvest looked set to be destroyed by the terrible rains. Worst of all, there were rumours that our Emperor, Henry, had died of typhus at Messina. He had no successor other than his three-year-old son. There was tension in the air. One could sense the foreboding amongst the ordinary folk as it appeared that civil war between Welf and Staufer was brewing again.

It is possible that I would have just drifted and eventually met my death in a brawl or a ditch somewhere if I had not come across Ewald.

I met him in the imperial town of Wimpfen, whose mighty castle and illustrious court I had once visited in an official capacity on behalf of the Graf of Frankenburc. Now I was far fallen from those days of glory and I confined myself only to the humblest of taverns, where I played whatever songs pleased the folk who went to them. I spent the money they gave me on drink until the moment came when I could neither play nor think, but fell unconscious, only to wake up in a bed in the inn (if the landlord was kind) or in the street outside (if he was not).

The evening in question, the weather had been filthy throughout the day and I had taken refuge in the one decent-sized tavern the town of Wimpfen boasts. I had already drunk a fair amount and had sung too much. I noticed Ewald while I was playing. He was in his mid-twenties, tall and very thin, with dark hair. He had been observing me closely, staring at me for the greater part of an hour. His manner combined a genuine, possibly learned modesty with a manic energy that caused his eyes to shine and dart back and forth no matter how hard he tried to contain whatever thoughts were enthusing him.

I finished a song. It was the song Friedrich von Hausen sang before setting off on Crusade with Barbarossa - the Crusade during the course of which the Emperor was to die. In the song he says how his heart and body were divided, since his heart yearned for the Holy Land whilst his body still wished for the familiar things of home: *'mín herze und mín líp diu wellent scheiden.'*\* I was lost in my drinking and the music, yet I was taking little notice of what I was singing.

Ewald, on the other hand, was taking it all to heart. He was drinking little, but he was more intoxicated than I was, nodding his head to the rhythm and grinning in appreciation whenever the death of a Saracen was mentioned. His eyes would glint fanatically at the point where the song deals with the recapture of Jerusalem.

When I finished he said to me, 'You sing like that, so what are you doing here?'

The question surprised me. I gave no reply, but stared back at him.

He continued, 'I said what are you doing here? What am I doing here? We are both fools. We know what is going on. We know the world is in a mess and we know why. You are an educated man, I can hear it from your singing. Surely you know what is wrong with the world, why there are bad harvests, why there are wars everywhere and rumours of war, why there is hunger, strife and pestilence, why no kingdom can stand, just like Saint John the Divine predicted about the Last Days.'

\* *My heart and my body want to separate.*

I stared at him, but he was not to be stopped. I drank more, trying to pay no attention though I could tell he would insist on an answer. Besides, I could feel his words stirring something deep within me, as though he were articulating thoughts that were really my own.

He continued: 'It is because the Last Days are already upon us. Has not the Antichrist already set up his throne in Jerusalem?'

I was annoyed by now. 'So,' I said, 'what are you going to do about it?'

'Haven't you heard? The German Crusaders, led by the Archbishop Conrad, have taken Beirut. It is said that even now they are marching on Galilee, that they will attack the great fortress of Toron, and that they will be sure to take it.'

'Good for them.' I tried to keep my distance, but I could feel the excitement stirring within. Of course I had heard of this Crusade. It was all the talk. It was, after all, the first Crusade to be led by an archbishop, a man of the Church, as opposed to kings and lords. At times I had felt the temptation to take the cross myself, but only in passing, for at the time I was too beset with troubles of my own.

'Don't you see?' Ewald insisted. 'They are bound to take Jerusalem back from the Saracen. We should be there, people like you and me, to fight with them, to encourage them, to be there when it happens. It is rumoured that the Pope plans to found a new Order at Jerusalem, like the Templars, a fighting Order, an Order of German Knights.'

'Who sent you?' I asked.

Ewald was thrown by the question. I was pleased that I had caught him off guard. It was obvious from the way he had approached me that someone had sent him. He probably meant what he was saying, yet at the same time there was something in the way he spoke that was too premeditated, too opportunistic.

He was not good at disguising this, for he was young and inexperienced, and certainly far too much himself to be able to hide his feelings of confusion at having been second-guessed so soon.

'I am sent by no one,' he said. 'I am just speaking the words that are in my heart, the words that should be in the heart of all Christians during these times.'

I was drunk, but not so drunk that my mind was dulled. In fact I was so used to my drink that I almost never managed to achieve what I hoped, which was to remain conscious whilst forgetting myself. In those days all my drunkenness achieved was to hasten sleep and mildly relieve the pain of being.

'Come outside,' I said.

He appeared surprised at my request. It was his turn to be uncomprehending.

'Come outside,' I said. 'I have something to tell you that I do not want to be overheard.'

I tucked my lute under my arm and exaggerated my stagger as we left the table. We stepped outside into the cold, windy November night. The frequent drizzle had reduced the road to a slush of mud and dead leaves. I felt for my knife.

The moment we were out of earshot of the tavern and I was sure no one could see us, I punched him as hard as I could in the stomach to wind him and then grabbed him round the neck, half choking him. I held the knife in front of his eyes so that he could see it.

'I'm going to kill you,' I snarled at him.

He put up no resistance. As I suspected, he was not a seasoned fighter but a cleric turned ministerial who had neglected to learn the arts of war. What use he thought he would be against the Saracen on a battlefield I dreaded to think. I had terrified him.

I jerked the knife with a sudden motion. He jolted and then began to whimper like a puppy.

'I said I am going to kill you,' I went on, 'unless you tell me who sent you.' He relaxed a little, but he was going to take some persuading yet. 'You are going to tell me who your master is, and you are going to take me to him. I will not let you out of my sight until you do so. And if you cross me I will kill you.'

He was still too scared to speak. I thought maybe it was time to be more reconciliatory.

'Don't worry,' I said, 'you can pretend that I came voluntarily, that you led me through your powers of persuasion, if that is important to you.' How was I to know that I was playing into his hands? Earlier in my life I do not think that I would ever have had it in me to speak like that to another man: to threaten and sneer would have appalled me. But by then I had much experience of the rough-and-tumble of tavern life.

'Yes,' he stammered, 'I'll take you there, now.' I had been sure that I was right to follow my intuition, yet even I was surprised that my threats were having an effect so soon.

Maybe I was falling into a trap.

I released him. 'Where to, then?' I asked.

He gestured to the castle of Wimpfen itself. The castle belonged to Friedrich of Swabia, the most powerful member of the Hohenstaufen clan, who would this moment be planning his strategy to become Emperor in the event that the rumours about Henry's death turned out to be true.

'Come on, then,' I said, and let him lead the way. I stayed just behind him and to his left, keeping my knife in my hand under the sleeve of my jerkin in case he tried to get away suddenly.

We made our way through the black streets, stepping through the mud, slime and excrement left after the market earlier that day.

The rain was falling harder.

We were let into the castle complex over the drawbridge. The guards must have recognised Ewald. I could see the lights shining from the torches in the great hall and I heard the sound of laughter. At least some people were eating well that evening, even if there was famine elsewhere. This was a court where Barbarossa himself had spent much time, and where the courtly arts had first been cultivated under the tutelage of his beautiful wife, Empress Beatrice.

We did not go to the main hall but continued along the ramparts, round the back of the castle. It was a black, moonless night. To my left I could just make out that there was a sheer drop, down into the cliffs, through the dark trees to the valley below. I became obsessed with the idea that this would be an easy place to throw a man at this time of night. He would fall to his death without any scream being heard, and it would be days before his body was found. I wondered if such a fate was in store for me, and whether I should hurry to inflict it on my guide first.

Yet he continued nervously, and I felt under no threat.

We were allowed through a back gate into the castle complex. I could hear laughter and singing in the distance, but where we were everything was pitch-black and it was hard to pick our way through the mud. At last we came to a door built into the side of the thick rampart wall. Ewald knocked and was ushered in.

At first I thought we would be entering some dungeon, and I was reluctant to go any further. Then, as I looked round the corner, I was surprised at the sight that greeted me. There was a lavishly decorated room, built into the wall itself. It was amply lit by candles. An oriental carpet was on the stone floor. There were two or three folding chairs, such as normally only a king or Graf would use. They were positioned in front of the largest writing-desk I have ever seen. Rich tapestries covered the walls, as well as shields and coats of arms. Above the level of the tapestries the walls arched up into a vaulted ceiling of roughly hewn stones, giving the impression of the inside of a cave. The table was decorated with many carvings: angels, lions and the faces of other monsters and animals. I was surprised to see such luxury in such a secluded spot of the castle, separated from the main hall and chancery. I wondered if it was some sort of Imperial observation post, the place where representatives of the higher powers of the Empire would come to make sure that the affairs of the court were being conducted in accordance with the will of the Emperor.

Behind the desk there sat a man. He was thin, energetic, strong-looking. His hair was ginger and curly, his face narrow and lined. He must have been in his early forties. He smiled at us in a kindly way, then continued writing. I noticed the rings he wore on his fingers. The smile could have been sincere or feigned, it was impossible to tell. He gave the impression that he was pleasantly surprised to see us, that he knew who we were, that he had been half expecting us, even at this time of the night.

We stood awkwardly at the door as he looked us over. It was he who spoke first. 'So, it is you, Walter von der Ouwe. You did come. Well done, Ewald, very well done.'

So I need not have threatened after all. Ewald smiled awkwardly.

'Who are you?' I said.

'Never mind about that,' he replied, with a politician's sham warmth and friendliness. 'So, Walter, you wish to go on a Crusade. That is very good.'

'What makes you think so?'

'Why, you would not be here otherwise, would he, Ewald?' There was something effete, catlike in the man's manner, which left me feeling even more ill at ease.

Ewald shuffled uneasily and attempted to smile.

I said, 'That's as may be.' In fact, as I was walking through the darkness with Ewald, and as the words he had spoken resonated in my mind, the thought of trying to join the Crusade had become more and more attractive. After all, I had nothing else to live for.

'I - we - know much of what has happened to you recently, Walter,' he continued. 'We know about the sorrows that have befallen you. We know about the circumstances in which you left the court at Frankenburc.'

I looked at him the whole time he spoke. What else was I supposed to do? His eyes were like a snake's. They moved, with his head, in a hypnotic motion, flickering in the candlelight as he talked, so that it was hard to avoid being swayed by the rhythms of his speech. I resisted as best I could, but I have to admit that I was fascinated by the man.

'What do you want of me?' I asked him.

'All we want, Walter, is for you to find your destiny.'

'What do you mean by that?' I asked defiantly.

'If you know, then you know, but if you don't, then you don't. It is as easy for you to play games with us as it is for us to play games with you.'

'But what do you want me to do?'

'We think that your destiny might well lie on the road to

Jerusalem. If you are who we think you are, then your heart will tell you that this is the case. If you are not who we think you are, then it is a matter of no consequence.'

'But who do you think I am?' I blurted out. There was nothing in his manner to give away what he was thinking. I thought of Antonius' ramblings about the Last Days; surely an intelligent man like this did not believe in such nonsense.

'I wish to tell you this. If you want to go to Jerusalem, and you lack equipment, as I know you do, I will provide you with the best horses, clothes and arms. We know your talents, Walter. We know how well you sing, how well you can fight. We understand there must be reasons why you keep yourself from us. Yet it seems to us now that we can help, and we are always ready to help.'

There was almost a pleading tone in his voice. Again I felt, as I had before when talking to Stefanus, to Quintus, and to Antonius, that I was being talked to as a potential superior, very much as a prince might be addressed by a regent during his minority.

I became aware that there was something beautiful about the room, the candlelight, the tapestries, the vaulted stonework... Then it came to me in a flash. Suddenly I knew just what to do. My future was there in front of me. My days of idle wandering were over. I would join the Crusade. I did not care who or these people thought I was, and whether they intended me or ill. If they could help me to achieve my purpose of taking part in the Crusade, then I would use them. But first I wanted to go and find Hildegunde. I would tell her of my intentions, bid her farewell forever in this world, and join the armies in the East to fight to regain Jerusalem from the Saracen, for death, or glory or both if God willed.

This sudden sense of purpose gave me strength. I no longer felt like the down and out wandering singer I had been until an hour previously. All that had been a false resignation. I thought I had given up hope, but I had not really. The self-indulgence and resentment were the result of my failure to accept my fate. I began to feel all that falling away. Or at least I thought I did.

'Your offer is very kind, sir. It is a generous and noble offer. I shall accept it. I shall be glad to accept it.'

I scrutinised the man for some reaction, but none came – or at least none that I could perceive. The meeting was taking on the air of a dream in which I was an actor playing a part that I had rehearsed, and knew by heart, yet had forgotten I knew.

The man smiled. 'You have many friends, Walter.' I remember the way he stressed my name, using it as though it were not really my own, as if it were some kind of secret code, part of a secret the two of us were playing. 'Now, would you like to stay the here in the castle?'

'Sir, you are very kind, but there is something I must do before I depart.'

Until then we had been speaking German. I looked to one side, at Ewald, as if to exclude him. Then I addressed the man, who was still sitting at his desk, in a deliberately formal Latin: 'Sir, you see before you a poor wandering singer, yet you say you know sorrows that have afflicted me - the death of my father, and of Uqhart the Jew. What do you know of these things?'

He considered for a long while. He looked as though I had set him a test. At last he said, also in Latin, 'You must forgive I speak in riddles. If you are the one we think you are, then you understand; it would be foolish of me to lie to you. If you are the one we think, then it would be pointless explaining, since you would not understand anyhow. Only remember, if you accept our help, the reward will be great.'

'What is the reward?' I asked defiantly.

The man sighed deeply. He hesitated, and then pronounced slowly the one word: 'Jerusalem.'

# XII

# The Hanged Man

✠

I returned to the tavern through the dark streets. I was pleased because I had had the presence of mind not to fly into a rage as I had done with Antonius, and I had judged the timing of my leave-taking so as not to lose my dignity. By the time I reached the tavern my mind was firmly made up - though I suspected that these people were responsible for much of the evil that had befallen me, I would play along with them, so long as it suited my ends.

I found that I had lost interest in the poor girl I had organised to spend the night with. I sent her packing, got out my lute and started planning a new Crusading song, my mind teeming with plans about how I should spend the next few days. I was so excited that I slept little.

From then on, every moment that passed saw my enthusiasm about the Crusade grow. According to the reports pouring in at that time, Archbishop Conrad had already taken the fortress of Toron and was now poised to march on Jerusalem. There was talk of a new Order of Knights being formed at Acre, an Order of Germanic Knights. Perhaps I would live to see the day when Jerusalem became part of the Holy Roman Empire, and was subjugated to our Emperor.

The next morning I rose early and set about making practical arrangements. As the sun was rising over the tree-lined horizon, I was already making my way to the castle. The sky was brilliant turquoise and pink over the town, and it was cold and windy. I saw the first tradesmen setting off to the market, still dazed with sleep, and priests hurrying through the cold morning air to their churches for the first service of the day.

The guards at the great gate of the castle recognised me and I was allowed straight in. Ewald was not present, but I was led before other officials who confirmed the offers of assistance that had been made to me the previous evening. None would tell me the name of the man I had spoken to; all I learnt was that he had left the court before sunrise. I was told that I could move to the castle the following morning if I wished. There I could practise arms and make preparations and arrangements for my departure.

That afternoon and evening I had time to kill. In the afternoon the tavern was quiet, and I used the time to finish the Crusading song I had started the previous night. I decided I would sing in the tavern one last time that evening.

I no longer felt the desire to get drunk. After the evening meal Ewald arrived with a couple of other men from the court. They wanted to hear me sing. I played my new song, which was well received. Then I launched into my old songs.

As I sang them, they began to take on a new meaning, or, as it seemed at the time, their true meaning. All I had ever sung of - Hildegunde, my religious aspirations, my military training at the court, my losses and sorrows - all these things pointed in one direction: I was to become a Crusader. I was to help free Jerusalem from the infidel. I was to help bring the Ideal to this earth. I was to be an instrument of the Last Days.

Quite a crowd gathered that evening. I sang and sang. I am sure that I never sang better, before or since.

The next morning I moved to the court at Wimpfen. It was freezing cold that December day, but the light was crisp and clear. It was almost as if I could already feel underfoot the energy stirring that would bring about the end of winter and herald the start of spring.

At the gates, Ewald greeted me with doe-eyed enthusiasm. He

announced that he and four other young men from the court would ride with me to the Holy Land. I said that if they were such competent fighters as he himself was, they would need training in arms first, and I offered to help with this. He agreed gladly.

From then on it was almost as though I were back in the court at Frankenburc. It is not difficult to pick up the threads of courtly life. I slept in the communal dormitory under the great hall by the kitchens. It would have been warmer to have stayed in the tavern, but I enjoyed the company of the young nobles, who continually pressed me to sing to them, and plied me with questions about the mêlée I had fought with Johannes of Ulm, and helped me with my plans for the Crusade.

We spent most of the day practising and choosing arms. The men I had agreed to take with me looked as though they would make poor soldiers. Ewald, for all his other qualities, completely lacked the temperament for fighting, and made little progress no matter how hard he tried. Still, I enjoyed being outside, charging about on the horses given to us, practising wielding sword and lance. It was as if the exercise were starting to cleanse my body of the bad humours that had collected within it during my months of debauchery.

The court was run by the ministerial Alfred of Wimpfen, who held the castle directly from Henry the Sixth. We had just received news of Henry's death, but it was thought that Alfred's position in the castle was secure enough. He had reached an age where he was so well respected by one and all that he could afford to be kind. He was a shortish man with a large, round, reddish face and longish, silver hair. If his wife had been a beauty in her youth, there was no evidence of this now. She was a small, hag-like woman, with a deeply wrinkled face. Still, she spoke graciously enough, and I flattered her in the usual courtly ways. She asked me to sing to the ladies, which I did on a number of occasions, including the great Christmas banquet that was held just before our departure.

There were many beautiful ladies present at the court, and it gave me a lot of pleasure to sing them my songs of courtly love.

Attractive though many of the women were, I made a point of steering well clear of them. I was surprised at how much my attitudes had changed since I was at Frankenburc. I was well enough acquainted with whores by now that there were few pleasures of the flesh I had not experienced, and the last thing I wanted was to compromise myself with any of the ladies here. Nor did I wish to discover any noble souls amongst them. My own soul could only just cope with the love I felt for Hildegunde. Any other emotional entanglement would have been quite contrary to my purpose in setting out on the Crusade. Instead, I concentrated my efforts on getting fit, practising arms with Ewald and the four other young men.

At that time a priest who was a follower of Joachim of Fiori was passing through the town. This man, whose name was Michael of Bruges, was very famous for his preaching, so a large group of people had gathered round him. It did not take much to persuade him to deliver a sermon in the church.

I had heard the theme of his preaching before: de Fiori's division of history into Three Ages. The first Age is the Age of the Father, or the Age of the Law, which came to an end with the coming of Christ. The Second Age, the present one, is the Age of Love, the Age of the Gospels. The former laws have been replaced by the law that we should love one another. Yet we shall not be able to fulfil this law until the coming of the Third Age, the Age of the Spirit. When this Age comes, it will become clear that even the Church was nothing more than a great whore. Then the Church will fall away, for all men and women will be able to speak to God directly, through the Spirit, without any need for the intervention of priests and sacraments. First, however, must come the time of the Last Emperor and then the tribulations of the time of the Antichrist.

Suddenly it all fitted into a pattern. I thought of my own talking in tongues. I thought of the Archbishop Conrad's Crusade in the Holy Land. I thought of the sudden death of our own Emperor, Henry the Sixth, at Messina. Some had thought that he was the

Last Emperor; indeed, some said Henry believed this himself. Yet he was dead now, and the succession of Philip of Swabia was by no means secure. There were powerful forces in Rome who were opposed to him. The present Pope, Innocent the Third, was amongst them.

The preacher implied that the Last Emperor would sit upon the throne of Jerusalem. I wanted to be in the Holy Land by then, so that I could see the Last Emperor for myself when these things came to pass.

Michael's preaching fired my enthusiasm for setting off to the Holy Land for another reason too. He said that all Crusaders, no matter what their birth or rank, would have the status of clerics so long as the Crusade lasted. That meant exemption from temporal law and service. As a Crusader I would be better able to gain protection if I continued to try to track down those who were responsible for my father's and Uqhart's deaths.

If only I could recapture the joy I felt in my heart that Christmas morning as I said confession, took Communion and, in the presence of Michael of Bruges, the Bishop and all the members of the court, took the cross, swearing never to rest till Jerusalem was once more in Christian hands. I was in a state close to bliss.

I spent the week after Christmas at the court preparing myself. I sang each evening and practised weaponry during the day. I found that I had lost little of my strength during my years of easy living and that I had not forgotten the arts of weaponry.

I discovered that my new enthusiasm was contagious, and I began to develop a considerable following. I recounted the story of the mêlée with Johannes of Ulm, sang of my love for Hildegunde, and also sang my bawdy songs of lower love, which were greeted with laughter. Ewald took it upon himself to act as my attendant. Soon I was treated as something of a hero by the younger noblemen at the court.

I had learnt enough by now to understand the precariousness of this situation. Alfred and his wife did everything they could to be kind to me and to make my stay comfortable. I was extremely careful in everything I did. I could not bear the humiliation of another fall from favour. To avoid this, I determined that we should leave as soon as we could.

Eventually a group of half a dozen of us was ready to set off. Our plan was to ride to Marseilles, where we would take a ship directly to the port of Beirut; from there we would follow the line of the army to Jerusalem.

But before I could leave there was one person I had to seek out and find, so that I could tell her what had become of me and ask her forgiveness for past wrongs.

Through the priests in service to the court and their monastic connections it was not long before we were able to trace Hildegunde to a small convent near Rothenburc.

It was late January when I rode out, alone, to see her, through the forests and along the bank of the Jagst. This was just three days before I was to leave for Marseilles. I had a new horse now, given to me by the Lord Alfred. Also I had a new set of courtly clothes. On the breast of the jerkin I had embroidered the insignia of the red cross of the Crusaders, so that everyone should know of the vow I had taken.

It was a while since I had last ridden through the land and it was distressing to see the hunger that the poor folk were suffering. I had been given more than enough food for my journey, but I could not prevent myself from handing out crusts and cheese to the starving, so much so that by the time I found the convent I was faint with hunger.

I kept thinking about the story of the knight who had sinned and become infected with leprosy; eventually he had been cured by the love of a simple village girl. I had lost that sort of purity, but I was determined to regain it, and that was what was going to make it possible for me to present myself to Hildegunde. The Crusade would provide the means of purification. I thought that I would die gloriously in battle or else that one day I would have possessions in the Holy Land, in which case I planned to travel back to fetch Hildegunde. Perhaps it would be possible after all for us to be happy together.

The convent in which she was now living was an aristocratic foundation. The nuns followed the Cistercian rule with which I was familiar from the time I had lived at the monastery in Frankenburc. The buildings were quite new, set some way out of the town in the midst of rolling fields.

I remember walking into the cell where we were to meet and talk. She sat across a table from me. All the time there was another nun in the room, presumably to protect Hildegunde from me, and to inhibit us from any excessive displays of emotion.

I remember the odd feeling of anticlimax when I first saw Hildegunde again after such a long time. I think that I imagined she would be surrounded by some magical aura of beauty, holiness and nobility. Instead, when I was ushered into the little room, with its bare, vaulted roof built of hard, uncompromising stone, and its few sticks of simple furniture, there she sat, hands placed in her lap, a pale, young woman, nervously huddled in her white, woollen Cistercian robes. If I had not known her I would probably have passed her by without noticing her. Was this pathetic creature really the object of my thoughts day and night?

As I sat with her and talked, I realised that it was not going to be easy, and that I was going to have to get to know her all over again. She had changed. At first she was very still. She kept her head covered, though at one point in our conversation she cupped her face in her hands, pushing back the hood a little and revealing that her beautiful hair had been cut short. Her cheeks were sunken so that her eyes seemed large as they stared up at me.

Yet she was beautiful. If anything, I fell in love with her even more then. Her paleness made it seem that death had her marked out already, in the same way that I felt that death had marked me out for the Crusade, unless through Grace we both survived to be together again. Also, I noticed consciously for the first time that there was a certain scent about her; I do not mean a perfume or herbal substance but a natural scent, which I found intoxicating.

We spent about an hour together. At first she said little, and I did all the talking, about Quintus and Antonius, how I had met Ewald, my life at Wimpfen and how I had taken the cross.

At this she smiled. 'So, you too have found a noble cause...' she said. But there was more pity in her eyes than pleasure.

'Tell me,' I said, 'what happened to you?'

'Life was hard at the convent at Hohenfeld. It was healing for me to be on my own in my cell, for a while. I thought I would find God, peace. But I became ill – I was always coughing and feverish. They thought I might die. I would not have minded. But they moved me here.'

'How are you now?' I asked.

'Well enough.' She brushed my question aside. 'My uncle was furious because I had already taken vows. I cannot marry without special dispensation...'

'I see,' I said. It was her way of telling me that there was no hope. Not now.

'My uncle is still very angry with me. But at least, Walter, if we are not to be together, then I won't have anyone else inflicted upon me.' She reached out her hand to touch mine. I bit my lip to stop the tears. 'Besides, I am happy enough here. Surely it is right to pray, to study, to seek God.'

As she spoke, I remembered my days at the Frankenburc monastery. I remembered my aspirations that through prayer, study, music, work and a pure life, it might be possible to break through the barriers that are set between us and the Eternal, and to glimpse, even for a moment, the world of the Divine, the True, the Perfect. For me, this world *was* Hildegunde's world, and there was a rightness that she should seek fulfilment here.

Then I noticed that she had stopped talking. I looked up and saw that she had turned almost completely white, that her breathing was irregular. Then I saw that there were tears in her eyes, and she fell forward, sobbing. so I tried to console her, to find out what the matter was. I was concerned that the other nun in the room might react by stopping the interview. I kept looking over in her direction. But she sat impassively while Hildegunde continued to weep.

'Please speak to me,' I said. 'We have not got long together. You know I am leaving for the Holy Land in just a few days. It might be years before we meet again. We must say everything now, before it is too late.'

'Walter, my life is so empty without you.' she said. Then a look of anger flashed across her face that made me recoil involuntarily. 'I have heard about your life of sin,' she went on, 'with prostitutes. My uncle and his people know all about you...'

I could not deny the truth about my dissolute life. In some ways I felt relieved that she knew about it.

'How do they know all about me? Why?' I interrupted.

'How should I know?' she replied through her tears. 'When he told me, I was angry and jealous. You should have kept yourself pure for me, as I will always keep myself pure for you. Don't you know that debauchery debases love?'

I hung my head. How selfishly I had behaved, how stupidly!

'Hildegunde,' I said, 'what you say is true. I cannot understand myself. All I can ask is that you try to forgive me.'

'I will forgive you,' she said. 'It will take time, but I will forgive you.' I sensed once again the rift, the darkness between us, like that first night we made love beneath the linden tree, when I told her about Katrin. 'But, Walter, you must be careful. For my sake, please. My uncle says the most terrible things about you. He says that many people follow you. Some say you are a man of destiny, but he thinks it will not be long before you are hanged as a common criminal.'

'Who says these things?'

'I don't know, Walter. I don't want it to be like this. I just wanted for us to be together. But they will never let us...' We both fell silent. There was little left to say now. Nothing had changed. I tried to choose my words carefully. 'I will go on pilgrimage to the Holy Land,' I said. 'That is the only solution. But believe me, Hildegunde, if ever I do anything good, anything noble, it will be for you, and you will always be with me in my thoughts.'

I stood up. The nun in the corner sat impassively. I embraced Hildegunde one last time. I felt shaken, almost burnt by her love and judgement, which had penetrated to the very depths of me.

As I left her, I felt dazed, sad, judged, loved, more attached to her than ever, yet strengthened in my purpose. I was almost glad that I would not be able to be with her for a while, for her goodness was more than I could bear.

I returned to Wimpfen. Three days later, as planned, the five of us who were to leave together packed our weapons and provisions, loaded our horses, and set off for Marseilles.

From the very beginning we were beset with bad news. We learnt how the new Pope, Innocent the Third, was bitterly opposed to the Staufer Philip of Swabia's succession. Instead he was in favour of Otto of Brunswick, who was being supported by the Welfs and the English. We heard that Henry of Champagne, who was in charge of the garrison of Acre, had fallen out of a window and been killed, together with his dwarf, Scarlet, who had clung on to his clothes to stop him from falling. Such news troubled me; how could such bizarre accidents be part of God's plan for the recapture of Jerusalem?

We heard further details about the siege of Toron. The town had been Conrad's for the taking. The garrison had even offered to surrender, provided that their lives were spared. Conrad had refused, whereupon the garrison had fought even harder. Then the Crusaders had heard rumours of a great Saracen army marching north towards them from Egypt. Word had it that Conrad's men had panicked and fled all the way to Antioch, and had given themselves over to the brothels there, whilst waiting for ships to take them home.

My party was disheartened by this. What was the use of going on a Crusade if there was no army to join? Then Bernard, the youngest of our group, fell ill with fever and we had to leave him at Besançon.

As more bad news reached us from home, the rest of my party

deserted one by one. All the young aristocrats had interests to defend if it should come to a civil war. Then there was the famine, which made them worry about the welfare of their families. Eventually, by the time we reached the territory of the Montferrats, whose court is famous for the poetry and songs that have been written there, only Ewald and I remained.

We continued, mile after mile down the Rhône valley, until at last, in early spring, we arrived at Marseilles. It was the first time in my life I had ever seen the sea. I was overwhelmed by how majestic and beautiful it was; the great mass of water which was in perpetual motion, as though driven by some incomprehensible, restless spirit, reaching out towards infinity.

I was fascinated by the port of Marseilles. If anyone had told me that such a place existed on earth, I should not have believed them. What took my attention most was the boats. There were so many that the sight of them quite took my breath away; so many different kinds, everything from tiny fishing vessels, small craft for transporting men and animals, to massive ships that carried great war engines and had room for more than a hundred soldiers.

Yet more bad news came. The rumours we had been hearing were confirmed: because of the failure to capture Toron, and because of the death of Henry the Sixth and the fear of civil war at home, the Crusade had been disbanded. When we asked the master of a ship to take us to the Holy Land he merely laughed at us, saying we were too late. No more ships were taking men out to the Holy Land, they were only bringing them back.

We stayed at the port for some while, trying to decide what to do. I felt so dejected at times that I considered launching myself once more into a life of debauchery. There were many fine-looking women about. Most were not born in the port but came from further inland, because of the opportunities to earn money from the sailors who were constantly passing through. I was still smarting from Hildegunde's rebuke, and now that the Crusade had collapsed I felt depressed and lethargic, so I did not fall.

Instead, I spent some of my time playing songs, either in taverns where the landlord was friendly or in the open air. I also spent a lot of time familiarising myself with the Provençal language spoken in that part of the world. I knew how to read it, from my study of the poetry of the region, but training the ear to hear and the mouth to speak was harder.

Eventually Ewald persuaded me that we should abandon the pilgrimage to Jerusalem for the time being, and go instead to Santiago de Compostela. His reasoning was that if we remained on the pilgrim route we would be the first to hear the next time an army was raised to free Jerusalem. Meanwhile, the pilgrimage to Compostela was said to be rich in spiritual benefits. There was also the fact that the Saracen still occupied a part of Spain and good soldiers were needed to drive them out. I remember him saying that perhaps the last Crusade had failed because the time was not yet right for it – perhaps because certain forces, like the one who was to become the Last Emperor, were not yet in place.

So we pressed on through the marshy lands of the Camargue towards Arles, where there are vast buildings left by the Romans, including a massive amphitheatre. Then on to Montpellier, where there are many shrines to our Lady, and colleges where men of great learning gather. Then we headed for the imposing fortified cities of Béziers and Narbonne.

Ewald turned out to be the ideal companion. He was enthusiastic but quiet, a rare combination. He showed great affection towards me but did not overpower me with his fondness. He was someone with whom it was easy to be silent. Yet when appropriate we could talk together about everything under the sun. He was one of the few people to whom I ever confided all that I felt for Hildegunde. I also told him about Katrin, the burning of Uqhart and my father's suicide. I told him about what had happened to me with regard to Antonius and my suspicions that the various events in my life might be linked.

I remember him still as he was when we rode through the beautiful country, never far from the sea, overlooking cliffs and bays, day after day in the hot sun, with his long, brown, curly hair, and those big, doe-like eyes of his glinting in the light.

It was September when we entered the heart of Cambrai, where the predominant religion is not Christian but Cathar.

Poor Ewald.

We were not far from Carcassonne. We had had bad luck finding an inn, but since the weather was still fine we were happy enough to sleep rough.

That evening was just like so many others we had shared. We ate bread, cheese, drank wine, chatted, I sang for him, and then we fell asleep on the ground, listening to the chirping of the cicadas. How was I to know it was to be for the last time?

The next morning I was woken just before dawn by shouting. The sun was just rising brilliant red between the trees. It had been so warm during the night that there was hardly any dew on the earth.

I sat up lazily and looked in the direction of the shouting. A group of ragged men had entered the copse where we were sleeping. Some of them were carrying sticks and one or two had swords.

At first I thought they were just passing by, but one of them saw me, shouted something to his comrade and started over in our direction. I shook Ewald to wake him up, but he was too slow.

I shouted first in German, then Latin, then in the Provençal language. They made no reply. It was obvious from their bearing that it was our possessions they were after. Or so I thought at first.

There was no point in running because as I glanced round I saw that there were men on the other side of us.

From the look of them they were probably not very good fighters, but they outnumbered us and surprise was on their side. Ewald was awake and on his feet before me, but he panicked and started running. If he had made any effort at all we might have managed to fight them off, but that was not to be.

I decided to try to forestall them and ran into their midst. I struck out at two of them and knocked them over. The others were not expecting any resistance and took fright. I held my sword towards them threateningly. There were six or seven of them, but none of them dared approach me. I stood there, holding the sword in two hands, daring them to make a move.

By that time they had caught Ewald and dragged him back, whimpering. I can still remember those big eyes of his looking pleadingly into mine as they manhandled him.

I asked them in Latin what they wanted of us.

They signalled to our money and our horses.

I shook my head. If they were common thieves I was not going to give up without a struggle.

There was a moment of silence as they looked from one to the other. I thought of shouting aloud in the hope of attracting attention, but we were miles from anywhere.

Then the man who looked like the leader gabbled something.

The others nodded. I was pleased that so far they still had not had the confidence to attack. Then they started making threatening gestures towards Ewald in order to make it clear to me that unless I threw down my sword immediately they would hurt him, probably kill him.

Ewald understood this also and, rather than keeping calm, he began to struggle. The reaction of the robbers was cruel. They pushed him from one of them to another. Then he was knocked to the ground, and another produced some rope, tied it round Ewald's feet, threw it over the branch of a tree and hoisted him up, so that he was hanging upside down. All this time I hesitated, knowing that if I attacked anyone of them this would leave me open to attack from the others.

They started beating Ewald, who screamed pitifully as he hung there. At last I lost control and, just as the man was tying the rope to the tree, I charged at them, with my sword drawn.

I did not get very far. There must have been someone behind.

No one in front looked like he was going to put up any resistance.

I remember a sudden jolt, a feeling of sickness and frustration, then a shocked, searing pain. Then I remember falling forward, and then darkness.

I have an odd memory of waking, or half waking a number of times, looking up and seeing Ewald swaying above me, still hanging. I could not tell whether he was alive or dead. His eyes were wide open as if he was looking down in order to decipher some message written on the ground where I was lying, as if there were sacred runes there, lying around me, and he was Odin or some pagan sacrificial victim, hanging, staring down from the Tree of the World, trying to see down through the ground, to the roots below the earth.

The pain in my head was unbearable. Each time I saw him I tried to move, but the pain was so appalling that soon all I craved was the comfort of unconsciousness. As my mind returned to the blackness, I heard the hissing of meteors, and sensed a fluttering like burnt parchment in front of my eyes. It is curious how this impression has stayed with me so strongly and for so long.

I do not know how many times I woke and saw him there, above me. I do not know how long I must have lain there. Eventually, I woke and the pain was more bearable. But by then Ewald had gone. I made an effort to stand up, but was too weak and fell unconscious again.

The next time I woke after that it was dark. I was aware that someone was giving me water to drink. There was no sign of Ewald. Then I was stretched, stomach down, over the back of a horse. I just remember the beginnings of the movement of it walking, before my mind spun off once more into the blackness.

# XIII

## Death

✠

I woke to find myself chained to a dungeon wall. The heat and the pain in my head were terrible. I could remember the events leading up to the fight. I could remember seeing Ewald, hanging upside down, swaying over me. But I could remember nothing about how I came to be in that dungeon.

The same vision came, over and over again. When I closed my eyes I saw above me a great scythe swinging to and fro. It was as if Ewald, swaying above me, had become the scythe. Yet also in the blackness there was the appalling grimace of a bleached, white, skeletal face.

Then in the darkness I would see the dismembered limbs, hands, feet, legs, arms, heads, of those I loved, of those I had wronged. Katrin, my father, even Hildegunde was there, dead, disfigured.

The dungeon was tiny. There was just a little light from a grate, so that I could distinguish night from day. I could see nothing through it, for I could not get my head in the right position. All I could hear from outside was a dog howling in the distance. I was fed only on the foulest crusts and leftovers of pottage, which were pushed to me through a flap by a hand whose owner I never saw. I called out, but no one ever came. I was left to fester in my own filth.

After a while I noticed that they had not taken my money. The purse was still tied to my belt.

Then they came for me. They wore masks. I thought they would kill me. They were rough at first but they quickly realised that I was in no fit state to put up any resistance, so they treated me well enough. I supposed they must have been hired from the town and that they had no reason to bear me any malice.

They led me to a vaulted room, which was like the chapter house of a monastery, though deserted, with its vast, arching pillars. It was hot, even though we were in a stone building.

Light poured in through the narrow windows from behind the table where my judges were sitting. The light dazzled me so that at first I could not make out the features of those who accused me. I remember the odd echo in the room as a voice spoke that I recognised. It struck terror into me. It was Tremgistus.

'These are the crimes of which you stand accused:

'The first charge is Arson. Whilst still a student at Babenberch you took rags soaked in oil to the scriptorium and lit them. The destruction of the cathedral and the cathedral school at Babenberch was your doing.

'The second charge is fornication. You wantonly fornicated with the whore Katrin. You led astray the virgin Hildegunde, who is of noble birth. Truly our Lord said that it is better for a man that a millstone were tied round his neck and that he were cast to the depths of the ocean than that he should cause one of His little ones to stumble. Since then you have fornicated with numerous whores. Moreover, you have glorified fornication and adultery in vile songs, sinning against God with your blasphemy, and against his Creation by wanting to add to it your filth.

'The third charge is necromancy and heresy. You learnt the black arts from the magician Uqhart. You used this knowledge to charm spirits and used them to kill your own friend and companion Pauli, stepson of Uqhart.

'The fourth charge is parricide, for you used the said arts to torment your father with evil spirits, driving him to take his own life.

'The fifth charge is treason, for, despite the trust granted you by

the Graf of Frankenburc, you made adulterous advances to his wife
the Graefin, abused his ward, Hildegunde, and killed Johannes of
Ulm during a tournament, by trickery and witchcraft.

'The sixth charge is murder, that you killed the ministerial
Ewald for the love of killing and for gain.

'Do you have anything to say for yourself?'

My head was throbbing with pain and my vision was
swimming. I became convinced that I was dead and that this was
the first stage of my Judgement. I began to recognise the faces of
my accusers.

They all sat behind a great table beneath the window through
which dazzling sunlight shone directly, so that I could only just
make them out amidst the dancing, golden rays of light. On the far
left sat Antonius, the blind visionary I had met at Zell. He remained
in total silence, his head making a rolling motion as the charges
were read. On the far right I could easily make out the Abbot
Quintus, who nodded sadly throughout the proceedings, as if he
had been personally hurt by my crimes. Fabricius was to his left,
dressed in fine clothes, thin, alert, at times giving the impression
that he was bored, drumming his fingers on the wooden table. At
other times he would give the impression of having been, like
Quintus, hurt and appalled by my crimes. To the right of Antonius
there was a tall man, dressed in black, but he was wearing a helmet
so I could not tell who he might be.

Occupying the central position, standing to read the charges,
his white hair standing out like the rays of the sun, and his tawny
eyes burning like coals even brighter than the sunlight, was the one
I most feared – Tremgistus.

I said nothing. I remained still. Perhaps they mistook my
behaviour for defiance, for strength of will. Nothing could be
further from the truth. I was exhausted and confused. I accepted
the charges. They might have been true. I was curious. Was this the
explanation for my behaviour, for the unhappy course of my life,
which I had hidden, even, perhaps, from myself?

Day after day the trial proceeded. I was barely conscious for much of the time. The pain in my head was sickening. I did not so much hear the words of my accusers as see in front of my own eyes the acts they accused me of. I certainly did not have the strength to disagree with them.

I saw myself that evening at Babenberch, my heart full of hatred and resentment towards all those who had tried to help me. I saw myself taking rags from the place where the women did the laundry, then making my way furtively, late at night, to the kitchen where the oil was kept, then soaking the rags in the oil and hiding them under a stone by the scriptorium.

Then, just before compline, when I knew that those who loved the good would be setting about their devotions, I stuffed the rags down the front of my smock and ran to the scriptorium. I took them out and lit them, fanned the flames by waving the rags in the air, threw them into a pile of dusty books. As soon as I was sure that the flames had taken, I ran out into the night, across the quad, and joined the compline service, praying to all powers of evil that the flames would take. Such was the creature I had become even at the age of fourteen.

Already, in the library, despite my tender years, I had found texts about necromancy, and this act of burning was a summoning of spirits, which would accompany me in evil throughout the years. I knew that there were those who had offered me this education for the purposes of good. Yet even at that age I had my own plans.

My fornications with Katrin were linked with rites I had learnt by studying with Uqhart. I saw myself with her, there at the mill, relived the demonic embraces we shared, heard again the music we played together, the music of the dead. We knew that the mill, a place of discord and strife, was suitable for worshipping the things of evil, which would be drawn to us as they witnessed our satanic couplings.

I remembered how it was from Uqhart that I learnt the magical arts of sacrifice, and it was through him and for him that I killed Pauli, falling on him one day in the forest and beating his face with a stone until it was unrecognizable, then tying him to the horse and sending his body off into the forest. It was clear to me, now that I was dead, what an evil person I had really become. Yet I would not repent, for to do evil was the only way I could be myself.

At the court of Frankenburc my plans were thwarted for a while by Hildegunde. I recognised that she was an angel of goodness sent to challenge me. Yet I used philtres and charms so powerful that eventually I managed to seduce her carnally and thus destroy the angelic essences she possessed.

Johannes of Ulm, the strongest warrior they could find, was to have dispatched me, for there was no one else thought to have the courage and virtue to take me on. Yet I summoned devils during the fight against him, and these devils actually severed his hand from his arm. The Graf and the Graefin had fled the castle for fear of my powers.

Next I had attempted to kidnap Hildegunde, so that I would be able to sacrifice her and use the powers this would give me to further my evil purposes of gaining dominion over others. Yet she had managed to trick me and had taken refuge in a convent, where the holiness of the place meant that I no longer had power over her.

When this failed I turned to debauchery and tried to hide from those who were aware of my true nature. Now, at last, they had caught up with me.

I saw all these things. I had no strength to fight them. They had to be true, since I saw them.

I was made to think of the events four years before my birth, when Barbarossa was returning to Germany from Italy, when malaria struck down the army, when Rainald of Dassel died, along with two thousand other knights, crying out in the stifling heat as the thunder struck overhead. My spirit was there. I could see the scene still in my mind's eye. The heat, the exhausted knights lying, waiting for death. And the Brotherhood knew I was there too.

This was how I came by my powers. Like Judas, I had revolted against the gifts entrusted to me. All the powers I ever possessed were turned to evil. Now I was corrupt beyond redemption.

Every night, I was cast back into the cell. I would lie there, half conscious, half unconscious, watching the great sweeping movement of the giant scythe, recognising parts of people I had once known amongst the dismembered limbs and the grimacing death's heads. I tried to avoid the hollow eyes of the skeleton, because of the appalling voids they contained, each an accusing abyss of a deeper hell, into which I was being drawn.

The day came when sentence was pronounced. I was confused and bewildered. I was sentenced to death by being broken on the wheel. That meant that my bones were to be broken one by one, until at last I suffocated, in agony. The execution was to be delayed by three months, so that I should have time to reflect on my wrongdoings, and in case the fear of death brought about repentance. But there was to be no appeal against the sentence.

I could not believe what I heard. Surely I was dead already. I had the stench of death about me. I felt my limbs, my face. I was dizzy. The pain in my head was still excruciating. In a way the pain was so much a part of me that I no longer felt it. I was that pain. Yet as the sentence was read out, I had to conclude that, yes, I was alive after all. After all this time I felt cheated. I had accepted my death. I could not go through the process of acceptance again.

So that was what I had to look forward to: three months of rotting in the damp cell, and then that awful death.

I thought of Hildegunde, how I had wronged her. I realised that I deserved what had happened to me, for that, if nothing else. Just for that one moment my tears were pure.

After my trial the conditions in which I was kept improved. I was not chained and the food I was given was better. As my strength began to grow, so my head also began to clear. The pain was less acute. There were even some days when there was no pain at all.

The memory of the trial haunted me every moment I lay there. I would sleep, and each time I woke to find that I had been dreaming of the trial. This happened so often that now I find it impossible to distinguish in my mind between real memories of the trial and the nightmares it inspired.

How did my accusers come to wield such power over the innermost workings of my imagination? I was ill and exhausted, yet that was not reason enough. Much had gone appallingly wrong in my life and there was every reason to believe there were evil forces at work in it. I had always assumed that those forces for evil were outside myself. Was I to believe that the source of these forces was my own volition?

It was as if I now had two selves, the self I always thought was my own and then this other self, this self which was more aware, more evil, more coherent. I had admitted it was mine, but I was only just beginning to understand it. During the course of the trial I accepted it utterly.

Only very slowly did I begin to reflect on the mistakes in what they said about me. I searched and searched my mind for any memory of setting fire to the scriptorium when I was a boy. There was nothing. I relived every moment. I was not responsible for the fire. I had been at compline the whole time.

I had studied books of occult knowledge when I was at school. It was true also that I had pursued such studies with Uqhart. At the time, however, as far as I could remember, I had done so out of love for knowledge and truth, not with any deliberate aim to achieve evil.

The charge of fornication was true. Yet if I had loved, it had been at first out of true love, and latterly out of desperation. I had never known a woman with the intent of doing evil in acquiring illicit powers. Yet I had known that fornication was a sin of the flesh and that the flesh is evil. On that count I deserved whatever punishment was to be meted out to me.

As time went on I regained strength. The food was much better now, some of it delicious. My headache had almost gone. I was still feverish, though there were times when my body was at peace and I could think clearly just as I can now as I write this.

During these hours I remembered myself as I truly was. I could not understand how I had given in so easily, how I had so easily accepted my own death, the exclusively evil nature that was ascribed to me.

Then there were moments when I would feel real anger. I would shout and rage against my accusers and the sentence they had passed against me. No one came though.

At other times my mind would teem with the words I would have so loved to say to them, to accuse them in return. Then I would feel the great pressure of self-pity. I would become thirsty for the life I had known, and bitter with a sense of injustice about the judgement passed against me and the appalling death that awaited me.

Still no one came. I was fed by the invisible hand. Once, when I called out, as food was being thrust under the door for me as usual, I saw the hand hesitate for a moment. But that was all.

At times I would become desperate, scream and shout, cry, hoping that someone would take pity, at least come and talk to me, listen to what I had to say. I had sinned, but not as they thought.

Then again the scythe and death's heads would return, and one of the death's heads would be the face of Saint John, as I thought I had seen him as a boy, telling me that I should have become a priest of the Most High.

I tried to keep track of time by making a mark of each day on the stone wall. The stone was hard. All I had to rub it with were my bare fingernails. The light was poor and it took a long while before the mark became visible. My fingers would sometimes be bleeding by the time I finished.

There were days when I would become so distressed that I would forget whether or not I had make a mark. I would hesitate for hours, trying to decide whether or not to make a new mark, just in case. There were days also when I was so beside myself that I might well have forgotten to make a mark at all.

# XIV

## Temperance

✠

I remember the change distinctly because it was like a miracle, a sudden re-becoming. One day I woke up and felt well. My headache had gone, completely this time. Suddenly I could think clearly and calmly about where I was and what had become of me. I was still distressed, yet the irrational feelings of guilt had disappeared. The distress became something I could cope with.

I remember also becoming aware of birdsong, or rather the singing of one bird, above the grate that provided the only source of light and air in my cell. Whether or not the bird had sung there before this time I honestly do not know. If it had, I was unaware of it.

The following night I slept well and there were no more dreams of the scythe and the death's head. Now that my mind was clear I ceased from doubting. I began to think clearly about which crimes I had and had not committed.

Instead of seeing everywhere images of death, I began to remember the good moments in my life, like those first hours with Katrin, memories of schooldays in Babenberch, the innocent hours spent with Hildegunde when we first met, times during my childhood spent with my father and in the forest with the ex-priest Josephus... Everything came back to me with an incredible lucidity. I came to be able to imagine moments of my past so strongly it was as though I had returned fully to them. The present fell away, becoming irrelevant. I still possess that capacity now. This explains how these thoughts that you are now sharing with me came to have the quality of endurance. In some ways it is like travelling through time, and in other ways it is as though time does not even exist to travel through, but rather that I had become one with my greater self, that is the sum total of all I have ever said, felt, thought, and done.

As I became more adept at this form of time travel, I became less prone to emotional excess. I was able to take better care of myself, rising at a regular hour each morning and carrying out a plan of regular exercises to try to regain my strength.

I began to keep the hours of the monastic services, which of course I knew by heart. Doing so became a great solace to me. Between offices, at fixed hours of the day, I took also to singing through a set number of myriad songs. I sang the songs aloud, then organised and categorised them mentally in terms of their different themes and styles and the time at which they were written. In doing so I came to understand myself better. The categorization of my songs was like a spiritual anatomization.

My songs also turned out to be a privileged means of time travel. As I sang through each, I was present contemporaneously at all the other times when I had sung it, also at the time I had written it and the time of its conception. It was like an arrow shooting through time, and time was not like a continuous sheet of seamless manuscript but rather a parchment folded in such a way that, if one sheet were pierced by the arrow of a song, then others would necessarily be pierced also.

At other times of the day I would turn my mind to composing new songs. I composed several in the prison on the subject of courtly love, thinking of Hildegunde and how our love could and should have been.

No one came to my cell. At a regular hour, once in the morning and once towards the evening, a hand would push a plate of food beneath the door. I noticed that the quality of the food continued to improve. I gave up shouting to attract attention. Instead, I thanked the unknown bringer of food courteously in a loud voice, to make it clear that I was well and that I was in control. Otherwise, I was quite alone. I had every reason to expect that the punishment prescribed for me would soon be meted out. I still feared death, but I had reached the stage where I accepted that I would die.

All that separated me from others was not the knowledge that I would die, for that is common to all men, but the fact that I knew the manner of my death and that it was imminent. Now that I had become so adept at revisiting scenes from my past life, it seemed more likely that my past would survive my body, and that in death I had nothing to fear, only pain and a transition.

I remained in this state of balanced euphoria – it is hard to think of a better word for it – for about three weeks. Then one night, I fell asleep as normal after saying compline and singing to myself. I do not know how long I slept before the dream came. At first, I was sure it was Hildegunde. For the first time, in my imagination, I did see her face clearly. I saw that she was wearing a long robe, which was blue on one side and red on the other. The knowledge that she was there filled me, for the first time since I had been with her, with warmth, a spiritual warmth such as one feels when angels pass. This is the opposite of the feeling of coldness that surrounds the apparition of ghosts of the dead. It is the warmth of wholeness, of completion, whereas the ghostly cold of the returning dead is redolent of the dissolution of the grave.

I could see her face clearly, every feature distinctly, and at the same time I could sense, rather than see, that she was making her way through the deep stone corridors of the monastery in which I was held, down the dank stairways and along the narrow passages.

She was alone, yet I knew that it was her and that she had the power to release me. At the same time I did not believe that I was to escape death. I thought rather that this vision was another aspect of death itself, the death to which I had now resigned myself, agonising though it would be. At least, at the end of all the horror, I believed there would be some justification for me, since I was dying the victim of injustice. I thrilled to what I expected to be the beauty of release from the body in death, as one might thrill to the beauty of the touch of a lover. Therefore, I thought it was wholly appropriate that death should come to me in the form of Hildegunde.

In my dream I followed Hildegunde's progress through the corridors of the dungeons to my cell. At the very moment when I knew that Hildegunde would be outside my cell, I opened my eyes. Then I knew that I was waking, not sleeping, and I heard, albeit dimly, the chain of the door to my cell being rattled.

I was startled by the coincidence, that I should have dreamed of Hildegunde the moment my executioners and torturers came for me. Yet I was grateful for this consolation. I even wondered if perhaps Hildegunde had been praying for me then, and her prayer had taken on the form of her body as it sped its way to me, to appear to me, to make known to me the presence of her soul.

The rattling at the door to my cell continued. I wondered what sort of men my executioners would be, whether they would be stupid and brutal, whether they would be clever, evil people who take pleasure in causing the maximum of suffering, people who would sneer gleefully as I choked with agony; or perhaps they would be merciful souls, who would prefer to get their work done with a minimum of fuss, to take their money for killing me and be gone. Whichever, it would soon all be over, and at least I should have the memory of my vision of Hildegunde to console me during my suffering. Perhaps this vision was a sign of her forgiveness.

I looked up at the grate and saw that the sky was a dull, reddish grey. Dawn must have broken only a very short time ago. I had always imagined that my death would take place at dawn, and for that reason, every day, when dawn passed, I would relax somewhat. This was the time of day I expected them to come, and there they were.

The rattling continued and yet still no one entered. I broke into a cold sweat. The thought of the torture to come was suddenly real. I became acutely aware of my body, of what it is to experience one's own body without pain. I tensed muscles, tested nerves, each, I thought, for the last time. I felt the sweet flow of the blood, the running of the spirits from mind to limb, directing movement. It was as if I were taking leave of my body, saying farewell to all those sinews, that skin and those bones I had come to love so much. I sensed its beauty, the magnificent, cathedral-like ordering of its tiniest parts, and at the same time I imagined it as it would soon be. I imagined the yanking at my guts, the burning, the breaking of my bones and the final consumption by the flames. It was an obscenity, a profanation to do such a thing to a creation of God's that was so intricate, so complex. I wondered how much I would take before I fell into a faint, before I died and slipped into the other world. I wondered how I would take the pain, whether I would be able to keep my dignity, or whether I would rant and rave and say things in my agony that would disgrace and betray me. I wondered if this state of equanimity I had been enjoying for the past few weeks was not in fact a deceit, the last of my self-deceits before the true horror of my worldly existence was revealed.

At last the door opened. What I saw was not what I expected. There were three young men and a young woman. They were all wearing black clothes, yet there was nothing of the executioner or torturer about them. The woman's eyes were beautiful. It was the sight of them that gave me most confidence. Surely they would not have sent a young woman as one of a gang of torturers.

Slowly they came up to me, looking at me with curiosity. Then they signalled to me to be silent and to follow them. They did not strike me or humiliate me in any way. They did not read out my sentence. They did not lead me away by force. They appeared unprepared for the eventuality of my putting up a struggle. Their eyes betrayed neither cruelty, nor pity, but rather worry, fear of being seen.

I did as they said, hoping against hope that perhaps my time in prison was to end mercifully. My legs felt weak. This was the first time I had walked anywhere for a long while, and I feared that I might collapse at any moment. I felt light-headed, so incredulous that I was not in the hands of torturers that now my waking was more a dream than my dream of Hildegunde – when I had dreamt of her, though I dared not to admit this to myself, it had been as though she were coming to release me – precisely what these people were doing.

We walked on and on down the corridor. They whispered amongst themselves in their dialect, which I found impossible to understand.

At last we came out into a courtyard. I can still remember the effect of the brilliance of the sunlight on my eyes, which had not seen anything but darkness for so long. It was a pain filled with pleasure, an explosion of gold and white as if a million angels had suddenly rushed to populate the space just in front of my eyes.

As soon as my eyes adjusted, I made out arches and cloisters. I tried to judge the nature of the place in which I had been held. A monastery perhaps? The style of the building was old and heavy, but it was not without beauty, for the stone was an elegant sandstone.

It was curious that there was no one else about. I had assumed that I was the victim of a considerable and involved juridical process, and that my cell must be in the dungeon of a castle or monastery of some importance. Yet there was not a soul to be seen, despite the fact that the sun had now risen. Over to my left I could see the church. I listened for singing but could hear nothing. I was almost disappointed.

There was no one to stop us leaving the courtyard and going straight out into the streets of the small town. Here there was the bustle of people setting about their daily tasks. Some looked towards us, greeted us in their language and were greeted in return by those who had released me from the cell. I felt uneasy at first, but the people nodded towards me, as though it was quite natural that I should be there. They gave no impression that I was anything or anyone special. They certainly did not react towards me as if I were shortly to be the victim of torture.

I was led through narrow streets to a house. It was large and built of stone, unlike the other houses in the village, which were wooden. I was led through the front door and then up some spiral stairs. On the wall of the stairs I saw the SATOR AREPO sign both as it is normally written and extended out into a cross shape to spell PATER NOSTER, with A and O representing the Alpha and Omega.

I was allowed to sit on a bench before a trestle-table on which a meal was set out. There was a lentil dish, pastries, some onions, fruit, bread, even grapes; but no meat. The young woman had unveiled her face by now. She was beautiful. Her hair was very dark brown, long and curly, and her eyes were almost completely black, so that her stare was intense. Having gone for so long without seeing another human being, let alone a beautiful young woman, I found it hard not to stare at her.

She smiled at me and gestured to me to eat. I waited to see if the others would be joining me but, on a gesture from the young woman, they left the room.

I looked round. It was a magnificent room in a magnificent house. All the walls were stone. There was quite a large window, much larger than usual in a house of this size, and it let in a fair amount of light. I noticed that there were tapestries on the wall.

One of the tapestries represented a unicorn.

What attracted me most was the food and drink. The wine was excellent and I found it hard to stop myself from drinking too much. I feared that I might become drunk and unable to cope with whatever was to follow. I wondered why there was no meat.

I had soon eaten my fill and was trying to relax, wondering what was going to happen next.

Then, tired of waiting, I decided to venture down the stairs; but I had just stepped out of the room when I saw, coming up them towards me, an elderly man flanked by two of the younger men who had released me from the dungeon. He probably had them with him for protection. The elderly man was also dressed in black.

He nodded towards me in a friendly manner, to communicate that he wished me no ill.

I asked him who he was, in German, then in Latin, then in the dialect used in Marseilles.

He would say nothing, however, until he had beckoned me to sit down, and was seated comfortably opposite me. I was impressed by his calmness as well as by the solemnity and dignity of his bearing.

'It seems to me, young man, that it is rather you who owe us an explanation as to who you are.' His Latin was polished.

After all I had been through, I saw no reason why I should be anything other than honest. I told him how I had been a pilgrim, how we had been set about by robbers, how I had been beaten, had woken to find myself in the dungeon, was then subjected to a kind of trial and told that I would be tortured to death.

The whole time he nodded. He was a good listener and I probably told him more than I ought to have done.

'Do you know who my captors are?' I asked him.

He did not answer my question directly but smiled and shook his head. 'I despair of the ways of Christians,' he said.

I was taken aback. He did not look like a Jew, and I had never heard of anyone other than Jews denying that they were Christians in public, no matter what their private thoughts about religion might be. 'Are you not a Christian then?' I asked him.

'Not in the sense you mean,' he replied. 'My name is Markus. I am the ministerial in charge of the town of Aletus and the surrounding lands. I am answerable to the Lord of Toulouse. In this area, the majority of people practise the Cathar religion, and I hope soon to become a perfect of this faith.'

'You mean you have renounced Christ, and the Church?'

'The church, yes, but not Christ. We grew tired of the barbarism, hypocrisy and rapacity of the Catholic Church. The Cathar faith offers a purer, more spiritual way.'

'So there are no Catholics hereabouts?'

'Yes, quite a number. We try to live in harmony. But the monastery where you were held was closed around about the time the town was converted. The townsfolk were aware of comings and goings there though, at strange times of the day and night.

Some thought that the monks were returning to make sure property they had left behind had not been tampered with. My view was that the monks were hoping to find damage to their property to give them an excuse to persuade Catholic nobles to attack the town.'

'But how did you find out I was there?'

'Rumours reached me that at certain hours of the day and night singing could be heard – sometimes the monastic chants of the Christian religion and sometimes courtly songs of love. Many of the simpler townsfolk had become afraid, thinking that there were spirits dwelling in the building. These rumours also reached Gervoise. He was paid by the monks to provide you with food. The poor man was torn. He had converted to the Cathar faith with the others, but was scared of betraying the monks who paid him. Eventually his conscience got the better of him. He said that your singing moved him to tears sometimes, and that he was touched by the way you would always thank him for the food he gave you. The first thing he did was to stop drugging your food. Then eventually he came to see me.'

'They were drugging my food?' I repeated... So that explained my fever and the bizarre visions I saw. Then I remembered the story of Orpheus. It was my singing that had saved me. If this Gervoise had not heard me sing, and if my singing had not moved him, who knows what would have become of me? 'You know they tried me, and condemned me to death,' I said.

'Have no fear,' he said. 'No court has jurisdiction in the town other than mine, and no court in the region has jurisdiction other than those appointed by the Lord of Toulouse.'

'What do you think was happening to me then?'

'If you want my opinion, you are the victim of a barbarous trick played by a group of foolish Christian monks with nothing better to do.'

As we continued to chat, we became as friendly as it is possible for an older man and a younger man to become on first acquaintance. He told me how he had once thought of becoming a Catholic priest but had found the ways of the Cathars more plausible philosophically. According to him, the Christian faith could not provide adequate answers to questions like why there is so much evil in the world. He said the only possible explanation was the Cathar one, that there was a good God and an evil God, both eternal and as powerful as one another, at least until the Last Judgement. He argued that our souls were born of the good God, and were left behind in heaven, but that our spirits had chosen to become part of the created world and that we were therefore now subjugated to the evil God. The only way to escape the power of this evil God was to accept the *consolamentum*, the laying-on of hands by a perfectus, which would reunite our soul and spirit, so long as we remained pure, confessing all our sins, desisting from carnal acts and refraining from eating the products of coition: meat, milk, eggs and cheese. Only then could we earn the right to say the Lord's Prayer, to address the good God as 'Father'. He said that some, if they were in adversity, would take to their beds once they had been given the *consolamentum*, and starve to death, rather than risk losing the spiritual benefits the sacrament bestowed. I learnt later that this practice was called the *endura*.

I was not sure what to make of these ideas, but when he mentioned the corruption and hypocrisy of many so-called Christian clergy there was nothing I could do but agree.

He did not attempt to inflict his views on me. I learnt that the Cathar perfecti desist entirely from sex, since this is regarded as being part of Satan's creation. He said that the good angels imprisoned in Satan's creation had wept bitterly when they found that the bodies Satan had given them were of different sexes.

Then the talk turned to the events in the world. I heard that a preacher called Fulk of Neuilly was travelling round the country preaching a new Crusade. To think that it was from Markus that I learnt that Halberstadt and the Count of Katznellenbogen had taken the cross, as well as Baldwin of Flanders and Hainaut! All this was the result of that tournament held by Thibault of Champagne. At the time I reacted with enthusiasm, but Markus rebuked me, maintaining that all war and killing are wrong. This is another of the beliefs of the Cathars. Rather than kill, they would prefer themselves to be killed. I did not understand him then. I do now.

I also heard more news from Germany. Otto the Welf and the Staufer Philip of Swabia had been crowned Emperor at rival ceremonies during the time I was a prisoner. Philip was crowned at Mainz on the eighth of September, with the Emperor's insignia but without the blessing of the Pope. Meanwhile, in July, Otto had been crowned in Aachen with the blessing of the Pope but without the proper insignia. The situation did not promise well for the future.

The young woman returned shortly and served us more food. Her name was Margarite. She was Markus's stepdaughter.

She left the room and then returned once more with a lute.

'Will you sing for us?' Markus asked me.

'Of course, I would be delighted.' I could not take my eyes off the lute. It looked incredibly like my own, which I had supposed lost for ever at the time of my capture.

Markus handed it to me. 'We found this on the road outside the town some two or three months ago.'

'I cannot believe it,' I said. 'You know, once it was mine.' I felt that it would have been too impolite to insist on its return.

'Then you must have it,' he said. 'We suspected as much, didn't we, Margarite? But there is a condition. You must prove it is yours by playing and singing to us.' He smiled kindly.

It was hard for me not to weep as I sang for them. I was saved. I was reunited with my lute. I was free.

At first I sang some noble love songs in Provençal, which I knew they would be able to understand. I looked at Margarite as I sang and was pleased to see her blushing and averting her eyes from mine, especially when I sang:

*Alais! tan cuidava saber*
*D'amar, e tan petit en sai,*
*Car eu d'amar no'm posc tener*
*Celeis don ja pro non aurai…**

**Alas, I thought I understood so much / Of love, and yet how little I really know / For I cannot cease from loving her / From whom I should expect nothing.* (Ventadorn)

Markus insisted I should stay until I was well and strong. He asked nothing of me but that I should sing to him occasionally and that we might talk to one another about philosophy.

So a routine was gradually established, whereby we would meet over lunch, and after supper, to talk. He was interested in the systems of thought I had learnt as a monk. I, in turn, learnt much of the Cathars. For example, they think beasts and birds are miscarried foetuses of pregnant women, which fell from heaven during the battles between the forces of God and Satan. Therefore they eat no meat.

They believe too that Satan used beautiful women to inflame the good angels with lust, and that is why they fell from paradise. Despite this, many women became perfecti, and there were houses in which such women lived together, like the one in Toulouse where they earned their living by making clothes and shoes for the townsfolk.

One day I was allowed to attend an *apparellamentum*. This was the monthly meeting in Markus' house of those who were adepts or perfecti of the religion. The meeting took place in an upper chamber. The whole of the service was spoken in the vernacular, and was more like an informal meeting, with no singing, no crossing, no incense, no candles. The believers prayed together and confessed every one of their sins to each other, even tiny things, like failing to say the requisite number of paternosters or eating eggs by accident, all of which would lose them the right to the *consolamentum*.

We sat in a circle, so each could see all the others. There was a true atmosphere of peace at the meeting, and I still often remember looking from face to face, and then at the wood of the rafters and the floor and the chairs. The grained texture of the wood seemed to form a pattern that swirled so as to extend out beyond the wood, engulfing those there and reaching out into infinity. Amongst the perfecti were women, some of whom were strikingly beautiful, pale and thin, all dressed in black. They seemed already close to death, part of another, eternal world.

Many of their ideals, and particularly their way of life, appealed to me, but I would not have been able to convert. I could not believe that the created world is entirely evil. Nor could I believe that the soul wanders from one body to another finding release only when it dies in the body of a *perfect* in possession of the *consolamentum*. There are spirits and spirit voices, but the matter is more complex than they realised. Also the Cathars believed that Christ was pure spirit, an angel perhaps, but not one with God.

What I discovered from this was that I did believe, in my heart of hearts, that Christ was flesh as well as spirit, and that His Resurrection was the guarantee of salvation for humankind.

After a week or so I asked if I might meet the man who had fed me for so long, in order that I might thank him for fulfilling his duties so kindly. Markus approved the plan, and so it was that I came to meet him the very next day.

Gervoise turned out to be a large, rather awkward man in his mid-thirties. He had dark hair and a bloated, asymmetrical face. He was married and had three daughters. The family lived in a small wooden house near the market. Gervoise had been a shepherd in his youth, but now he found it hard to get round the countryside as he used to, so he lived instead by doing odd jobs around the town. He helped with the building of new houses, repair work, setting up stalls for the town markets, and so on.

He was a simple but kindly fellow. He was nervous when he first saw me. I said little and let Markus do the talking. I could just about make out some of the dialect by now, but I still could not grasp all the words.

Markus spoke very kindly to Gervoise. To begin with, Gervoise eyed me suspiciously, or rather with fear. Then, when Markus explained that I was grateful to him for feeding me so well and for helping to secure my release from the prison, something seemed to melt within the man and he ran up to me, threw his arms round me and would not stop hugging me and kissing me, tears in his eyes.

Hesitatingly, Gervoise described the men who had employed him: the blind priest and the tall one with the white hair and fiery eyes, the ministerial with curly grey hair and the man with a square jaw, who fitted the description of the Abbot Quintus. They had sworn Gervoise to silence. It was hard to tell whether Gervoise was more ashamed because he had betrayed them or because he had served them in the first place.

'Where are they at the moment?' Markus asked.

'I don't know,' said Gervoise, hanging his head.

'When are they due to return? Do you know that?'

Gervoise became embarrassed. 'One of them usually turns up every two or three weeks. Recently it was only the tall priest with white hair and fiery eyes.'

'What does he say when he is here?'

'He just asks, "Is the prisoner well?" and I reply, "He is well fed and sings a lot, sir." Then he gives me money and goes.'

After the interview Markus gave Gervoise food and drink to take with him back to his family, and dismissed him.

Even before Gervoise left I had formed a plan in my mind. As soon as he was out of earshot I said, 'May I wait here until Tremgistus returns? I wish to confront him with his crimes, in person.'

'You are free to do as you wish. But if you must confront him, please do not do so on our territory.'

'Surely, though, he committed the crime of false imprisonment, and should be punished.'

'According to secular law,' Markus replied, 'but not ecclesiastical law. There is nothing I can do. And I do not want to provoke a situation which could give our enemies an excuse to wage war against us. I witnessed the attack seventeen years ago led by Henry, the Abbot of Clairvaux. I do not want to see anything like that again as long as I live. But of course you are welcome to stay here. It is already as if you were part of my family. Only please confront Tremgistus away from the town.'

# XV

## The Devil

✠

For the next two weeks I lived, enjoying all the comforts of domesticity, with Markus, his wife, and his stepdaughter Margarite. Then, one breakfast time, Gervoise came rushing in, forcing his way up the stairs to the room where we were accustomed to eat together. Even Markus seemed shocked at first.

Gervoise was out of breath and something was clearly the matter.

'I must speak,' he said. 'I just stepped out of the door and was going to set up stalls in the market, when I saw him...'

'Saw who?' Markus tried to encourage him, while he got his breath back.

'The tall one, with the white hair. He's come back. What am I supposed to do if he sees me? What shall I say?' He had lost his composure completely.

'Don't worry,' Markus said, 'you can stay here and he won't find you.'

'But he saw me. That's what I meant to say. He's following me.'

'What?' This was the first time I ever saw Markus flustered. 'Gervoise, you must tell him that the prisoner died of fever two weeks ago, and that he was buried in the town cemetery.' As he spoke we heard footsteps on the stairs.

'Walter, in there!' Markus said, signalling to me to go to the far door leading into a small room where there was a ladder, which led up to an attic. I grabbed my lute and just got out of sight as he strode in - the man I feared most in the world. There was no time for me to climb the ladder, so I pressed myself against the wall in the shadows. My heart was beating so loudly that I worried in case they might hear it in the other room. Markus had the good sense to motion to Gervoise to sit where I had been sitting, in case any questions were asked about the half-eaten meal on the table. Gervoise would normally have been delighted at the food, but under the circumstances he was too nervous to eat anything.

There was a small crack in the door behind which I hid, and through it I could just make out what was going on. Tremgistus was fierce, domineering, his eyes wild, staring from one of the men to the other. Gervoise was clearly intimidated, but Markus remained calm.

'So,' he said, talking directly to Gervoise without greeting Markus in any way or apologising to him for bursting into his house, 'since when have you taken to breakfasting with those above your station? Or have you too become a miserable Cathar?' He turned to Markus. 'I never knew that the Cathar faith recommended eating with peasants.'

Markus and Gervoise remained silent.

'Gervoise, I need to talk to you,' Tremgistus demanded.

Gervoise looked desperately at Markus. It was clear to me that Gervoise would not be able to stand up to Tremgistus on his own. Fortunately this was clear to Markus also. Markus intervened. He spoke calmly, definitively: 'If it's your illegal prisoner you want to talk to Gervoise about, he's dead,' Tremgistus glared threateningly at Gervoise.

'And don't think it was Gervoise who told me,' Markus went on.

'The whole town knows. Your illegal prisoner did a lot of screaming before he died. I authorised some men to go and see what was going on. It was too late. He was delirious by the time we reached him. He died shortly afterwards.'

'So, what did he die of?'

'Fever.'

'Where is the body?' asked Tremgistus, clearly shaken but trying to make it clear that he was not willing to take Markus' word at face value.

'In the cemetery,' Markus remained calm.

Gervoise managed to nod.

'Show me,' said Tremgistus, staring at Gervoise.

Gervoise made to get up, looking pleadingly towards Markus as he did so. But Markus chose his moment well. He stood up, leant towards Tremgistus and shouted, 'You have no right to give orders in this house, or in this town. I tell you your prisoner is dead. And you know what that makes you? It makes you a murderer. And if I see you or any of your kind in this town again I shall have you arrested and tried.'

'You,' said Tremgistus, 'you understand nothing. You are not even a Christian. You are a heretic. You are the one who will face judgement, a terrible judgement.' He stared fiercely, his eyes rolling. Gervoise recoiled with fear. Yet Markus' ploy worked, for Tremgistus did not insist. He turned and strode out of the room.

None of us moved until we were certain that he had gone and that he was quite out of earshot. Markus went over to the window and satisfied himself that Tremgistus was on his way down the narrow street before he called to me to come out.

The time had come for me to depart, to follow Tremgistus. I embraced both Markus and Gervoise and said, 'So much for his powers of divination, if he cannot even sense my presence behind a door.'

Markus smiled, but he was in no mood for joking. 'Don't underestimate him,' was all he said, quietly, under his breath. 'Go now, but remember that if you confront him it must not be on land which is under my jurisdiction.'

I nodded, then I took my lute and my few belongings. Markus gave me money, which I accepted on the condition that he would let me repay him as soon as I was able. I did not even take the time to say farewell to Margarite, but set off straight away on Tremgistus' trail.

I followed Tremgistus for nearly a month. He headed for the

mountains, for the high places, which were wild and uninhabited. As soon as he was sure that he was out of the sight of men his behaviour would change. He would often sit or kneel for long periods, motionless, muttering to himself. Then he would spring up, like a man half his age, and dance and sing and roll on the ground, then go running off over the rocks and scrubland, a wild glint in his eye, as if he were possessed by a legion of supernatural forces. This state would persist for hours and hours as he half ran, half strode over the high places and through the ravines of the Pyrenees. I could not get close enough to hear whether the words he muttered were angelic or diabolical. I supposed the latter and so kept my distance in case the spirits with whom he intercoursed told him of my presence.

It was not difficult to track him; I was younger and fitter than he was. My strength had soon returned after my prison ordeal. I had learnt the arts of tracking during my time in the forest as a boy and then from my military training at the court of Frankenburc. Tremgistus had no such training, or at least made no attempt to avoid pursuit by me.

He was very good at setting traps for animals, though. I saw him using fixed and moving nets to trap birds, rabbits, hares and other small creatures. In this respect he was more like a wily peasant than a noble priest and visionary.

On the first two evenings I saw him build a fire. On the first night I suspected that he was burning bodies of small animals - mice, lizards perhaps. On the second night I saw him catch a bat. He literally plucked it out of the air. I was too far away to be able to tell for certain what he was doing, but what I heard and smelt was enough to make my flesh creep. As he caught it he cackled, and then sang songs in languages I could not understand, but which were perhaps spirit languages. I heard the bat squeak pitifully and I am sure I saw him pluck off its wings. I have heard it said that there are those who rub the blood of bats into their eyes to give them power to see in the darkness of the spirit world. It was not long before I smelt the burning of the animal's flesh.

On the third evening, the last he spent in the deserted parts of the mountains, he caught a ram. He kept it tied to a tree until nightfall. I was watching from a considerable distance, but I swear that he knew the beast carnally before cutting its throat and consigning its body to the fire. I remember that the sky was an unearthly purple colour that evening.

I was tired by then and fell asleep not long after the animal had been killed, and the smell of its burning flesh began to sweep up the mountain to the rocks where I was hiding. Suddenly, from the depths of my fitful sleep, I was woken by the sound of my own name being called out in a blood-curdling, shrill voice. I looked up. Tremgistus was standing by the fire, hands stretched up, in some kind of trance. For a horrible moment I was sure that he would come straight over towards me; I was sure that he knew exactly where I was. Nothing of the sort happened. He screamed my name three times more, then he lay down motionless, asleep or unconscious.

After Tremgistus left the next morning, I inspected the site of the fire. The charred remains of the carcasses were still there.

Round the fire, in the earth, was drawn the shape of the pentagram.

After the days in the mountains he went back down towards one of the main roads on the plain and headed north-west towards Roncevalles, occasionally joining with groups of pilgrims on their way to Santiago. From then on he behaved quite normally, walking with a stick in his hand, like an ordinary traveller or pilgrim.

When amongst other pilgrims he would act the part of the Christian priest and prophet. I would see him preaching and exhorting pilgrims, telling them to mend their ways, telling them that the end of time would soon be upon us, saying that the time had come for the reign of the Last Emperor and describing the afflictions that would soon befall the world. I know this because I made a point of talking to people he had talked to, in the hope that he might have divulged his eventual destination to them. The pilgrims were overawed by the man, and I saw many of them kneel to be blessed by him.

In the mountains, the tracks Tremgistus left were obvious. Down on the plain, on the pilgrim route, there was only one main road to follow, which was part of the main pilgrim route to Santiago. Here he left many human clues, since he was unable to resist talking to any groups of pilgrims he came across. His appearance was so striking that even those he did not speak to could not fail to notice him.

I followed him from shrine to shrine, from church to church and from hamlet to hamlet. He would stay in a great variety of places, sometimes sleeping rough, sometimes in great and noble monasteries and sometimes at humble inns. The one time I nearly lost him was when he stayed at the hill-fort town of Saint Bertrand, in the castle of a powerful local aristocrat. The fact that he was welcome in so many monasteries and amongst such nobility brought home to me that he was a man with considerable connections, a man to be feared because of his influence.

It was already late October by the time I tracked him to his cave in Roncevalles.

We climbed steeply up the path and high into the mountains, where I imagined Roland's scouts must have looked for signs of the armies of Spain. I shall never forget the sight of the clouds and the mists rolling through the valley, swirling and mysteriously white against the dark greys and greens of the hills, as if the spirits of the armies that had fought over the pass were present in the majestic rolling motion of the whiteness, as if the battle now being fought was no longer between two earthly armies but between the present world of matter and the spiritual world of the dead. I remembered the words of the Song of Roland:

*Halt sunt li pui et li val tenebrus,*
*Les roches bises, les destreiz merveillus.* ★

★*The mountains are high and the valleys dark, The rocks sheer and the gullies full of mystery...* (The Song of Roland)

From the top of the path where I had followed him that night, I saw that he had descended a narrow path into a deep ravine, yet for the first time he had left no clear tracks. I was beginning to panic, wondering if I had lost him, or if perhaps all this time I had been tracking a spirit, or maybe a figment of my own imagination, since he had disappeared from the face of the earth as if he had never existed in the first place. I was relying entirely on guesswork.

I decided to keep going down and down, as far as I could, into the ravine, for there was no obvious place to head to on the mountainside. I was just about to give up when I saw the entrance to a cave. Sure enough, there were tracks. Just one set, not enough for more than one person. Then, to my relief, I noticed that there was some of the wool from Tremgistus' habit caught in a gorse bush. I felt that the time had finally come to confront him.

I bent down to enter the cave. Inside, it was not entirely dark. Round the bend there was an eerie light shining. There was a chill in the air, the chill of evil, as if this cave were one of the entrances to hell itself.

Nonetheless, I refused to allow this place to intimidate me. As I made my way along through the rocky passage, strange shadows loomed about me. Now I saw the image of the ram that Tremgistus had sacrificed. Then I saw Tremgistus himself outlined on the rock wall, only now with horns like the ram's and with a tail like that of a lizard.

I heard the sound of singing, or rather a low, droning incantation coming from round the next bend. It was Tremgistus' voice, and it was unearthly, unnerving.

I rounded the corner and saw him sitting, cross-legged, dressed entirely in white, eyes glazed over, in front of an altar, which was made of rough stone. There was no cross on the altar, but there was the smell of burnt remains in the air. Five candles set out around the altar at regular intervals provided the light.

At first, Tremgistus did not see me. Then, suddenly, his chanting stopped. After a second or two more he turned his head to look at me. His eyes glinted an appalling tawny yellow in the candlelight.

His gaze chilled my whole being. My instinct was to turn and run, but I stood my ground.

'Are you alive or dead?' he said.

I did not answer. I realised that I had taken Tremgistus by surprise. He seemed to fear me as much as I feared him. I stared at him as fixedly as I could and said, 'You are going to tell me why you have been meddling in my life. What do you want from me?'

As my eyes adjusted to the light I noticed that there were many books and parchments round the outside of the cave. Three or four which Tremgistus was using that moment were held in place by stones laid on top of them.

Tremgistus continued to stare at me, as if trying to judge whether or not I was spirit or flesh and blood.

'I have power over you,' I said, 'I can kill you or I can let you live. I can bring you to justice in front of the church authorities or I can let you go. Which is it to be?'

'You are flesh and blood. Those fools at Aletus lied to me.' Angrily, he threw dust towards the altar. The candle flames swayed and the shadows danced crazily on the walls.

'I want to know why you have been interfering in my life. You tell me now or I shall kill you.' I produced the knife that I carried with me and pointed it towards the old man.

'If you do not already know the answers,' he said, 'you would not understand them even if I pronounced them to you. If you know them already, then there is no need for you to ask.'

'Tell me or I'll kill you.'

Tremgistus remained silent. Then he seemed to come to a decision. He spoke, slowly at first. 'The visions. They never lie. First they came to me, then to Antonius. We know this world is irredeemably corrupt. All must end. All must be swept away before the millennium. The sooner all is swept away the better. We knew that you would come. I suppose it is possible that you do not know yourself yet. I have seen it already. We have checked your astrological charts. They confirm the visions. Do you not see visions yourself? Of course you do. So you understand our interventions, with the whore Katrin, with Uqhart, with Hildegunde. All here below is corrupt and passing. You know that as well as I do.'

'Who do you think I am? What are you talking about?'

'If you know the arts, you will know the answer.'

'I have seen you practise black arts yourself,' I said, 'in the mountains, in the high places, and I saw your altar there, the ram. Do you worship Satan?'

His eyes glowed like coals as he stared at me. 'No one could worship those evil ones, the princes of hell and of the air. Yet I know them. And it is true that I have conjured them. I am a man of occult knowledge. What I have seen and what I know few would understand. It had been my quest, throughout my life, to understand the Last Things. This desire has been mine ever since I first read the Revelation of Saint John when I was a young boy. The knowledge contained here has been sealed from most men, and from the angels, like the secret books of Aristotle, which only the Antichrist will be able to read when he comes. Yet the demons know, for what terrifies them, what drives them to ever greater excesses of evil in this world, is the knowledge of the punishment which awaits them. That is why I summon the demons, not because I worship them, but for the knowledge they are able to impart about the innermost workings of the End, of the Last Things, in which you are to play an important role.'

'Why then did you have me arrested? Why was I drugged, tried? Why was I kept so long? Why was I threatened with death?'

'We needed to test you, and your powers. You did very well.'

'Who else is involved in this game of yours then?'

He stared at me. It was like talking to a sphinx. He was motionless, his face ashen in the candlelight, only his tawny brown eyes shining out of his head with the light of the flames of hell. He might tell me that he did not worship the forces of evil, but it was hard for me to believe that he was not possessed by them.

Images crowded in on my mind of all that I had lost in my life. It was all through this man here. I felt the flames of anger rise within me.

'I said I want to know who else is involved in this charade of yours.'

'I am sworn not to divulge their names. Not to anyone. Not even to you.'

'We'll see,' I hissed at him.

As fast as I could I stepped behind him, put my arm round his face and held my knife at his throat. His flowing white hair had a smell not unlike that of musk.

He remained motionless. If only he had struggled, I might have found it in me to kill him. 'Tell me,' I hissed once more.

'So,' he said, 'you know how to behave like the demons. Then you must know as I do that Lucifer is the harbinger of the True Light.'

As I thought for a moment about what he was saying, he raised his hands and prised my arms away to free himself. Was I stunned by what he had said? Was he really too quick for me? Or had he charmed me in some way? In any case, my arm felt like jelly and there was nothing I could do to stop him slipping, ghost-like, from my grasp. For a moment I felt the humiliation of being a young man outmanoeuvred in a fight by an older, frailer man.

There was a dull roaring sound. A chill gust of wind blew through the cave. Suddenly, as if of their own accord, all the candles went out. The cave was in total darkness. Tremgistus had moved not in the direction I thought he would, towards the outside of the cave, towards the light, but even further into the rock, downwards, towards the bowels of the earth.

It took me a while to come to my senses - to pick up one of the candles, then to grope my way to the light, find a flint, strike it in order to get the candle alight, then to make my way back into the cave.

By the time I had the other candles alight I could see the passageway down which he had disappeared. I followed it only to discover that it branched off in different directions. I called after Tremgistus. There was no reply, just the distorted echo of my own voice, which mocked me.

Although Tremgistus had gone, I could still look through the papers he had left behind.

I took them out to the daylight and spent until sunset reading through what I could. There was a variety of texts: a number of astrological charts, some Latin books on the arts of necromancy, some books in Greek on Neoplatonic magical practices, as well as other texts written in a language I could neither understand nor recognise. What was most interesting to me was a pile of papers written in what must have been Tremgistus' own hand. These made up a diary of the meetings of the Brotherhood. Each was dated. Only the names of those present at each were not stated. The individual members' names were represented by symbols, five symbols in all, which corresponded to the signs of the four elements plus a distorted version of the sign of the quintessence.

The dates of the meetings were clear. They took place annually, always on the Eve of Saint John. They went back to the year before my birth. The places where they took place varied. The first had been in Rome; then there had been one in Padua; another was in Paris.

I decided to try to find out the date of the next meeting. I found out that it would be in the Navarrese town of Soria, at the Church of San Saturio, and it would take place on Saint John's Day the following year, the year of our Lord 1199.

This was all I needed. The candles were burning low now, and the light was fading outside. I replaced the books in the cave. I planned to return here in a day or two with the Church authorities; in the meantime I did not want to be found in possession of the books, for fear of incriminating myself.

I climbed up the winding path to the main road through the mountains. The mist was already low, but soon I reached a path that rose in a zigzag to the monastery dedicated to the memory of Roland. I went to pray in the chapel.

I felt that the atmosphere of evil from the cave was still clinging to me. I prayed repeatedly to be cleansed. It was not until midnight that I began to feel a sense of peace. I fell asleep in the chapel, propped up against the wall.

Before dawn I was woken by a monk, who asked me who I was. I said simply that I was a pilgrim. Many passed this way over the Pyrenees on the way to the shrine of Saint James at Santiago. The monk showed me to a large hall full of snoring men and women. I found a corner and slept for another hour or two before the rest began to stir.

That morning I avoided conversation. I did not want anyone to see where I went, in case I was followed and myself accused of necromancy. As soon as I was sure no one was looking, I made my way once more down the ravine. The sun was like a brilliant, golden flaming ball over the mountains. The sky was crystal blue and the grass was like emerald, glimmering in the dew.

By the time I reached the cave, the air had already grown quite warm. For the first time in years I felt myself able to pray, properly, as I walked.

The cave seemed a different place from the previous day. There was no longer the atmosphere of fear, of foreboding, of evil. I made my way inside lighting a candle I had from the monastery.

I listened carefully. The cave was deserted. I crept to the central chamber where I had confronted Tremgistus the previous day. My plan was to make sure there was sufficient evidence to be able to report his wrongdoings and evil to the authorities. But when I entered the chamber, there was nothing left. The rock which had served as an altar was still there, but that could have been just by chance. All the books and papers and candles were gone. There was nothing to prove that this might have been a place where evil spirits had been summoned.

I looked down the tunnel where Tremgistus had disappeared the previous day. I considered venturing down, but found that it led to a labyrinth of tunnels where I would be sure to be lost.

As I stood, in silence, I was suddenly convinced that I heard the sound of laughter coming from deep inside the cave. It was quiet and distant. I might have been mistaken. My instinct was to run down and try to trace the source of the sound, yet I stopped myself, realising the danger of losing myself forever in the labyrinth.

I returned to the chamber of the cave. For the first time I noticed a painting on the wall. The colour of the paint was brownish black in the light of the candle; it could easily have been blood. The painting depicted the outline of a horned, winged creature, standing on a plinth of some sort, to which were chained two other creatures, both also horned but without wings. The central figure had breasts and male sex organs. In its hand there was a wand.

The legs of all the creatures were like those of animals.

As I stared at the picture I felt once more the sense of evil creeping over me, not so strong as the previous day but more insidious. I was sure that I heard the sound of laughter once more coming from deep within the cave.

I ran out into the comfort of the light and the morning.

# XVI

## The Stricken Tower

✠

I was determined to find Tremgistus once more. But how?

I made friends with the monks at the hostelry in Roncevalles, and became one of those helping to care for the pilgrims, preparing food and deciding who should sleep where. Also, I composed songs about the pilgrimage and helped provide entertainment in the great hall in the evenings.

I used the opportunity to ask all the monks and nobles passing through on pilgrimage, or returning from the pilgrimage, if they had seen anyone answering the description of Tremgistus. But all my inquiries came to nought. I decided the best course of action would be to make directly for Soria, and make inquiries there. Otherwise I would just have to wait until Saint John's Day at the Church of San Saturio. Was I being foolish to pin so much hope on those writings of Tremgistus' I had found by chance?

By autumn the flow of pilgrims had all but dried up. An atmosphere of intense melancholy settled on the pass. The low, rolling clouds engulfed the hostel most days and the monks told me that soon snows would come, which would make the gorge impassable. So I took my lute and my few belongings and made my way down the treacherous, winding path, out of the English kingdom and into the kingdom of Aragon. I spent the winter drifting from one inn to another on the pilgrim route between Roncevalles and Pamplona. The snows were heavy, so I put off heading further to the south.

Time passed very slowly. I soon tired of making inquiries about Tremgistus. Instead I became fascinated by the language of those who lived in those parts. At Zubiri I lived at an inn whose landlord was very learned. He was a local man, had lived as a monk in his early days and knew Latin. He taught me much about the language of the region. He had observed that, whilst most languages have at least something in common with one another, and are formed using similar rules to Latin, this language possessed words and patterns all of its own. It was a language he loved, and he wondered if perhaps it was the language originally spoken in Eden, or the language all men spoke before the Tower of Babel was struck down.

By the end of February I was living in Pamplona, where, to my surprise, much of the talk was of bulls. The people in this part of the world were truly different from those I had known in Franconia, dark and with fiery eyes. I learnt that each Easter herds of bulls are driven through the streets of the city and men, women and children run with them, though it is very dangerous and each year many people are killed. Some talked of festivals, too, where bulls were ritually slain. In these rituals the bull represents the base, material body, and the one who slays him is the triumphant spirit of man.

Now the weather was finer I pressed on south over the plains through Olite to Tarazona, which was a beautiful city, built on rocks rising up steeply from the river, with brightly coloured houses that looked like giant flowers on the face of the rocks. I was pleased that I had learnt some of the language of the locals, who welcomed me and never ceased from plying me with questions about my life in Germany.

No longer on the pilgrim route, I missed the company of other pilgrims. It was possible to walk for miles, without meeting a soul. The land was rich where it was not rocky, but much was uncultivated, for many peasants had moved away, fearing that the Moors would soon be coming to invade their country and take their lands from them.

After crossing the Lodesa the countryside became like nothing I had ever seen. The great plain extended for miles, but then, out of it, massive cliffs and ravines would rise, which were the dwelling-place of strange black and white butterflies, enormous eagles and trees with unearthly shapes perched in the oddly twisted outcrops of rocks. At last the road began to descend towards Soria and I saw the tall towers of its churches and cathedral reaching up out of the plain in front of me.

As soon as I arrived I asked everywhere after the Church of San Saturio, only to be told that it was some way out of the town along the banks of the River Duero.

I had pushed myself quite hard on the journey over the rough terrain and realised that I was beginning to feel ill, so I decided to rest at an inn not far from the cathedral. I had been thinking much about what the innkeeper at Zubiri had said about the language people had spoken before the Tower of Babel was struck down.

During my first night at the inn I remember dreaming distinctly that I could speak a language that would be understood by all men, but that for this I must be punished as the people in Babel were punished. I awoke sweating and feeling greatly afraid. I wondered what this language could be. Was it my ability to speak in tongues, or my music? What was the punishment that awaited me? That day I went for a walk to the market square a little way outside the centre of the town. There the masons were building a fine frieze into the tympanum above the main entrance to the church. The stonework had not been painted yet; nonetheless I could make out, not only the saints and angels of our Lord, but also musicians playing instruments - harps, psalters, fiddles and flutes. The musicians, as they had been represented by the master masons, looked lifelike, not at all idealised but as if they were real. They had each been assigned an individual place in the structure of the arch. They were not high up in the order of Creation as it was depicted there, below the angels and many of the other orders of men. But at least there was an order, and looking at the structure of the tympanum one might think that it was their music that bound together the other orders, because of the way it reflected the mathematical relationships in the bows and geometry of the arch.

The frieze set me thinking about myriad hopes and aspirations. I remembered how in my youth I had seen myself as part of a universe where the music I played reflected the divine harmony running through the whole of Creation. Yet my life had slipped into chaos, and it was hard to see what order there could be. I looked forward to Saint John's Day, when I hoped at last some order might be restored to my life.

The next day I felt strong enough to undertake the walk to the church where the Brotherhood's meeting was to take place. It was built on a cliff overlooking the River Duero. In fact its tower-like, octagonal shape seemed to grow out of the rock, like some geometric deformity.

It could be reached only by a narrow path winding its way along the rocky side of the valley. The church itself was entered by going into a cave in the rock-face at the end of the path, and then climbing endless spirals of stairs that were roughly hewn into the rocks inside the cave.

Other caves branched off on either side of the stairway. Some had been turned into small votive chapels. Others were meeting rooms. Others still led off into darkness. After my previous meeting with Tremgistus it was not difficult to see why such a place should have been chosen for a meeting of the Brotherhood.

The walls of the church proper were covered with strange painted pictures and symbols, including butterflies, chrysalid shapes and octograms. I noticed that a representation of the crucified Christ had a halo that was round like the moon, not trinitarian.

I spent some time getting my bearings in the church. Finally I found that one of the caves led off the main staircase and then doubled back on itself, opening out on to the staircase at knee level with an aperture of about one foot. It was just possible to squeeze round in such a way as to get a view of anyone coming into the cave. I decided that this would be the place where I would await the arrival of the Brotherhood on Saint John's Day.

I satisfied myself that the view was good and that I would be well enough hidden, even at night-time when the light would be coming from different sources. Then I decided that the time had come to leave Soria for the time being. I did not want to become known in the town.

I went back to the inn for my belongings.

I set off in the direction of the Abejar and Burgos in order to rejoin the pilgrim route. I travelled slowly and reluctantly. The weather was becoming hotter every day. That naked, dry heat drained me, bending the very rocks with the same power that robbed all living things there of their strength and energy. By the end of April it was impossible to ride between Sext and Nones. So I followed the custom of the locals and took to sleeping a little each afternoon.

After Abejar I travelled for miles through the desolate and uncultivated landscape to a tiny village called Quintanajar. There I met an elderly priest called Father Mateo, who took me to see a very ancient church built by the Visigothic people, those who, according to history books, had driven out the Romans. He pointed out the ancestral patterns on the wall, curious interweaving branches with leaves and animals, and showed me how the patterns suddenly stopped at the point where the Moors, in turn, had driven out the Visigoths.

I was elated to reach Burgos at last, where they were building a magnificent cathedral. It was thrilling to hear the great choir sing the new polyphonic music, in which parts interweave like vines or branches, creating the impression of a living thing.

I felt at ease in Burgos, so I stayed there for a month instead of continuing on the pilgrim route. Yet I was obsessed with returning to Soria. All my attention was focused on that Saint John's Day. By the time it came to leave I was counting every day, every hour.

By the beginning of June I was back in Soria, lying low and killing time. It was all I could do each day to stop myself from going out to the church to check my plans, or to see if there was any sign of the Brotherhood. I spent my time drinking in low taverns, riding out on futile excursions to the lands around the town, making up songs, practising the lute – anything to keep me occupied and unnoticed.

The day did come. I set out for the church in the early afternoon, since the meeting was due for the evening. The sun was still beating down. It was not the usual dry heat. It made me feel uncomfortable and I sweated a lot.

My plan was to climb the hills opposite the church on the north side of the river and keep a lookout in case any of the Brotherhood should arrive early. Then, an hour before sunset, I would cross the river by the main bridge and see what I could see.

From my lookout on the hill there was a good view of the church on the other side of the river. I was still fascinated by the way it rose out of the cliff face and by its octagonal shape, by the way its geometry contrasted with the unordered, flowing shapes of the rocks. I had a good view of the path leading to it. No one went to the church all the time I was there.

I made my way down the hills towards the bridge earlier than I had intended. There was a Cistercian monastery just to the east of the point where the bridge reached the other side of the river. I had heard that the monastery possessed the most beautiful cloisters, where there were arches that seemed miraculously to hang in the air; yet so far I had deliberately avoided making my presence known there. The monastery controlled all access to the path leading up to the church and I feared that perhaps there might be some connection between the monks and the Brotherhood. So, instead of using the bridge, I swam across the river, and then decided to make my way up to the church at a level just below that of the track leading to it, in the hope that I might not be seen.

I got down to the river and swam across without difficulty. When I reached the other side, I noticed that the atmosphere had become close and humid. The heat was going out of the day, but I still found myself covered in sweat. Swarms of tiny flies stuck to my face and clothes and hair. I looked up. Dark clouds were rolling in from the plains. I felt the first few drops of rain. There would be a thunderstorm later that evening or during the night.

In spite of the discomfort, I felt more secure in the rain and in the close, misty atmosphere, which made it less likely that my movements would be perceived. I climbed up to the church, confident that no one would have spotted me.

There was no door at the entrance leading into the church; the cave just swallowed up the path like an enormous, dark mouth.

By now it was pouring with rain. There was no one in sight. I made straight for the cave.

As I entered, there was a chill in the air that made me feel ill at ease. The atmosphere was even less that of a Christian place of worship than on my previous visit. Saturio was supposed to have been a saint who lived in the mountains here, and was distinguished by the fact that the holy life he had led meant that he had not aged, but still looked like a young man when he was martyred in his seventies. Yet the name was so much like the name of the Roman god Saturn. Nearby there was another church called San Polo, like Apollin, the pagan god in the Song of Roland who was worshipped by the Saracen. I wondered if this valley was still a place where pagan rites were practised. Something within me wanted to run away. I had come thus far, though, and I was determined to see it through.

The floor of the cave sloped up to the flight of roughly hewn steps leading into the main body of the church. At the bottom of the steps someone had placed two wooden pillars surmounted with carved geometrical shapes: a cube set on a cylinder on the left side and a sphere set on an octagonal plinth on the right. These had not been there at the time of my previous visit in March.

The church was deserted. I made my way up the steps. At the top I could make out the light of a candle burning. My eyes were adjusting to the darkness and now I could make out that on either side of the stairway there were openings in the walls that led off into further caves. In the distance I could hear the drip-dripping of water.

The sound echoed in the chill atmosphere, creating a sense of desolation and loneliness. It was only five minutes since I had entered the cave, yet already it seemed to me that perhaps there was no world beyond the cave's walls, that I was trapped in a region in the very depths of the earth from which there could never be any escape.

The light of the candle caused me to fear that maybe someone was already here after all. Then, beginning to worry in case any of the Brotherhood arrived earlier than I expected, I made my way to the cave where I had chosen to hide during my previous visit, and I squeezed my way into it.

I can still remember every nook, cranny and crevice in that cave where I lay, waiting for them. I can still smell the damp stone and see the trickle of water winding its way down the rock to the left of me, continuing down another crevice in the floor and out of sight, presumably to flow eventually, by some tortuous route, into the river below us.

The waiting lasted an eternity. I could just glimpse a zigzag of grey sky outside from which I could tell that night was closing in. It was still pouring with rain out there. I settled down for a long wait. And my mind drifted back over the past. In the meantime the monotonous pitter-patter of the rain outside and the drip-dripping of the water inside the cave had a hypnotic effect.

I must either have fallen asleep or gone into a trance-like state, because when I first heard the sound of human movement, everything was pitch-black.

It was the sound of footsteps in the distance that shook me out of my torpor. Someone was coming up the path to the entrance of the cave.

Then I heard voices. As the sound of the men walking and the voices became clearer, I realised they must have been carrying torches, because the cave was no longer pitch-black; I could see the opposite wall of the cave again. The lights weaved eerily and unpredictably in and out of one another at first, like will-o'-the-wisps. Then they became brighter, and eventually I made out ghostly, hooded human shadows dancing menacingly on the wall of the cave.

The first pair of men entered the cave. Each of them was bearing a torch. I could smell the pitch even before I saw them. The light was good and cast long shadows. I was frightened because the light would have been strong enough for me to be seen if they had looked down in my direction. Yet I did not dare move for fear of being heard.

I saw clearly that one of them was Fabricius; the other was Quintus. They had pushed back their hoods now that they were out of the rain. They were soaked to the skin. Their dress was strange. They were both wearing long black robes, with hoods attached, like Benedictine monks, only the material was much more costly and embroidered round the skirt at knee level and round the chest. The pattern was a series of joined and interlocking circles, like the Arabic sign for eight. Their belts were tied with gold or bronze chains rather than the usual hemp or leather belts. On the thongs round their necks they wore not crosses but two interlocking rings, one of which was silver and the other bronze or gold.

They went straight past where I was hiding and on up to the church.

Next came Antonius and Tremgistus. They were dressed the same as the other two, but their bearing was more formidable. Tremgistus was a tall man, and his deeply lined face and white hair exuded a spiritual, or rather occult, power. I remembered our previous meeting. It was not difficult to see how easy it was for him to exert over others the power he did. He was the one most at home in this place, himself an embodiment of the menace of its atmosphere. It was as if this were his territory. Both in Tremgistus and in this place were the same tensions and energies, the same ambiguous combination of the occult and the mystical.

Antonius was small and old, hunched, blind. There was still vigour in his step, though. He too was in his element here. I remember that, as they passed, Antonius' unseeing eyes turned directly towards me. They were all but glazed white, and I became terrified, feeling that he could sense I was there even though he could not see. Yet he did not react. Either he was unaware of my presence or else he had chosen not to let on. His blind eyes struck real terror into me for a moment. Then, as soon as the moment of fear passed, he looked once more like an ineffectual little old man. Could he really have been responsible for all the ill that had befallen me?

After they had passed I heard Tremgistus reassuring him that all was ready for the rite this evening. This was all I overheard them say to each other as they passed.

Only one more man came, a giant of a fellow whom I could not recognise. He was not bare-headed like the others. It was the helmet that made it impossible for me to recognise his face. He was wearing the helmet and the clothes of a knight, and was dressed all in black. His bearing was not that of a young man, but he did not appear to have lost any of his strength. He did not speak.

Outside, the rain was still pouring down and in the distance I could hear thunder from the east. I remembered the saying that thunder from the east means there will be bloodshed the following year.

Soon all five men had gathered upstairs. I could hear them talking. I decided that the time had come to observe whatever it was they were doing.

Slowly, painfully slowly, I crawled back down the cave and stepped out of my hiding-place. The presence of the tall man in the knightly helmet made me wish I had come armed with more than the small knife I had tucked into my belt underneath my habit. He had a sword and armour. If it came to a fight I would be hard-pressed to defend myself against him, but it was too late to worry about that now.

I crept up the stairs, one step at a time. As I approached the candlelit room where they were meeting, I overheard something of their conversation.

'How can you be sure about these visions?' Fabricius was asking.

Tremgistus' voice was harsh and cutting as he retorted, 'If you have so little faith in your spiritual elders, then you have no business here...'

'It is hard,' Antonius intervened, his odd, singsong voice almost cracking in an attempt to sound conciliatory, 'for someone to understand, who does not himself have the powers of prophecy. Yet I pray with all my heart that as you attend the rite this evening, you may come to know the truth more deeply.'

'I pray so too,' Fabricius said with false humility, 'but what am I to say to my Staufer masters? They are the lawful Emperors and will brook no competition.'

'Our interest is not in the rulers of this world but of the world to come,' Tremgistus snapped.

At this, Fabricius fell silent.

Next the conversation turned to talk about a person they referred to as 'the One'. I was deeply worried by what I heard. Quintus assured the others that 'the One' was kept under watch and that all 'the One's' movements were being followed.

'He did well,' said Tremgistus, 'to come through the trial. The signs that he was the chosen one are even more promising now than before. Yet there is still doubt...'

'Perhaps, this very evening, all will be revealed,' said Antonius.

All the time, the tall man with the helmet was silent. Quintus, too, looked uneasy.

I shuddered. By 'the One' surely they meant me. Did they know that I was in the church? As I reflected on Fabricius' words, suddenly I realised what great danger I was in, not just from these people but from the Staufers. I thought of what Fabricius said. If the Staufers truly thought I had any pretence to power, they would seek me out and kill me, unhesitatingly, whether I posed a real threat or not.

I stood in the shadows as the candles flickered and cast shadows that danced and weaved weird patterns on the bare rock walls of the corridor outside the room in which they were sitting.

At last Quintus raised his hand and said it was time to begin. They went up the main body of the church.

I followed. As I went up the stairs I became aware of where the candlelight was shining from. It was a small side-chapel built into a cave leading off from the main stairway. There was an altar. Behind it was a wall-painting representing Saint Catherine: something was missing from the chapel; it took me a few moments to realise that there was no crucifix.

I looked into the room they had just left. It was a largish chamber, half cave, hollowed out of the rocks. In the middle of it was a carved, oblong table surrounded by the chairs where they had been sitting. A window looked out over the hills on the other side of the river. Through it I could see that the rain was still beating down and in the distance, over the hills, every now and then there was lightning followed some time after by the distant rumbling of the thunder.

I made my way further up the winding stairs, past another chapel, and then I saw the main body of the church.

The five of them were sitting in a half-circle in front of the altar. They had brought their torches with them and I could see the paintings on the walls of the chapel dancing in the light of the flames. In the eerie light, the caterpillars and butterflies looked uncanny, almost alive. I noticed the pictures of Christ, one of Him turning water into wine, another of Him rising from the grave, and another of Him sitting, meditating. To my mind there was a look of hurt about the face, as if He were a sad figure, not triumphing but in some way unable to reconcile himself to the material aspect of his nature.

I noticed too that all round the ceiling of the church there were signs of the zodiac. Also there were several depictions of Moses, or at least a figure I took to be Moses, since he was horned and bearing a stick or wand round which was wrapped a serpent, such as Moses used when he was in Egypt.

I saw all these things from behind a pillar as the five Brothers began chanting. To begin with, the ceremony followed the pattern of a normal mass, and I was reassured. Tremgistus was officiating. Then I noticed that were no references to our Lord as the Messiah. Instead they used the formulae Lord of Sabbaoth or Lord of Hosts. Also, there was no host to be consecrated.

On the altar there was a wooden statue of San Saturio. The saint was bearded and bearing a staff, like a bishop's staff, yet curiously formed so that it could easily be mistaken for a scythe. His face was an extraordinary mixture of youthfulness and age, and was so life-like that in the candlelight I almost thought I could see it move.

Then the prayer departed from the usual pattern. At the point when the consecration would normally have begun, they called, chanting after Tremgistus, upon the spirits of Saturio, of Catherine of the Holy Wheel, and of the Pure Ones who had gone before and who would return, purified by flames. Then they called on the spirits of the circling planets, the sun and the moon. Then Tremgistus and Antonius went into a trance, and began a chanting in languages I could not understand. Their chanting was a low, other-worldly droning, which every now and then would rise in pitch as they became more and more excited. They raised their arms as they prayed.

I head the others calling rhythmically on the god they addressed as the Thrice Great. As far as I could make out, the litany was in a mixture of Latin and Greek and vernacular languages of sorts. I picked out odd phrases: 'Thrice Great One... Send us the spirits... send us the Emperor... send us Carolus... the Majestic one... send us the Singer... King of Jerusalem... the New David...' The rite was a bizarre mixture of Catholicism, Catharism and necromancy. All the time I could hear the thunder and the sound of rain beating down on the roof of the church. Through the narrow windows I could see the flashes of lightning.

I became aware of the appalling coincidence. They had been, and perhaps still were, under the impression that I was chosen for some special role in an event involving mysterious powers. There they were, by means of their rite, trying to summon the spirits in which they believed. The coincidence was that I was there, as if they had evoked me.

As I realised this, there was a deafening clap of thunder, which stopped them singing and chanting for a moment. A chill ran through me and I wondered if I was not after all a spirit summoned from the cool of the earth. Yet I fought the feeling, forcing myself to remember my past, who I was, forcing myself to feel the warm flow of blood through my veins, reminding myself that I was a creature of flesh.

At last I decided that I could stand no more. I had nothing to thank these people for. Whatever it was they believed in had led them to interfere in my life in a way that had jeopardised, not only my happiness in this world, but also my immortal soul.

I had been toying with the idea of creeping down the stairs, rushing back to town and there denouncing them to the Church authorities. If I were quick they could be caught in flagrante, celebrating the rite.

This was not to be, however. I was just about to turn and run: when I heard one of them, I think it must have been Antonius, half shouting, half screaming the words 'He is here!' The sound of his voice cut through the chanting and brought it to a sudden halt.

I did not know whether this shout referred to my presence or whether it was part of the rite. As he shouted I became aware also of a loud crack as lightning struck outside. The flash was just outside the window and for a moment the whole of the church lit up with a brilliant, jagged light, then plunged back into darkness.

The torches and the candles were still burning, but in contrast to the lightning the darkness was total.

Instead of running, I decided to confront them. I stepped out from behind the pillar and stared at them.

Their reactions varied. Quintus was pale and shaken at the sight of me. Fabricius looked nervous, though not to the same extent. I could not judge the reaction of the tall man, who was still wearing his helmet, though he stood up. Tremgistus smiled at me. It was a wild, mad smile. He took Antonius' sleeve and pointed him in my direction. Now Antonius' blind eyes also stared, right into the very depths of my soul. He smiled a smile of satisfaction.

Tremgistus continued, still in the role of officiant, addressing me as he would a summoned spirit: 'Are you He, or are you the Traitor?'

His eyes burnt right through me. I felt paralysed. What was I supposed to say?

'I ask you the second time. Are you the One, or are you the Traitor.'

By now my fear was beginning to turn to anger.

'I ask you the third and last time. If you are the One, then give us a sign; if you are the Traitor, be gone or prepare to meet your death!'

The lightning was moving away. The thunder was less loud. I lost control and began shouting: 'Who are you? Who do you think I am?'

'He is the Traitor,' said Tremgistus slowly, menacingly. He turned to Antonius, whose expression had changed, the moment I spoke, to a look of ashen disappointment and repressed, smouldering anger.

'Not yet,' he said. 'He may be putting us to the test.' The others looked on. Probably they were out of their depth, and intimidated by the storm and the strangeness of their surroundings.

'Are you not the One, the Chosen, the Anointed... ?'

I did not understand what they meant, so I pressed them further.

'I am Walter von der Ouwe, son of Adam von der Ouwe, a cartwright. I am a wandering singer and soldier. Nothing more. Not to my knowledge. Who do you take me for? Tell me. For God's sake!'

Tremgistus' eyes glowed fiercely. He grabbed a torch from the wall and came towards me. I drew my knife and held it out to threaten him. I was the closest to the stairway and had the advantage of being able to see them all. I feared none of them, should it come to a fight, with the exception of the tall man wearing the helmet.

Tremgistus looked round from one to the other. 'My friends,' he said, 'it might be that we were mistaken about this boy. We, the Brotherhood of Prayer of Charlemagne, gave succour to this child, paying for his education, keeping him from the ways of sin. Yet he is ungrateful. He hates us. It was written that there would be a traitor, a betrayer, a harbinger of the Antichrist. Seize him!'

This last order took me by surprise. I should have turned and run, but I was so mesmerised by Tremgistus that I did not expect violent action.

It was the helmeted man who, before I had time to think, had grabbed the hand in which I held the knife, grasping it with an iron grip and twisting my arm behind my back so that I was forced to let it drop. The man, whoever he was, was inordinately strong, and for the time being I could do nothing to resist.

It was Antonius who spoke next. 'Do not judge too soon. I say he might yet be the One. This might be a test of our faith, of our art. We must not judge too soon. We need a test, the trials of fire and of water.'

'What is that?' Fabricius asked. He was looking from me to the others, nervously.

'If he is of the Reborn,' Tremgistus answered, 'then it is written that neither flame nor water will hurt him.'

'And if they do?' Quintus intervened.

Tremgistus smiled cruelly. 'Then,' he said, 'he is no more than a cuckoo in the nest, the Traitor, one who, uninitiated, impure, has witnessed one of the Brotherhood's rituals. Such a person might betray us to those who would not understand. If he is such a one, then he will not survive the trial.'

Tremgistus came towards me, brandishing the torch. He described circles with it before my face. At any moment he would thrust it into me, and was delaying only in the hope that I would say something which would show I was who he thought I was – or maybe he was just enjoying watching the fear and suffering on my face. The helmeted man hesitated, yet seemed deliberately to be loosening his grip on my arms.

'Wait,' said Fabricius. Even as he spoke I could hear the thunderstorm growing closer. The lightning lit up the room every few seconds. 'Surely there is no point...'

The sequence of events that followed took only a split second. First I struggled free, or was allowed to go free. Tremgistus saw this and lunged towards me with the torch, aiming to thrust the flames into my face. I ducked under the flame, grabbed the old man round the middle and pushed him backwards towards the window with all my strength. As he fell to the floor, he took the blind Antonius with him.

I fell forwards and lost my balance also. As I did so the whole building was shaken by a deafening crack of thunder. The room was lit brilliantly with dazzling white light. A charge of raw, destructive energy ran through the chapel. I felt my hair stand on end and all my skin tingled with shock.

The next thing I remember was scrambling to my feet and seeing that the two old men, Antonius and Tremgistus, were engulfed in flames. All else was dark. They fell over and rolled on the ground, but the flames grew stronger. Flames began to lick up the painted walls of the church.

The two men were still screaming, Antonius was huddled and uttering little, bitter yelps as the flames burnt him. Tremgistus was howling, more like a wild animal than a man. He was writhing, moving about the floor in unpredictable lurches. Suddenly he lunged towards Fabricius, who until that moment had been staring on, transfixed. Tremgistus grasped Fabricius, whether intending that he should share his fate or hoping for help no one will ever know.

Nor could I tell whether the fire had been started by the torch that Tremgistus had brandished at me or whether the cause had been the lightning. In any case, the fire was already spreading throughout the church. The smoke was appalling and the stench of Antonius' burning flesh was sticking in my throat, bringing back memories of that appalling day when I saw Uqhart burn.

I turned round. The helmeted man had already turned to make for the stairs. Quintus and I were left standing together.

I grabbed him round the throat. 'You tell me the truth now and I might let you go. Were you responsible for keeping me at Frankenburc while Uqhart was tried and burnt?'

'What can I say?' he stammered.

'The truth,' I said. 'Only if I think you are telling me the truth will I let you go.'

'No,' he said, 'I was told to keep you at the monastery, that much is true, but I did not know why. I did not find out about Uqhart and your father until afterwards.'

'Tell me now. Who is behind this? Is it them?'

I signalled towards Antonius, who was motionless now, his flesh still burning, and to Tremgistus, who had released Fabricius and was collapsing to his knees, still engulfed in flames. Fabricius was not on fire, though he had been burnt by Tremgistus' embrace. He was staggering towards us. I held my sword out. He was sandwiched between my blade and the fire.

'You too,' I said to Fabricius. 'If you want to live, you must tell me exactly what you want from me.'

Quintus replied, 'We do not know, Walter. Surely you must know. Antonius' visions, Tremgistus' charts...'

'Or maybe Tremgistus gets his instructions from other sources,' Fabricius butted in.

'You mean from the spirits of the dead?' I asked.

'No,' said Fabricius, 'there are more powerful forces still. Powers of this earth.'

'You must know,' said Quintus. 'You must know there are powers within powers, wheels within wheels. In all of this we are just as much victims as you.'

'But what do you want from me?'

'What do we want from you?' said Fabricius. 'Surely we should be asking what you want from us. Whatever it is that binds our fate together, it is not over yet.'

I did not push them into the flames. For that moment I believed they were as confused as I was. I looked once again in the direction of Antonius; surely he was dead now. Tremgistus was still burning, though less fiercely. He lay still, face down on the ground. I was convinced he would not be able to survive. He and Antonius would take whatever secret they bore to the grave with them.

The wall in front of us was beginning to break away and the whole of the floor seemed to be trembling. I realised that it would only be minutes before the whole of the rest of the structure of the church collapsed on our heads.

I turned on my heels and ran down the stairs, through the pitch dark, as if I were descending into the very depths of the earth, the smoke billowing all round. I heard the sound of running behind me, so someone must have escaped, certainly the helmeted man would have been able to follow closely. Yet he never caught up.

I stumbled out of the church, and ran down to the river. I swam across it to wash the stench off my clothes and because I still feared the monastery, which I would have had to pass if I had used the road. By now the monks would surely have seen the fire and would be on their way to the church.

Only when I reached the opposite bank did I stop to see the spectacle of the tower, the roof and part of the walls now partly collapsed, burning like a torch against the black night sky, as the lightning continued to zigzag overhead and the clouds which the flames and lightning illuminated rolled past angrily like giant, clenched fists.

I thought for a moment about the other fires that had determined my life: Babenberch, Uqhart, now this one. Two fires had destroyed what I loved, and now a third destroyed the destroyers.

As I looked up, I was sure that I saw, tumbling down the hill, three balls of flame, which I took to be the burning remains of Tremgistus, Antonius and - who or what else? At that moment the thought was a satisfying one.

I walked off into the night, back up towards the town, which I planned to skirt before continuing on my way.

# XVII

## The Star

✠

I walked all through that night and the next day, over the rocky plains in the burning heat of the day, along rivers in which I bathed to cool down, through tiny villages with their clusters of poor houses and fields where meagre crops were withering in the heat.

The peasants all looked pinched with hunger and this look was exaggerated by the swarthiness of their skin and the way their eyes seemed to stare from vast sockets.

I wanted to get back to Germany to find out more. The questions were going round and round in my head. Was there another power behind the Brotherhood? If so, was it spiritual, occult or political? Who was the man in the helmet? What did they mean by 'the One'?

I rested at an inn on the second night, walked again all through the next day until the heat became unbearable, and finally reached a little town called Villatoro.

The town consisted of twenty or thirty shacks, three of four larger wooden houses arranged in a square, a large church, which was quite newly built, and, attached to it, a stone house with an octagonal tower. It was so hot that the white stone of the house seemed to melt away and then grow again in front of my eyes, like a living thing.

I was pretty sure that this must be the house of a religious community, and I was desperate with thirst, tiredness and hunger.

So I knocked on the great oak door. Perhaps it was just chance that I stumbled on this place; yet it all seems to fit into a pattern.

I was welcomed by a tall, bearded, white-haired man dressed all in black, with a simple steel crucifix hanging from a thong round his neck. His complexion was ruddy and his face deeply lined. I explained in my best Latin that I was a wandering singer and scholar, that I had once lived as a Cistercian and that I was in need of food and a bed, for which I would be willing to pay. He told me that he was the almoner, Father Joano, and that this house belonged to the Knights of the Temple. Only three men lived there, who had grown too old to fight, and they ran the house as a staging-post for those heading in and out of Spain. They stored equipment there and took in travellers like myself.

I had heard of the Order of the Knights of the Temple, yet I knew little about them other than that they were a wealthy military order and that their aim was to recapture the Holy Land.

Father Joano led me up wooden spiral stairs to a small attic room. The walls were of white painted plaster and the high window let in plenty of light. The floor was wooden and there were straw mattresses for travellers to sleep on, together with linen sheets and woollen blankets. The room was clean and I was to have it all to myself.

I was the only traveller there and I never saw either of the other two Templar knights. I stayed in the room, ate in silence with Father Joano and tried to make plans. My past seemed entirely unreal to me, probably because I was so tired. The only future I could envisage for myself was to return to Franconia, or maybe to try to attach myself to a lord on the way.

On the third day I woke to find someone else in the room with me. On the mattress opposite me sat a man, probably in his late fifties, with short cropped grey hair. He wore a long grey robe. Round his neck hung a chain with an octagonal gold pendant at his chest. The man's brow was deeply furrowed, and his eyebrows formed a V-shape above his eyes. From his bearing I could tell that he was someone used to commanding respect.

It was obvious that he had not slept in the room but had been waiting for me to wake up.

'Walter, I am the Master of the Templars in this region. I make this suggestion to you. Take this map and follow it to Richerenches. There is one of the larger Templar houses. You will see others marked on the way where you may stay. At Richerenches you may join the Templar community. If you are patient and diligent you may become a full Knight of the Temple. We know that you are seeking, Walter, and we may be able to help you find what you are seeking.'

I tried to interrupt, saying, 'But how can you know about me? What do you know?' He raised a hand to silence me. He said, 'I am only the bearer of a message. But if you take up our suggestion I am told that a Visitor will come who will make everything clear – not here but some time in the future. All I can give you at the moment by way of answers is this.'

He gave me a piece of parchment, bowed and left. I was too sleepy, too much taken by surprise to stop him. The parchment had odd figures, half hieroglyph, half pictures, arranged into a circle and numbered from one to eleven. The first figure was like a Fool chasing a butterfly with a net. Then there was a young man performing magic of some sort. Next there was a beautiful woman dressed as a priestess sitting on a throne. There was something familiar about the pictures, but what it was I could not tell.

Later, I pressed Father Joano to tell me more about the Master. I showed him the parchment.

'In my view, there are two things you should bear in mind,' he said. 'Firstly, what you are given on trust you should show to no man. Secondly, I know nothing more about this man than you do, but if I did I should not reveal anything to you without instruction; that is the way our Order works. The enemy we fight is great and merciless. One day I am sure you will understand this need for secrecy. All things have their time and their place.'

I spent the rest of the day on my own again, playing my lute and trying to decide what to do for the best. At Nones I went to eat with Father Joano and told him that I would accept the Master's offer. Father Joano smiled broadly. He led me into the yard between the house and the church, where there was a stable. Three fine horses were there and I was allowed my pick. I chose a strong looking horse called Astrum. We drank wine together that evening, and I probably told Father Joano too much about my past life. He was a good listener, smiling and commenting in just the right way to draw me on.

I left for Richerenches early the next day. The journey was uneventful, though at each new place I arrived I could not help wondering if this would be where I would meet the so-called Visitor, or if there would be some clue as to what was expected of me.

But nothing happened.

By and large, I tried to keep myself to myself. Now that the Templars had, for whatever reason, taken me under their wing, I felt a need to prove myself worthy, and it seemed that the best way of doing so was to draw as little attention to myself as possible.

Whenever there was an opportunity to sing before others though, I must confess I found it hard to resist, since this is such an important part of my life.

I spent much time studying the chart I had been given. There were eleven signs in a circle. The first three I have mentioned. Others looked to me variously like an emperor, an empress, a priest, young lovers, an angel bearing scales, a chariot, a hermit, and a massive wheel. I tried to understand what they meant. They seemed both full of meaning and meaningless at the same time. I wondered if they referred to me, and whether or not the chart was complete.

When I arrived at Richerenches I was welcomed as if I were expected. Two of the younger brothers, a German called Wolfbert from Saxony and a man from the north of France called Oliver, befriended me and helped me to get used to Templar life.

The Master of the House there was Raymond of Perpignan, a fierce-looking man with silver hair and a tall, graceful head, which contrasted with his strong, athletic body. He said that initially I should live as a sergeant. He explained everything that it was necessary for me to know and was very kind, yet at the same time showed me no special favours. Every time I tried to direct the conversation towards the aspects of the past that most interested me, he smiled and evaded the question. Yet he seemed to know a lot about me.

Since much of the day was spent in silence anyhow, conversation being, by order of the Rule, restricted to necessities only, I had to work up courage to mention these things.

I slept in a draughty corner of the hayloft, with two other sergeants for company. One was a surly, silent man, a peasant who was nonetheless, in his way, intensely religious, and another man, whose father had been a ministerial in the service of the lords of the region, and who was well-meaning but so methodical that it was almost painful.

The Templar buildings at Richerenches consisted firstly of an entrance hall with a door leading on to the main street of the town; this hall was built of stone. Leading off it was the large wooden building in which the ordinary knights and men slept, the knights at floor level and the rest of us in the hayloft. Annexed to this was one of the stables. Opposite our wooden house was the stone-built accommodation where the leaders and important visitors slept, and where, it was said, there was an underground treasury. To the left of this was the octagonal chapel and a series of other smaller buildings, some of which were used for administration and others for reasons I never discovered. Behind these buildings were more stables, and then there was the heathland we used for military training.

The day started at midnight, when we got up, put a mantle on over our shirt and pants, and made our way, in silence, to the chapel. There we said thirteen Our Fathers. Next, strictly observing the order of silence, we went to the stables to be sure that our horses were fed and watered properly. I loved this moment when the night was fine and there were stars in the sky, but when there was frost, it could be misery.

We slept a little after that until dawn, when we said mass. After a short period of study, there followed the canonical services of Prime, Terce and Sext, which were said one after the other, not spread out over a period of hours as had been the custom of the Cistercians. This was so that we could devote the rest of the day to our tasks: administration, looking after the horses, military training, practising fighting with lance, sword and mace, going on rides and marches to build up our endurance, engaging in small tournaments where one side would play the Saracen and the other the Christian knights. Sometimes, too, we would receive instruction in siege techniques and would learn how to build the great war engines that could knock down town walls and breach ramparts.

At the first meal of the day we, the knights and sergeants, were served first and the squires and stewards afterwards. We had our own bowls and cups, unlike at the monastery at Frankenburc, where we had to share. We ate well, for we needed good food to survive the rigours of the training. Any leftovers were given to the poor. We observed silence during meals, while a brother would read from the Bible or another sacred text.

In the afternoon we continued our tasks, breaking only for Nones and Vespers. At sunset, when Compline was rung, we assembled to drink watered-down wine and to receive our orders for the following day. Thereafter, from Compline to Prime, silence was kept.

The discipline was very strict. We could do nothing without permission. I even had to ask to set down songs that were in my head. I consoled myself with the thought that the purpose of this was to make us a well-organised fighting force when we were in the Holy Land, and that there were other Templars, in the Holy Land at that very moment, who were living by exactly the same rule, waiting for a larger Christian army to come so that they could lead the final overthrow of the Saracen in Jerusalem.

One evening, shortly after I arrived, I asked for an audience with the Master of the House. I was going to ask him directly if he knew anything about the Visitor I was to expect, or if he could tell me about the chart I had been given. I still remember the way he stared at me, smiling, weighing me up, his eyes glinting in the light of the candles burning on the table, next to the earthenware cup of milk and herbs that were served to us as a nightcap.

He said that there were secrets he could not divulge until I was a full member of the Order. He said that, in spite of the expense, I was to be made a full knight, since reports he had of me were extremely good, and it was certain that I would be a valuable asset to the Templars.

He told me in more detail about the new Crusade, how regular meetings were taking place in Compiègne under the leadership of the young Thibaut, Count of Champagne and Brie. He told me the names of many great ones who had taken the cross. The names meant little enough to me then, though now they are all too familiar.

It became clear to me that I would get no more information from this source. Yet there was hope for me. Perhaps, just perhaps, when I was made a full knight, I would find out more.

There were periods of instruction with the older knights, during which we would learn about the exploits of the Templars and the situation of their various fortresses. I loved the sound of the names of the Templar castles in the Holy Land: Tortosa, Krak des Chevaliers, Chastel Rouge, Belfort. I delighted in the stories told by the other knights about the great deeds of the Order, even those they told about their rivalry with the Hospitallers. At times I wondered if the Templars did not hate the Hospitallers more than the Saracen. Yet that was all talk. The brothers' idealism was tempered with hard-headed practicality when it carne to military matters. For example, it was on the advice of the Order that Richard of England had refrained from taking Jerusalem in the year of our Lord 1191, though he was just twelve miles away from the city. This was because the Templars knew that, once taken, it would have been impossible to defend with the forces available.

When I had time, I wrote ballads based on the anecdotes I heard, and sang them back to those who had witnessed or performed them. This won me a number of friends, though there were those who regarded singing as a superficial and wasteful luxury when there was serious military work to be done in order to recapture Jerusalem from the Saracen.

I read what Bernard of Cîteaux wrote about the military Orders, comparing our life with that of lay knights. He mocked the lay knights for having soft hands in their iron gloves, for their beautiful, perfumed hair, their finely wrought helmets, the way they wore cloth of the latest fashion, coloured or quilted silk, draped over their chain-mail, bearing blazoned, almond-shaped shields as symbols of their own vanity, galloping through fields of flowers towards eternal damnation.

We Templars, on the other hand, he described as shaving our heads so that our helmets would fit more closely, allowing our beards to grow, wearing no coloured garments, bearing arms without decoration, hunting ferocious animals only in our spiritual battles, being as terrible as lions to our enemies yet meek as lambs towards Christians.

The thought of Hildegunde and how much I loved her never left me. I tried to resign myself that I would never see her again and to turn my thoughts instead to Jerusalem, to tell myself that to work towards the recapture of Jerusalem was in every way more noble than trying to lure Hildegunde away from her convent. Yet there were times when I was tempted to walk out of the house and do just that.

I was interested in what many of the older knights had to say about the Saracen. Those who had been to the Holy Land respected our mortal enemy as being fine knights in every way; only they did not love Christ.

I was reminded once more of Uqhart, and how much I had learnt from him. How could it be that such good men, and there were many more besides Uqhart, were condemned to eternal fires and damnation because they did not know Christ? I asked one of the other brothers this. He laughed at me and quoted the verse from Matthew's Gospel: '*Judge not that ye be not judged.*'

Often the thought had occurred to me that there is more to

the relationship between the Saracen and the Templars than is admitted. Could it be that there is some complicity, some deeper motivation to the history between our peoples, which goes beyond, which goes deeper than the superficial struggle for Jerusalem?

During the spring of the year of our Lord 1212 there was more and more excitement as we heard news of the plans being made for the new Crusade. Thibaut of Champagne, who was to have led the campaign, had sent emissaries to Doge Dandalo in Venice. There, after mass in Saint Mark's, the Doge had received the envoys as supplicants, raised them up in front of the cheering crowds, and promised them food, drink and lodgings for four thousand five hundred knights, nine thousand squires and twenty thousand foot, and in addition fifty galleys to transport them to wherever the leaders decided. All for eighty-five thousand silver marks.

When I first heard this, I was overjoyed. At last the great expedition was to start that would free Jerusalem, in which I would be able to take part. It never occurred to me, or to any of us, that eighty-five thousand marks might be too much money to raise. It was, after all, less than the English paid for the release of King Richard. I knew that there were some, like the Bishop of Autun, who were suspicious. He was planning to sail directly from Marseilles to Syria. But I thought that he was just being churlish.

It was only later, when Thibaut had died and Boniface of Montferrat took over the leadership of the Crusade, that I too became suspicious. Could it have been that Thibaut's untimely death was divine punishment for the rashness with which he concluded the treaty with the Doge? Or was some human hand involved? At the beginning of Lent I was called once more to the Master.

He told me that I was to be received as a full knight at Whitsun.

At one point during our interview I remember him musing, 'It cannot be easy for you, all the things that have occurred to you during the course of your life. But one day everything will become clear to you, if not to the rest of us.'

I was taken off guard and did not press him further. Besides, I had grown used to waiting. All those midnights in the chapel, the mornings mucking out the stables, seeing to the horses, chopping vegetables for the communal soup, teaching the use of the bow, practising close combat, reading and meditating – those months seemed to last an eternity. Yet there was something good about the waiting.

The one regret I had was that to take orders would signify a final break with Hildegunde. It would not be an act of betrayal, for it was probably what Hildegunde would have wanted. Yet as a gesture, as an act of commitment, it was even more final than marrying another.

At last Whitsunday came. How I hoped that this ceremony would provide the key that I would eventually be able to use to unlock the knowledge I sought.

I shall remember what happened till my dying day.

I thought I was fully prepared for the ceremony, yet this is what happened.

I woke before dawn as usual, and tended the horses. Then I went to the antechapel and waited alone, spending an hour in silent contemplation as instructed. The doors were bound with ropes. The stewards and grooms were never admitted into chapel at this hour of the day. They either rested or began work early.

It seemed an eternity before the very first rays of dawn broke over the horizon, which I could see from the narrow slit window. The sky slowly turned from black into a dull, greyish mauve. There was no other light in the antechapel and, despite the time of year, it was quite cold.

The moment the first gold of the sun appeared on the horizon the doors were opened. First of all the Master and another knight approached me and asked, as was the custom, 'Do you seek the companionship of the Order of the Temple and participation in its temporal and spiritual goods?' I replied that I did.

'You seek a great thing,' he continued, 'yet you know the harsh precepts of the Order. From the outside we appear well dressed, well mounted and well equipped. Consider, however, the austerities of the Order, for when you wish to be on this side of the sea, you will be beyond it, and when you wish to be on the other side of the sea, you will be here. When you wish to sleep you must be awake, and when you wish to eat you must go hungry. Can you bear all this for the honour of God and the safety of your soul?'

I said I could and would. I remained kneeling on the flagstone floor, according to custom.

I was asked the usual questions: whether I was married or promised to another Order, whether or not I was born a free man and legitimate, whether or not I had bribed anyone to gain admittance to the Order, whether or not I had any secret infirmity that would inhibit my service, whether or not I was in debt, and so on and so on... Anyway, I was able to swear allegiance to the Order with a clear conscience.

Then the Master undid the ropes that bound the doors to the chapel. Two brothers came from within and led me into the chapel itself. I knelt in the centre facing the altar, as I had been instructed. In the chapel there was an unearthly deep-red light. It was as if the dawn sun were shining through a sea of blood. The scent of the incense was acrid, and the smoke from the incense thick in the air. The other knights were all assembled, and were sitting or kneeling, lining the walls of the chapel. Each was reciting or chanting a different Templar prayer, quietly, so that the chapel seemed to hum, as with the sound of giant bees.

I could make out the master of ceremonies in the odd light. It was not Raymond of Perpignan but another man who was of medium height and build. I noticed straight away that his eyebrows almost met in the middle and formed a V-shape. His lips were thin, and the shape of his mouth echoed that of his eyebrows. His nose too was long and pointed. It was the same man who had visited me in my room at Villatoro. He frightened me.

I was presented to him and told that he was the Grand Master of the region. It was then that something unexpected happened, or at least something of which I had not been warned.

He picked up the crucifix from the altar and carried it to the centre of the chapel where I knelt. He told me that I was to spit on the crucifix to prove my allegiance to the Order. As he uttered these words the chanting of the other knights stopped. All eyes turned towards me.

I was horrified. In fact I nearly panicked as memories of Tremgistus crowded in on my mind. I began to wonder if this man was a successor to the Brotherhood, a new Tremgistus. Yet I controlled myself. Rather suffer any humiliation, I thought, than run the risk of losing the thread, of living a life without answers. I remember the atmosphere of tension. A brighter, pinker light was beginning to stream in through the narrow windows of the chapel now. There I was, a young man, untried as yet in battle, surrounded by these hardened warriors of body and of soul, being ordered to profane what we all held sacred.

I did not spit.

The Master ordered me again.

I said I would never spit on the spiritual idea of the Crucifixion of Christ. There was no movement from the other knights. I detected neither sympathy nor antagonism. They just stared.

'Then spit on the wood and metal!' shouted the Master.

I did so. But to this day I swear it was only on the wood and metal I spat, not on Christ Himself.

The Master smiled and said that we should press on with the ceremony. He asked me to swear an oath, 'I will imitate the death of my Lord, because as Christ laid down his life for me, so I am prepared to lay down my life for my brothers.' I did this without hesitation.

Then I was asked if I knew the source of all true meditation. I replied that I did not.

No sooner had I spoken than three of the younger knights walked up to me and stared at me for a moment or two. Then two of them moved suddenly to grab my arms, forced me forwards so that I was lying flat, face down on the ground, then the third stripped me from the waist down. I hated being naked and tried to struggle. I almost got free before the Master ordered me to be still if I wished to be admitted to the Order.

I craned round and saw one of the older monks come forward. He knelt down and kissed me on the base of my spine. I was shocked. But as soon as he had returned to his place I was released.

There was silence.

Then the Master pronounced gravely that unless I released the power of contemplation in such a way that it would run throughout my whole body, I would never fight like a true Templar, and never have the strength to serve God.

Now I know that this refers to the secret Templar spiritual method, which anatomises the body into spiritual zones, locating a source of spiritual energy in the base of the spine which, when released, can be led through the spine and into the head, the seat of intelligence. These disciplines enhance the powers of travelling through time which I acquired in the cell at Aletus, and which, in my way, I am now using. Yet I should write no more of this, for it is secret knowledge.

Then I was enjoined to preserve chastity, the good usages and the good customs of the Order, and never to allow any Christian man or woman to be killed or unjustly disinherited, to give good account of any property that the Order might entrust to me, and never to leave the Order without the permission of my superiors.

By now brilliant golden light filled the chapel. The rest of the ceremony took the form of a normal mass. After I had taken the bread I returned to kneel once more in the middle of the chapel. Two knights came up to me. One of them moved slowly behind me. He grabbed hold of my arms so that I would not be able to struggle. The other raised his hand and struck me as hard as he could on the side of the head. It was a sharp, hard blow and nearly knocked me out.

I tried to regain my senses, though the room was still spinning; I stared in front of me. This blow was the *collée*, which signified that I had been accepted into the Order. I was overjoyed.

After the final chants I was led from the chapel to the antechapel on the far side. I had never been there before, since it was part of the house accessible only to full members of the Order.

This was the moment I had been waiting for. At last, I thought, there would be some word. Could it be that the Brotherhood of Prayer of Charlemagne was linked with the Templars? Or were they opposed to one another? What had it all to do with the Crusade that was being planned, or with the previous Crusade that had failed?

Firstly the Master Raymond explained formally the disciplines and routines of daily life. Then he explained the constitution of the Order, how the masters and grand masters were elected by colleges of twelve, so as to represent the Apostles. There were of course other matters, of which I should not write here.

Next it was the turn of the man with V-shaped eyebrows. What he said seemed to be all in riddles. He said I must take everything he said on trust and ask no questions, for what he had to tell me would become clear at the right time. He said that he was not the Visitor, but that the Visitor would come and that I would recognise him when he did. Then he said that I had a mission to fulfil, and that I would understand it when the time came. He said that I would have a role to play on the Crusade. He said my role was this: '*You are to be a Watcher over the Blind One. If he transgresses, you are to slay him.*'

Then he gave me another chart, similar to the first, only this time there were two circles, linked together, consisting of the letters of the Hebrew alphabet.

While I was looking at it, he left without saying goodbye. I have never seen him since. Father Raymond took over once more.

I was fitted out with clothing and equipment: two shirts, a narrow-sleeved tunic to be worn over them, two pairs of shoes and pants, a long jerkin divided below the waist, a long straight cape tied at the neck, a light summer mantle, a winter mantle lined with wool, a broad leather belt, a cotton cap and a felt hat. I was provided also with two towels, one for the table, the other for washing, and with a heavy blanket. Unlike my sergeant's equipment, everything was black or white, the colours of the Order.

All this equipment had once belonged to a fellow knight, a countryman of mine, who had been slain in the Holy Land. His name had been Brother Manfried. I was told that I should keep his death constantly before my mind and pray for his immortal soul, so that he in turn would pray for mine.

Then Raymond said, 'Walter, tomorrow you will leave Richerenches. You will dress as an ordinary lay knight for the first part of this mission, and as a Templar only later. Money and clothing will be provided. You will travel to Venice and help with the preparations for the Crusade. You will receive further orders on arrival.'

We spent another hour discussing the practicalities of my journey. At the end of the discussion he passed a letter to me. I nearly collapsed. I recognised the writing. I remembered that beautiful, ornate handwriting from Frankenburc. It was Hildegunde's writing. This is what she had written:

*Walter,*
*It is important that you should not believe what you hear about me. I shall come to you when the time is right. Only remember me and do what you know is right. Then all will be well.*
*Hildegunde*

I thanked the Master, who smiled. What did she mean? Why was I not to believe anything about her. Who would want to lie to me about her? How would she come to me? How had the Order come to be a means of communication between us? I would have been overjoyed, only in some ways it is more painful to hope than to despair.

That was to be my last evening at Richerenches. I remember, during the service of matins at midnight, looking around me, at the chapel, taking in every detail, the odd angles of the walls forming the chapel's octagonal shape, the cross on the altar, the simple arches of the windows, the dusty, smoky smell of the place.

My thoughts kept turning towards Hildegunde.

After the office I had to go to the stables to check that my horses were fed and watered. When I had done so, instead of returning directly to the dormitory, I stood still for a while and looked up at the stars. It was a clear, fine night, and I thought that I had never seen them shine so brightly. I followed the patterns of the constellations and looked out to where I would be travelling the next day.

I remember the silence of that night. There was just the spring breeze stirring the leaves of the trees, the breathing of the horses and the barely audible sounds from the dormitories where the others were settling down to sleep again.

There, due east, shone the most beautiful star of all. It was a lovely orange-red colour. I knew from my lessons with Uqhart that it was Aldebaran, the eye of Taurus. Now it made me think of the star that announced the birth of Christ. I thought that now, at this very moment, it would be visible also in the night sky over Jerusalem.

I looked back towards the star. It was not difficult to imagine cascades of angels rising and descending between that star and Jerusalem, all those miles away. I wondered if the sound of their singing was that silence. Then I saw seven stars that perfectly formed the shape of Hildegunde's face, and it was as if her face was there in the heavens, shining like jasper and carnelian, ringed with an emerald rainbow. This vision lasted for a moment only, then vanished, and it seemed those same stars veiled some secret sorrowing known only to the heavens.

My journey was about to start. The very next morning.

Suddenly, for the first time in years, I felt worthy of Hildegunde. For a moment I entertained the thought of trying to visit her on the way to Venice. Yet that would have been unthinkable.

My gaze fixed on that one star. I remembered what Aristotle had written about the stars and planets being made of the fifth essence. And then, for a moment, that star was the focus, the vanishing-point, of all my hopes and aspirations. Just like

Hildegunde. She had become the quintessence of all my other thoughts, just as that star over Jerusalem was made of the quintessence of all that was created. Then I felt that there was something of myself, my own true self, which was for ever at one with her. And it was joined with her at a point that was infinitely small, eternally vanishing into nothingness. Another poem came to mind:

> ich wolt daz ich doheime were
> und aller werlde trost enber,
> ich mein doheim in himmerlrich
> do ich got schouwe ewenclich... ★

As I returned to the dormitory I was sure I heard a nightingale sing, for the first time in years. I thought of Jerusalem and smiled at the thought that Jerusalem would provide the answers to all my questions, though in what form I could not be sure. And I thought of that first night I spent beneath the stars with Hildegunde.

Jerusalem. Would we ever get there? Would I ever be with Hildegunde again?

★ *I wish that I were at home / and away from all the consolations of this world / I mean at home in the heavenly kingdom / where I might gaze upon God for all eternity...* (Walter von de Vogelweide)

# XVIII

## The Moon

✠

As I travelled I was overwhelmed by the extraordinary works of man and nature I saw each new day. In so many places new churches and shrines were being built to the glory of God, with bright paintings of spiritual visions. I saw great mountains, reaching up to the heavens, cliffs overhanging wild seas, great forests and strange animals. I met men and women of different races and of different social stations. Yet in all my dealings with my fellow men I was circumspect, wondering at each new encounter if this might be the Visitor. And these words were constantly before my mind: *'You are to be a Watcher over the Blind One. If he transgresses, you are to slay him.'*

I travelled to Venice as a lay knight, as if I had never become a Knight of the Temple. At times I stopped at inns and earned a little money by singing. Sometimes I slept rough. Yet the fact that I was leading a double life gave me an immense sense of purpose.

Whenever my spirits ebbed, so long as I could be sure that I was not being followed, I would stop for a day or two at a Templar house, where I would slip back into the daily routine, as one slips back into familiar clothes. I would make new contacts amongst the brothers, find spiritual refreshment and talk about the activities of the Order, and its secret designs.

As for myself, I suffered hardship at times, hunger, thirst, the freezing cold of the early morning and the burning heat of the afternoons. I suffered temptations of the flesh, for there were many alluring women who would have made themselves available to me.

The journey took two months, and you can imagine my joy when at last I arrived in Venice, whose magnificent buildings seemed to rise out of the waters in which they were mirrored like the most splendid illuminated manuscripts suddenly come to life. The atmosphere of marble stillness created by those waterways, on which glided boats of all shapes and sizes, seemed to absorb all the bustle, as if there were powers beneath those waters, which cradled the city, nourished it and gave it strength, yet smiled at its transience.

Other knights and their men were already beginning to arrive at the same time as me. They came from Italy, France, Spain, the Empire, even England. There was great joy as we set about preparing the island of San Niccolo de Lido to receive the influx of the Crusading armies.

Jerusalem. It was as if we were all of one mind, many hands but the same body. This is one of our songs. It pains me to think of it now; I was so full of hope:

*You who love truly, awake! Sleep no more!*
*The lark's song tells us day is here*
*That the day of peace has come*
*Which God, in His tenderness,*
*Will give to those who so love Him,*
*That they take the cross for their burden*
*And suffer pain both night and day.*
*Now God will see who truly loves Him.*

In those days we were granted free access to the centre of Venice.

I was intoxicated by the smells of the city. Each waterway, each street, each square had its own particular scent, which blended with all the others to form a symphony of scents quite unlike that of any other city. It was a rich harmony of the smells of the waterways, food being prepared, spices as they were unloaded, the resin of wooden casks, the salty tang as the sea lapped against the wooden foundations of the buildings. The docks were the focal point of the tapestry of scents, the smells of the sea, the exotic fruits, the perfumes, the fish, the wooden chests and casks that were used for storage. Even the refuse had a tart sweetness to its stench, and was like a solvent, the essential spirit into which the other smells were dissolved, yet which preserved them. All together, there was a musky aroma that was at once full of life, redolent of the passing of time, harmonious, yet differentiated; I thought a man who was blind and deaf would be able to lead a full life in that city, walking round the town, negotiating his way by tracing the geography of smells.

My eyes too were ravished by the wealth of the cathedral, the palaces, the churches, all miraculously rising out of the waters, as if hovering there. Then there were the ships, which came from the East, a thousand masts bobbing in the waters of the docks, ships carrying fine wool from Syria, silks from Byzantium, leather from Phoenicia, precious stones, glass, spices, precious foods, dates, figs, almonds, ointments, medicines, jewellery, anything to satisfy the smallest whim of those who dwell in the city. I could not imagine how Jerusalem, how any town, could be more rich and full than this.

At first we crusading knights were welcomed by the populace. Perhaps they saw in us what we saw in ourselves, heroes who would destroy the infidel, make the whole world Christ's, free Jerusalem and make straight the way for the coming of the Lord. Perhaps these things will come about one day, though not in the short time still allotted to me.

In those early days in Venice the Doge would organise great services for us at Saint Mark's. From the outside Saint Mark's is the greatest cathedral I have ever seen, with its massive archways, great minarets and the five domes, which some said represented the four elements and the quintessence. On the walls there were reliefs of strange winged creatures, birds and trees that must live in paradise. Inside the walls and domes were like the vaults of heaven itself, painted with the Apostles, stories from the Bible and the angels of glory with many wings seeming to hover over the crowds. How intoxicating the atmosphere of devotion was, the power of the singing, the glory of the incense and the sheer joy of all us knights and soldiers as we offered our souls to God during those early services, as we promised to carry out His will in our march against the infidel.

Perhaps you can imagine my excitement. The music in the cathedral seemed to come from beyond this world! It was sung by many choirs, each positioned in a different part of the church, some at ground level, some in galleries high above the ground, each singing a different line of music yet each in harmony with the others. It made my senses reel. I thought I was in heaven, listening to the harmony of all the choirs of Creation resounding throughout the ages of man, mingling with the rich, harmonious scent of incense. The Doge spared no expense on the music and I wondered if perhaps such songs were some compensation to the Doge for the sense of sight that he had lost.

I remember how once during an evening service I closed my eyes on the richly decorated, painted walls of the church, on the pictures and candles. I fell into a trance and when I woke I saw a girl on the other side of the church who had long blond hair. I could not see her face at first because her head was turned away from me, but I imagined it shining like jasper and carnelian, framed by the twinkling light of the candles, like stars. I tried to push my way through the crowds towards her, to make sure that it was not her, but I could not manage to do so because there were so many people. At one point she turned. It might have been Hildegunde, yet I could not be sure. From then on I returned to the central parts of the city every day just in case I caught a glimpse of her.

Each evening, when I returned to the island of San Niccolo di Lido where we were encamped, I would look back over the city towards the magnificent domes of Saint Mark's, silhouetted against the purple of the evening sky. I remember how the air would fill with the smell of smoke from the fires in our camp, where food was being prepared, and how this smell would mingle with the salty breezes of the sea. Then there was the sound of the waves lapping, the look of satisfaction and tranquillity in the eyes of my fellow knights, and the magnificent sight of the town, fading against the hyacinth, purple and gold of the evening sky, like a vision of the New Jerusalem.

There was sadness in that beauty though, as in our yearning for Jerusalem. For as the sun set and we returned to our camp-fires beneath the stars, there was a sense of fragility and transience about the scene, as if we knew that in this world ideals and beauty are things that are only glimpsed, and only rarely come to fulfilment.

Did we foresee, deep within ourselves, the tragedies and the treachery that were to beset us? Around about that time I purchased a sturdy white horse for myself. He was taller than most warhorses, with eyes like jade and the proudest temperament I have ever known in a horse. I imagined riding into Jerusalem on his back. I called him Sîger, Vanquisher, and he became very dear to me.

I remember how much I used to admire the Doge in those days. I was so busy with my work, and so filled with hopes for Jerusalem, with the belief that everything that happened would fall into a pattern, that just for a while I lost myself in the role I was playing. I worked hard and sang much, both as a means of getting to know people and as a way of keeping abreast of affairs in the camp, so that I could report back to the Templars via the network of watchers we had. At first everything proceeded in good order. Count Baldwin of Flanders had already arrived, as had Count Hugh of Saint Paul, Geoffroy the Marshal of Champagne and many others.

My forebodings began on the twenty-seventh of November of that year. A Templar messenger came to tell me for certain that the company of Villain of Neuilly, Henry of Arzillieres, Renaud of Dampierre and others had decided to make their own way to the Holy Land by ship, shunning Venice and our armies there.

I remember the moment exactly. I was organising a group of foot-soldiers, who were preparing large boughs of trees to make the temporary accommodation - accommodation for those who had already set sail for Apulia. The day had been clear until then.

The sky was blue but tinted an odd brown and purple. As I tried to work out the full implications of the news about de Neuilly and his followers, I noticed that many of the men were looking up at the sky and were slacking from their work.

I was about to chide the soldiers when I witnessed a terrible sign, which struck me to the core. Though it was daytime, the moon was plainly visible in the sky, and it was turning black, and growing larger and larger at the same time, as it moved closer and closer to the sun. We all stared, wondering what would happen if the two heavenly bodies were to collide.

At last the moon grew so close to the sun that it did touch it, and then began to cover it, as if eating it. The sun turned black and a terrible chill darkness fell across the land. Many of the soldiers crossed themselves and threw themselves prostrate on to the ground and prayed for their souls, howling and weeping in their fear at this prodigy of nature.

I stood stock-still. Soon everything was pitch-black. I do not know how long the darkness lasted, but it felt like an eternity. An evil had fallen to the earth, which was not to leave us.

At last the sun began to reappear and light and day returned. But the chill remained. I feel it still.

That night the clouds in the sky formed the shape of a bloody red horse, which seemed to ride out across the lands to the East.

My worst fears turned out to be true. By the time everyone had arrived, our army consisted of only four thousand five hundred knights, nine thousand squires and twenty thousand foot-soldiers. They could not provide enough money to honour the contract with the Venetians. Some fifty thousand silver franks were raised, but nowhere near the eighty-five thousand we were supposed to find.

The camp of Geoffroy of Villehardouin blamed those who had gone to Apulia. Others were openly critical and suspicious of the treaty that Villehardouin had signed on our behalf with the Doge. They said that the whole plan for the crusade had been ill conceived and should be abandoned. This was the beginning of the dissent that was at times to break out into overt hostility.

Month by month the bitterness in the atmosphere increased. There was less military work to be done, but at the same time I became busier gathering information for the Templars. The main debate as far as we were concerned was whether we should align ourselves with Villehardouin's party and try to make the best of a bad job, or whether we should join with those who wished to abandon the Crusade there and then so that we would be able to make a fresh start later.

By June everyone in the camp knew of our plight. We would have been ready to set sail, but because of the money still owed to the Venetians, we had to wait until our debts had been paid. So instead of celebration, all the army felt was stifling anger and bitter helplessness. For as far as we were concerned we had already paid for our passage. Just because there were so few of us we were being asked to pay all over again, and more besides.

The situation was saved, in the short term, by some great ones like the Count of Flanders and Count Lewis, who began to give all they had and all they could borrow. This shamed the others into - a resentful silence. But there were so many who had already spent all their money, and who were overwhelmed with the debts they had run up in the last few months. Many of them were good knights, whose intentions were noble enough, but who lacked the discipline imposed by membership of an Order like the Templars, and who had long since spent what they had on food, so-called precious objects sold to them as mementoes by wily merchants, and of course on wine and the services of local women.

The Venetians clearly felt they had been wronged. Merchants would come in increasingly large groups to harass their debtors and try to get their money back. Often there were fights. Some of our number got into brawls. Some were even ambushed and killed if they dared leave the camp. Tempers boiled over and I feared there could even be a full-scale battle between the Venetians and the Crusaders from other parts of Christendom.

By June we were being kept on the island under close guard. None of us was allowed to leave. Most of us were hungry and exhausted. Some were practically starving. Our spirits were vexed by the way the Venetians would charge extortionate sums for food.

Illnesses began to break out: many suffered from phtisia and languor, and many too were struck with scrofula, Saint Lawrence's fire, tuberculosis and so on. Some made fortunes by claiming to be doctors of medicine, and they carried out bleedings, sold purgative medicines and the like, most of which made the men worse than they had been in the first place.

Then there were the rumours that we would not be marching directly on Jerusalem, as we had expected, but that we would first be attacking Egypt. These rumours, along with the debt situation and the sense of frustration, all added to the feeling of discontent. Jerusalem was our goal. Jerusalem was the purpose of our sacrifice and all our strivings. What use to us was the distant land of Egypt? Certainly those who lived there were heathen. Yet it was God's own City that we wished to liberate, and with God's help we felt sure that it would fall to us if only we had the courage of our convictions and marched on it directly, trusting in God. We could not see the point in taking a cowardly, roundabout route.

Even that would have been preferable to what actually happened. I found out from my secret sources (of which I must refrain from writing) that the Doge had come to an agreement with Al-Adil promising that he would allow no attack on Egypt, and in return he received important trading concessions.

By the end of June the Venetians were threatening to cut off our food supplies altogether. Still I could not judge the situation. Who was to blame? Those who left without us for Apulia? Or was it Thibaut's and Villehardouin's recklessness? Or was it all part of the Doge's grand strategy? Had he realised that he would be able to appropriate the army of God and use it to his profit to settle private scores?

Next, in return for continued support from Venice, the Crusading army was to act as the Doge's own private army and attack the Christian town of Zara, which had, some years previously, fallen to the king of Hungary. This was to be the first stage of the Crusade. The Venetians drew lots consisting of wax balls to determine which of them would take part. It was extraordinary how well ordered the process was.

The response of my fellow Franks was initially to despair. Why should we fight against a Christian king for a cause that we did not understand? Yet we had debts, and so we had little choice. Besides, anything was better than staying on that island, and if we were successful at Zara, at least there was a chance that we would be able to carry on, as planned, to Jerusalem.

I tried to organise an interview with the Doge. By signs I let it be known to him that I was a Knight of the Temple, and normally this would have been enough to allow me access to him. But his officials always claimed that he was busy, and the earliest time offered to me was not until the Feast of Remigius, in October. I agreed to wait, thinking that this would give me time to find out more about what he planned in advance, so that I could head him off by argument, or – I am going to write it – if I felt that I was justified in my perception that he was the Blind One, and if I felt that his plans were going to lead the Crusade off its true course, then I would be able to dispatch him by other means.

Would I kill him? Not straight away. I had to get information first, find out what his plans really were. Then I would see.

The time I had to wait seemed to go on interminably. I grew more and more melancholy. I no longer joined in the training and skirmishing and mêlées, which we German knights organised amongst ourselves. Others came to neglect them too and soon they ceased.

Also I avoided singing and reciting stories and courtly epics for the others. I continued to write songs, though I spent as much time as I could on my own, brooding on what might happen during my meeting with the Doge. I had made friends through the military training and through my singing, yet I refrained from drawing too close to them, since I did not want my connection with the Templar knights to be known. All my dealings with my Templar masters took place in secret. Messages were passed using secret writing. Nor did I want others to be implicated in any action I might have to commit. If I did kill the Doge, I would have to take responsibility and spare the Order.

The situation in the camp worsened too. More and more of the men began to give themselves to brawling, drunkenness and whoring. It was like a cancer, spreading through the camp. I was not immune. Even my horse died. I bought a black one to replace him. I called him Justus, and he was strong but cold of temperament, like a machine, and his face made me think of a death-mask.

Shortly afterwards, in spite of my vow of chastity, I took a prostitute from the town. She was a slim, dark girl, not very old, very graceful in her manner. I used her to slake the lusts that had been pent up inside me for all those years, then sent her packing. I sank into a state of melancholy and took up drinking once more. I neglected my military duties and spent hours staring out to sea, or at the outline of the city of Venice, plucking desolately at my lute, singing songs to myself that I would not care for anyone else to hear.

I would have left Venice, I suppose, if I had had anywhere to go. I was without money, without connections other than the Templars, who wanted me to stay there, and I was reluctant to return to any of the scenes of my past life where there might be connections with the Brotherhood. My commission from the Templars was the one thing I had left, together with the most desperate of hopes that everything might, after all, turn out for the best.

The day of my interview with the Doge drew closer and closer, yet the time I waited seemed to grow eternally longer. How should I present myself to the Doge? Directly, openly, honestly? Or should I be diplomatic and use phrases containing hints and innuendoes so as to be able to cover myself? Would I have the courage to slay him there and then? Was that really what I was supposed to do, or were my thoughts those of a madman?

All my worrying was to no avail. The Feast of Saint Remigius was to be the day of our departure to Zara, and I was sent a message to say that my meeting with the Doge would have to be postponed. It was too late for me to do anything about it.

I sailed in one of the ships set aside for knights, with our horses in the hold. We spent much of our time on the deck. It was an awesome and beautiful sight. All the ships sailed close to one another. The quantity of equipment we had amassed was vast. Our vessels carried more than three hundred petraries and mangonels.

The fleet was led by the Doge's own galley, which was painted bright vermilion. His throne was set up on the poop and covered with a canopy of silk. It was as if the sea had come to life, and we, the ships, the army and the people, were creatures of the sea moving across its surface.

All the way, during the daytime, there were drummers beating and trumpeters sounding over and over the sequence of notes that could only be employed to the honour of the Doge. The noise was deafening, and only when it died down could we hear the priest singing the hymn to the Holy Spirit, '*Veni creator spiritus*'. Their voices were as often as not drowned by the sound of the trumpets which seemed to be summoning other spirits, strange spirits of the sea, to which the Doge is wed at his inauguration ceremony.

Looking back now I see the sea as a pale horse, and our ships and armies as its deathly riders bringing destruction to the inhabitants of Zara.

We arrived before Zara on the Eve of Saint Martin. Its high wall rose like cliffs directly out of the sea and it was impossible to see how anyone might attack it. Also, the Zarians knew we were coming. They had appealed to the Pope, who had decreed our army would be excommunicated if we attacked the city. Great towers and minarets stood even higher than the city wall. On each of these, and all along the ramparts, the inhabitants had set up crosses to make clear to our army that it was a Christian city we were attacking.

So, we blockaded the port, and landed the troops to the north and south of the city, who managed to surround it by land after a few minor skirmishes, and we prepared for a siege, hoping all the time that a settlement would soon be negotiated and we would be on our way to Jerusalem.

At that time I talked much with one Bertrand of Ray in Burgundy, the minstrel of Count Baldwin, who said it was certain that his lord would be the Last Emperor of the Apocalypse, and asked me what I was doing there on the Crusade. I tried to fathom whether or not he was linked to the Brotherhood of Charlemagne or if he had any connection with the Templars. I discovered nothing, only I began to wonder if he was mad, or if the story I was involved in was being played out in other places.

There were complex negotiations before the battle, but the Doge made it seem that the Zarians had first accepted terms, then I reneged on them. I was very busy at that time, trying desperately, with the Templars, to sue for peace. But the leaders would have none of it.

The night before the battle I felt that I was losing my mind. How could we, a Christian army on the way to free Jerusalem, attack a Christian town? The question drove me into a state of frenzy. It was as if the earth would not stay still, the sky was being rolled up like parchment and the stars were all falling to the earth. Somehow I managed to conceal my state, which I feared might be misconstrued as cowardice. The next day I was just well enough to fight.

I watched as wooden towers were brought up, together with the mangonels, which were used for hurling massive stones. I saw walls being mined by sappers and ladders strapped to the masts of the ships, reaching to the top of the city walls.

The city held out for five days before surrendering. They said I fought gallantly. I was one of the first over the walls of the city when the main attack came. I killed three or four men, God rest their souls. Sometimes I forget my own strength, and the impression of confidence and power I give because I am tall and have a strong physique. Yet what those who praised me witnessed was not so much heroism as an urge to self-destruction, which came to possess me more and more.

There was no honour or gallantry in what followed. The Venetians appropriated most of what was of value in the town: the shipyards, the ships, the port and the area around the port. The Flemish and Prussian troops were given free rein to riot and destroy, despite the terms of surrender agreed with the Zarians at the outset of the battle. The soldiers lived in the houses of the ordinary citizens, reducing them to whores and slaves.

Three days after our so-called victory, a pitched battle broke out between the Venetians and the rest of the Crusading army. There was fierce fighting in nearly every street. Swords, lances, crossbows and javelins were used. The fighting went on all night and many were killed. Even after a form of peace was agreed in the morning, the fighting still continued, and it did not stop completely for at least a week.

I was possessed by feelings of shame and disgust at what I had seen. I made it clear to my Templar masters in the secret messages I sent back to Venice that I thought every effort should be made to abandon the expedition there and then.

Some men did try to escape. One boat set sail, but it capsized, drowning five hundred. Some tried to escape inland, but were killed by peasants. There were other knights who begged to be sent to Syria, but they were never heard of again.

Most to be pitied were the women and children of Zara. I wonder if they will see light again in the Resurrection of the Just.

About three weeks after the initial rioting was quelled, things had quietened down a little. Now there were just sporadic outbursts of fighting and looting as individual houses were raided by semi-organised gangs, the inhabitants dragged out, and raped, killed or set free, depending on the whim of the soldiers.

One incident in particular sticks in my mind. I was out walking one evening just as the sun was setting. The light was a sickly brownish yellow because of the smoke still billowing from some parts of the town. With the stench and the filth, the atmosphere of evil was almost palpable.

I was walking along a street of wooden houses where relatively wealthy Zarians lived. Suddenly, I heard shouting. A group of young Flemish soldiers, louts no more than eighteen or nineteen years old, were leading a girl out of a house in which she must have been hiding. She was probably about sixteen or seventeen. Though her hair was dark, I saw in her something both of Katrin and Hildegunde. She was beautiful.

At first she kept her dignity. She shook herself free of the men and tried to smile at them, to win them round. Then she tried to make a dash for it, to get away through a small gap that had appeared in their ranks. But they caught her easily, pulled at her long hair and pushed her from one of them to the other, tearing at her clothes.

Then they made her dance, clapping their hands. The sky had turned a sick, orange-red colour, tainted brown by the smoke from the fires still burning in the town, and it was as if a terrible hail of fire and blood was pouring down from the setting sun.

I do not know how long it went on for. Soon she was dancing naked. Then there was a movement of bodies, pushing, shouting, as they piled on top of her.

At first she screamed, but soon her cries stopped, either because she was already dead or because her screaming was being stifled.

Why did I not intervene?

There was a writhing mass of bodies – something that seemed to take on a life of its own. Then they were all still. One by one they climbed to their feet, no longer shouting. Some of them were hitching up their breeches, using each other for support. One of them began singing drunkenly but was shut up by the others. They walked off, looking for their next victim, their next drink, their next debauch.

All they left behind them were twisted tatters of flesh in the growing darkness, tatters covered with blood, and a broken head with eyes still wide, still staring, though, mercifully, now seeing nothing. They had practically torn the girl limb from limb. She had been so lovely, a unique and beautiful creation of God, yet, minutes later, she was a heap of dead flesh, filth to be cleared up the moment its stench became intolerable, and now there was nothing that could ever return her to this world. Nothing, I supposed, but the saving power of God. Yet this is a power He is loath to use.

Of course there were many rapes, many murders; yet I am haunted by the memory of that girl dancing, in the last few minutes of her life. To me it is a symbol of all that our armies, our Christian armies, did, and are doing still. And it is a symbol of my own failure: why did I just stand there and look on?

Later that night, restless with self-disgust, I walked out of the town and made my way over the fields, then up the coast to the north. I do not know how far I walked, only a mile or so.

I sat down on the beach and looked back towards the town, which had become like a stifling, infected wound on the face of the earth. It was chilly. Even the stars seemed to have grown dark. A great, sickly yellow full moon was hanging over the sea. In the distance I could hear dogs barking, howling into the night.

I tried to think of Hildegunde. I wondered if she was still alive. I wondered if she was comfortable, asleep in her convent back in the Rhineland. I wondered if she ever thought of me, or ever prayed for me.

I tried to imagine her face spread out over the sky. I took my lute and tried to play some of the songs we had shared. Yet everything I played seemed out of tune, and the resonance of my playing mingling with the howling of the dogs created an impression of unutterable loneliness and emptiness, so I soon stopped. As I sat there I realised that I was far from well. I had stomach cramps, my head span and the earth seemed to shift beneath my feet.

I looked towards the sea. Its waters were calm. There was the gentle lapping of the waves. I followed the line of the water. My gaze was drawn as if by a magnet to the body of a man, which was rolling backwards and forwards with the movement of the sea.

I do not know if it was my imagination, but I was sure that the body was infested with crabs, lobsters, scarabs, all tearing at the dead flesh.

I stared. Then the creatures were making their way towards me. I began trembling and at the same time I caught the stench of the body full in the nose. The cramps in my stomach became unbearable and I turned to retch. And as I retched it was as if a massive ball of fire, like a star, fell into the sea, exploding with searing pain in my head.

I shook myself and tried to walk back to my tent and to the warmth and companionship of the camp. But all the strength had gone from me, and I was only able to manage a few steps before collapsing and passing out.

# XIX

## The Sun

✠

The next morning I woke to find myself in the small house where I was sleeping rough. I do not know who found me or who brought me back there. Next to my bed I found the message again: '*You are to be a Watcher over the Blind One. If he transgresses, you are to slay him.*' It was attached to another chart. It was like the first two I had been given, only extended. Now the letters of the Hebrew alphabet were arranged around the figures of the upper circle of the chart. The Magician was next to Aleph, the Priestess was next to Beth...

The lower circle had no images. What did that mean? Was I to confront the Doge immediately, or wait until the chart was complete, or until I could understand it?

I stayed in that house throughout the winter. It used to belong to a carpenter who lived alone. It was a simple wooden house, draughty when it was cold, but it suited my needs, unless I had fever, in which case it was miserable. Still, it was vastly better than what most of the soldiers had to put up with - there was plenty of straw and the food-stores were nearby.

I remember that awful morning when I returned from mass to discover from my fellow knights that the whole army had been excommunicated by the Pope. It really seemed that everything was lost, even my soul. It was bitingly cold and we were all beginning to suffer from the lack of food.

Like many of the men who had opposed this expedition to Zara, I felt utterly dejected. There was no hope for us, no hope of salvation, either in this world or the next, no meaning in anything we had striven for, only darkness and the prospect of an ignominious death. It was as though all the waters of life had been turned bitter by some angelic poisoning.

I realised I still had the taste of the bread and wine on my lips. I was terrified. Had I sinned, by taking the Eucharist whilst excommunicate? Even if I did not know it at the time? Was this the sin against the Holy Spirit that cannot be forgiven?

For weeks after, there was nothing to do, just exist on the meagre rations, make fires of whatever was available – the smell of burning always seemed to be in my nose. No one had any energy for military training. I used to spend hours watching an eagle that flew over the camp, hovering against the chill, marble sky, and his squawks and cries seemed to herald nothing but desolation.

Then, to add further to our doubts and our foreboding, we learnt of the death of Fulk of Neuilly, the holy man who was amongst the first to preach the Crusade. He had died just as we were taking Zara. This too seemed to be a portent. Before, he had healed the sick and caused the blind to see; now that our pilgrimage had gone astray, like the rest of us he was unable to save himself. Was this too a sign of God's wrath?

I thought of my early days at school and in Frankenburc, how I sincerely believed that there was order in the universe. I thought of how I expected to find this reflected in music and song. What had gone wrong? Everything was discord, and everything I did added to the discord. It seemed that even the stars had grown dark. Only the sick, ghostly yellow moon gloated over the town through the clouds and the smoke.

In February we learnt that young Alexius of Constantinople was to join us in Zara. He had been thrown into prison with his father, whom he had seen blinded by his usurping uncle. Our next destination would not be Jerusalem after all, but Constantinople.

All because this fourteen-year-old made vain promises of support if ever we returned him to the throne.

Next the Pope lifted his ban of excommunication, on the condition that we never again attack fellow Christians unless they actively opposed the Holy War!

I dared hope that perhaps, after all, I was foolish to have doubted, that my trials were all over, that the Church would shine, like a great sun, all over the world, not just from Rome and Constantinople, but from Jerusalem too.

Something else. I received a message from the Templars that a young noblewoman with long blond hair and blue eyes had been inquiring after me in Venice. She had given her name simply as 'H'.

Alexius arrived in Zara on the twenty-fifth of March and we set sail on the seventh of April, Easter Monday. That year Easter Sunday had fallen on the anniversary of my first meeting with Katrin.

I was extremely busy with the preparations for our departure and, curiously, my health improved as a result. On the advice of the Order I moved to a new part of the camp and attached myself to Halberstadt's regiment. I made friends with a group of knights from the Rhineland. One of them had been on Crusade with Friedrich Barbarossa and had known the singer Friedrich von Hausen.

At the end of each day, by the harbour at Zara, when the first fires of the evening were lit and the food was prepared, I would sing for these knights. They were grateful to hear Crusading songs in their own language. No one suspected my connection with the Templars.

Some evenings, considerable crowds would gather to hear me and to join in the singing. In a way, these were happy moments for me. The power of the singing, the words and the music, would emanate from me in spite of myself, and charm the spirits of these warriors, so they would become like docile children, sitting there wide-eyed, dreaming now of glory, now of battle, now of home and loved ones.

On leaving Zara, we sailed along the coast to Constantinople, keeping close together. There were so many ships, and so many of them brightly coloured, that it seemed that the sea was in flower. We passed beautiful bays and islands. I used to watch the sun as it set and as it rose. Passages from Virgil repeatedly came to mind, and I would delight in reciting them to myself or to any fellow knights who cared to listen.

Even before we set sail there was much dissent regarding the fact that we were not going directly to Jerusalem. I suppose it was partly in response to this that news reached us from the Doge that the young Alexius was to be crowned Emperor of Byzantium before we reached Constantinople.

So we put in at Durazzo. There all the armies gathered to see the coronation ceremony. The pomp and splendour overwhelmed and heartened many of the men in the camp. Those who were suspicious kept their own counsel. By then rumours were rife that our leaders had no intention whatsoever of going on to Jerusalem after we had completed our mission in Constantinople.

There was all the pomp of the coronation ceremony beneath the blazing sun, the precious jewels, the brilliant garments and the fine words. At the same time there was that nagging doubt: would we really be going to Jerusalem?

I had been in contact with my superiors in the Order. The message I received from them was that they were out of sympathy with the expedition.

I remember that evening vividly: the clear skies, the smoke rising from the fires and the smell of pinewood in the air. It was our last chance, and we failed to grasp it. The men had gathered as usual to eat and talk. I was surrounded by my group of friends and was singing songs about what a true Crusade would be. Between songs, we talked of sailing directly to the Holy Land, bypassing Constantinople.

The sun was turning deep yellow as it descended towards the mountains, and the lingering smell of our meats and breads and fires mingled with the scents of the long grass, wild flowers, heather and herbs that grew in the valley. Then, suddenly, there were hundreds, maybe thousands of voices shouting, as if with one voice, 'Ire Accaron! Ire Accaron!' – 'Go to Acre!'

The rhythmic cry spread throughout the camp – even the knights who were with me joined in. The sun set, and the blue sky turned purple. Smoke from our fires billowed up towards the wispy clouds.

As if with one mind, more than half us took our horses and belongings, and marched away from the main camp and into the next valley. We used our swords to cut paths through the rich purple gorse and heather that grew on the top of the highland separating the valleys.

Some wanted me to lead them. 'Walter, Walter,' they were all shouting, 'you could be the one. You could lead us.' I would have none of it. But those words 'you could be the one' set my nerves on edge.

I slept only fitfully that night, wondering what was in store. I remember I became obsessed with the vision of great beasts, larger than horses, with tails, like scorpions, flying through the night, then creeping over the earth, harbingers of the destruction to come, some red as fire, some blue as sapphire, others yellow as sulphur. I was in no fit state to lead a rebellion.

Next morning, just after dawn, as we were sharing breakfast together, we saw thirty or so horsemen riding over the hill towards us. All were wearing full ceremonial regalia, and the sight of them was dazzling in the morning sun. The men included Boniface, the Marquis of Montferrat, Baldwin, Count of Flanders, Louis, Count of Blois and the young Alexius.

All eyes were upon them as they rode through the light mist that swirled round the gorse and heather on the hill, between the small, black silhouettes of trees, and over the lingering dew.

At some distance from the camp Boniface dismounted, then the rest of the company did the same. Unarmed, they walked towards us, and great crowds gathered about them, curious to see what they would do. When they were in the very heart of our camp, Boniface and his entourage threw themselves down on their knees. Bald and fat he might have been, and given to women, good living and the company of poets - but Boniface was no fool. The effect was brilliant. The clothes which Boniface and the others wore were of the richest reds and purples, and the sunlight glinted on the precious stones studding their chains and rings. Yet there they were, abasing themselves before us.

Boniface waited for silence before announcing solemnly that there was much he wished to discuss with us. Shock and astonishment shot through our camp like a volley of arrows. Of course, we agreed immediately.

Boniface rose. He was a brilliant orator. He begged us, pleaded with us, cajoled us. He presented the young Emperor to us and said that it was right and proper for a Christian army to restore him to his throne, that it was our Christian duty. He said surely this was the will of God - because of Alexius' offer of money, ships, food and extra men if only we helped him. Once this duty was performed, he said, of course we would sail on to the Holy Land.

Thus Boniface drained the enthusiasm out of us as death drains life from a corpse - the rebellion came to nothing and we returned to the main body of the army, preparing to sail as if nothing had happened.

Within days our ships had rounded the Peloponnese and turned northward to the island of Andros. There we were able to refill our water-tanks from the springs. The Dardanelles were undefended and we found the Thracian harvest ripening. We put in at Abydos to gather what we could, yet even here there were intimations of what was to come. The peasants were so terrified of us that they let us take what we wanted without offering any resistance whatsoever. Nonetheless, I saw hundreds of them rounded up by our Christian armies, taunted, beaten, raped, killed. Whole families were left bleeding and dying in their pillaged fields. All for no reason.

Was this really part of the divine plan? Were these people really so wicked that they deserved such terrible retribution?

The morning we arrived before Constantinople the sun rose on a pillar of cloud with shimmering circles all round it, rainbow coloured, like haloes round the head of an angel standing over the sea on fiery legs.

There was much din and excitement amongst the men as we drew closer to Constantinople - Constantinople, the Golden City, the City of the Virgin, where my father had told me that the craftsmen knew how to make automata that moved of their own accord, angels blowing trumpets, clocks with horsemen signalling the passing of the hours, trees cast in bronze on which sat metal birds that knew how to sing, each according to the species they represented, even miniature thrones of Solomon guarded by metal lions, which beat the ground with their tails and roared.

As we arrived before the city, every drum on every one of our ships was beaten as we sailed past, and every trumpet sounded a fanfare. The noise was deafening. All the Greeks were standing on the roofs of their houses, watching in amazement.

I had never imagined that so rich a city could exist. I gazed upon the high walls and noble towers that ringed it, and the splendid palaces and towering churches. There was such an extraordinary number of beautiful buildings that I would never have believed it had I not been there and seen it with my own eyes. We first saw the city in the early morning of the twenty-third of June. I remember that in the distance all the buildings were the colour of honey, shimmering and golden in the morning light.

We turned back, and later that day we anchored in the Sea of Marmora opposite the Abbey of Saint Stephanos. There were bad winds, but we found that we could land at will on less populated areas of the coast and gather all the food we needed.

I remember, that night, I dreamt of the woman in the Apocalypse whose dress is the sun and who had the moon beneath her feet. I saw her pursued by the red dragon with seven heads and ten horns. I woke, sweating and disturbed, for the woman could have been Constantinople, or Hildegunde - which would mean that I was the dragon.

There were still grounds for hope in those days, however. We believed Alexius and we believed the Doge. We really did think that the inhabitants of Constantinople would be pleased to welcome back the legitimate Emperor, that they would wish to rid themselves of the usurping tyrant who had blinded and tortured his own brother in order to be able to take over the throne.

The first blow to these hopes came when the Venetians decided to stage a spectacle. They sent ten of the most splendid Venetian galleys to approach Constantinople under a flag of truce. On the deck of the most magnificent of these the young Alexius was displayed, sitting on an imperial throne and dressed in imperial robes. As they passed in procession under the walls of the city, criers called out, 'Do you recognise the young Alexius as your lord?' Far from welcoming Alexius, they reviled him. They taunted the Venetians, saying that they did not recognise him, that they did not know who he was.

A few days later, a Venetian ship, the Aquila, succeeded in breaking the chain across the mouth of the Golden Horn. The tower of Galata and the Greek ships anchored there were captured. This was our great chance. That evening, the whole army was blessed and, in the deep blue stillness of the night, to the sound of the lapping water, we entered the special transport ships that had been designed so that our horses could be ridden directly off the boat and on to the land. No one talked. No one slept. We all just gazed at the sky, at the stars, listening to the sounds of the sea and the neighing of the horses.

The next morning, at dawn, under a clear sky and brilliant sun, we were ferried across the straits from Scutari to Galata at the mouth of the Golden Horn. I was on one of the ships assigned to land on the beach facing the northern walls of Constantinople. There was the Doge's ship. I saw its ensign: a leopard with bears' feet and a lion's mouth. I saw the Doge with my own eyes, on the prow, leading it to a point where the fighting was at its height. Two hundred trumpeters sounded the advance and there were twice as many drummers. The noise was deafening. I saw the Doge jump down, the first of all, though he was over ninety years old and blind, quite fearless of the enemy. I understood why he was so much admired, why his soldiers would do anything for him. He was beyond the categories of good and bad, generous and rapacious. He was a force of nature.

I saw too the extraordinary sight of the Venetian flying bridges, attached to the high masts of the galleys, which were swung up by a system of tackles and counterbalancing weights to reach up to the parapets of the high walls. Some of the bridges were up to a hundred feet long, and three men abreast could walk along them in full armour. Some of the bridges were covered with hides, which protected them from arrows and from Greek fire, and others still were in the form of tunnels, so that it was possible to walk the whole way to the parapets completely protected.

The fighting I was involved in by the walls was fierce and made little progress. The attacks at the gates cost us many brave men. Eventually some of our men scaled the ladders and took control of the wall. There was terrible fighting, hand to hand, but our men would not budge.

I tried to climb one of the ladders, but I was struck a glancing blow in the chest, on the left side, by a crossbow bolt. It did not fix in my body but fell to the ground. My chest bled, but I did not seem to be seriously injured. Anyway, I was led away and told to direct the men who were constructing other ladders. All the time the Venetian ships were drawing closer, shooting mangonels, crossbow bolts and deadly arrows at the Greeks who were still manning the walls, and trying to land and attach their ladders to the walls. The din was so great that it seemed the very earth and sea were melting together.

By the end of the day twenty-five towers had been captured. Given the number of Greeks set against us, it would have been impossible for us to hold them. However, scouting parties who entered the city by means of the flying towers managed to start a fire. The flames were fanned by a wind blowing from our side, and they rose so high that the Greeks could soon no longer see our people.

I remember lying there at Galata, all night long, whilst the flames leapt higher and higher into the night sky. I was feverish as a result of the wound in my chest, and my fever seemed to be an extension of the heat of the flames. The light of the burning dazzled my eyes. It was as if the sun had refused to set, or rather as if it had been caused to fall to earth in an act of terrible judgement on the people of that city.

That night, the Emperor Alexius fled, taking his jewels and his daughters, and did not stop until he reached Mosynopolis. The next morning we learnt that Isaac, the blind brother of Alexius, whom most of us thought must be dead by now, had been returned to the throne by the palace officials.

An embassy was sent from our army and it was agreed that the young Alexius, who had travelled with us from Zara and for whom we were fighting, should be crowned as co-Emperor along with his blind father, Isaac. The ceremony of his crowning took place at the church of Saint Sophia on the first of August.

So it seemed that Constantinople had become our ally after all, and that there would be no further bloodshed.

From then on we had free access to the city. It was like walking through the streets of heaven itself. The churches and palaces were filled with gold, silver and ivory. The very streets shone with a golden light, so that everywhere were textures of chrysolite, amber, honey, and saffron. I could not believe how many of the ordinary houses were built of stone, and not of wood like those in Nurenberc, which were mere huts in comparison. There were many learned people, and one could tell also from the bearing of many that they knew how to live well.

Yet it was easy enough to discern the corruption in the town, which was twofold. Firstly there was the corruption of the Greeks themselves, who were dishonest, self-obsessed and effete. Then there was the corruption caused by the presence of our army. There was plunder, murder, rape – it was becoming like Zara all over again.

In my mind I have relived countless times the day I visited the

Blachernae palace, how I walked across the courtyards paved with marble, saw the gold decorations everywhere, the main halls faced with porphyry. There was a huge maze of royal residences, offices, state chambers, baths, gardens, shrines, churches, barracks, dormitories, workshops, kitchens, stables, museums, a university, art galleries and a zoo. I had never seen anything like it. I even saw the semi-spherical close-fitting crown the Emperor wore on special occasions, richly encrusted with pearls and jewels, some inserted, some hanging, and I saw the two lappets of pearls that would hang down the Emperor's cheeks.

It was on the way out, just through the gates of the main exit, that I saw her. She was exactly as I had seen her at the convent, wearing a simple dress, only her hair was longer and her head uncovered. She did not see me and I was so surprised that I stood for a long while, not sure what to do. I was almost scared, as though it were some apparition. She turned to walk down the street before I could make a move. I ran after her. I was sure that I glimpsed her amongst the crowds on the street, and I tried to push my way through to the river. But she, whoever it was, had gone.

From then on, whenever I had a spare moment, I would search the camp and the city, hoping to catch a glimpse of the one who had looked so much like Hildegunde. All my senses, and instincts were at war with each other. Part of me was convinced that it had been her. Part of me was almost terrified that she might have come, and that part wanted to prove that she had not been there.

I spent that autumn based at the camp in Estanor. We hoped that we would be setting off for Jerusalem at any moment, but the Doge insisted that we should not leave until the young Alexius had fulfilled his promises of men and money for the Crusade. Alexius delayed. He could not raise the money, and he needed the Crusader army there to bolster his power.

Later that autumn, after a fight between the Latins and Greeks who lived in Constantinople, a fire was started, which burnt through a massive swathe of the city. It burnt for two days and nights. Great churches, palaces and libraries were all destroyed. How many men, women and children were killed I do not know. The stench was appalling even from Estanor. I had terrible nightmares, fearing that Hildegunde might have perished in the flames.

The fire lit up the whole sky. We thought the Church of Rome was the true light, which would shine like a sun, on this place and throughout the world, whereas it seemed we had unleashed forces that were far more terrible. Would our punishment be that this burning light in the night sky would never go away, that it would be day for ever?

In January, Geoffroy of Villehardouin, the Marshal of Champagne, Conon of Bethune, Miles the Brabant of Provins and three of the Doge's men went to Alexius to try to make terms. In the palace itself, they were manhandled by the Greek officials, and a scuffle broke out that could have turned into a full-scale fight. Only by defending themselves with their swords did they manage to hold off the Greeks, and they only just escaped from the palace with their lives.

We waited and waited. There was talk of revenge, but by January nothing had happened and we were starving again. My fever had returned and the lack of food caused it to grow even more severe. Many of the men were afflicted with sores that were horrible to look at.

It was in late January that Murzuphlus, the Emperor's steward, who hated us Franks with a vehemence knowing no bounds, sent fire-ships against our fleet. They did little damage because of the direction in which the wind blew. I saw the flames licking hundreds of feet above the sea. It seemed the whole of the sea had caught fire and turned red with blood.

Then there was rioting in the city, during which the great statue of Athena, which stood in the forum facing west, was hacked to pieces by the drunken mob because they thought she was beckoning to our soldiers to invade the city. The statue of Helen of Troy was also taken away by the mob and broken up. I almost wept when I heard this, for I had seen the statue and it was fairer than the evening air, and clad in the beauty of a thousand stars. It made me think of Hildegunde when I first saw it. Every moment of every day I tormented myself wondering if she was in the city, desperate to know that she had not been hurt.

Next we heard Alexius had been thrown into a dungeon. Murzuphlus had Isaac beaten and starved to death. Alexius was strangled with a bowstring. They were buried with great honours, though what had really happened soon became common knowledge.

Murzuphlus ascended the throne. We learnt this from a note bound to an arrow that was shot, ignominiously, into our camp.

I was part of the foraging party led by Count Henry of Flanders which took the town of Phile. We found good provisions there and the Greeks put us little resistance. On the way back to the camp Murzuphlus' men attacked us near the entrance to the wood.

I fought hard that day, leading a company against the front lines. Many were killed. At one point I saw Murzuphlus himself. We gave chase through the rich woodlands, which were still damp from recent rain, and where countless birds fled, rustling through the treetops at our approach. We drove him towards a company of Venetians. Murzuphlus himself just escaped, but his standard bearer was unable to fight off the Venetians, who knocked him to the ground, stabbed him with their pikes and took the imperial insignia, the golden helmet, the imperial standard and the icon of the Virgin.

The Venetians took great pleasure in this. Every day from then on a Venetian galleon moved slowly up and down the straits in front of the town walls with the helmet, the standard and the icon roped to the masthead, to taunt the people of the city.

Yet what did I care? I wanted Hildegunde. I wanted Jerusalem. The petty quarrels between Greeks and Latins meant nothing to me. It was no longer safe for us to go anywhere near the city. There was no sign of Hildegunde in the camp. Surely she could not have been staying in the city.

Throughout March counsels of war were held in Galata to decide on the next move. All the time, I was busy gathering information for the Templars, and trying to find ways of stopping a further attack, all to no avail.

Then, when the invasion was fixed for April, I had to give my time to military duties, training with other knights and preparing the engines and petraries. I watched the Venetians building the great ladders on their ships. We saw the Greeks were building wooden defences on the top of the walls, which were already so high it did not seem possible that we would ever be able to take the city. I was afraid - not for myself but for Hildegunde. Even this fear would have been easier to handle had I been absolutely certain it was her I had seen; the doubt made me all the more desperate.

The first attempt to invade the city took place on the sixth of April, exactly one year after our arrival. It was the fifteenth anniversary of the day I first set eyes on Katrin. I fought beneath the walls at the very centre of the fortifications.

By Nones we had lost many men, we were tired and were making no progress, so we withdrew. During the counsels that followed it was decided that the mistake which had been made was that only one ship was assigned to each tower. For the next attack, fewer towers would be targeted, but they would each be dealt with by two or three ships.

The next attack was on the following Monday. The Greeks had lost all their fear and were lining the walls and towers to get a better view of the battle, as if it were all some sport.

It was dull and overcast as we drew closer to the walls, and the arrows and bolts began to rain down upon us. From that distance they did little enough damage if one took care. Even though we had been repelled before, the men's spirits were bolstered by the sheer size of the army, the vast numbers of ships, all brightly painted, and the din of drums and trumpets as we went into battle.

I was attached to a party that was to attack the lower part of the walls. Spies had reported that some of the sea-gates had been bricked relatively thinly and that we might be able to break through.

This was our job. I helped to organise the men under the

command of Robert of Clari. Getting to the wall was no problem. The Greeks did not seem to be aware of us. We landed under the steep stone walls and unloaded the machines. Only when everyone was on land did all hell break loose. I do not know whether the Greeks were slow to register that we were there or whether they wanted to take us by surprise, and so to kill as many of us as possible, but all of a sudden the air was thick with bolts, stones, rocks and burning pitch, all pouring down on top of us.

News reached us that two Venetian ships, the *Peregrina* and the *Paradiso*, had managed to get knights and men on to two of the towers, and that they were holding them. Andrew of Dureboise, an oaf of a man I once had the misfortune to meet, distinguished himself by being the first along one of the catwalks.

Meanwhile we continued our appalling job, the burning oil, arrows and rocks still falling around us like a plague from heaven. The sound of the screaming of those burnt by the pitch was enough to make any man think about turning and running, but somehow we managed to protect ourselves with our shields. Aleaumes of Clari, Robert's brother, worked like a man possessed as we hacked away at the brick.

After two or three hours we did get through to the other side. The wall was as thin as we had hoped. My instinct was to call back for reinforcements and work at making the hole bigger so that a number of men would be able to charge through at once and put up a stronger fight, but there was no stopping Aleaumes of Clari. As soon as he saw the hole was big enough for an armoured knight to pass through, he hurled himself into it. For a while his brother held on to his feet, telling him not to be so stupid and cursing him with every name under the sun. Eventually he was knocked backwards by a kick from his brother. Aleaumes went through and then there was a mad scramble to follow him. Whether the intention was to attack or to get the fool back, it is hard to say. In any case, soon there were a dozen or so of us on the other side and more still coming through.

Then, think of the sight that confronted us. As we prepared our arms we saw, coming towards us down the narrow streets from two sides into the square where we had emerged, the Emperor Murzuphlus himself, dressed in full regalia, and the mounted soldiers of the imperial bodyguard.

If you think that I played a coward's part in the battles, you should think again. I had my quarrels with the cause of our fight, but when it came to fighting I was every bit as brave as the next man. For we did not flee at the sight of them but, encouraged by Lord Peter of Bracuel, we stood our ground, waiting for the Emperor to charge at us and preparing for whatever fate had in store.

And our bravery was well rewarded for, when he was halfway to our lines, the Emperor stopped still. There was a wait that seemed to go on forever. We prepared ourselves for a fight we would surely have lost. Yet the Emperor himself gave orders that his men should withdraw. They did not withdraw in an orderly fashion, but fled in disarray. A great shout went up, the rest of the wall was broken down and our men set about occupying the towers and the buildings nearby.

In the meantime Peter of Amiens broke into the city through another set of sea-gates. He met with no resistance and was able to ride directly to the scarlet-coloured tents from which Murzuphlus had been directing military operations. In the tents there were coffers full of treasure. This was the first booty of the battle.

I was amongst those following the Greek army up the main street. The Greeks who had turned out to watch, including women and children, were still fleeing in terror.

It was in the upper storey of a tall house that I thought I saw Hildegunde through a window. It could only have been her with that blond hair, those eyes, the graceful way she moved her head, so beautiful it was like a bolt of fire from the sun shooting through me. I stared, but she did not see me. She moved away from the window, and her form was lost amongst the shadows of the inner room.

I banged on the door, but it was locked firmly. Other soldiers saw me and must have thought I was mad when there was so much booty to be had from Murzuphlus' tent. At last I knocked the door down and rushed through the house, searching every room. It was quite empty. The occupants had moved out all their possessions.

Was I going mad? Had I seen a ghost? Perhaps Hildegunde had died in Germany and this was her spirit, which had come to seek me out. Yet she looked so real, so lifelike.

I joined the other soldiers. There was plenty to do. They had to be restrained and regrouped, in case there was another attack. We took up positions in and around the monastery of the All-Seeing Christ, the Pantepoptos.

There was no more fighting that day; all the Greeks had fled from that district of the city. Yet another fire started, this time greater than any we had ever seen before. It began in a part of the city we had taken and where we thought the Greek army would be. It spread faster than we had expected, and we were lucky that the wind did not change to blow the fire back into our camp. We felt vulnerable as the smoke billowed over the city, and the cries of those who were burning could be heard.

I spent the night in the monastery itself. I was exhausted but did not sleep. We were subdued. There was no feasting and no celebration. We were conscious of the fact that it was the Monday after Palm Sunday. Rather than riding in procession into Jerusalem, we, a Christian army, had just fought, and were just about to fight once more, another Christian army. We had spent the day in carnage and slaughter, and for all we knew the next day would be just the same. And we dared lodge in the monastery of the All-Seeing Christ.

How would the All-Seeing Christ judge us? Would it be with defeat the next day, with a slow, lingering death, and were the fires outside harbingers of the eternity of damnation we had before us? Throughout the camp there was a deathly, fearful hush in anticipation of what was to come. The Greeks who had been captured, mostly monks, were rounded up and kept under guard in a great hall, but they were not hurt or mistreated, not that night. They were holy men. And I suppose we feared that soon we might be in need of their prayers. We knew well enough that we might be their prisoners the next day.

The next morning when dawn broke, the sun rose through the choking, acrid smoke that hung so thick over the city that it was scarcely brighter than at night-time. There was nothing but an eerie silence. No battle. No attack. We kept to our positions, waiting.

Then, towards the middle of the morning, men from the Emperor's guard, themselves mostly Franks and Englishmen, came to offer their services to our armies, saying that Murzuphlus and his wealthy attendants had fled from the Bucoleon Palace, where they had attempted to gather their forces but failed.

As soon as the news got round there was pandemonium. The men went on the rampage. There was no more real fighting then - only murder, pillage, rape.

# XX

## Judgement

✠

The next two days were utterly darkened by the smoke from the fires burning throughout the city. I wandered hither and thither in a desperate state of mind, seeking Hildegunde.

It was worse than any vision of Hell my imagination could have conjured, worse even than Zara. Everywhere there was burning, destruction, soldiers with faces frog-like with greed, running riot, their bags and pockets stuffed full with precious objects, women and children screaming, corpses left to rot, old men sick and weeping, sitting outside their gutted homes, girls bleeding, rocking back and forth in anguish, violated and debased, children's little bodies littering the streets like refuse.

The earth seemed to quake with the masses of people running to and fro, and thick clouds of ash fell everywhere like hail.

On the second day I tried to go to the palace library. Hildegunde might be there, amongst the books. No one else, I thought, would seek knowledge in libraries at such a time, except perhaps Hildegunde.

But it was too late. The libraries were already burning. If the secret of the Music of the Spheres had been contained there, now it was gone, floating up to heaven in the plumes of smoke.

Great fires were lit in open squares for the melting down of statues, so that the soldiers could fill their pockets with gold and silver. No one thought of the beauty or the craftsmanship of the objects they were destroying, only the value of the metal.

On one street I saw Greeks, young and old men, women and children, lined up by Frankish soldiers. They were rolling dice to decide how to kill them, and taking bets on how long they would take to die. So, for the sake of a few pieces of silver, men, women and children were stripped, stabbed, hanged, beaten, stoned and burnt to death, with a callousness that beggared belief. Their screaming and shouting and weeping in the agony of their deaths just made our soldiers laugh.

On the third day I decided to go to the palace to see the throne of the Holy Patriarch. A large crowd was gathered and at first I thought that one of the great ones was about to make a speech. But no, there was a whore, dancing and cavorting half naked on the throne itself, twirling her robes of purple and scarlet round her, her pimps shouting that the price to have her on the holy throne itself was twenty pieces of silver. Dozens were queuing for the privilege.

I thought of Katrin. Was there someone like me in this girl's life, someone who had betrayed her as I had betrayed Katrin? I vowed that if ever I got any money, if ever I got back to Germany, I would seek out Katrin and make sure that she was provided for.

The stench of the city was overwhelming.

I walked away from the palace, through the wrecked and looted streets, craving some air, some space. There is a great tower in the centre of Constantinople, or at least there was one, for I do not know if the inhabitants will have left it standing, since this was the tower from which the Emperor, Murzuphlus, was thrown to his death. I felt impelled to go to that tower, to climb it, to look down from above at the horror of what had once been a lovely city, to reflect on how I had contributed to this terrible perversion of history. Then I would decide whether or not to cast myself from the tower, and so judge myself by paying for these terrors with my own life.

I thought of how we should have taken Jerusalem. I climbed the tower as if in a dream, then sat on one of the steps at the top of the tower and looked out towards the hills, far beyond the centre of the city. I imagined a true army, an army of the poor, the sons of Lazarus, a remnant of the debauched army of Constantinople, setting off there and then on a march that would be long and arduous, but would lead eventually to Jerusalem.

The more I thought, the more clearly I could see in my mind's eye what we should have done. I imagined us marching on and on, through the lands to the east, then Syria, caring nothing for the hardships, singing all the while, our faith purified and increased with every step, every trouble, the atmosphere amongst us like that vision I had when I was at school, of people walking through the great forest, collecting more and more people on the way, our faith constantly growing, then arriving before Jerusalem, where the air would be clear as crystal, the sun brilliant as the most precious gem, radiant with gold shafts of light that would pour out to illuminate the city, its massive walls, its towers and minarets.

I imagined how we could take Jerusalem, not with weapons but with the power of holy love and song. Because of our faith, as we marched, others would join us; even the Saracen would want to be one with us when they saw the purity and holiness of our ways, the true joy we shared.

Some, including Hildegunde, those who know the secrets of the Last Days, would have gone before and prepared the inhabitants for our coming. Therefore, because they would know that we were the Good Army, the Army of the Poor who came in the name of the True Christ and of Justice, the Saracen of Jerusalem would not arm for battle, but would come out to greet us, and set out tables before us covered in rich foods, oranges, apples, pastries, sweets, milk, sweet honey, wines and dishes the likes of which no one ever dreamt.

Then I imagined the sun setting, beautiful music filling the air, some playing the harp, others lutes and pipes, others fiddles, trumpets, cymbals, still others singing, so that the music was like that of a whole host of angels. The sky was a beautiful crystal blue, the stars were shining deep in the firmament. Beneath, I was walking hand in hand with Hildegunde. She wore long, white garments and her eyes were like the pure waters of paradise. We walked to the Holy Sepulchre, which began to shine forth all on its own with a mysterious light. This was the sign to us and to the people that we were to be Emperor and Empress, until the time of the Antichrist, from which would proceed the glorious day when Christ Himself would come to reign forever.

Such was my vision. There was no more death, rape and destruction, but men and women rebuilding the Temple, some working with gold, silver, bronze and iron, others with blue, purple and red cloth, some making musical instruments, harps and lyres with juniper wood from the Lebanon, and trumpets and flutes from gold and silver. I imagined them recasting the bronze columns, decorated with the pattern of a thousand pomegranates, the inner rooms of the Temple being panelled with cedar and juniper, overlaid with gold, decorated with flowers, chain patterns and the winged creatures which will appear one day, but not for many years.

For a moment it was almost as if I could see the walls of the Temple rebuilt with stones of jasper, sapphire, agate, emerald, onyx, carnelian, yellow quartz, beryl, topaz, chalcedony, turquoise and amethyst.

All this was so vivid in my mind that I had almost forgotten where I was, at the top of that tower, from which I had planned to throw myself. I was alone, or at least I thought I was alone. I looked up into the dull blue sky over Constantinople, the smoke curling, then down at the roofs, spires and domes of the city. Whole swathes of the city were now little more than rubble and the wrecked carcasses of houses and buildings, because of the appalling fires that our armies had caused to burn.

In the sky, above the sea, there was a cloud that seemed to possess the shape of a walled city. I imagined I could stand and, reach out, walk, fly towards it, from the top of the tower.

I knew that I would fall, and that the fall would kill me; but I did not care. I did not see it that way. I would be walking towards the cloud. After the fall there would be Jerusalem, or hell, or the terrible void of nothingness. Anything was better than the real

Constantinople, the death, the destruction, and the sense of failure and self-disgust that all my ideals had come to this.

As to what happened next, Philippos, you will understand that I thought I was going mad, that everything normal in reality had been stripped away and that I would remain forever a prisoner of strange and obscure illusions. I was about to stand up, and I am sure to this day that I would have thrown myself from the tower, when I felt hands resting on my shoulders. The touch shocked me. It was as though I had been surprised in my thoughts, and I felt suddenly guilty, ashamed of them. I did not dare look round at first.

Then there was the voice. So familiar and so chilling: 'Do not fail us, Walter. Remember all that you learned at school, from Uqhart, and at the monastery of Frankenburc. You know how dangerous it is to fight your destiny, to follow the wrong path, the selfish path. You remember what Pauli drove himself to. I am sorry for the pain we caused. But you will understand.'

I felt so stunned, by the voice and by what it had spoken that I did not move. Yet it was so clear, so distinct, I could even feel the hairs on the back of my neck bristle at the touch of his breath. Or was it the breeze? No, there was the feeling of his hands on my shoulders. Was I going mad? Was it a vision?

Then, as I sat, to all intents and purposes paralysed, suddenly every detail of my young days returned – my studies at Babenberch with Uqhart, the great patterns of the cosmos, the meaning of the numbers, Boethius' vision of eternity, his distinction between the foreknowledge of God and predestination, chance and Providence; then I remembered poor Katrin and her music – but now, in my mind, what I learnt from her, of music and of love, was no longer separate from and opposed to all else that I had learnt, but in harmony and at one with it.

I glanced up, briefly, at the cloud that I had taken to be the New Jerusalem, and saw, projected against it in my mind's eye, Uqhart's face, and then Katrin's as she was when she was young, when we were lovers and she taught me how to sing.

All these thoughts came in a split second, much less time than it has taken for me to set them out here.

The Abbot Quintus. His voice. My mind continued reeling back to my school-days, to my time in the monastery, to that beautiful, deceptive peace, going to and from chapel, where the only sounds were of the water-mill, of the birds singing, the cowbells in the distance and the chapel bell ringing for services. It was his voice. I felt the pressure of his hands leave my shoulders. Then, for a few minutes, I simply could not move, and I stared, out into the blue of the sky, towards my cloud, which now looked just like any other.

I summoned my strength and stood up. The Abbot, or whoever - whatever - he was, was already gone. I turned and ran in leaps and bounds down the spiral staircase. I caught up closely enough to catch sight of the squareness of his head, the greyish white of the habit. But how could he be running so fast? Was I chasing some disembodied spirit? There was a group of soldiers coming up the stairs. They blocked my path and jostled me, but I was determined to force my way through. Were they there just by chance? The Abbot must have passed through them like air.

Now there was no sign of him. Only too late did I realise there were doors, just smaller than a man's height, on the side of the stairwell where the wall was thickest, and that these doors led to other chambers. The Abbot could have entered any one of these. I looked inside one that was unlocked and saw there were ladders leading from each room to the one above and to the one below. He could have gone up or down.

Then the concentrated memory of my young days returned, not as intensely as before. It began to occupy my mind and I lost heart as far as pursuing the Abbot was concerned. I felt elation and dejection, both at the same time.

I made my way back down into the streets and the sunlight and continued my wanderings through the city.

That night my sleep was feverish and disturbed. My mind teemed with memories of my past, and I was tortured by the desire to find out if I truly had seen Hildegunde and the Abbot Quintus.

Early next morning I set out through the streets again, this time with the certain intention of confronting the Doge of Venice. Increasingly I sensed that he was the Blind One, and that everything centred on him. What I would do, when finally I confronted him, I did not know. Would I inquire politely if he could help me trace Hildegunde and Quintus, or would I allow myself the satisfaction of losing my temper and accusing him of failing us; of being responsible for the perpetration of all the horrors that had taken place at Zara and Constantinople?

I reached the Blachernae Palace, where I knew the Doge would be staying. I had heard that he would often leave the palace to ride about the city, to direct the acquisition of booty or, by his presence, to help quell fights between rival factions of the Latin armies. I waited for an hour outside the palace, squatting on a low wall beneath a tattered lemon tree. I was in a terrible state of fatigue, almost shaking with nerves, yet staring wide-eyed, expecting at any moment to glimpse either the Abbot, the Doge or Hildegunde.

One hour went past, then another. I took out my lute and began strumming a song about Jerusalem, slowly, sadly, and it created an odd dissonance with the shouting and screaming coming from the city. Then, towards the middle of the day, I glimpsed him, the Doge of Venice. He was wearing rich clothes and was at the centre of a procession of nobles and soldiers.

This was my opportunity. There was the monster responsible for all the carnage and desecration. I felt full of rage as I strode towards him, pushing my way through the crowds.

For a moment the Doge seemed to look towards me with his blind eyes. Something snapped within me. I felt something between fear, hatred and fascination. But he and his retinue did not leave the enclosed area of the palace. They were simply processing from one hall to another.

I thought of trying to push my way into the palace grounds, to whichever chambers he had appropriated; but I realised they would never let me in.

I looked up at the sky. The sun had been shining brilliantly all morning above the smoke which rose from the town, but now clouds began to gather, which took on the same sickly brown hue as the smoke rising up towards them.

Eventually I could stand waiting no longer. I decided I wanted to walk the city walls by the sea. I never got as far as the sea, however.

Just as I was walking through a quieter courtyard round the back of the Great Palace I thought I saw Hildegunde again. Now she was wearing blue, like the first time I saw her. It was a simple dress. How gracefully she moved! How she stood out from the crowds! But what was she doing there?

I called her name, but she did not hear me. Again I felt that I was seeing a creature from another realm. There was a stillness about her that contrasted strongly with the sickening scenes going on all round. She seemed to be looking for something, someone.

I called after her once more, but she turned a corner. I ran to where she had stood and just saw her back as she went into another garden in the palace complex. I shouted her name at the top of my voice, but by the time I reached the garden she was no longer in sight.

The only place she could have gone to was back out on to the street, amongst the crowds. I got up and started walking across the outer courtyard of the palace, beneath what remained of the palm trees, and then round the back towards the sea, which, since the clouds had gathered, had changed colour from deep blue to a foreboding greeny grey.

Then, almost as if it had been planned, coming out of a side gate, wearing a dull, russet red cloak rather than the normal crimson, I saw the Doge of Venice himself, in the company of just four men, who wore ornamental helmets and whom I took to be high-ranking officers. Once more it was as if his blind eyes were turning towards me, as if he was aware of my presence, and I felt a chill run through me.

The little group was heading towards a wealthy quarter of the town. Why was the Doge walking about the town in secret? I decided to follow.

The light over Constantinople was dull now. The clouds were coming in low and eerie, warm rain was beginning to fall. At least, I thought, it would put out some of the fires. Yet I was still haunted by my vision of Jerusalem the previous day, and in my feverish, trancelike state I thought I could smell the scent of the cedars of Lebanon.

I stalked the Doge's small party, trying to spy the right moment to confront him, yet always uncertain, hesitating. What would happen to me? Would he listen to me? Would he simply have me arrested? Would I manage to do any good?

They continued to walk further and further from the centre of the city. We picked our way over the rubble of buildings burnt to the ground, past shallow graves of loose earth and boulders marked with crosses, then into another district where all seemed to be as it had been before the invasion, where the people still dressed in fine clothes. Next we reached an area where there must have been looting and fighting the previous night, for there were bodies of Greeks still lying in the streets. Then our strange party, slipping along the narrow streets in the shadows between high houses, arrived in one of the wealthy outskirts of the town. There seemed to have been little burning or looting, yet there were no people anywhere to be seen. There was something ghostly about this place.

Eventually the Doge's party halted at a small, domed church. It was a squat building, undecorated other than with the dog-tooth on the arches. One of the Doge's men fiddled with the chains on the doors. Even from outside I could sense an uncanny atmosphere. I watched the Doge go in. The oak entrance door was left ajar.

As soon as I thought it was safe, I crept up to the door and looked inside. I saw why the church had such an odd atmosphere. It was no longer fit for worship but was stacked high with plundered treasure; it was being used as a warehouse.

In the light shining through the few slit windows that remained unobscured by great piles of treasure, the walls, the boxes, the chests and the massive canvas sheets all seemed to be stained the colour of blood, the blood of those who were killed and maimed so that the Doge could add yet more to the superfluity of his wealth and power. Or so I thought then. From somewhere nearby, just one or two streets away, I heard howling and screaming once more.

Then there was the smell of smoke.

My eyes adjusted to the gloom. There was straw scattered on the floor and the smell coming from within made me think that horses must have been stabled there recently – unless there were more sinister reasons for the smell. I noticed that there were precious objects scattered on the floor, only half covered by the straw, here an icon, there an ivory, there a cross.

I reflected briefly on the Eastern Church's doctrine that icons are doors to the spiritual, signs of the redeemability of matter made possible by the Incarnation. Yet they had not saved this church from the evils of this world.

Suddenly, as if in a dream, I heard a voice intoning my name. It was the voice of the Doge himself. 'Walter von der Ouwe,' he said, 'come in, you are expected.' He had turned towards me and even in the gloom I could see how his unseeing eyes seemed to fix on me. How did he know I was there? What interest could he possibly have in me?

My first thought was to run. Had I been tricked into following them? Perhaps I had been followed. Perhaps, behind me, there would be more soldiers. Besides, this was my great opportunity. Perhaps now everything would become clear. Even if it cost me my life.

I stepped forward and looked over towards the icon screen. The paintings were still just visible beneath the grime, but I could not see what these icons depicted because they were covered with filth.

A deep red cover had been thrown over the altar. In the centre of the altar there was just one candle burning, in a simple bronze holder. Next to it was a chalice.

Just to one side, there he stood, in the darkness. Now, though, he was wearing long robes, all crimson, and a gold chain that hung round his neck. The pendant was a pair of large, interlocking gold rings. How had he managed to don such robes so quickly?

No matter. For the first time, I had my audience with Dandalo, the Doge of Venice, and at a moment I least expected it. The first thing that struck me was that, in spite of his age and blindness – he was over ninety - he was tall and strong. His hair was grey and his face wrinkled, yet there was an extraordinary air of youth about him. He was a man whose energies were far from spent. An eerie light seemed to shimmer behind him.

I remembered how brave he had been during the battle at Galata, how he had been the first to jump from the ship on to the beach, leading the armies. At the same time I remembered the words of the Master of the Templars: '*You are to be a Watcher over the Blind One. If he transgresses, you are to slay him.*' Was this to be required of me now? Had he transgressed? How was I to judge?

But I was unarmed.

He was the first to speak. 'Well, Walter von der Ouwe, what is it that you desire of me?'

My mind raced. I had to keep him talking. I had to find out. But what? I looked round the church, at all the objects strewn about, piled in the dark, and thought of myself becoming history, in this airless storeroom of history.

I thought, and sometimes still think, that this is all there is to us, that we become history. We begin our lives with the illusion that we are individuals. Then great events take us over, like the rape of Constantinople, and all we can do is to play our role in them, a role fixed from the outset.

What was I to say to the Doge? I simply blurted out the first thing that came into my head.

'Do you really think I am Walter van der Ouwe? There are those who seem to think I am something or someone else.'

He stared. Then, slowly, he intoned, 'The Last Emperor, perhaps?' He spoke in a monotone, whether mockingly or quizzically I could not tell.

'Who do you think I am?' I said.

'You are a fool,' he said, 'a true fool.'

Again I could not read his voice. Was this a simple insult? Was he telling me that I had missed something obvious? Or was he trying to tell me that I was a fool in the way that Parzifal was a fool, that I was the sort of fool who would inherit the world, maybe as the Last Emperor? Was I reading too much into what he said? My mind spun round and round.

I began to feel a deep anger welling within me. The voice – *if he transgresses you are to slay him* – rang in my ears.

He continued. 'One of the reasons you are a fool is that you have always allowed yourself to be led. The Brotherhood only had power over you because you wanted them to.'

There was a smile on his face that disarmed me. It was not cruel or sardonic; rather it was human, humorous, loving even. Or so I thought. His blind eyes seemed to look past me, through me. What did he know about the Brotherhood? Was he one of them? Yet surely he was a man like any other, even more vulnerable because of his blindness. I dared hope for sympathy from him, for some kind of answer. I thought of all the Brotherhood had done to me: Uqhart's burning, my separation from Katrin, my banishment from the court, my imprisonment at Aletus... Yet, deep within me, I sensed a reflection of the Doge's smile.

I tried to return that smile. But the mask had returned. Then there was a flapping, a rustling and squeaking above me. I looked up. It was a bat flying across the dome of the roof of the church. The bat caused a chill to run through me, and I wondered if perhaps I had already died and this meeting was part of my descent into hell. I wondered if there was no world outside this desecrated church. There was an odd scent in the air, the scent of sulphur.

I said nothing. I was trying to think how to respond. The Doge had mentioned the Brotherhood, openly. I half understood what he said about me needing the Brotherhood as much as they needed me. Had I not created the Brotherhood for myself? Had I not given them their power over me? Had I not, somehow, wanted my life to be like that?

'There is someone you must meet, your Visitor...' Now the Doge was speaking as though he held me in total disdain. 'For you still do not understand...'

As he spoke, soldiers stepped forward out of the shadows, grabbed me by my arms and led me downstairs towards the vaults below the church. I cried out and tried to struggle. Eventually I managed to get one arm free, but during the course of the tussle one of the soldiers lashed out and caught me a blow across the left temple. I felt all the strength drain from me and a blackness engulfed me.

But it was not as if I had lost consciousness, rather that I had passed directly from one realm into another, for I found myself in what must have been a dream or vision. I saw myself doomed to an underworld, a hell, which was a castle with a thousand windows, yet there was no light, no sky, only blackness, and each window of the castle was lit by the faint light of one candle.

There was a ghostly musician silhouetted in each window. And each of the musicians looked just like me, and sang of some vice, some sin, some act of cruelty or lechery I had committed. The pandemonium of their tuneless playing and singing filled the stifling, sulphurous air, and the damned howled in the dungeons below the castle, as they descended into the lake of flames.

I was led to enter the castle, where there was a pit. It was in this pit that each of the damned was forced to confront Satan himself. They would climb, or be pushed, down a ladder, and then forced to enter a dark cave. There Satan would greet them. He would take on different forms: for example a vain, prattling priest, then a beautiful woman half eaten by worms, then a prince of power, then an inexorably grinding wheel, then a hanged, rotting corpse mouthing dumb words, then a winged creature with cloven hooves, then a vile scarab, then a serpent, hissing and covered with filth and slime - and the damned would each have to kiss that serpent.

I shook myself. I tried to force myself to recover consciousness. The vision passed and I could see normally again.

Next to me I heard a groaning, whimpering sound, and the metallic clunking of chains. I forced my eyes to look into the darkness and I saw, opposite me, the chained figure of a man. In the shadows I could make out that he was tall, and that he was trying to hold his head up, but his back was arched awkardly so it was not easy for him.

I tried to move, but I realised that my hands too had been bound to the pillar against which I was slouched.

'This is your Visitor,' said one of the soldiers.

The pain in my head was abominable. Then, recognition came like a flood of trembling which possessed all my body and mind. The Visitor. There, in flesh and blood. Yet it was so obvious that, but for the pain in my head, I might have laughed.

Though I recognised him I did not recognise his manner. He was a changed man, and what he did took my breath away.

He twisted round, so that he managed to achieve an uncomfortable kneeling position, then he looked at me and wept, as though I were some noble person he had wronged.

Then he looked up towards me and began muttering. I recognised the voice, but it was broken. Slowly I began to understand what he was saying. He talked to me as a long-lost brother, begging me for forgiveness. I thought I was dreaming, that this was another hallucination. I realised too that he had been the fifth man at Soria, the tall, helmeted man wearing black. Why had I not recognised him then? It was almost as though I had deliberately chosen not to.

He seemed to be in pain. I could not tell at first whether he was ill or whether he had been injured. I was soon to find out. He was short of breath and his face was bruised and scarred. All his haughtiness had gone, his power to command. I remembered how fine he had looked at court astride his white horse. How far he had fallen to come to this. It was the Graf himself.

'Forgive me, Walter, please forgive me,' he repeated the same words over and over again. The light from the torch licked eerily over the stone wall in front of us and lent an odd glow to his face.

The Graf fell silent and breathed deeply as he tried to compose himself. Then he said, all in a rush, 'We were responsible for so much, Walter. I helped Quintus set up the plan to abduct you via the ex-priest Josephus. He wanted you for his monastery, even as a child. Yet Joseph and the woman took pity on you and returned you to your father's house. You know the rest...'

As he spoke, it was as though I had been transported out of that place and back to the forest of my dreams, with tall, interarching trees, and sunlight pouring between the branches as through a million crystals of emerald, and I saw myself, as a young boy, running over the rich brown earth, smelling the fresh, rich smells of the German forests in springtime, not the filth and decay of hoarded treasure, nor the stench of sulphur that curled round me in the vaulted gloom of this place.

Then in my mind's eye I saw Josephus again, the day he was hanged, how his feet seemed to run away into some distant realm, and my feet were his feet. And then, again, it was though I was running, through the forests...

Suddenly a question formed in my mind, a question I had forgotten for years and years. 'Who was she, the woman who was with Josephus?'

'A young noblewoman, the daughter of one of my vassals, who had left her home and family to live with the priest because she said she loved him... Because Josephus kept his word, and did not betray us, she was spared. She prays for him now at Hohenfeld.'

Hohenfeld. I thought of Hildegunde. I remembered that moonlit night when I had, without knowing what I was doing, delivered Hildegunde there, how the convent stood like a ghostly, silver silhouette against the deep blue sky, like an unreal realm beyond and above this fallen world of ours. To think that she had been there, in the same place as the lovely woman who had looked after me in the forest, my second mother, the woman who was perhaps the first to inspire in my young mind something of the true love of women. I wondered if they had known each other. I wondered if they had ever talked of me.

'Hildegunde,' I said, 'is she here? What has become of her?'

'I did not go to see her. Not after what happened between us.

But I have news of her. When she heard you had taken Templar vows, she accepted the suit of a young noble. She has born him two sons. Those who know her say she often sings your songs.'

'But surely she is here. I saw her, twice. And at Zara.'

'I do not think that can be possible, Walter. I know that she is married. I saw the documents. And with young children she would never... Unless it was her soul you saw,' he added wistfully.

While he spoke I remembered all that was lovely about Hildegunde, particularly those days before we became lovers, when our two souls seemed to weave together into a oneness through our learning and our pursuit of the ideals of courtly life. Then I remembered the fateful joust with Johannes of Ulm, my awful separation from Hildegunde.

'If only I could say that the others were manipulating me,' the Graf was saying. 'But that would not be true. I am as guilty, perhaps more guilty, than the rest of them. I am most to blame. I repented, but I repented too late. We watched your every move. For years. Then at last it fell to me to look after you. I did my best for you, but I failed you. All through my pride, my jealousy, my foolish desire for revenge...'

For a moment I lost track of what the Graf was saying. It was not so important as the memories his voice stirred. I saw myself back there once more, that beautiful starry night when I first loved Hildegunde, the feeling of anticipation before the mêlée as I rode out against Johannes of Ulm, the sense of youth, strength...

'I should have realised you were innocent. I was not sure until one morning, in chapel, when I was trying to say my prayers, and I saw a vision of you and Hildegunde, separated, each walking the surface of the earth, poor, hungry and lost. That was when I decided to follow you. I traced you to Soria, through the Brotherhood, then I became separated from them. At last I traced you to Venice, then Zara, then here. The moment I arrived at Estanor they sought me out and kept me in captivity, threatening me that I might be tried as a spy. Then they told me the truth about you, that you were here. They say they will only forgive me if you forgive me. You are my judge.'

I was reflecting that without the Brotherhood I would have been a cartwright in Nurenberc to that very day. Is that what I would have wanted? 'Walter, I failed you, and I failed them. And I failed Hildegunde... I cannot see like the others in the Brotherhood, yet they used my power in this world...'

Another question. I had to find out after all these years: 'Graf, my father,' I said, 'why did he die?'

'We do not know. We had not planned for it. Maybe it was despair at losing you. Or maybe... he had other beliefs.'

For a moment I could glimpse my father's face, smiling as he had when he looked at me when I was a little boy. For the first time in years I felt a great surge of love for him. I felt reconciled with him. There was a sense in which nothing else really mattered any more. I turned towards the Graf once again.

I felt strangely detached. His words of explanation did not matter so much as the textures of the days they invoked, and as he spoke I continued to be lost in spiralling dreams of my past. There seemed so much to take in, as so many images from my past flickered before my eyes.

After a long silence, I said, 'I forgive you, for what it's worth...'

'Thank you,' he said, and a tension seemed to go out of the air. No one came.

I began to realise just how alone we were – in the damp, earthy dungeon below the church. The Doge and the soldiers must have gone while the Graf spoke and I was dreaming. The Graf was no longer speaking now but making sounds which were perhaps sobs – I could not be sure.

Did I really forgive the Graf? It was the only way I would ever be able to forgive myself.

The Graf was lying back now. He grew calmer. Quietly, I hummed some of my old songs. At last, the Graf slumped, asleep I presumed.

I closed my eyes and tried to dream of the happy times I had spent with Hildegunde, before all this, and an immense calm descended on me too.

As the day wore on, what little light there was in the cell faded. Still, no one came. I called out to the Graf a couple of times, but he was asleep or unconscious, dead for all I knew.

I wondered if forgiveness could kill a man.

Then, a terrible image began to form in the darkness, in front of my mind. It was the Doge's face, only with great metal hooks hanging from his lips and his ears, his face turning coal black, those eyes of his flaming, his ears then suddenly like those of an ass.

Then I saw him as the ten-horned beast, the last of worldly powers. I tried to remind myself that it was written that the true Antichrist would be a Jew of the tribe of Dan, and that he will be born of a harlot in Palestine, and educated by sorcerers who have remained true to the old arts. It was written too that he would found a church that will be called the Whore of Babylon, 'the woman drunk with the Blood of the Saints'. Surely none of these things applied to the Doge. Or were they still to come? Was he, perhaps, a harbinger of the Antichrist, and not the Antichrist himself? Wrestling with these thoughts, these visions, I too must have fallen unconscious.

I came to my senses as someone was tugging at my arm, hands undoing the fetters that bound me to the pillar. Then I remember being made to walk, stumbling in a haze, through arches, vaults, corridors, sewers and passageways, a city of dank tunnels, mantled in silence, beneath the very streets of Constantinople itself. I was exhausted and feverish, and I had no way of telling how far we were walking or in which direction.

For a time I became aware of what sounded like the lapping of the sea. Then we were climbing endless steps, half lit by torches. I tried to speak to the soldiers who were leading me, but I received no reply.

Eventually a door swung open and I was half led, half pushed, on to a soft bed in a nobly decorated, candlelit room. Out of a narrow window I glimpsed moonlight. Next to the bed there was fruit, bread and some cheese. There was a pitcher of water and another of wine.

The men who had led me there left immediately. I was quite alone.

I got up and walked round. There was a door leading to another room, then another door leading to another chamber, which was slightly larger. In the corner there was a place for ablutions.

I splashed water on my face, then looked out of one of the windows, through which I could just make out the dark horizon of the sea and a black sky in which no stars shone.

The rooms must have been on the top floor of a townhouse belonging to a noble or a wealthy merchant. All night long I could hear the waters of the sea lapping at the walls.

These rooms were to be my prison, and my refuge, for the next twelve weeks.

Though I was a prisoner, I lacked nothing. I had the three rooms to myself and was provided with fresh clothes, food, water and wine. My lute was returned to me, and my writings.

But there was no way out – just one stairway to the ground floor.

The door to it was locked and I knew it was guarded by soldiers because of the response when I shouted. It would have been possible to force my way through one of the windows and jump, but it was so high that I would certainly have been killed. Outside, the walls were steep and smooth. There was nothing to hold on to, so climbing would have been impossible. Besides, soldiers guarded the house on the land side day and night, so I would have been unlikely to escape even if, by some miracle, I had reached the ground below.

Each day, I tried shouting to the soldiers, but they understood no language familiar to me. They were certainly not Greeks. I supposed they must have come from somewhere in the distant East.

On the fourth day I began to receive visits from the man who called himself Father Martinus. He always came with one of the soldiers. I presume this was in case I tried any violent tricks to escape. He made it his business to look after me, and was kind in every way, bringing me books to read, and music. He even offered to provide me with women; though I was tempted, I refused.

During the first few days I tried to ply him with questions about where I was, why I was being held prisoner, what was to become of me. Whenever I did this he fell silent, kindly asked if there was anything else I required, and left with the guard.

For a week or so, this man was my only contact with the world.

He came once a day, in the early evening, when the light was such that I could not see him very clearly. He wore robes, not unlike those of the Cistercians, though he said that he did not belong to their Order. He would not tell me what Order he did belong to. He responded to none of the secret signs and I was certain that he was not a knight of the Temple. At first I was afraid of him because his face was so deeply scarred and flecked with yellows, browns and reds. There were folds of skin that made his face less like that of a man and more like that of a reptile.

His eyes were an odd, yellowish colour, and it was certainly hard to look for long at that twisted, pock-marked face of his without feeling revulsion. I supposed this was a result of some deformity of birth, and I knew that I should not judge by appearances. Nonetheless, his presence did make me feel uneasy. Something about him was familiar, and stirred some memory in my mind – something uncanny, which I could not quite place.

Yet, as I said, he was very kind and made it his business to provide me with anything and everything I wanted – except information about the reasons I was being held, or my freedom. He brought me a hot meal each day and left bread, meat and fruit, and plenty of water and wine. When he had gone, I had everything I needed.

At times I felt sure they would kill me there; but deep down I sensed that something else would happen, that the words spoken to me about the Blind One would be fulfilled.

I tortured myself about my failure to kill the Doge. It would have been so easy, yet I sensed that I had done the right thing.

Then I wondered what had become of the Graf. Was he still down there in that vault, dying, dead maybe? Would the Doge have released him?

I could take all this and wait patiently for my fate. In spite of what the Graf had told me though, there were those three occasions on which I was sure I had seen Hildegunde. I tried to convince myself it was a trick of my mind, and I tried to relive every detail of those sightings, just in case. The thought of her being present in this dangerous city, no matter who might be protecting or manipulating her, filled me with dread. I wondered if the forces that were holding me had brought Hildegunde here. And if so, to what purpose?

I still remember how at certain times of day sunlight flooded the rooms. Outside, the spring must have been beautiful. At night, when there was a full moon, the sky was filled with a blue shimmering light, and all the stars seemed to shine more brilliantly than I had ever seen them shine before.

Nothing could have prepared me for the shock that was to follow.

One morning there was a knock on the door at the same time as usual. The door was flung wide open, but this time it was not Father Martinus.

I could scarcely believe it. I saw in front of me a young man with brown hair, maybe just a little younger than me. Those bright, doe-like eyes I had last seen closed, swaying above me when we were ambushed near Carcassonne. Ewald.

'How are you?' he said, and crossed the room to embrace me.

His complicity in my imprisonment was immediately obvious from the fact that he was carrying with him my daily provisions.

I returned his embrace, but though I was pleased to see him I was deeply suspicious. I remained silent.

'Look,' he said, 'I have brought you these.' In addition to the food, water and wine, he had with him a very large scroll, writing equipment, and reams of paper.

I glanced at the scroll. On it was depicted a chart just like those I had been given at Richerenches and subsequently at Zara. This one was even more detailed. The hieroglyphs, beautifully drawn using different coloured inks, were set out in a vast figure of eight, or rather the sign for eternity, and on this chart it was so much easier to see what each figure represented.

'Why are you here?' I asked eventually.

'Have you not realised yet? I am one of the elect, one of you. After Antonius was killed by the lightning.'

I was still looking at the chart, and my gaze fell on the hieroglyphs of the wheel of fortune, the hanged man, the stricken tower. I began to remember all the time of my wanderings, round the Staufen lands, then across southern Franconia to the Pyrenees, that cruel mock trial, and then how I had followed Tremgistus to Soria. So, Ewald too was one of them.

'What do you want of me?' I asked.

'Walter, we have so much in common. All I want, all any of us want, is for you to accept that you are one of us, to join us formally.'

'But who are you?' I could not understand it. After all they had done to me, after all the pain they had caused – now to hear that I was already one of them, that I should join them formally... What did it all mean?

'You already know who we are. The Brotherhood of Prayer of Charlemagne.'

'What if I say no, that I will not join you?'

'You do not understand yet. Or at least you think you don't. That is why I brought you these.' He pointed to the chart, to the writing implements. 'Study the chart, Walter, and write down what you know of us, of yourself. Then decide.'

As he spoke, I looked beyond him, through the window, at the infinite sky above the sea. I thought about the infinite movement of the waters of the sea and about my wanderings – all the inexplicable moments of my life. I began to wonder if there was a pattern after all, only a pattern I had not yet grasped.

I talked at greater length to Ewald, who was kind and

affectionate, and sincerely wanted me to say that I was part of this Brotherhood which had caused me so much hurt. Why did he think I was one of them?

As for Ewald, he told me that he had been rescued from the tree where he had been left hanging by someone he referred to obscurely as 'a wise old monk', an Augustinian from Germany called Brother Foden. He refused to elaborate other than to hint that hanging there, expecting to die, waiting for me to come and cut him down, had been an experience that had changed his life. This Brother Foden had looked after him, he said, and set him on the path that had led, eventually, to his presence here.

The last question I asked him that day was about the Doge. I wanted to know how he could possibly serve such a monster, who was directly responsible for all the horror that had befallen Constantinople.

Ewald stared long and hard at me. All he said was, 'Ah, then you do not understand the Doge. You must write, as I have been told to instruct you. Then all will become clear.'

'What about Hildegunde? Where is she?' I cried passionately. 'And the Graf, what has become of him?'

'They are safe and well.' This was all he would say before, sensing I was becoming excited, he got up and left.

I was annoyed at his departure, but straight away I set about the task he had set me. I wrote down everything I could remember, and studied the chart deeply.

Father Martinus came as usual, and I received more visits from Ewald. They were both always polite and friendly. They would talk at length about anything to do with art, music, literature, philosophy, the attempts to establish order in Constantinople, news from our home countries, but as soon as I began to ask questions about how much longer I was to be detained, or about Hildegunde or the Brotherhood, they fell silent and made an excuse to leave.

What I wrote during those weeks forms the basis of these pages, Philippos, though, as you will see, there is much that I have corrected in the light of subsequent knowledge. Then, as now, writing was a great help in settling my spirits, and in discovering patterns in things, so much so that I have often wondered if perhaps what we call reality is in fact a great book, written and read by God, in which we are hieroglyphs. And I wonder too if perhaps our writing is an echo of the divine writing.

During that time of imprisonment, this is how I would spend my days. I would rise at dawn, say or sing Prime and Matins, then start writing. I would write until I received a visit from Martinus or Ewald. I would share breakfast with them, and wash as soon as they left me. Then I would study the chart or read until midday, when I would eat lunch. After lunch I would write again until I was tired, then I would sleep a little. On waking, I would study the chart or read other books, until it was time to say Vespers. After saying Vespers, I would eat, drink wine, read and sing songs until I was tired enough to sleep.

This life began as torture, for all I wanted was to escape and go looking for Hildegunde, and to settle score with those who were holding me captive. Then, in my writings, in the charts and in my songs, patterns began to emerge. The more I pursued these patterns, the more fascinated I became. There were correspondences everywhere, particularly in the charts. It was like an uncanny dream, sense and nonsense all rolled into one.

I wondered if there was anything diabolical about the chart. Maybe it contained some formula for the summoning of the spirits of evil, or of the dead. Or maybe it was a pattern for tracing the development of the soul towards perfection and union with God, or another version of the zigzag of lightning Uqhart used to describe the anatomy of God.

Then I remembered the threaded cone I had seen in the air when I was travelling with Ewald. I remembered how the cone seemed to epitomise the shape of all knowledge. This chart I now had in front of me seemed to reflect the same shapes, and I imagined that in the twenty-two hieroglyphs I could see pictures of the thrice seven subjects of the liberal arts.

Then again the hieroglyphs would glow in my mind and I would see in them the stages through which base matter must pass as it is transformed by the alchemist into gold.

Then the images I saw in the hieroglyphs would weave their way into my dreams, so that I imagined whoever composed them must have seen the course of my life in advance.

Eventually I became convinced that each of the pictures referred to some specific time of my life. The Fool stepping off a cliff was me as a child; the Magician was me proud of my knowledge at school; the Papess was Katrin, who first showed me the link between love and music... Even the Stricken Tower was the church at Soria; the Star, Aldebaran, the star I saw on the night before my departure for Venice; the Moon was the moon I saw over Zara; and the Sun was the fire at Constantinople.

Gradually I began to see all these things of my past as an outsider, dazzled by a presence, a burning presence, to which I could not be reconciled because of its fiery brightness. Everything – my childhood, my father, my learning, my singing, my loves, my wanderings – was all contained in it.

Yet the very consistency inspired me with fear and terror, for it was as though I had no control over it all. For that reason I could not distinguish what was good and evil in it all, what was mine and what was not mine.

I remember how I became fascinated by the mysterious angel-like figure at the centre of the Arabic figure of eight. She was surrounded by a kind of wreath and four strange creatures. But then I did not understand what she represented. I thought of gold, perhaps, or death. My own death.

There was something else, something that began to cause me great fear. I became aware of memories I possessed, which came to me at times, memories of long ago, from far in the past. Once, for example, I saw myself leading a great army, which was stricken with a terrible plague. We were in the great plains of northern Italy and I was dying. I wondered if I had been touched by the spirit of the Sleeping Emperor, who will return one day. I began to feel too that

I could glimpse the future, and talk to those who are yet to come, to warn, to tell. For example, I saw great iron monsters over the skies of my home town, pouring out fire. I began to see those who one day will sing the songs I wrote, how they live in strange, heavenly places, in rooms that glow with their own light.

Also, I wondered if there are those who do not die but who wander in the world for ever, weaving repeating patterns, seeming to die, sometimes living through others, sometimes in their own right, until at last the Work is complete. Tremgistus, Antonius, Quintus, Stefan us, the Graf, the Doge. And my own spirit. I remember another prophecy about the Last Emperor, '*vivit et non vivit*'*. Perhaps, I thought, this could refer to them and to me. But now, perhaps, I have written too much.

I distinctly remember the day I first began to formulate these thoughts, for something else happened at the same time.

Father Martinus paid his regular call. At first he was his usual, kind self. Then, as I tried to explain to him my thoughts about the chart, albeit in a jovial, detached kind of way, I became aware of his eyes. Because of his deformity, I had never dared look too closely into them, in case he should think that I was staring unkindly.

Had his eyes changed, or was I just noticing them for the first time? They seemed to have lost all their usual kindness and were glowing a hideous, tawny yellow. I recognised that look. He started laughing. It was not his usual laugh. It was a laugh I had thought I would never hear again. And it sent ice-cold shivers down my spine.

I remembered the fire at Soria. The scars, the pock-marks, the blemished skin of the bald head, could all have been caused by burns. I tried to see Tremgistus in him. He was the right build, but the face was so altered. Yet those eyes could only have been his.

He stopped laughing, and spoke. 'You see in me two persons. Two of many. It is true that I have the capacity to change. Like quicksilver.'

*'*He lives and does not live.*'

I tried to speak. So many thoughts wanted to explode in my head. At first I desired revenge for all the pain he had caused me, for the way he had stood between me and Katrin, my father, Uqhart... Then I realised that if he had been burnt like that, in the terrible fires at Soria, then I already had my revenge. Then I remembered all the kindness he had shown to me in the last few weeks. He had nursed me, kept me informed of events in the outside world, fed me, brought me food and wine, even helped me with my writing.

His laughter gradually subsided. 'Do not ask, Walter. You know the answer. There is no answer. Only the patterns you perceive. And there is no need for you to say sorry' – he gestured to his face – 'for this... It was the lightning, and it was because of what I am. You remember what Uqhart used to say: "*Solve et coagule*" – dissolve and distil. Rather, I should say sorry to you, for all the pain I caused. But now you probably do understand.'

I found myself unable to move. I did not know whether to strike him or embrace him. As it was, he stood up, placed a hand on my shoulder and left. I heard the door close. I was still their prisoner.

You can imagine the state of turmoil my mind was in by then. Thoughts of our armies, of Jerusalem, of Constantinople itself, were far removed from me. My past, and the patterns formed by my past, these surprise confrontations with those I never thought to see again, heaved and bubbled in my mind like the molten rocks in a volcano.

# XXI

## The World

✠

That night I did not fall asleep until the moon was high above the window. There had been a strong wind during the day, which caused great white crests to appear on the choppy waves of the sea. All that evening, much louder than usual, I was aware of the sound of the waters beating against the rocks beneath my window.

Yet when I did sleep, the sleep I fell into was so deep and at the same time so clear, that it seemed, even as I was dreaming, that I had died and was about to pass into a different realm.

I shall describe enough of this dream for you, Philippos, so that you will be able to deduce the rest, for it is hard to put such a vision into words.

I began to see, in the distance at first, then growing closer, the last of the hieroglyphs in the chart, floating towards me. At first I was aware of the four creatures depicted there. There was an Eagle, a Bull, an Angel and a Lion. Though I knew, as you do, that these are symbols of the four Gospels, the four elements and so on, I can assure you that these were not mere symbols, but living creatures.

Not only were they living, but from each there issued a strange music, which was both harmonious and still. It was as if they were creatures guarding a door – not a door in the ordinary sense, but a kind of space that it was necessary to pass through.

As their music grew in volume, I began to realise that the sounds were melting together into a new sound, more lovely than the first.

This music was the source of the music of the creatures, yet it was different again from it, and infinitely more lovely, because of a feminine quality it possessed. It was still yet shifting, harmonious yet timeless and serene. All worldly music, even the music I had heard when singing in strange tongues, was only a pale reflection of this. It came from a fifth creature.

I had not seen this creature clearly to begin with, because he, or she, was a long way behind the others through the door I spoke of, and because of a funereal wreath made of laurel that hung in the way. Who was this creature? She was Hildegunde, and she was Death and she was Music. Or maybe she was the true quintessence, unifying each of the other elements yet separate from them, the true goal of the alchemist's seeking, the element through which the lead of matter is changed into the gold of eternity.

As I woke, she was beginning to dance. I began to understand that the music she danced to was the source of all music, which runs through all Creation if only we had ears to hear it. Again, as I woke she was beginning to change. She was no longer just Hildegunde. She became androgynous, for in the vision her body, and her features had become one with those of Christ.

I awoke feeling that I had been bathed in some pure, serene light.

It is a feeling which, ever since, has never left me.

That morning I spent much time pondering what I had dreamt. I remembered the stillness the music had evoked and I tried to recapture it. I stared out at the sky above the sea and imagined that beautiful creature floating there, above the clouds.

This state of mind explains, in some ways, my reaction to what followed.

Towards the middle of the morning there was a loud knocking at my door. I stood to greet whoever should come in, but I did not bother to open it, since I had no key.

The knocking persisted. Eventually, I began to lose patience and walked with the intention of shouting that, whoever they were, they should get the key from the guards.

As I pressed against the door, it fell open on its own. I wondered how long it had been like that.

Behind the door were Fabricius and the Doge of Venice. I recognised Fabricius immediately from his reddish, now greying, curly hair and his extravagant dress. I should not have been so surprised, since he was the last of the five of the Brotherhood. But I was surprised.

As for the Doge, he wore crimson robes embroidered with gold. He was the taller of these two and his deeply lined, bronzed face looked more like that of a wooden statue than that of a man

He was the first to speak. 'Come with us now, Walter, it is time for you to leave this place.'

Behind Fabricius and the Doge there was a retinue of some dozen soldiers. Some were tall and blond; I imagined they must have been members of the Vangarian guard. The others had the yellowish skin and sharp eyes of those who come from the distant East beyond the land where they say Eden lies.

I was led down the steps, and out into the streets.

There seemed to be more order than in the days just after our conquest of the city – no screaming or shouting – but also a sense of emptiness and desolation far from normality.

'Come, Walter, we are to see a burning,' said Fabricius.

I began to feel real fear. I remembered Uqhart's death. Was I to witness the death of some enemy of theirs? Would I once more have to support the stench of the burning of human flesh?

Then came an even more terrible thought: perhaps I was to be burnt. Would this be the outcome of all I had suffered?

I remembered my dream from the previous night, and it seemed to me that perhaps, if my death were to come now, that dream would become a reality, or at least the first stage of a new reality, so much greater than this worldly realm.

Soon we came to a large square. We were not in the centre of Constantinople but in the suburb where many rich Greek merchants had lived. There was a great church.

We stopped on the opposite side of the square to the church. Fabricius said, 'The priest of that church refuses to accept the authority of the Pope, and the people of this district are rebellious. Therefore our armies will burn their church. The priest says he will remain inside. That is his choice. No one is forcing him. No one else is there. The soldiers have cleared it. Maybe you would like to join him.'

All around there were soldiers standing guard. Many Greeks had assembled to look on. They were neither angry not spiteful. They were beyond that. They looked exhausted, fascinated that everything they had ever held dear should be brought suddenly to an end in such a cruel way, too dazed to be angry, only curious to see it all through, to see how the process would come to an end.

'Why should I want to burn?' I asked.

'Who knows?' said Fabricius, and looked towards the Doge, who shrugged and smiled, whether cruelly or kindly I could not tell.

'If you do not wish to burn,' Fabricius went on, 'you can always join us, or admit that you are already one of us.'

I understood. Again the challenge was being placed before me.

I stared over towards the church. All those years of craftsmanship – the finely cut sandstone, the perfect dome. The sun was still just managing to shine, though low clouds were already beginning to roll in from the east.

'How can I admit that I am one of you?' I asked. 'All this barbarism. All this cruelty...' Despite my fear, the stillness of the vision of the previous evening had not left me. I did feel at one with them. And I did want to live. Only I did not want to admit it. Not yet.

There was a murmur from the crowd and I saw the first of the thick, acrid smoke rising from the window of the church. Why had they threatened me with burning? It was already too late for me to go into the church. Or was this just a jibe, a hint of some other worse fate they had in store for me? I thought of the priest inside the church. What must be going on in his mind?

'Power is cruel, Walter. You wanted to take Jerusalem, to be one of a Crusading army that would free Jerusalem forever from the infidel?'

'Of course.'

'The only way Jerusalem can be taken from the Saracen, and kept from the Saracen, is for there to be a direct line, an uninterrupted flow of trade between the Holy Land and the seat of power in Europe. The only way this can be achieved is by destroying any powers opposed to us. And you understand that the Greeks always have opposed attempts to free Jerusalem, because of their own trade interests with the Saracen.'

I reflected on what he said. I could not deny the logic. Then I remembered my hopes for an army of the Pure and the True, the Sons of Lazarus...

'I know what you are thinking, Walter.' It was the Doge speaking now. 'We are powerful. But we are not all-powerful. We can do nothing to alter the rules of power. Only renounce them. Yet then we renounce power itself. And then we can no longer influence the course of history, pursue any ideal. I, for one, have chosen not to renounce power. Will you?' He was speaking kindly to me, like an equal. Why did he need to justify himself to me like this?

Now there was not just smoke, but livid white and yellow flames licking out of the roof of the church. I could feel the heat. I thought of the beautiful paintings on the walls, which no one would ever see again.

Just then a figure rushed from the church. I heard the sneering laughter from various parts of the crowd, and from the soldiers. It was the priest, who had not been able to face that death and who had run out to save his life.

Those words, the instructions entrusted to me by the Templars, which I had forgotten for so long, returned to me: '*You are to be a Watcher over the Blind One. If he transgresses, you are to slay him.*'

I began to tense, to remember my military skills. I wondered if I might find a way of dragging the Doge with me into the flames. I had to be sure, however, and besides, there were too many soldiers about.

What the Doge said next took me by surprise. 'We have all wept because of these things, Walter, those of us who, like you, can *see*. I see visions and wish for truth, beauty, justice, no less than you. Maybe more. You have to choose, Walter. My power, the power I wield through those such as Fabricius, political power, the power of trade, of soldiery, of terror, intrigue, blackmail, espionage, will always be there. It is a question of who wields it. Consider the priest who has just run from the church. And tell me this: if you amplified the consequences of your actions, your loves, your songs, your treacheries, your pursuit of Jerusalem, so that the effect of these things were commensurate to the power I wield, would the result be better or worse than what you see before you?'

As I listened, I gazed into the fire. One of the neighbouring houses was about to catch fire. A woman started screaming. It must have been her house. But no one stirred to help her. The loss of just one more house was nothing to these people now. A couple of Latin soldiers stepped forward to bar her way – not so much because they wanted to protect her, but just because they happened to be there. She screamed more and tried to fight them. One of the soldiers struck her hard across the face. She collapsed on to the ground.

I thought of all the people I had hurt, callously, selfishly – the men I had killed – all for the sake of my ideal of Jerusalem.

'I ask you no more,' said the Doge, 'than that you should forgive us and accept that you are one of us.'

The fire in the church was raging out of control, and was spreading to more and more of the neighbouring houses. The crowd was still silent. Would it ever stop? The heat from the burning was becoming unbearable and hot ash was blowing in our faces.

Could I forgive the Doge? Could I forgive myself and the world? The questions, in my mind, were melting into one, and I resented it.

The sky was beginning to cloud over.

'Come now,' said the Doge. He took my arm and led me away. My mind was spinning. It was as though I was there, and I was not there, both at the same time. Soon we were walking through streets unfamiliar to me. Tall houses arched up on either side of us. Above us angry clouds rolled through the sky.

What was I to say to the Doge? That I forgave him? Or was I to try to find some way of killing him?

As we walked through the streets I began to wonder why I was being treated with such favour. For most mortals, to be allowed to walk in such company, at the head of such a retinue, with the Doge of Venice himself, would be the highest of honours. I observed how everyone, Greek and Latin, made way in deference to us, shrinking, back to the walls of their houses or bowing, depending on their station. How fearlessly the Doge strode at the head of our small procession. And yet it was this same, great man who had just asked me for forgiveness.

I thought I had lost my bearings, but eventually we turned a corner and I found that we were in front of that same church to which I had followed the Doge some twelve weeks previously. This time we entered by the door on the other side, above which was a frieze engraved by some Greek sculptor probably long since forgotten.

The frieze was of the orders of Creation, and above them, the four creatures of the gospels and the elements: the Eagle, the Bull, the Angel and the Lion; air, earth, water and fire. As I looked I saw yet another pattern: in the faces of these creatures I saw the faces of Quintus, the Graf, Antonius and Fabricius.

'Let us go in,' said the Doge.

I looked up at the sky. The clouds were low now. In the distance, out over to sea, to the east, there was lightning.

We stepped into the church. It had changed since I was last there.

Now all the plundered treasure was stacked at the far end, opposite the altar. Dim candlelight lit the church.

In front of the rood-screen were seven seats. The seat furthest to the left was occupied by the Graf of Frankenburc. What was he doing there? He seemed quite recovered, quite composed. Was it truly my forgiveness that had the power to rehabilitate. I wanted to speak to him, but he nodded formally, signalling that I should remain silent. In the next seat sat Quintus, and Tremgistus in the next. The large seat in the middle was unoccupied, as was the one to the right of it. The next seat was occupied by Ewald.

Fabricius and the Doge advanced. Fabricius occupied the seat to the far right and the Doge took, not the central seat as I had expected, but the one to the right of the centre.

I tried to take in my surroundings. The rood-screen had been cleaned, and on it I saw, not the usual icons of the Greek church, but odd patterns of butterflies and caterpillars weaving round pictures of Catherine and the Wheel, Mary Magdalene and Lazarus. There were some pictures of Eastern saints, but I recognised none of them.

Behind me the wall was packed high with chests, boxes, treasures of all sorts. The soldiers who had accompanied us all remained outside, except two, who stood guard by the walls on either side of me.

I noticed that there were precious objects strewn on the ground beneath the piles of treasure. Amongst them I saw a priceless gold cross, encrusted with blood-red rubies. Also, on the altar behind the Doge, was an ancient chalice.

When he had sat down, the Doge began to speak. 'I asked for your forgiveness, Walter. I am sorry for all this. More sorry than you will ever know. We saw this darkness coming. And we would have averted it, by a pilgrimage to Jerusalem. We thought you might be the one to help. But the power of events is too great for us.'

I remembered the last time I was in this place, the sense I had of being in a storeroom of history, of losing myself, of becoming history, becoming the past, in spite of myself. But my vision of the previous night kept returning. It took the edge off my despair. There was the same odd smell in the air. Sulphur. As if, from below the church, the fumes of hell were penetrating to the surface of the earth. Again I remembered Uqhart's words: '*Sulphur and quicksilver, sulphur and quicksilver - solve et coagule.*'

The Doge, continued. 'If you will not forgive, then judge me, judge all of us. That is your right.'

I tried to marshal my thoughts. What questions still remained? I already foresaw the outcome, yet my mind was still divided between an understanding that had resulted from my study of the charts, that I was indeed already at one with these people, this so-called Brotherhood, that in some way they were me. Then there was still the old hatred, and that voice: '*You are to be Watcher over the Blind One. If he transgresses you are to slay him.*'

'Are you the leader of the Brotherhood?' I asked the Doge.

The reply came quickly, proudly. 'Why should I want to be their leader? I am the Doge of Venice. I am greater than all of them, I can insinuate myself wherever I want. I am the nexus of a whole network of watchers. I am the point at which all this knowledge meets. There are wheels within wheels, and pyramids overarching other pyramids. My will is my own. Yet I, like you, am one of these.'

'You recognise nothing higher than your own will?'

The Doge was still smiling, but his smile was sardonic now. I was beginning to feel that I was in the presence of something awesome, blasphemous. It had grown even darker now, and the light of the single candle made his face look yellowish, like that of, a wild cat – or like a tiger I had seen at the zoo in Constantinople when we first landed.

'I once sought a will higher than my own,' he replied. 'And I found none. That is the secret of the power I acquired.'

I had to know if this was the transgression, the blasphemy I was to avenge, according to the command of the Templars. I accused him openly. 'You actively opposed the Crusade,' I said. 'You wanted to stop us from getting to Jerusalem. Venice, Zara, now this…'

I noticed that his unseeing eyes were rolling and that his breathing was rapid and uneven. The thunder overhead was louder now, and through the narrow slit window I could see that the sky was a fierce, dark, purple grey. Chill air blew in from outside.

I continued. 'You could have lent us the fifty thousand marks. We could have gone straight to Jerusalem. There would have been profit enough there. True profit…'

'I am power,' He intoned these words slowly, carefully. The lightning outside was bright enough now to shed light inside the church, a ghastly, silvery white light that contrasted with the sickly red and yellow of the candle.

I remembered the vision of hell I had had. The serpent. The serpent I had to kiss. I shouted, 'You are not telling me the truth. For God's sake tell me the truth!'

There was a long silence. Then he breathed, deeply. Suddenly, all his worldly charm, all his veneer of humanity and friendliness left him. He spoke these words, in a cold, hissing voice, which echoed in the dusty half-light of the empty church: 'I have said enough. And it is for you to judge now. I have begged you for forgiveness or judgement.'

Bitterness surged through me. I felt the stench of evil, true evil, more icy than anything I had felt in the cave at Roncevalles or in the church at Soria. I understood his denial. This was Cain unpunished, Judas without remorse, a messenger of Satan, the Fallen One, the Prince of the Air. The words of the Templars went round and round in my mind: '*You are to be a Watcher over the Blind One.*'

I bent down and picked up the gold crucifix encrusted with rubies and raised it high above my head, holding it in my right hand. I started to move towards him. Had I struck him as I intended, I have no doubt that I should have killed him.

Curiously, no one stirred. As I approached him, he began to smile. And as he smiled, the smell of sulphurous evil seemed to leave the place. The vision of the night before, the sense of peace, the patterns I had learnt, all flooded back into my mind. The Doge was part of all this. Why were the others not moving?

As I approached the Doge, it was as if the course of time had slowed to a standstill. With every effort I made to move, the will to destroy his life began to leave me. I no more wanted to kill him than to kill myself.

I looked up and saw the dark vault of the church arch above me in the gloom. Outside now there was only the bleakest glimmer of light. I saw my hand with the crucifix, reaching up, the Doge in front of me, all my movements like the slow flight of a bird through the air. Then I froze, for what seemed an eternity.

Still no one moved. Neither the Doge, nor the other members of the Brotherhood, nor the soldiers.

I looked into the Doge's eyes and they seemed to have changed. Now it was as if they could see. Or rather, that I could see with them, beyond, in spite of it all. And there was laughter in them. Not the mocking, hollow laughter of just a few minutes before. Instead, there was a warm, human laughter.

I lay the crucifix carefully on the ground. Then, obeying some deep instinct, I stepped forward to embrace the Doge. My embrace was returned.

Something had passed between us, something vast, something within and beyond all the patterns and the charts, and to understand what it was, Philippos, you must read these pages, for it is all encoded here.

In short, it was at this moment that I accepted the chalice, and truly joined the Brotherhood of Prayer of Charlemagne, the Brotherhood of those who know what it is to move through time.

The Doge and I led the way out of the church, followed by Tremgistus and Quintus, then Ewald, Fabricius and the Graf. We were flanked by the soldiers. The clouds had dispersed and now a brilliant sun was shining from behind the clouds. We went to the Blachernae Palace, where food had been prepared.

On the way there, a beautiful girl joined us. She wore a blue dress and her hair was long and golden. My heart leapt. Hildegunde.

Yet only for a split second did I mistake this girl for her.

She looked to the Doge for leave to speak, and then said, 'You must forgive me. I followed their instructions. They did not explain at first. I had not understood, but I do now. I know the girl you love is married to another. I am sorry. I know that I could never take her place. They asked me to give you this letter.'

She spoke Latin, and her voice was beautiful. Had I been younger, had so much else not intervened, I might easily have fallen for her, as I had fallen for Hildegunde.

Then I realised they had used this girl to entice me. She was right, of course; I could not have loved her, though she was lovely. Besides, I had realised that what I loved in Hildegunde was not something just in Hildegunde but something inside all women, and something inside myself. I remembered the androgynous Christ in the chart, and in my vision. I had understood.

I read the letter. It was from Hildegunde. It confirmed what the Graf said, that she had married another, that she had two sons, that she still sang my songs and that she would always remember me.

Even a day before, I would have reacted wildly and angrily at this. Now I smiled, feeling full of warmth for the girl because she had helped me.

At the palace, in the great hall with the busts of Roman emperors, brilliant mosaics and rich marble columns, all seven of us conversed about the past and about the future, only now, at last, we were as equals.

Then others joined us. The Master of Richerenches was there.

He embraced me warmly and I understood from our conversation how there was no opposition between the Templars and the Brotherhood. Walter of Montbeliar was also present. You know of him, Philippos, for he was the regent of this island for many years. I learnt much from him about how the Brotherhood works, using and creating organisations that cross and recross, many of which appear hostile from without, yet which in fact form a complex mosaic through which the Brotherhood wields its power.

It was during the course of these conversations that it was decided that my role would be to re-found a base for the Brotherhood on Cyprus, since the old Templar stronghold had been overthrown – rightly so in view of the corruption of the Master there. Because of this a Templar House would have been out of the question, so it was decided to use the looser umbrella of the Augustinian Order.

I cannot write to you of the details of our discussions, yet there is much that you must discover for yourself, Philippos, by looking carefully at what I have already written.

In short, at the end of the evening I was asked to sing. This was the last of the songs I played them:

*Vro Welt, ir sult dem wirte sagen*
*daz ich im gar vergolten habe.*
*Min grôziu gülte ist abe geslagen,*
*daz er mich von dem brieve schabe...* *

What happened next is well known to you, Philippos, how I founded the monastery here in Bellapais the year after our armies took Constantinople, how I spend much time riding throughout the island on the business of the monastery, how we have provided a haven for brothers driven from Jerusalem and done many good works here.

There is much, of course, that I have failed to achieve. The building of this monastery in stone according to my plans has scarcely begun. We still live in wooden huts and worship in a wooden church. How I would have loved to see the great refectory I have planned, with a view out over the sea, and the arrangement of the courtyard and cloisters, all following the patterns of the sacred geometry. I am sure that one day these plans will come to fruition, though I shall not live to see it.

You know, too, how much I love this place, every last bit of it, down to the last stone and the last lizard. I love the view out to sea, watching the colours of the sky change from rose-red and gold to blue in the mornings, and from blue to salmon pink, green, violet and purple in the evenings. I love the great mountains which arch behind me, how they catch the colours of the sunrise and sunset every day. I love the ancient shapes of the vines and the fig-trees, the abundance of lemons, oranges, grapefruit.

At this time of year there is such a wonderful profusion of yellow flowers - yellow poppies, great mesembryanthema, and the

---

* *Lady World, you should tell the innkeeper / that I have paid my dues. / And my great debt has been repaid. / So that he can wipe clean the slate...* (Walter von der Vogelweide)

mimosas – which echo the gold of the sunlight amidst the brilliant green of the grass and the trees. I love too the myrtle, the dog-roses, the periwinkles and many-coloured orchids which grow amongst the rocks; so too the violets, the clovers, the cyclamen, the irises – to look at the countryside is like looking at the inner flowers of the soul after long periods of contemplation. In the garden of the monastery I have trained a rose and a vine on the same trellis – here is a mystery.

There are even golden butterflies here. You remember, Philippos, the story of the Fool on the cliff-top chasing a golden butterfly? Only here, in this island, have I ever seen a golden butterfly fit for a Fool to chase.

Life is so simple. If one wished, one could live like John the Baptist, eating only the carob nuts and wild honey.

Of course there is evil here. One senses it at dusk in the packs of wild dogs roaming the hills below the monastery, and in the beautiful houses and churches burnt out, wrecked and looted by Richard of England when he was here, and the memory in the stones of the blood of those killed in the many battles that have taken place in this island. But it is a quiet evil, a necessary shadow cast by the golden sun, which shines here throughout the year. And you know from our study of music, and the distillation of substances in the athanor, how such things are to be quietly transformed.

I have never seen Jerusalem, nor did the Doge's army ever get that far. Here, though, I am closer to Jerusalem than most. Besides, it matters little to me now if I never see Jerusalem. The reason why it does not matter is part of the message encoded in these pages, Philippos. It is up to you to understand, if and when you can.

So much has come full circle. Even the sunrises and sunsets here, the bays, harbours and mountains, put me in mind of the descriptions I used to read in Virgil when I was a child. It seems to me that now at last I actually understand all that I learnt in those days – the philosophy of Boethius, the science of number, all these things I have taught you.

Or maybe I am wrong to write '*now* I understand', for there is always more to discover. I do know that all I passed through, all that I have set out here, was necessary for me to acquire what little knowledge I possess.

You have probably realised by now that I am, and always was to be, Uqhart's successor. Of course he was not killed by the Brotherhood as I originally thought, but by order of the Bishop of Babenberch, who had heard the rumours about Pauli's death and gave full vent to his hatred of all Jewish people. I know you will say it is strange that my predecessor was a Jew, yet consider the biblical writings about the Temple, and you might conclude that perhaps the chalice is older than is usually maintained.

They say that when his time came, Uqhart died joyfully. I write this so that you should know that when my time comes, however it comes, it will be in harmony with my will, and you should not suffer the same fears and resentments I suffered.

I never saw Katrin or Hildegunde again, but when I think of them I look back and smile, and contemplate Love, Amor, or Caritas – there are so many names for the different loves that weave together the magnificent fabric of our lives. When I first arrived here from Constantinople I sent messengers to Germany in order to trace them both. I organised for money to be paid to them, should they need it. Katrin used the money to settle debts she owed, then tried to become a nun. Soon, however, she met a wealthy merchant and is now his wife. She is happy by all accounts. She lives with him in Nurenberc.

Hildegunde was married to a wealthy knight, as the Graf said, and as she wrote in that letter. She bore him three sons before he died some years ago. When her children could fend for themselves, she re-entered the convent at Rupertsberc. She is still there – as far as I know.

As for me, since you asked, I can assure you that I have kept my vow of celibacy. Here it is easy. The island was once said to be Aphrodite's and I can believe that this is the case. She rose from the sea at Paphos, just at the spot where the evening star so often shines in spring. In many places in the hills there are temples to the honour of Aphrodite. Dare I say it, venerable abbot that I am? I can feel her presence here in the evenings, especially in the springtime, in the scent of the orange blossom and the jasmine.

I remember clearly one day when I first arrived here and rode out on my donkey along the coast to the ruined Roman theatre near Soli. You know the place, because I once showed you the mosaic where there is a swan, with a lily, and I used the picture to illustrate Plato's notion of the pure Idea of a swan. You in turn pointed to the rich, interweaving patterns of the mosaic and commented that, when you closed your eyes, you saw such patterns in your soul. You remember how much that heartened me...

Anyhow, behind the theatre there is a winding path leading over the foothills and up into the mountains. There is one of the grandest temples to Aphrodite. They say that on spring evenings her rites were practised in the hills beyond.

As I rode up the path I could feel the presence of crowds of young people who, hundreds of years before Christ, would make their way up to the hills to worship the goddess with their bodies. Suddenly I was at one with one of the young men, and I could see the face of his lover-to-be in the torch- and star-light, smell the perfume she wore and the perspiration on her light dress, the scent of anticipation. I could see, as he had seen, the shape of her breasts beneath her dress and the look in her wide eyes - like the look in Katrin's - as she turned towards him, leading him up to the place beyond the Temple where they would become one.

I record this vision for you, not with any lascivious intent, but so that you should understand how easy it is to sense the presence of the feminine, especially in the air here in Cyprus. But the source of this femininity is within us, just as in that vision the feelings of both the young man and the young woman were contained within me. This is part of our secret, and the secret of the songs of mine you say you love so much. You might consider that for some of us celibacy is not self-denial but rather, given the nature of the visions that are granted to us, a necessary self-indulgence.

You must forgive the ramblings of an old monk, but you will understand from my songs, from these writings and from the writings and visions I have set down, that Venus, the Virgin, and the androgynous Christ on the chart I gave you are all signs of the key to the door we seek.

Our masters, the Lusignans, who control the castles high in the hills - Kantara, Buffavento, Saint Hilarion - also possess a sign for this. One of their forefathers fell in love with a maid he met in the forests one day, whilst out hunting. He did not know she was a fairy when she returned his love. The queen of the fairies was angry but allowed the marriage between them to take place, on two conditions: the fairy bride was to relinquish her immortality, and once a week she was to return to a fairy form, that of a dragon. During this time, of course, the count was forbidden to see her. The marriage took place and for a while the couple continued to live in great bliss. Then, one day, it was time for her to regain her fairy shape, and she hid in an inner chamber. The count was unable to bear being separated from her, and burst through the door behind which she was cowering. He saw her as a foul dragon, the sight of which sent a chill to the very marrow of his bones and made his hair turn white there and then. She, weeping, breathed two words - 'Your promise...' and flew out of the window, leaving him to pine for her for the rest of his life. Now, whenever death or ill fortune besets the Lusignans, she is seen flying round the turrets of their castle.

Here is a question for you, Philippos. When did he love her most, before or after he knew what she was, before or after she became, once more, a spirit of the air? If you understand this, you will understand how I now feel about Hildegunde, and why it is not difficult for me to remain celibate.

As you know, since my arrival here the Lusignans have been very kind to me, in their generous gifts towards the founding of our little monastery here at Bellapais. They have been very kind too in their support for my music and my songs, and in having books shipped to us. I count Walter of Montbeliar amongst my closest friends. How many times, when I first arrived here, must I have ridden out with him into the mountains, to hunt mouflon or to dine with him at Saint Hilarion, where I sang my songs to his great court there.

I am told that my songs are sung in many courts throughout Europe, and that many great ones would be glad to have me live at their castles. They do not understand how I am most truly with them when they hear and play my songs. They do not need my old body to come and drink their wine for them. Besides, I am at peace here. If I were to return they would tear me to pieces, like Orpheus.

You will realise how fortunate I have been, to live here in peace, while in Constantinople so many disasters have befallen the greedy Latins, who have craved only riches. You asked how I could ever have embraced such a man as the Doge, who is held to be responsible for all the suffering and destruction caused at Constantinople. The answer is set out here, if you care to seek it.

In any case the Doge is long since dead. He perished as Baldwin was captured in battle and dragged off to be killed by Greek and Bulgarian rebels.

In Europe I hear of endless wars. I hear too that they have been burning the Cathars, whom I once loved so much when I was with them, and that everywhere there is hatred and bloodshed.

Do you remember how, at our last meeting, I told you that I am haunted by a vision of a young man, playing a flute by a river, at night-time, in a cold, distant land, while mists swirl about him? The song he is playing is mine. I know he is, or will be, connected to us; though I am not sure, yet, how or when this will be. This is only one of a multitude of visions of which I should not write. There are many doors, and, when they present themselves, the art is to move through them at the right time, and just see what is on the other side.

I write this during my beloved period of study between prime and Terce. Now, as I sit outside on the terrace in front of the wooden cell that has been my home these twenty years, as the cocks crow and the air is filled with the singing of the birds, as I hear the shepherds' pipes as they lead their flocks up into the hills, as the brilliant golden sun rises over this enchanted world of seas and mountains, and as I gaze out towards the infinite violet blue of the sea and sky, which is still tinted with the rose light of the dawn, I give thanks for all that is past, and for your future, Philippos.

They say that the Emperor Friedrich will be here soon, on his way to Jerusalem. Some believe that he is the Last Emperor of the Apocalypse; yet I have *seen* too much to believe this. There are too many loops and spheres and circles in the world for it to take the sudden end some have predicted.

Still, sometimes when I ride past the charcoal burners, and see the smoke billowing from the cracks in the domed ovens like smoke from hell, I do fear the worst...

The bell is ringing for Terce now; then will follow the business of the day. I shall put away these writings now, Philippos, for I do not want you to find them before it is time, when I am no longer of this earth, and when the chalice has passed to you. You know you were chosen because of your many gifts, which I recognised in you the moment I saw you working with your father in the harbour at Kyrenia, when I invited you to visit me here in order to learn from me as you desired.

I must go now, Philippos. I wish you well in this life.

*Bellapais, 6th April 1227*

*I, Philippos, Brother of the Abbey of Bellapais, was with Walter von der Ouwe when he died, just before the feast of Saint John in the year of our Lord 1227. His mortal remains were buried in this place on the Feast of Saint John that same year.*

*These manuscripts are my copyings of the parchments he left, and which I have ordered according to his wishes.*

*There is no monument to him save these writings, this abbey, and the many songs he composed and which are now sung throughout the whole of Christendom.*

*En seintes flurs il les facet gesir. May his soul too rest amongst heavenly flowers.*

*Bellapais: the year of our Lord 1227*

# APPENDIX 1

## The Resurrection of G

✛

## 0 The Fool

It all started on the sixth of April last year when I surfaced from sleep and switched on the ghetto-blaster. Radio Three was playing a concert of medieval music.

As I dozed back off into semi-oblivion, the music interfered with my dreams. I dreamt of beautiful forests, of a woman with long blond hair, wearing a blue and gold dress. Then there was a room in the upper storey of a castle where there were lovely tapestries and the smell of fresh herbs and flowers. There was a wonderful scent of spring in the air.

Then I began to dream of grotesque faces, burnt, mutilated. I could smell burning in my dream.

I shook myself awake. It was springtime. But there was no castle; just my grotty bedsit with the usual mess of clothes and coffee cups all over the floor, and the litter of half-read books and the 'yet-to-be-organised' research papers on my desk.

I tried to listen to the music, to return to the visionary landscape in order to postpone the moment when the memories returned of who I was, with all my worries and insecurities. They congealed in front of my mind like scar tissue, or the inevitable message on the display telling you that your computer still has the terminal virus you thought you had cured it of.

I was twenty-five and had a first-class degree from Oxford.

Instead of getting myself a proper job, I had insisted on pursuing a research project on medieval poetics, which was going spectacularly badly. So, while my friends were off buying flats and houses and swanning around expensive London restaurants, I was still slumming it in bedsit land, and counting the pennies of my cheapskate grant even if I went for a beer at the local pub.

Contrary to garret romances I had read, I was finding that being twenty-five and broke impressed no one. My father despised me. The girl I wanted to marry, Rosemary, had just left me. The small time rock band I sang in had folded, further diminishing my chances with women, since 'being in a band' had always been a fair pick-up line – or at least a confidence boost.

As I got out of bed, I made the usual vows to myself about embarking on a regular programme of exercise. I even promised myself a more varied diet than the peanut butter and Marmite sandwiches to which I was addicted.

These were the thoughts that tormented me as I listened to the dying medieval song. I caught the announcer saying it was called: '*De moi doleros vos chant*', 'I shall sing of my sorrows.'

I went over to the sink and washed quickly, tried to comb the knots out of my matted, curly, brown hair, struggled to put in my contact lenses (my one concession to vanity), pulled on a T-shirt and jeans and looked out the window. My great consolation in the mornings was the massive lime tree that grew in the front garden of this appalling bedsit house. It made me think of Schubert, first love, all my favourite medieval poems...Then the neighbour's black poodle started barking its head off again. That dog annoyed me beyond measure.

I knew I was heading for a downer if I did not get out as soon as possible, so I popped a vitamin B pill, grabbed my reading list and note file and was about to face the big, wide world, or at least the streets of north Oxford and the library when, on the mat in the corridor at the bottom of the stairs, I found a letter from Rosemary.

I felt excited as I opened it. Maybe she had not meant all those things she had said to me. Maybe she wanted us to get back together.

But no. My heart sank. She apologised if she was hurting my feelings (perceptive of her) but assured me that I was a really great guy - though I really ought to make something of my life. She said she hoped that we could be good friends now we had split up, and that she really felt much happier now, so I shouldn't worry about her (heart-warming!). By the way, she said, she was seeing someone else. She would explain later.

So, not only had she left me, but she had added insult to injury by patronising me. Something kept coming back to me, something she said, reflectively rather than hurtfully, during the closing stages of our final, fateful row: 'Do you know, I used to think that you knew everything. Now I know you know nothing, just like the rest of us.' What Rosemary said was usually clear, concrete, to the point. Yet I could not fathom this. I suppose that was why I kept thinking about it.

Then the phone rang. Chance? If I had got up any earlier, if Rosemary had not written, if I had not hung around in the corridor getting resentful, dreaming, pondering, regretting, I would not have met Lilian when I did, and the next two days would have taken on a different shape, and who knows what would have happened after that?

It was a message from the college to say that my supervision with G was cancelled. It was one of the college secretaries speaking. This was odd, because G himself would normally have phoned to cancel a tutorial. He was supposed to have returned from Spain a couple of days ago.

I felt uneasy even then. I reflected that G was an arrogant bastard, and cancelling things in person added to his sense of superiority; though to be fair, he was usually punctilious over arrangements for supervisions and took them very seriously. They gave him a chance to put his students down and to indulge in his favourite pastime of self-congratulation.

I should not really write about G like that. The whole point of writing this is to get a balanced view. G had always exercised a power over me, ever since I first met him, which was during my interview to come to Oxford when I was still at school. Then, when he was my tutor as an undergraduate, and supervisor when I was a graduate, I spent half my time hero-worshipping him and the other half hating and resenting him. Yet I was never able to free myself of the influence he had over me.

No sooner had I put the phone down than it started ringing again. No one ever phoned me at the house. If people wanted to get in touch it was usually through screwy bits of paper in my pigeon-hole in college.

The voice at the other end of the phone was young, female, charming, with a hint of a foreign accent. She said she was one of the junior partners at a firm of solicitors called Arott and Marcanu in St John Street. I had never heard of them and asked her, probably too apologetically, if she was sure that it was me she wanted. The voice insisted that I was the right person, having confirmed my name and address. But she would not be drawn as to the reason why I was being contacted in this way, other than to say that money was involved and it was to my advantage. I was assured that it would be best if I could come to the firm's office in St John Street as soon as possible because there was an important matter that needed to be discussed face to face.

Even before she mentioned money, I had decided to go. I suppose that even then I was allured by her voice and by the prospect of being involved in a story that had nothing to do with my research project.

## I The Magus

Before I go into detail about what happened at the solicitor's office, I ought to mention something about G and my relationship with him.

The first thing that needs to be said about G is that it was almost impossible to tell whether he was a brilliant intellectual or a charlatan. He was immensely well read, but he was not really a scholarly man; he was too full of his own ideas.

He had written on any number of topics, but he specialised in the philosophy of historical criticism and Medieval History. He was tall, fairly thin for a man pretty well over fifty, had a full crop of stylishly swept back silvery hair, and features which were lined in a way that made his suntanned face look distinguished, expressive and smiling all at the same time. He was something of a dandy, favouring bow-ties, tailored suits and striped jackets.

One of the things that made G so popular was the fact that he was such a showman. He was unlike most of the university lecturers, who would read out their notes, mumbling, looking at their watches and not caring whether they were communicating anything to anyone. Even if he was making a relatively superficial point, G would do so in such a way that you felt the universe would never seem quite the same to you again.

Take, for example, his first-year lecture called *What is Number?* which ranged from Plato to Hawking, the kabbala to post-structuralism. During this lecture he would consider different views of what numbers are: divine essences, angelic beings, innate qualities, mechanical principles determining the functioning of the universe, occult magical presences we only dimly understand, rational *a prioris*, linguistic conventions, and so on. Then he would point out how important it was to bear in mind the difference between the pre-Enlightenment world-view, when numbers seemed to exist in the world, and the present state of affairs, when it is possible to locate numbers only in our *descriptions* of the world.

He would remind his audience of the fact that in medieval times the study of arithmetic meant the study of the mystical significance, of the quality of numbers, which were perceived as having an individual existence, whereas in the present day we never ask ourselves what numbers are, and instead train ourselves to become virtuosi at doing things with them. He wondered if this was not a tacit admission that numbers no longer *mean* anything.

Then he would suggest that maybe modern science had got it all wrong. Maybe the discovery of mathematical patterns in the universe did not prove that the universe functioned mathematically, any more than it proved that the universe 'knew' maths. Maybe all it proved was that we, as human beings, were only capable of seeing it that way.

Or maybe the opposite was true. Maybe quantum mechanics was wrong and the kabbala right. Maybe the universe does not consist of waves and/or particles, but number. That would explain the effect of music, which is, after all nothing more than mathematically sequenced wave patterns. Music could be spirit if spirit were number.

At this point he would swoop down from the platform like a great bird of prey and grab a couple of unsuspecting students, male or female, by the scruff of the neck. Then he would drag them up on to the podium.

Next he would shy the rest of the audience by asking if anyone could count the number of students who were on the podium with him. Of course no one would answer. Everyone was too embarrassed. I suppose they all expected some kind of trick. Then G would rant and rave about how appalling it was that the university admitted students who could not even count up to two.

Finally someone would crack and say that there were two students on the podium. Then that person was told to come up on to the podium also. Once there, he or she was asked again how many students there were now. If the poor victim said two, he or she was mocked because, of course, now there were three of them, or if they were fast enough to spot this, the victim was asked to justify why they had changed their mind since coming on to the podium.

Next, G would ask them in turn what it felt like to be three rather than two. He would tease them, asking why standing on a podium should make such a difference to their threeness. Why should getting on a podium make so much difference? Why not stand on chairs, jump up and down? Would that make any difference to the number of them? Then he would organise for his audience to form groups of different numbers, holding hands, standing on chairs, tables, window-sills, trying to experience the essence of their twoness, or threeness, or fourness. He would transform a hall full of earnest undergraduates into something more like a playground full of junior school children, or a pantomime audience, or a quiz show. Just as pandemonium was about to break out, he would slip away.

G's manner labelled him very much a product of the English public school system, if system isn't too flattering a word for it. Myself, I went to an old grammar school. I was one of the very last years to go through before the school was turned into a sixth form college. For me, school, learning, exams, knowledge, have always been something acquired with difficulty, as a means of escape. For G, though, things academic were part of his birthright. He might question the value of what we call knowledge on a theoretical basis, but never personally. Or at least, that was what his manner implied. He always seemed to be at ease, as if it were all a game.

There was one side of him that did leave me feeling uneasy, even in the early days, and this was his interest in the occult. He used to collect occult systems, everything from treatises on alchemy to the tarot to the kabbala. He would mostly justify this in terms of his academic interests in structuralism, arguing that such things were interesting examples of social, mythological, intellectual structures, of means men and women have used in the past to come to terms with a world in which meanings have seemed constantly to change and shift, or when meaning has seemed impossible.

Which was all very well. Yet there were times when I saw his dark side. Then he would become depressed, tired, pale, lifeless. He would say that his whole life's work was a fraud, that all recent movements in academia were a kind of exorcism, an attempt to drive out the ghosts, devils and voices from the past, which, he said, were more real than any modern theory of the self as an illusory product of social interaction.

On more than one occasion he asked me if I heard the voices.

I did not know what he meant. He said that he heard spirit voices, voices from the past that told him of their lives. This was so out of character that it shook me the first few times it happened. In a day or so he would always have rallied and would make light of what he said to me. I noted, though, that he was a regular attender at college chapel – odd behaviour for one whose official academic position was strictly anti-transcendental.

## II The High Priestess

As I cycled through the streets of north Oxford on my way to the solicitors' office, my mind turned again towards Rosemary. We had been together for about six months. We met through mutual friends at a party in London. For some reason, still not clear to me, she made a beeline for me and we ended up sleeping with one another that same night. We had been together ever since, though the fact that she worked in London as a freelance music teacher and session player limited our meetings to weekends, when she would come to Oxford and stay with me in my bedsit.

What can I say about her? She was beautiful, slim, with long, flowing curly black hair. Oh, yes, and she was highly sexed.

She had studied music at one of the London colleges. Her speciality was the flute, but she also had an excellent soprano voice.

She was talented in other ways. She could draw extremely well. She was so well read it was not true, especially since she had not studied literature since she was fifteen. She could also improvise brilliantly at the piano.

Yet she never really seemed to want to make anything of these gifts. She just coasted along, drifting from one man to the next, playing and singing when she felt like it, amateur stuff and some session work. She picked up and learnt pieces with consummate ease, and then just forgot them again, like her relationships.

That was the great contrast between her and me. I have this need to fix everything, to make it permanent. Maybe that is what drew me to research for that wretched D. Phil.

The difference between us came out too in our different approaches to music. What I like about music is the sense of timelessness, permanence, that it gives me. I like to read, note, analyse scores so that the text becomes permanent in my mind. When I studied music, what I enjoyed was the structure of the harmony and counterpoint. Performances did not really interest me: they were too fleeting, too intangible, unless of course they were on record or CD. I found it infinitely fascinating to compare one recording of a particular piece with another.

I have often wondered if there are fundamental, eternal rules underlying the construction of music, which we glimpse only imperfectly, but which it is given to some to glimpse more perfectly than others. I remember G once wondering aloud if a Mozart symphony could have existed before Mozart wrote it down.

I suppose that was what frustrated me about Rosemary. Such thoughts meant nothing to her. And why should they? She was off the scale as far as my own thinking was concerned. Part of me saw her as the possessor of some great truth from which I was excluded. At the same time, I tried to see in her too much of myself and I got annoyed when she did not reflect back what I wanted. Perhaps I tried to change her too much and that was what drove her away.

During those weekends we spent together, we did not make enough effort to go out amongst people. All I wanted was to marry her, to make things permanent between us, to trap her, she said. So we stayed in the bedsit, which to me became heaven on earth when she was there, had wonderful sex, and talked. Yet they were not real conversations. We talked about ourselves so much that we became less like a couple and more like two psychoanalysts staring into one another's eyes.

I was jealous of her talent, her ease, and her former lovers. She was my first 'serious' relationship, while she was anything but inexperienced. I resented her for that. I cannot explain why. Maybe it was my upbringing, some odd religious aspirations I had. I used to think that there was some dimension of the self, something like the soul, or the evestra that Paracelsus wrote about, that would become polluted by illegitimate sex. I never mentioned that to G. He would have laughed me out of court. Or would he? Maybe, as Rosemary said, this was an unhealthy obsession resulting from my puritanical upbringing. Or maybe there was some truth in my intuitions after all.

Something about my relationship with Rosemary makes me think about G's lecture on Caillois' praying mantis. When the mantis is in danger, it freezes, motionless, using death as a defence mechanism, feigning death to save its life. But what if, whilst in this state, the mantis actually dies? This would be a mirror-image of the way life had mimicked death in order to preserve itself.

Apparently, though, a dead praying mantis can still carry out certain functions appertaining to life. It can walk, keep its balance, even lay eggs. Here death mimics the life that life had feigned to lose in order to preserve itself. The insect, like the marathon runner, has not noticed that it is no longer alive. It is dead but too busy; it has not had the time to realise that it is no longer alive.

The final degree is reached when, amongst the signs of life that the dead insect continues to exhibit, there appears what Caillois calls 'sham corpse-like existence'. This is the return to the starting point. The insect is playing dead again. But now it is dead. It has lost the life that it is continuing to protect. In death, it feigns life only because in life it feigned death. It is a double death, simultaneously real and feigned: the corpse pretends to be what it is.

Somehow that describes what became of my relationship with Rosemary, what becomes of most things I touch. It is also what happened with G.

But more of that later.

### III The Empress

I sometimes wonder if there is a conspiracy amongst interior decorators to make solicitors' offices as similar as possible to Indian restaurants. This was exactly the effect achieved by the red plush of the offices I walked into in St John Street. I immediately felt out of place in my jeans and T-shirt, and wondered if perhaps I should have put on a suit for the occasion.

Yet the receptionist, who was in her forties and a bit tarty, gave me a too-good-to-be-true welcoming smile when I told her my name, and beckoned to me to sit in one of the pseudo-silk-covered red sofas arranged at calculated non-square angles from the wall. As I lowered myself and fell backwards endlessly into the soft upholstered void, I experienced something of what astronauts must feel when space walking. At last, when I was convinced that my fall had been arrested and that gravity was once more treating me with some degree of normality, I studied the pseudo-antique coffee-table from the new, lower angle. There was the traditional pile of Country Life magazines, together with the one, neatly folded and untouched copy of the Financial Times to flatter clients into thinking of themselves as men and women of worth.

I leant forward and managed, with some difficulty, to get hold of the *FT*, as I had heard my sophisticated City friends call it. To compensate for my jeans and T-shirt, I pretended to look at the stocks and shares columns. Little did I guess then how much those little numbers would soon mean to me.

At last the telephone on the reception desk rang and I was directed to the office bearing the sign MISS MARCANU. Until that moment I had subscribed to the prejudice that all solicitors are boring middle-aged men who wear stuffy suits that smell of Yorkshire pudding and who balance half-moon spectacles precariously on their noses. I was taken aback, as I stepped through the door, to find myself in the company of two very beautiful women. Sitting behind the desk on the far side of the room was Miss Marcanu, who had long brown hair, a pretty, smiling face, and wore a tightish white cotton blouse and a shortish black skirt. She sat with such easy grace and dignity that she commanded authority, and her beauty lent her a presence that went beyond the merely sexual.

The other young woman was turned towards me. She had medium-length blond hair. She was wearing a shortish blue cotton summer dress with a yellow pattern. At first the pattern seemed to consist of dots, but I noticed later that they were birds of some sort, possibly eagles. She was also wearing a summer scarf round her neck.

There was a heady, almost erotic scent in the air, a mixture of the young women's perfume and their perspiration. It was musky, oriental, somehow more what one would associate with the boudoir than a solicitor's office.

'Please sit down, Mr Mothing,' said Miss Marcanu, pointing to a chair next to the blond woman. I recognised the voice from the telephone earlier. 'This is Miss Koenigin,' she said, nodding towards the blond woman.

I looked from Miss Marcanu's face to Miss Koenigin's. There was no doubt that Miss Koenigin was the more beautiful of the two. Her skin was blond but lightly tanned, her cheek-bones strong in a way that added to her dignity without being too pronounced in any way. But more than that, her features had a kind of harmony about them, a stillness that put me in mind of Italian Renaissance paintings, Michelangelo, da Vinci.

'Call me Lilian,' she said, and smiled.

'Miss Koenigin is the late Professor G's publisher,' added Miss Marcanu.

I was so intoxicated by the two women that at first I did not take in what was being said.

I turned to Miss Marcanu. 'What do you mean, "late"?'

'Haven't you heard?'

'Heard what?'

'I am so sorry. I thought you would have found out by now. Professor G died two days ago, in his hotel in Toledo, at the conference he was attending.'

She told me the rest. He had been at a conference on the significance of mystical numbers in Arabic architecture and the legacy of these systems in Europe. He had dined well one evening and retired early, apparently in good spirits but saying that he was feeling a little unwell. He had been found dead, in his bath, the following morning. The doctors were saying it was a heart attack, though they would not know for certain until they had the results of the autopsy, which was being performed that very morning.

My head was awash with the usual thoughts that mark the beginnings of grief. I tried to remember the last time I had seen him, our last conversation together. This vied with the picture forming in my mind of the autopsy; G, who was always so full of life, stretched out in a hospital somewhere in Spain, cut open, passive, lifeless. I thought of what the autopsy room must smell like, I reminded myself where I was. Suddenly the feminine scent in the office was comforting rather than erotic, and I felt embarrassed, trying to gauge how much emotion I should show.

Miss Marcanu had a further surprise for me. G's will said that he wanted to leave all his estate to be divided equally between myself and Lilian Koenigin, on the condition that I, as his most trusted student, should make it my life's work to edit and organise his papers, and that Lilian should make it her life's work to ensure the publication of his work and its promotion by whatever means possible – advertising, lecture tours and so on.

The sums of money involved were staggering. I had had no idea that G was so wealthy. There was enough money to live extremely well for as long as it would take to edit G's work – and maybe even buy up any publishing house refusing to accept his books.

## IV The Emperor

I thanked Miss Marcanu and told her that I would have to think about the implications.

I have been trying to remember why it was that I did not say yes immediately. I remember that the thought of my own father came to mind. These thoughts were no more than impressions, fleeting – more a feeling than anything else. But it was enough to stop me from committing myself straight away.

I thought about how my father had worked all his life for a firm, that, at the end of his career, had left him with a gold watch and a couple of drinks at the pub. He had just enough money to live off and to run a small car - nothing more. I was feeling a kind of resentment that G had turned out to be so much more powerful, rich, important, in the public eye at least, than my own father. They were similar ages. Every moment G had been alive, thinking, doing something, my father had been too. Why was G so much more significant than my dad?

Was it just money? Was it the quality of their thought and experience? My father watched television: G read books. Was there really such a difference? My image of G's death would be unread books. The image of my father's death, far more terrifying, was a television unwatched by him.

What was it that gave G the power to fascinate me, to command me even from beyond death?

Miss Marcanu said there was no need to make a decision immediately. She said that Miss Koenigin had asked for time for reflection also. In the meantime, however, the two of us had been named as executors of the will, so there would be some affairs that it would be necessary for us to settle.

Thus I found myself walking through the streets of Oxford in the company of Lilian Koenigin, a beautiful stranger, with a list of tasks to carry out, papers to find, the funeral to arrange, officials to notify.

The first stop was to be G's college, to see if there was any mail to collect. Then we would return to his house in north Oxford, where we decided we would make an initial survey of G's papers and possessions, and see if there was anything that needed tending to immediately. Then I would see the chaplain about the funeral.

On the way, pushing through the hordes of tourists and shoppers, we talked about G.

Lilian was as surprised and bewildered as I was about the terms of G's will. I kept wondering if Lilian had been G's mistress, yet there was a kind of wide-eyed innocence about her that suggested she could not have been. Also, she kept asking me questions about G's family. Surely, if she had been his mistress, I thought, he would have talked to her about other aspects of his private life. Yet I found it impossible to judge, and I was so much enjoying her company it hardly seemed to matter.

G had never talked much about his family to me. I understood that he was half Jewish, that he had spent his early years in Germany and that his parents had been killed during the war, when he was very young. Somehow, as a child, he had been brought to England and sent to a major public school on a scholarship.

I had always been so intrigued with G in the here and now, with the ideas he was playing with at the time and, I suppose, with my image of myself in his eyes, that I never thought to ask questions about his past. This was odd, in retrospect, since the whole point of writing a D.Phil., at that time my excuse for being alive, was precisely about raking round in past lives - but always of the dead. I had never thought of employing the same skills on the living. Now he was no longer there to be asked, G was threatening to become an object of study.

As we walked and talked, I began to wonder myself if perhaps G's intellectual ease had not been acquired so effortlessly after all. On one level he was the sort of man who, if he knew you, would happily reveal details of his inner intellectual and dream life, yet he hardly ever let out any details about his personal or family life. It was not that he clammed up, rather he always turned the conversation round, if it came to the discussion of such things, so that you were telling him about yourself rather than vice versa. Besides, it is hard to ask about a man's family if you suspect they met a dark fate.

On the way to the college I found out a little about Lilian. Like me, she was twenty-five. She had studied at the University of Sussex. She had turned down the opportunity of studying for a doctorate and gone straight into publishing. In the short space of four years she had risen to the position of senior acquisitions editor of the philosophy, art, criticism and education section of the university publishing house for which she worked. I looked at her ring finger. No ring.

There was a quality that Lilian possessed, a quality rare amongst English women: it was impossible to categorise her. She was not a yuppie, or a hippy, or middle class, or working class, or naive, or worldly-wise. She was obviously intelligent, but there was no affectation about her. She was not obviously an intellectual. When she laughed it was because something was funny. When she joked, and she could be very amusing, it was in a way that left her, as a personality, intact, undistorted. She possessed a breadth. The strength of her presence was that of a potential rather than something defined. I noticed even then, as I walked with her, pushing my bike, feeling and probably looking like an amorous sixth-former, that it was not going to be possible to pin her down to a character-type, a cliché.

I became aware of a sense of adventure. It was as if I had suddenly been granted magical powers to enter a kingdom that had hitherto been closed. This was partly the excitement of being able to find out more about G, but it was more to do with grief. I noticed that grief came in odd wafts, or waves. At the peak I felt distressed, bereft. I lamented the passing of the dead person, cried, tensed myself, all the traditional and obvious things. Yet when the wave was either approaching or moving away there were other, more subtle states of mind. One of these was precisely this boyish sense of adventure, excitement, the feeling that I was, after all, exploring new territories, both emotionally and spiritually, the sense that I was learning something. Then I realised the selfishness of such thoughts and there returned that other feeling which so often accompanies grief: self-loathing. Oddly, even this was cheapened because I was so stunned by the thought of the money I stood to inherit.

We arrived at G's college and made our way across the quads and the winding passageways leading to his rooms. Painted on the door was a big number four and over the door was G's name. Using the keys supplied to us by Miss Marcanu (I could not help wondering what her first name was) we entered the rooms.

I commented to Lilian that possessing rooms like this at an

Oxford or Cambridge college was one of the highest honours that can be bestowed upon a man or woman in the academic world. It was as if their learning, all those hours poring over books, writing, thinking, had somehow been transformed alchemically into a privileged physical space, in which the body attached to the mind was allowed by others to move and have its being. Lilian smiled inscrutably. I really could not tell whether she was agreeing, disagreeing, registering amusement or a superior detachment.

Most of the time I had spent with G was in these rooms. Usually there was a chaos of books and papers strewn about the place. To my great surprise, the rooms had been totally cleared. Could he have known? Or did he always tidy up before going away? On G's desk was a sheet with four poems printed on it. I passed the piece of paper to Lilian. She studied it in silence.

'I didn't think he wrote poetry,' she said.

'Well,' I said, 'it's not exactly what I would call poetry. Unless you like that kind of Victorian symbolist stuff. Do you really think he wrote it?'

'It's not his usual style. You don't know what it's about, do you?'

'No. I suppose we could look it up in a dictionary of symbols. It reminds me of the kind of verse you get in kids' fantasy novels, where the dwarfs get given clues by the magician so that they can go and slay the sulphury dragon.'

Lilian smiled. 'Maybe you're right,' she said, and for the first time I caught her eye, and a kind of electricity passed between us. I wanted to hold her hand, to kiss her, but I concentrated on freezing every muscle in my face and body until the feeling passed.

The poems are reproduced at the end of this book.

## V The Hierophant

On the way to G's house we talked some more. Lilian told me about some of G's books that she had published. She was particularly keen on the one called *The Impossibility of Knowing*. In it he systematically debunked the assumptions underlying all the main forms of knowledge: Religion, Aesthetics, Ethics, History, Human Sciences, Mathematics, and, finally, even his own brand of philosophy.

It was a *tour de force* of sustained sceptical argument, most admirable perhaps for the sting it had in its own tail, when G turned his brilliant tools of criticism in on themselves, and exposed assumptions underlying his own critical methodology, leaving the reader drifting on a sea of ideas with nothing to hold on to. At the same time this structure, that of the snake eating its own tail, illustrated the philosophical method underlying the arguments in the book, the idea that the collapse of knowledge was caused by the discovery, or invention, of self-referentiality in theoretical structures.

The book was, needless to say, pilloried by the Establishment. G's methodology was ridiculed. He was accused of superficiality, lack of respect, even nihilism – this latter in spite of the fact that the last words of the book were 'Perhaps true knowledge, and true goodness, start beyond nihilism'.

I knew that G had gone away to Spain at about the time the reviews came out. I had not realised, and only found out from, Lilian, that he had gone to recover from what amounted to a nervous breakdown.

The book had sold well.

At last we arrived at G's house. It was one of those monstrous Victorian edifices, halfway between a medieval castle and a public loo, which had been made briefly socially acceptable during the seventies by Betjeman and his neo-Gothic cronies. The ugliness of the patterned red brick, the asymmetry, the inauthenticity of the imitation of a bygone age, the theatricality, crankiness and sheer size of the house made it the ideal setting for G and his thoughts.

I had only been there once before. G had invited me to coffee one morning when he had first become my supervisor. Then, my visit had been confined to the one downstairs room, the reception room, with its rows of books, leather armchairs and seventeenth century Italian paintings.

Suddenly I realised where I had seen Lilian's face before. It was on one of the paintings. She was Ceres, scattering flowers and bearing fruits.

I felt nervous and awkward as I turned the key and we entered the house, as intruders. If I had been on my own I doubt I would have had the courage to go there. With Lilian I felt, oddly, like a host.

I asked her if she had been to the house before. No reply.

As we entered the hall there was a deathly silence. No one had been here since he left it. All the objects were as he left them. He was the last person ever to have seen them. I felt tearful. It was almost as though I could feel the objects in the house around me lamenting his passing.

I could not tell what Lilian was thinking, but I could see that she too was overawed. I suggested that we should sit in the front room for a while, the one with the Ceres picture. I looked round at all the books, the paintings, the astrolabe, the globe, the 1930s style standard lamp G presumably used for reading. I tried to think of something to say. Yet we both remained silent.

Suddenly I realised I felt hungry and thirsty. I suggested that maybe we should go to the kitchen and see if we could get hold of some coffee and a bite to eat. Lilian smiled at the suggestion, so that is what we did.

The kitchen was vast, overlooking a massive terrace with white painted wrought-iron garden furniture, which in turn overlooked a garden that could more aptly have been described as a park.

For a moment I was daunted, angry even. I did not know the first thing about gardening. How was I expected to take on all that? Then I realised that someone as wealthy as G must be able to employ all the gardeners he wanted. I was about to feel the usual twinge of envy, then I realised that I too could soon be in his position. Half of all this could be mine, if I wanted.

In the meantime Lilian had been rummaging in the kitchen and had found some coffee. She had got the coffee machine going and it was beginning to make a comforting glug-glugging sound.

She was busy opening tins that she had found as if by magic in the pantry. Her colour was returning. It was as if she was taking possession of the kitchen in an archetypally feminine way. Or is that an unacceptably sexist thought?

She was so graceful, her smile, her pure complexion, the shape of her legs, her thin waist. But more than that she seemed to radiate a presence that made everything around her seem good, seem to fit into place. It was as if the darkness G's death had brought to the house could be dispelled by the brightness of her presence. I have often tried to locate that brightness. She was blond. Her eyes were a bright, light blue, usually wide open. Her skin was fair but slightly tanned. Also, she smiled easily and moved lightly on her feet. This lightness was emphasised by the short dresses and skirts she favoured. These in turn added a girlishness to her presence that offset the stillness and dignity in her face. In any case, the sum of her presence was greater than the whole, and the radiance about her seemed to come from within, rather than to be anything easily definable in her appearance.

'I'll fix something for us to eat,' she said. 'Why don't you look round the rest of the house? It will be ready in a quarter of an hour. You can report back over lunch.'

I took up her suggestion. Wandering from room to room, I found that I too needed to take possession of the place, to force myself to feel at ease. Each new room I went into for the first time made me feel nervous, as if G might be there, a ghost, a monster from childhood fantasies, who lived in the house and would not have expected us to be there.

In every room there were vast numbers of books, papers, paintings, artefacts. I was surprised by the large number of books on the occult. Also, on the walls there were many odd charts, some alchemical, some astrological, Chinese and Indian physiological anatomies, all sorts of variations on the kabbalistic Sefirot, and some I could not understand at all.

There were some rare objects too, which one would have expected to see in a museum rather than a private house. In one room there was a display of medieval artefacts: drinking goblets, swords, riding equipment, two shields, one bearing a massive black eagle and another of a different shape with red stripes and a half moon. Could it have been a real Saracen shield? There were also several fine Byzantine ivories.

I soon became aware that different rooms in the house concentrated objects and styles from different periods. The room at the very top of one of the towers was almost perfectly Victorian. One of the drawing-rooms had nearly all Georgian artefacts. Another of the bedrooms was perfect 1930s style, and so on. Going from one room of the house to another gave an odd feeling of travelling through time.

I remembered one of G's more curious speculations; that the space the earth travelled through was not just space but time also, and that this space-time had a perceptible psychic geography. If the earth could be physically moved back to where it was, say, fifteen hundred years ago, the same *Zeitgeist* would take over, since it would be part of the geography of that area of space-time. Various gods, mythological beasts, states of mind and so on would become real again, since they are the real psychic flora and fauna (I think that is the expression he used) of that area. They are beings who occasionally try to contact us but are perceived only subliminally, surfacing primarily in the work of artists and musicians. That is why artists at various points in history all suddenly became interested in the same things, like nymphs and satyrs, angels and archangels, elongated reindeer or abstract squares. These things were the psychic forces current in the area of space-time through which the earth was hurtling. It explains why certain types of harmony come to dominate music at certain periods. These were our way of perceiving the psycho-geometric formations prevalent there. I remember G adding wearily that the area of space-time we were currently traversing must be full of binary code, but otherwise rather dull.

On another occasion I remember his saying how strange and oddly apocalyptic it is that this point of history, of human development, is the first in which human culture has been entirely obsessed with the systematic (as opposed to idealistic) cultivation of the past – 'classical' music, history of art, literary studies, the pursuit of doctorates, architecture, medieval novels, to name but a few.

Over lunch I described the house in detail to Lilian. We talked about another book of G's. It was called *The Middle Ages and the Way Things Seemed: a Phenomenological Study*. In this book his theme was that we could not know anything about the Middle Ages, but we could attempt to evoke what he called myths of the Middle Ages. Instead of the usual academic analyses, he had set about providing a series of sketches, impressions, what he called phenomenologies of life in the Middle Ages, from the point of view of a priest, a peasant, a wandering singer, a bishop, a duke, and so on.

For G, this world was inaccessible – dead to us. Since the Enlightenment, science and the critique of reason, only *belief* in a Platonic world order has been possible. There can be no *knowledge* that the world is cosmologically ordered by a Divine Being, since the nature of knowledge has shifted, become self-reflexive, turned in on itself.

G's fascination with this world, this inaccessibly ordered universe, explained all the charts, the astrology, the alchemy, the fascination with system, structure, order. It also explained why, though a philosopher, he delved so deeply into astrophysics. G was a seeker after Order, after the Answer, and he was serious about it. His frustration explained the vehemence of his attacks against comfortable yet untenable thinking.

It was wonderful talking to Lilian. She was a marvellous listener. She had a way of drawing ideas out of people. I suppose that is an important gift in a publisher. Then there was the way she spoke, carefully, sympathetically, without hurry, but without ever being boring or simply stating the obvious. Her voice had a lovely, open, relaxed clarity. She managed not to affect any accent, though she was obviously from the south. There was no nasal drawl, no residue of cockney, no Oxford plum or private-girl-school tweeness. It was such a pleasure to hear her.

## VI The Lovers

In the afternoon we decided that Lilian should stay in the house and start to prepare an inventory of its contents, paying particular attention to the papers we would have to handle if we decided to accept G's posthumous offer. While she did that, I would go into town, since I knew my way round better, and begin to deal with the bizarre bureaucratic rituals attending death: filling in forms to gain probate, sorting out death certificates and the rest.

First, we decided, I would call on the incurably Anglo-Catholic college chaplain. An hour later I found myself in his overdecorated, oak-panelled study, with carved Victorian panels, little bells, engraved wooden boxes, incense holders, and sub-Pre-Raphaelite prints, which I found sentimental and obnoxious. To be fair to him, he seemed genuinely upset about G's death. In his will G had insisted on a quiet funeral at the local crematorium, and specified certain details. He left money for a reception at the college afterwards.

I chatted with the chaplain for a while about G. The two of them had been relatively close, and I managed to fill in some details about G's life. Apparently G had spent his early years in Nuremberg. G had told the chaplain that his Jewish father had managed to escape the Nazis by forging his papers. With the help of these papers he had managed to live relatively openly throughout the war, only to be killed by Allied bombs in 1945. The chaplain thought this accounted for G's uncompromising pacifism. G used to say time and again that no one had the right to take anyone's life but their own. I wish I had paid more attention to that qualification.

My personal view of G's pacifism was that he really did value human life. He thought that since we were deprived of absolutes in our present world, we would have to invent them. The absolute value of human life was a point G thought it worth starting from.

G was four at the end of the war. His mother found comfort in the arms of an English colonel at first, but eventually suffered a nervous collapse, as a result of which she killed herself. In retrospect his mother's suicide explained a lot.

The English colonel felt sorry for G, took him back with him to England and, using family money, set up a fund for him, which made it possible for G to be sent initially to what in those days counted as a good prep school, and then a 'top' public school and Oxford, in all of which institutions he had shone.

Under any other circumstances I would have been fascinated to hear this story. It explained G's fascination with German culture, which he knew as well as anyone, and also Jewish traditions, like the kabbala. To be honest though, I found it hard to keep my mind on what the chaplain was saying. The signs were unmistakable, though I had only been afflicted twice before in my life.

I was in love with Lilian.

When I returned, it was to find Lilian sitting at the Bechstein in the lounge. She was playing a Mozart sonata, the slow movement of the early F major. She was playing beautifully. I crept in, for fear she might stop.

Light was pouring through the window. She was turned away from me and the sun was just catching her face. She had taken off the red scarf she had round her neck and had thrown it casually over a chair. I noticed that it had a motif on it: it was another yellow eagle, this time in a swirly art nouveau design. Lilian told me later that day that she liked collecting clothes, jewellery and accessories with eagle motifs.

Lilian looked relaxed and so graceful. There was a happy-sad quality to the music, typical of Mozart at his greatest. It seemed to be perfectly reflected in Lilian's personality, light and graceful, yet with a depth, a mystery that made it perfect, beautiful rather than merely pretty. For a moment Lilian was the music, and the music was Lilian. It is an experience I shall never forget. I do not know if there is such a thing as love at first sight. These are, in any case, the only words I can think of to describe how I felt for Lilian.

In our rational age we like to imply that when we fall in love the mind plays tricks. I could easily be convinced of the contrary. Perhaps it is when we are in love, when we perceive the beauty of another with all the obsessiveness, joy and enthusiasm that implies, that we perceive the truth about the person we love. Perhaps it is then that we see them as God would see them, if only He existed. Perhaps that is what it is like to be God - to be madly, head-over-heels in love with everyone all the time.

Though some maintain that the state of being in love is brought about by vitamin B deficiency...

## VII The Chariot

I made some tea and we sat together in the kitchen again.

Lilian said she would have to be getting back to London soon. For some reason this panicked me. I did my best not to show it.

'You will come back, won't you?' I asked, trying to sound casual.

'Maybe. I mean... probably. I'm not sure.'

'But...' I tried to force myself not to show how I was feeling.

'It's so sudden. I've got to think about it. Giving everything up for G. It's a big decision. I can't rush into it.'

'Giving up what?'

That was a stupid question to ask. It gave too much away. At least I said 'what?' and not 'who?', which would have been worse.

'My job, my flat in London, my friends, my way of life.'

'Are you married or engaged or anything?' I decided to throw inhibition to the wind and come straight out with it. There was no reason not to ask. I saw the ring finger was vacant. But you never know.

Lilian blushed slightly. 'No,' she said, 'nothing.' Her honesty was disarming - no apology, no '*well there was this man...*' and the usual endless stories. I admired her for that.

'You?' she added.

'No,' I said. 'Well, to be honest, I just split up with someone.' Whatever I said was sounding wrong, either like I was making excuses or I wanted sympathy. I felt myself blush.

I realised that all of a sudden Rosemary meant absolutely nothing to me. If she had walked in through the door, declared undying love, taken all her clothes off and thrown herself at me, I would have asked her politely but firmly to leave so that I could carry on my conversation with Lilian. So much for constancy.

'Do you want to... to accept G's offer?' she said.

Now that she put the question to me like that, I realised that up till that moment I had been avoiding facing up to it. What was the choice? I could carry on, doing my own work, making my own mistakes, living in my grotty bedsit, permanently broke, but free. Or I could move in, lead a life of luxury, never have to worry about money again... and be G's intellectual 'slave from beyond the grave'. But I would not be free. Instead of my own work I would have to commit myself to doing G's.

'Have you had a chance to look round? Is there much of the stuff? How long would it all take?' Lilian interrupted my thoughts.

'There's tons.' I said. 'It would take a lifetime. Several lifetimes probably.'

I realised that she was genuinely upset. She was not taking the choice lightly. I found her bewilderment even more touching. I wanted her even more then. Maybe I was relying on her for comfort. I was confused, bewildered too. Any normal person would be jumping for joy just at the money, and not worrying about the commitment. But not us. We seemed to be birds of a feather in that respect. We would want to make sure we earned that money.

'You're right,' I said. 'It does need thinking about.' Suddenly my main concern was to avoid losing her. I began to worry that if she did go back to London I might never see her again. I needed to think up some strategy to keep her there. 'Listen,' I said, 'you don't have to go back to London. We could have dinner here and you could go back later. Or you could even stay here.'

She looked at me askance. I could not tell if she was teasing or if she was wary, offended, on guard.

'I can always go back to my bedsit,' I added hastily as my mind looped the loop. I regretted saying 'bedsit' because it gave away my social and financial status, or rather lack of. Then I remembered that my social and financial status could be astonishing, as could hers, if only we went along with G.

'I'm not staying here on my own.'

I couldn't say I blamed her. What young woman in her right mind would want to sleep alone in the house of a dead man, a man whose body had undergone an autopsy that very day? Still, I did not want to let go. 'There's plenty of bedrooms. We could both stay. I'm quite respectable, you know.'

'I know,' she said. She smiled at me with big eyes. All my defences were melting. I loved her, I loved her.

'Let's see how it goes,' I said. 'In any case, I insist we go out to dinner first. We need to get out of here for a while, and we need to talk things through. Is that all right?' I added so as not to sound too domineering.

'Yes,' she said. 'All right.'

## VIII Justice

That was typical of me. I had to have my plans. Rosemary used to tease me. I remember her saying. 'Your trouble is that you can't enjoy time. You have to keep organising it away.'

I suppose she was right. I was attracted by the idea that maybe time was not linear but, as some modern physics theories have it, circular or imaginary. I have never really come to terms with the passing of time. Maybe that is why I am drawn to the written text. It is generous. Whether you are reading or writing, it always allows you another go.

We went to a smart Italian restaurant in a once attractive, now trendified street not far from G's house, often referred to as North Yuppie Street. We started the evening in great earnestness, thinking in depth about the pros and cons of the offer that had been made to us.

Then, as we drank more wine, our scruples and sense of honour began to wane. Somewhere between the second and third course (we made it to five in the end; I have always had a voracious appetite, and so had Lilian) we started to get giggly. We began to come to terms with, and revel in, our good fortune. All that money, that house, all ours to do what we wanted with. And all we had to do in return was sort out G's papers.

Suddenly my worries about getting a university teaching post seemed silly. G was offering more money than I could hope to earn in a lifetime of lecturing and tutoring. If I wanted status as a researcher and academic, it was there for the taking, for the thoughts and life of G were surely a worthwhile object of study.

Lilian was talking too about how good it would be to give up the petty power politics of the office and spend her time preparing G's work for print. We saw ourselves (under the influence of the wine, to my great joy at least, the pronoun 'we' was beginning to come into use) going on world tours, me lecturing on the ideas of the great G, Lilian presenting beautifully produced books of his works, all of which would bear our names as 'edited by...'

How can I describe Lilian? She was involving, exciting, and made me feel intensely alive. There was such understanding between us that, in a way, talking to her was almost like being alone, and our thoughts flowed as freely, perhaps more freely, than if we had been alone. By the end of the evening it was already as if we had known each other for months rather than just a day. Yet for all the familiarity of the way we spoke, there was still a distance, a respect, which made being with her all the more exciting, special.

We decided that we would sleep in G's house. Lilian would take a room on the third floor, in one of the turrets, like a maiden in distress, and I would sleep in one of the guest-rooms on the second floor.

It was a curious thing, but by then I was so in love with Lilian that I did not want to sleep with her. I wanted to leave her her freedom, to cherish her, to enjoy her company without any of the complications that can result from sex. I also wanted to be alone, just to be able to think about her and my love for her.

Only on the way home did the euphoria subside. It was a beautiful evening, the air mild and gentle, heady with the scents of flowers and blossoms. The moon was out. It was the ideal setting for love.

Yet there was a death to be reckoned with. Somewhere, miles over the sea, there was a corpse, in a morgue, cut open, a thing that had been a man.

When we got back, Lilian showed me some more poems of G's she had found during the afternoon. The poems were full of obscure references to astrology, Greek mythology and much else. I realised that if I were to undertake the editing of the complete works of G, I would have to puzzle them all out. I wondered if they constituted some mystical system G had discovered or invented. I noticed that the two women in the poem called 'The Lovers' made me think of Rosemary and Lilian. But when I am in a relationship, or just out of one, everything reminds me of the woman I love, or have just lost; so it was hardly surprising if this poem seemed to fit me like a glove.

I remembered the line from Eliot about measuring out one's life in coffee spoons. I wondered if the tragedy of this line lay in the fact that what men really use to measure out their lives is their women: mother, girlfriends, lovers, wife, wives, would-have-been wives. If so, the coffee spoon would be quite a good symbol for the sterility of sexual absence.

I was very virtuous. I gave Lilian a polite kiss on the cheek as she held my hand for a second, and we went off to separate beds.

## IX Hermit

That night, the images from the poems, hackneyed as they were, infiltrated my dreams. I woke up wondering what they were about. If they had not been G's (I assumed they *were* G's), I would have guessed they were about some form of quest for the inner self. Yet G would have laughed such an idea out of court. 'How would we know,' I remember him saying once on the topic, 'whether the inner self, once discovered, did not itself have an inner self, which might in turn have an inner self, and so on? Or perhaps we ought just to admit the obvious, which is that the inner self is just another way of seeing the outer self we had not noticed before.'

There was no sign of Lilian when I got up, so I made tea for her. By half past eight she had still not appeared, so I knocked on her door. I knocked again and called. I checked the bathroom. I called out again and again.

At last I could not take the waiting any longer. Gently, I eased the door open. There was no one there. The bed looked as though it had not been slept in, though I supposed she could have made it before leaving. I knelt down to check how it smelled. I caught a faint hint of her scent, of her own, very special smell.

I panicked. I could not believe that she would have just gone, without saying anything to me. I called her name. I checked every room in the house, calling for her over and over, then shouting until I became hoarse.

At last I gave up. I went back down to the kitchen, poured myself another cup of tea, and another, and another. All the time I was expecting her to appear, any moment. I sat there and moped.

Then I tried to convince myself that I was mistaken to be thinking so much of her. Certainly she was beautiful. But that indefinability about her - was it a form of haughtiness? When she was being so nice to me yesterday, maybe it was because she wanted to keep her options open. It would suit her for me to be soft on her. Then she could get just what she wanted out of G, financially and socially, and keep me as her lap-dog, to do all the work. I knew so little about her. I supposed she might have been G's mistress. I did not know where she lived, if what she said about being unattached was true. I tried to become suspicious of her, to disdain her, to distance myself from her, to dislike her even.

But none of it worked. She was the most lovely young woman I had ever met. There was no getting away from it. The problem was that I was not good enough for her. That was what hurt.

For some reason I started thinking about an interview G gave a couple of years ago. G was asked what he would have become if he had not become a famous philosopher, an intellectual. He answered that he would have liked to have become a monk. Everyone laughed at this. Everyone knew his reputation as a *bon viveur*, as a womaniser, as an intellectual iconoclast.

To me his answer made perfect sense. In fact I sympathised with him. One thing that created a bond between us, something we understood about one another, was the fact that we were both prone to periodic attacks of Christianity of one sort or another, mysticism, call it what you will. Throughout my adolescence, and my undergraduate days, I had often found myself drawn into religious groups. These flirtations always ended in self-disgust or disgust at the institution I had joined. G found consolation of sorts, as I said, in his visits to the college chapel, which was ironic, because few people in the university were ever more vocal than he in denouncing what he saw as the cant of what he called institutionalised Christianity in general, and Oxford Anglicanism, with its petty feuds, hysteria and self-serving self-righteousness, in particular.

He even expressed an interest in the charismatic movement. The idea of giving expression to our highest religious aspirations in a language we could not understand had an immense appeal for him. He wrote an article on the sheer logic of the illogicality of speaking in tongues. For someone interested in the structure of language, it was of course a gift of a topic. He wrote about tongues as a language of pure structure and pure meaning without syntax or semantics, the ultimate expression of the inexpressible, which thereby remained unexpressed.

His interest in monasticism was parallel. He was drawn to its wordlessness, its silence. For a man whose existence was entirely controlled, hemmed in by words, the monastic existence offered the ideal escape. The thought of endless days of not having to speak to anyone, of thinking in great slabs of silence, would have provided the ultimate adventure, the ultimate release and the ultimate expression of the inexpressible, unlike his own life, which he saw as nothing more than a professional quibbling with others' failure to express.

As to his own religious view, he said he subscribed to the 'Near Miss' theory of Christianity: the theory that if there was something, a Beyond, a God, then Christianity was sometimes partially successful, if not in expressing it, then at least in providing some sort of vehicle for it. A retreat into monasticism might provide an opportunity to seek out whatever that was.

I wondered if he had found whatever it was he sought in death.

As for me, I craved a life in which I would not be prone to such fits of passion as I was feeling then. I missed Lilian bitterly, though I had known her less than twenty-four hours.

## X The Wheel Of Fortune

That morning, without Lilian, the house was oppressive. It was only because of her presence in the place that I had felt able to sleep there. Now, without her, it was a dead house, a monument, eerie, like an Egyptian tomb.

I tried to decide what to do next. Any excuse to get out of the house. There were still a number of jobs to do in town. There were people to see at the college, things to sort out at the bank and with the solicitors.

The thought of starting with the solicitors appealed. I would be able to talk about probate and the technicalities of the inheritance. Besides, I wanted to know what would happen if Lilian were to pull out of the arrangement. To be rather more honest, I wanted to find out more about Lilian, where she could be contacted and so on. I did not want to lose her.

It was a beautiful spring morning. All the trees were bursting with blossom and the north Oxford gardens were aglow with colour.

I needed time to think, so I decided to walk.

My mind went round and round like a great wheel. I felt completely lost.

An anecdote G once told me kept coming to mind. I saw it so vividly that it was almost as if I had been there myself. It was a story from his undergraduate days in the late fifties. One long vacation he had been invited to spend a weekend with a friend in Ryde. The friend in question was a mathematician. He also enjoyed a reputation for knowing about rock and roll and for organising what in those days counted as riotous parties. One such was to take place on the Saturday of G's visit. The man's parents lived abroad and he had free range of their house. During the course of the afternoon and early evening, other undergraduate friends arrived as well as local friends – young men and women. The women were attractive and, allegedly, willing.

The first part of the evening was spent drinking and dancing. G had done a fair amount of both before getting into a conversation about a problem he was wrestling with at the time: the question of whether or not we have free will and what difference assumptions we make about free will have on the way we see the world.

I can imagine G as a young man, sitting in the corner of a smoke filled room, with a glass of wine in one hand, his dark hair falling over his eyes, arguing with his friend about the mathematics of probability, whilst all around him there was music, dancing, flirting and caressing. I can imagine G challenging his friend to imagine an event without a cause, to disprove that free will would involve infinite bifurcations of infinite universes... and so on.

To illustrate some point he was trying to make about freedom, G said that he was going for a swim, despite the fact that it was nearly midnight. It seemed like a good idea, and a number of them went down to the beach. G stripped to his underwear and started swimming out into the dark waters of the Channel.

The water was warm and dark and G felt, as he swam out further and further from the shore, that he was leaving everything behind him and entering a world that was beautifully private and enclosed, and that he was infinitely secure, infinitely strong .

He had heard noises from the shore, people shouting. He was dimly aware that he had swum too far out to sea, that he was in danger of being swept away by the current. But the people on the shore looked tiny, insignificant, and he was content in his enclosed universe. Soon he was out of earshot, and he could only just see them signalling frantically to turn back. They were so little, and the lights of the houses and the street lamps seemed to be shining from an infinite distance, as if from another world.

There was no reason to return. Only in a detached sort of way did he realise how dangerous this state of mind was, that it might be the onset of exhaustion, or some kind of black-out. Then he realised that the waves were growing higher, and that he was being drawn further away from the shore by the current. He turned round slowly and began to try to swim back. But it seemed not to matter.

At first he swam in a relaxed way. Then he realised he was not making any progress. He was just being dragged along by the current and the tide.

It was then that he had a vision of the infinite number of infinitely small atoms and molecules of water in the sea that were bearing the atoms and molecules of which his body consisted. That vision stayed with him ever since. It was beautiful and terrible; the movement of the waves, the infinitely complex criss-crossing of particles and energy, each unpredictable, uncompromising yet somehow forming a great drift, a dance, which was conspiring to his destruction and dissolution. It was a vision that was fascinating, comforting. There was no need to swim back to the shore. It was as if he was being drawn inexorably into the vast, ordered disorder of the geometric shapes and patterns of the vision, all the tiny dancing particles and waves making up the sea, the air, his body. He thought he had understood, that this vision was the truth, that he was seeing the truth about the universe, about what was all around him.

He was saved by fear, the sudden realization that he was losing control, and that if he gave way he would die. The fear inspired him to a supreme effort. The current was so strong that it took him nearly an hour to get back to the shore. Some of his friends cheered, but many, especially the women, scolded.

He tried to tell them of what he had experienced, but they were in no mood to listen – except one girl, who was a mathematician from one of the women's colleges. She led him back to the friend's house, gave him food, found him warm clothes, helped him to bed.

She joined him there. It was his first time. As they made love, he experienced once again the feeling of being part of a vast, random, yet inevitable ebb and flow of energy particles – pure energy.

He said he had *experienced* the sense in which there are no mathematical certainties. He said he now not only knew, intellectually understood, but had also seen and physically felt the implications. His understanding took the form, outwardly, of a nervous breakdown. On returning to his own home he went to bed and for days lay still, motionless. It took him a while to regain any motivation to do anything at all. The lethargy lasted throughout the rest of the vacation. Even for some time afterwards, he said he found it impossible to make decisions.

He recovered by rolling dice. Whenever he found himself confronted with a set of alternatives he could no longer choose between, he would simply roll dice, and always stick to what the dice said.

It was odd that, walking down through the spring sunshine, it was as if I was reliving this experience of G's. In retrospect, it all seems to fit into some kind of pattern after all.

## XI Fortitude

I turned off the Banbury Road, past St Mary's, into Little Clarendon Street with all its shopping attractions aimed at those for whom purchasing-power is a substitute for creativity – and into Wellington Square past the university offices.

I turned round the corner into St John Street and I swear I saw Lilian go in through the door of the office. Immediately my heart beat faster with excitement, and I ran in the hope of catching up with her. By the reception desk I was sure that I caught her scent in the air. But the receptionist denied that she had been in the office.

I was crestfallen and only just managed to maintain a semblance of amiability. Miss Marcanu was still charming and sexy, in her black miniskirt and tight white blouse. But all my thoughts now were for Lilian, and my visit was formal and business-like. I managed to release from G's account what by my standards was a not inconsiderable sum in order to cover the immediate expenses linked with the funeral.

The arrangement was that I should be the paymaster whilst the order of service and the details of the reception afterwards were to be left to the college authorities. I was amazed that everything was going ahead so smoothly. Apparently the autopsy in Spain had been carried out very promptly. The body was already winging its way to Heathrow.

Then there were a few other forms to fill in and sign and I was on my way. It did not escape my notice that Miss Marcanu was doing what she could to please me, to make herself attractive to me. Twenty-four hours ago I would not only have been tempted, but drooling with excitement. Now though, there was Lilian, and I could not help thinking that Miss Marcanu was interested in me because of the money I stood to inherit.

I could not work out whether or not there was something overstated in the way Miss Marcanu denied she had seen Lilian. So much about her was gushy and insincere, it was impossible to tell.

Next I went and treated myself to a bacon sandwich in the café next to the Taylorian where the traffic wardens relax, for hours on end, from their onerous duties. Then I walked through the centre of town, past the spot where Cranmer was burnt alive, and into G's college.

To get to his rooms it was necessary to trace one's way through a maze of passageways and tiny courtyards. I often used to wonder if G had chosen these rooms on purpose as some outward expression of the labyrinthine nature of his spirit.

Then it happened again. Just as I was coming round the pseudo-baroque corner into the quad where G's rooms were, I caught sight of a female figure going into G's staircase. I could have sworn it was Lilian. I rushed across the quad, into the entrance, then up the stairs and into his rooms.

I could smell her perfume. There were plenty of other rooms on the staircase and I suppose I could have been mistaken. I got it into my head that she had gone into his rooms and I spent a long while fumbling with keys, holding my ear to the door.

At last I got in and I could not stop myself from searching

everywhere, even in the cupboards and under the bed. I even pushed at some of the oak panels that lined the walls in the hope of finding a secret exit. But anyone could tell from the geometry of the room that that would have been impossible.

There was no sign of Lilian, but I was convinced I that was her scent.

It was like being haunted, teased by a ghost. Either I was going mad or I was falling very badly in love.

I sat down in one of G's pre-ecological leather armchairs and tried to recover my composure. Then I got on with the task I had set myself, which was to see what papers there would be here for me to sort out.

Almost nothing! I was surprised, because G was normally, superficially at least, an untidy person who would leave papers lying about all over the place. He seemed to have cleared everything out of his college rooms, though. There was something ominous about that, but at the time I could not think what.

The last place I looked was in the desk drawers. And there I found another crop of poems, this time labelled from eight to twelve.

I sat down in the armchair again and tried to read them, to concentrate on them. It is curious how the mind can divide. Part of me tried to make sense of the poems, but the rest of me was obsessed with Lilian. Now everything that could possibly be good about my future seemed linked with her.

I could not get out of my head the notion that the poems G had left lying round were clues of some sort. A kind of paper-chase. It was odd that I was discovering them in the right numerical order, as if my movements had been foreseen.

After a while I decided that there was nothing to detain me in his rooms any longer, and I decided to treat myself to a picturesque walk through the various colleges. But my mind was incapable of divorcing any of the beauty I saw from the thought of Lilian. The lines of the architecture brought to mind snatches of music - Mozart, Schubert, Beethoven, Monteverdi - and in that beauty I heard her voice, saw the shapes and curves of her face and body.

But most I was haunted by the medieval song I had heard on the radio the previous morning.

I tried to reflect on what it is to have ideals. I remembered an idea of G's that all we have left these days, when religion, politics, even art, have collapsed, become debased, are sexual ideals. Having no objective sets of values, no cosmology, no given social structures or hierarchies that make sense, all that we have left is one another. So those we find sexually attractive can tend to be invested with all the virtues, all the goodness, all the beauty and all the qualities we find so pitifully lacking in other aspects of our lives.

It is hardly surprising that loved ones rarely manage to live up to such expectations, and that so many relationships and marriages end in calamity. Curious, that just when religion was first threatened by science in the nineteenth century, romantic love got going in a big way.

Oh, to have lived before the age of science, in a Neoplatonic universe, where the whole of Creation was ordered into the shape of a giant pyramid, with God at the top, then the orders of archangels, angels, thrones, dominions, virtues, man, beasts, plants and inanimate matter. Then, values, lives, beings, relationships were not just invented, or by-products of social structures, 'inevitable accidents of social change' as G once called them. Everything had its place, an objective, verifiable value, and belonged to an order with a purpose and an end. So sexual attraction, love, had a role to play, but it fitted into the pattern, it had a place. It was not the be-all and end-all.

It is wonderful being human, that one can entertain such thoughts, think in such a detached and analytical way about one's own state of mind, and yet pursue one's obsessive emotions, in a mad state of excitement, obsession, deliberately, consciously and irrationally, until the bitter end.

Such was the dual aspect of my mind until I turned off the Banbury Road towards the river. For a third time I was convinced I saw her, just turning the corner a hundred yards or so in front of me. I called at the top of my voice and started running. But when I reached the corner, whoever it was had gone.

## XII The Hanged Man

Back at G's house, I started to reread the poems I had found.

To me it was extraordinary that, for all his need to debunk, contradict and undermine existing structures of knowledge, G should still have such an interest in this sort of semi-occult imagery. All the symbols were familiar to me, though I was not certain where I had met them before.

I made yet another cup of coffee and went to sit in the front room, where the Italian Renaissance-style portrait was. It had the same stillness as a da Vinci. I know little about painting techniques, so I could not tell if the painting was a recent imitation or really sixteenth century. The girl had beautiful hair done up in the sort of head-dress one often saw in prints and paintings from that period. She had a fine complexion, large, melancholic but brilliant eyes. And she looked just like Lilian.

Over the mantelpiece I noticed a small print of a young man. This looked like a Dürer, though the customary AD was missing. Maybe it was the school of Dürer. The picture was of a young man with curly brown hair. Surely it was a coincidence: the young man looked just like me.

I sat down again in one of the leather armchairs. Prompted by the contemplation of the print perhaps, I became lost in memories of happy days I had spent in Nürnberg while I was learning German. In particular I remembered the Dürerhaus up in the north part of town, towards the castle. On summer evenings the town became so animated, so much alive, so full of fun and friendship. Even the Frauentor, where the prostitutes displayed themselves at windows in order to attract custom, had an odd charm to it.

I had lived, briefly, in Nürnberg, in the days before I knew G. I often used to think of the terrors of the bombing of the city. It did not seem possible that such a thing could have happened. Even the Zeppelinenfelder, where Hitler had spoken, or rather ranted, at the Nürnberg rallies, now had an atmosphere of peace and tranquillity. What a monument to transience that place is. Hitler's Thousand

Year Reich. G was very keen on the history of the doctrine of the Last Emperor, who would reign before the coming of the Antichrist. And he was an expert on the occult in the Third Reich. Even the term Third Reich did not really refer to the third German Empire, but to an occult notion of the dawning of a New Age of Freedom for the Elect.

In some ways so little of the past stays in the air. Yet it was easy to tell where the bombs had landed in Nürnberg. The geography of old and new buildings was monumentally clear. One would have thought that a town which had suffered as Nürnberg had suffered would be full of ghosts, but that did not seem to be the case, not from the point of view of a visitor like me.

If ghosts exist, I suppose it is in our heads that they live, or rather in our wounds. I thought of what G must have suffered there as a child, the constant threat his father must have lived under. At least, that was how I saw it at the time.

Perhaps G's relationship with his father explains the schizoid needs that drove G's academic work. On the one hand there was the need to criticise, to pull to pieces, to show once and for all that there are no absolute foundations, no point from which grandiose claims can be made about anything. Then there was the meticulous investigation of the past, the need to collect, even create, systems and structures, like those in these strange symbolist poems of his.

There was more to his sense of the past, however. For example, I remember G once telling me how he thought the music of Mozart, Beethoven and Schubert was so powerful because it was a rehearsal for grief. He once told me about an experience he had listening to a Schubert song recital in the Queen Elizabeth Hall. He dozed off to sleep and imagined himself in a country house. It was built like the sort of house in the countryside near Vienna where Schubert might have spent his holidays. Yet this was a ghost house. It was dusty. In the basement were shelves of dusty manuscripts. Suddenly Schubert was there, telling him that he could help himself to the papers, for they would be valuable in the land of the living. Yet there was a penalty for doing so. After death he would have to join the company of the house. He would be excluded from heaven and from hell, for this was the house of Art, of grey spirits, neither good nor evil. Then a chill settled on the house, a greyness, and G woke up. He could not remember whether he had taken any of the manuscripts or not.

Another experience he mentioned has just come to mind. He was sixteen and had gone to the opera festival in Munich, sharing a room with a friend in a pension. They had just returned from a performance of Mozart's *Die Entführung aus dem Serail*. The two of them were lying in (separate) beds and talking about whether the source of art was diabolical or divine. Then, he said, it was suddenly as if the room had been detached from the world and was falling through a region that was evil, hellish. The walls seemed to fall away, to melt. There was a sense of loss. He felt frightened and wanted to cry, but did not want to show it. Eventually he could take no more and reached for the light switch.

His friend was quiet too. 'Thank God you turned the light on,' he said.

'Why?'

G's friend had just had an identical experience. He was looking at a photograph of the girl he loved and was convinced that it was weeping. G said that to him, also, the photograph seemed to have changed, seemed sad and haunted. How could they explain the fact that they both had the same feeling of loss and falling at the same time? They ended up saying the Lord's Prayer together - quite out of character for the two of them.

I know that G was very prone to such feelings, or states, despite the fact that, publicly, he was a representative of the 'no-nonsense' school of rational criticism, and all that implied. Yet he, and I, knew that such superficial thought did not even touch on the true nature of the past. There were voices, spirits, unexorcised, calling, haunting.

With a start I remembered that G was now one of these. It was so easy to forget that he was dead. His thoughts, his life's work, were so much present in this house, which made it seem almost impossible that he had ever lived as a real, breathing body. Dead now, he was his work, his thoughts. Yet dead, he was as finished as anyone dead. Though he had died only four days ago, the past he belonged to was as distant, as inaccessible, as that of the pharaohs, the Third Reich, the Middle Ages.

What he had wanted was to be allowed another, posthumous life. That was what he had been working for all this time. He wanted to be present in the world of academic thought in the way that Paracelsus says the astral bodies of the dead linger in air, in the way that the pharaohs wanted to live on in the effects with which they filled their pyramids, in the way that composers live on in their music.

That was another inconsistency. Why should he have wanted this for himself when he was so suspicious of others who had it for themselves? It was precisely that suspicion which led him to develop such incisive critical tools for dealing with texts. I remember him saying once: 'History is like sex: what people do and what people say they do is almost never the same thing.'

I thought of the last of the poems I had just found. Odin, the hanging God, hanging upside down from the great Tree of Life, the cost of learning to understand the runes. The only point from which understanding could be reached was from the point of view of the dead. Unless...

Then my mind turned to the terms of the will. That was where I came in. He was asking me to become possessed by him. The process had already started. I was beginning to understand why Lilian and I had been so afraid to begin with, maybe why she had disappeared. It was, to say the least, frightening to allow oneself to be possessed by a spirit like G's.

I had to make my decision. Yet it was already made for me. I could not resist. I had to go along with it. Not for the money. Not for the prestige. There was a deeper reason than that. I valued G. I valued his thought. In spite of this, I vowed, it would be on my terms. I would be no slave to G. I would be true to him, but true to myself also. I might decide to be his champion, but I would also be his sternest critic.

I was lost in these thoughts when the doorbell rang. I nearly jumped out of my seat. I went to answer the door. I could hardly believe my eyes. It was Lilian.

## XIII Death

I was so pleased to see her that I could not resist greeting her French-style, giving her a hug and a kiss on each cheek. She smiled. Again her perfume filled my head, and she looked even more beautiful.

'I went to London to pick up some things,' she said simply. She had a bag with her. I realised with joy that she was planning to stay.

'I wondered where you were,' I said.

'I'm sorry. I should have left a note. But to be honest, I was not sure what I was going to do. It's not easy to decide.'

There was a look in her eyes. The way she smiled at me – could it be possible? Could she reciprocate my feelings towards her, in no matter how small a way?

'It's not easy,' I said. 'I've just been thinking. I'm going to go through with it.'

'Well, at least one of us knows what they are doing,' she said.

'How about you?'

'I'm not sure yet. I had to come back, though.'

'Why was that?'

'There is a reason,' she said mysteriously, 'and it took me a while to come to terms with it. I will tell you. One day. Only not now.'

For a moment I could not think what to say. I wanted to probe more, but did not dare, for fear of being impolite, of giving too much of myself away. Fortunately, Lilian changed the subject and earthed the atmosphere that had grown between us.

'By the way,' she said, 'you know the solicitors, Arott and Marcanu?'

'Yes.'

'I tried to phone them, but I had forgotten to take their number. They were not in the phone book, and directory enquiries had never heard of them either. Next! tried the Law Society. Arott and Marcanu weren't even registered.'

'Maybe they changed premises recently. The place looked new enough,' I said.

'That's possible,' said Lilian, 'but the Law Society said their records were usually up to date.'

It was five o'clock. We decided to go out to dinner at seven, but in the meantime we would carry on working through some of G's papers. I showed Lilian the latest crop of poems I had found. In return, she had something to show me. It was a manuscript G had given her only three or four weeks ago. It was called 'Walter'. It was handwritten but, oddly enough, not in G's hand. It is the text that forms the first part of this edition.

'Did G write this?' I asked.

'I am not sure. It's not his style,' she said.

I flicked through it and noticed that there were a number of references to occult and mystical systems.

'What did he say about it?' I asked her.

'It was hard to pin him down,' she said. 'It was as if he was playing games. Sometimes he was very serious about it, and sometimes flippant. To begin with he said that the story of the book had been dictated via a spirit voice that had contacted him, and all he had done was to translate it into a modern novel format. On another occasion he said that the text was a study of why it is impossible to write about the Middle Ages. Another time he said that the book was a *roman-à-clef* and that it was really an exposition of a mystery – which the reader would have to puzzle out. Another time he said it was "just a thriller" a friend of his had "knocked off" in an idle moment. Then once he said that it was a serious study of social and power relationships in the late twelfth century.'

I spent three quarters of an hour flicking through the manuscript to get the feel of the story. I had an odd feeling about the main character. There was something too familiar about him.

## XIV Temperance

That evening at the restaurant, we talked about the arrangements for G's funeral. Then, as the wine began to take effect, we moved on to religion. I asked if Lilian believed in damnation.

'Oh, that,' she said jokingly, 'they say it was invented by male élites to keep women and the non-élite males in their places - by fear. Matriarchal societies did not have cosmologies with eternal punishment.'

'That's as may be,' I said, 'but it certainly worked on me. When I was thirteen…' What made me reveal all my adolescent religious and sexual hang-ups I have no idea. But I did. That was part of her charm. She was such a good listener.

'What do you think would be worst, then,' she asked, 'hellfire, total annihilation, or survival as a disembodied consciousness eternally shifting through its memories of this life?'

'What a dire thought!' I exclaimed. 'I think I would prefer heaven…' I nearly added 'with you', but stopped just in time.

'I remember seeing G take on an evangelical Christian one day. The woman had promised G eternal life if only he would do the usual things evangelicals say you have to do…'

'Which were…?' I asked.

'You know, say he was a sinner, ask God for forgiveness, let Jesus into his life, and so on.'

'What did G say?'

'He stared at her and said, "Which self would have eternal life? My present, thinking self does not survive from one moment to the next, since it is constantly changing. The self which is the sum total of my past experiences could survive, like some vast photo album, but then who or what would view it? It cannot view itself. Or do you mean the self which has a potential for new experience? But that self has no past, is defined only in terms of future experiences… So how can I, myself, have eternal life?" I think they were the words he used. You get the idea anyhow?'

'You've got G to a tee. How did the poor woman react?'

'The thing about evangelicals,' Lilian said, 'is that they can believe the most odd things, and be challenged in the most threatening ways, yet always remain sane.'

'Unless you see it not as sanity, but as a specialised form of stupidity or insensitivity,' I butted in. 'Sorry...' In conversation I am a compulsive apologiser. This annoys many people.

Rosemary, for example, once said, '*I don't mind you feeling guilty, Ian, but your paranoia is boring...*' Lilian, on the other hand, smiled charmingly, as though I had just paid her a great compliment.

'The Evangelical just said, "I know who I am and so does God."'

'How did G react?'

'Well, it was getting embarrassing by then, because the other people in the room started laughing. Only I caught G's eye. He was the only one who had thought about her answer and he was the only one who was impressed.'

I tried to work out why G should have been impressed, and decided to put it off till another day. Another memory was bubbling to the surface. 'Do you remember G's Orders of Morality?'

'You mean the Sunday Times "Philosophy you never knew you never knew" series?'

'Yes. I've got it pinned to the door of my loo.' Despite the wine and the excellent antipasti, I winced at myself for making that admission.

'Well, since it's confession time,' Lilian said, 'I've got it on the pinboard in my kitchen, amongst my favourite recipes.' She laughed.

'Can you remember the Orders?' I asked. 'I think I can, but I am not sure...'

The Orders were parodies of the Platonic Orders. The aim was to show that there are different levels of moral behaviour in society, which can be structured into a seven-tiered hierarchy. We quoted them in turn, imitating G's smug yet boyish way of speaking. Lilian began:

'Order one. Saintly: total self-sacrifice to a mystical or moral ideal...'

'Order two. Ideal: total self-sacrifice to a social role or ideal which actually benefits others...'

'Order three. Aesthetic: total self-sacrifice to an aesthetic ideal...'

'Order four. Honourable: the relatively successful, good, hardworking and boring fall into this category. These people are not motivated by any ideal but like to please. Therefore they do what is right in the eyes of their society...'

'Order five. Not harmful: those similarly motivated to four above, yet unsuccessful as a result of bad luck, ignorance, stupidity or a combination. These people try to live their lives in a way which, at least, does not do any harm, even if it does little good. This is a more noble and difficult enterprise than first appears...'

'Order six. Obsessive: those who should aim to belong to category five, but imagine they belong to categories four or above. These people justify mean, selfish and small-minded actions in terms of higher motives. They get away with this for years because everyone else is either too intimidated, bored or tired to point out to them the errors of their ways...'

'Order seven. Sadistic: those who actually do like hurting others and do not attempt to justify the fact. Such people can be refreshing because of their honest brutality (compared with those in category six), provided, of course, one is not on the receiving end of their sadism... That's all, isn't it?' Lilian asked.

It was so amazing for me to be eating with another G fan! It had never happened to me before, and I was having the time of my life.

By now we had reached the cheese course. I relished the sight of Lilian as she ate joyfully and without inhibition. None of the usual stuff about diets and this and that being good or bad for you.

'Which Order to you think you belong to?' she asked me.

'Five,' I said.

'You're too modest.'

'What about you then?'

'Oh, I am a five at best... six sometimes...' Lilian said, hanging her head.

I stopped myself from saying that if there were such a thing as an aesthetic of being, then Lilian would definitely be a three in my book... Instead, we tried to categorise people we both knew. G was hardest. Sometimes he fitted into categories two and three, at other times six or seven.

'Do you remember the next article?' I asked. 'The one about "*Futilitarianism and Confusionism*"?'

Lilian smiled. 'I know that one by heart,' she said, and quoted, whilst I demolished a splendid chocolate gateau: 'The difference between these two rival philosophies is as follows.

*The Futilitarian starts from the point of view that all things are futile. They are futile for the following reasons*

*1) Consequences are unpredictable*

*2) No matter how much effort we expend, there are no guarantees that we shall achieve what we want*

*3) No matter how well things turn out, we can always imagine them turning out better*

*4) Therefore we will never be totally satisfied with our lot, whatever happens...*'

I too knew some of the article off by heart, and so, not to be outdone, I continued, while Lilian started on her pavlova:

'*For these reasons Futilitarians argue that there is no point in doing anything. But by the same ticket, there is also no reason not to do anything. Therefore, being a Futilitarian does not affect one's behaviour on the outside. Only one is aware of the Ultimate Futility of Things...*'

At that point my mind went blank – probably something to do with the brandy. 'Can you remember how Confusionism works?' I asked.

'Just about. It's the more upbeat of the two. The starting-point is similar:

'*We know we can never know all about everything, that systems always contain elements which are unsystematisable, that we are not even aware how much we are unaware of, but instead of moping, which Futilitarians tend to do, though they should be the first to realise that moping would be ultimately futile - the Confusionist chooses to rejoice, to revel in the Confusion and Bewilderment (they are fond of using capitals for abstract nouns) which they see all around them. They live in a world full of*

*Wonderful Surprises, Unpredictable Reverses, and Mysterious Problems which, as soon as they are allegedly solved, immediately generate lots of other Problems, though of course this might not be the case...'*

'Do you remember the bit about Confusionist sub-theories?' I asked.

'If that was the following week, I think I missed it. I was away or something,' Lilian said.

'Then let me try to explain. The idea was that Confusionists spend lots of time inventing sub-theories, though they don't really believe in them - like the law of Intellectual Entropy, which states that all problems tend to the creation of even more problems, and the more effort one expends on trying to solve them, the faster this process becomes.'

Lilian smiled, and sipped at her brandy. She had drunk as much as me, but did not seem at all the worse for wear. 'Go on,' she said.

'There was another sub-theory, the principle of the Generation of Ontological Bewilderment (or the "GOB" principle). It is a development of Hofstaedter's law and states: *You are always more confused than you think, even if you take into account the GOB principle.* Do you want some more brandy?'

'Port, please.'

I ordered port.

'I just remembered another sub-theory,' I said, unable to stem the tide of my own enthusiasm. 'This one is called the "Bureaucracy" Cosmos Theory, referred to as "BUROCOSM", on the grounds that it sounds like a newly privatised monopoly. According to this theory, the Truth about Everything is that it is all a great bureaucratic muddle. BUROCOSM Confusionists state that the Neoplatonists were right about there being levels, hierarchies and orders in the universe, but they had missed the fact that these functioned, or rather failed to function, like the levels of management in a great bureaucracy, and that these levels were always in a state of SOS, or Sefirotic Ontological Shambles.'

'I see,' said Lilian, 'a kind of Platonism in reverse.'

'That's right,' I said. 'The Truth, according to the BUROCOSM school, is that the higher up the Platonic Orders one ascends, the greater the Confusion. One version of the theory has it that at the, very top of the pyramidal power structure there is an office door, swung wide open, with the notice "Sorry, Back Soon" pinned to it. No one is sure if anyone has ever been there.'

'Is that it?' Lilian asked.

'It goes on and on,' I said. 'For example, G said that the bureaucratic image generated the Higher Order, Higher Incompetence Principle (or HOHI Principle), which states that the Beings in each Cosmological Order are working Beyond their "Ontologically Normal" Competence ("BONC", hence "going BONCkers"). That is why they never get anything worthwhile done. Success results in immediate promotion to a higher level, at which the Being is bound to become incompetent. Hence the PIGGI Principle (Promotion In Order to Guarantee General Incompetence)... Anyhow, which are you, a Confusionist or a Futilitarian?'

'I like to think of myself as quite positive, so I guess I'm a Confusionist. How about you?'

'I'm afraid I'm one of your lyrical mopers, so I suppose that qualifies me as a Futilitarian,' I confessed.

And so the conversation went on all the way home. More important than the spoken content of these conversations was the body language.

To cut a long story short, it became clear that on returning to G's house we were going to sleep together.

## XV Devil

On the way home the conversation took on a more sombre tone. As we walked, arm in arm, Lilian asked me, 'Do you think G committed suicide?'

'I've been thinking that too,' I replied. 'Suicide was certainly part of G's character. For all his brilliance there was a dark side. Or perhaps "dark" is the wrong word. There was an absence, a void.'

'I think I know what you mean,' said Lilian.

I smiled. 'The trouble is there is no way to describe a void, because by definition there is nothing there…' I recognised it because it was in me. In G it was gnawing, corrosive, though this was what made it possible for him to be flexible, mercurial even. Lilian seemed to understand, and that drew me to her even more. Maybe I was wrong about Lilian. Maybe I was romanticising her. I often attribute to women I love some sense of certainty from which I have been excluded. I envy them as bearers of secret knowledge through which the void can be conquered. Curious, since what most of them want to do is just work for a few years and then get married and have children. Or maybe that is the Answer.

In any case, the streets of north Oxford were picturesque in the street-light. The scent of the trees and the flowers, mingled with Lilian's perfume, was intoxicating. I felt that I was no longer part of time, as though there was no 'now', but that we were just walking, disembodied, in a timeless plane, brushing shoulders with ghosts in the spring night.

'You know,' Lilian said, 'there are rumours about G being involved in occult practices.'

I had heard the rumours that he belonged to satanic cults, that he had become involved with groups that practised pagan rituals under the guise of therapy.

'One day – I remember he was depressed at the time – he said he had met people who knew of rituals which guarantee survival as a spirit after death.' As I spoke, an involuntary chill ran right through me.

'Do you think there was anything in it?' Lilian asked.

I tried to bring the conversation back down to earth. 'If ever he did go to occult meetings, it would just have been to see what was going on, to find out what system they were using. Attending is not the same as participating.'

I said all this, and normally I would have meant it. That evening though, I was not entirely convinced, and I could see that Lilian was not entirely convinced either. Yet how wonderful it was for me, after all the years of being alone in my thoughts about G, suddenly to have someone to whom I could talk openly, someone in whom I could confide.

On the way home, twice, three times, I stopped to kiss her. I was surprised that she kissed nervously, greedily, eyes closed, unsteady on her feet, like a sixth-former. In between kisses we looked up at the sky. I kept on thinking about Aristotle's theory of the crystal spheres, and I told Lilian how sad I thought it was that his theory had turned out not to be true.

Lilian nodded and we kissed again. She was trembling. So was I.

Walking into G's house was like walking into a dream, a fairy tale. It was all so rich, so splendid, so harmonious, that it seemed more like the projection of an inner landscape than anything in the real world. There were beautiful, urn-like vases, vast mirrors, oriental rugs and tapestries, polished wooden chairs and tables with carved animals on their backs and armrests, paintings, drawings – everything seemed to be speaking to me, as a sign, yet I could not tell whether it was warm and welcoming or more like a dream, a warning.

In any case, the house engulfed us. Lilian was very quiet. As if led, more floating than walking, we went up to the room in the tower where she had slept the previous night. The room was in perfect Victorian style, with striped wallpaper, a writing-desk with tiny drawers, a tiled fireplace with a bronze carriage clock on marble mantelpiece, even polished brass implements for making a fire in winter.

I closed the door. I hugged Lilian close to me, then kissed her and then stood back so that I could admire her. She was beautiful.

She let me undress her.

When she was naked, she said, 'Do you know, no man has seen me like this before?'

I put my hands on her shoulders and looked into her eyes. Frankly, I did not believe it. Not at first. Then I noticed that there were tears welling. I did not know what to do.

'What about you?' she said.

I had the good sense to say, 'Let's not talk about that now,' yet all of a sudden the presence of Rosemary, though she was not there, filled the room.

'You see,' said Lilian, 'I wanted to keep myself pure until I got married. Today, I don't feel like that any more.'

What was she trying to do to me? I almost felt like apologising, suggesting maybe we should stop, right there, take a cold shower. Then I looked at her. She was so beautiful. There is such a thing as a point of no return, and we had gone beyond that. I reached for her hand and led her towards the bed, planning strategic gentleness, wondering what was and was not a good approach with a virgin (I had never slept with a virgin – I had forgotten that there were such things, though logically I supposed there had to be).

I stared into her eyes, kissed away her tears, drew her closer to me, ran a hand down her side, from her shoulder, over her breast.

I was about to lift her into bed. Just then the noises started. From downstairs. Tapping, then the sound of a door opening and closing, creaking on its hinges, then footsteps.

We both froze, just as we were.

My mind began to spin as it sought rational explanations. The doors had all been locked. Could a cat, or dog, or hedgehog have got in somehow? Maybe it was a burglar, someone who had heard of G's death and consequently expected to find the house unoccupied.

I tried to imagine the house as it was downstairs, dark, empty. From the look in Lilian's eyes it seemed the same thought had occurred to her: G. The night before his funeral. His presence...

Then all was still once more. I whispered to Lilian, 'What do you think...?'

Then there were more noises, this time unmistakably footsteps. The movement was up the stairs, slowly, towards us.

'Get dressed,' I said quickly. Lilian's face had suddenly turned quite white. All the blood had drained from her complexion. She pulled her clothes back on as fast as she could.

My mind was teeming. I tried to remember the karate I had learnt during the five sessions I had attended in my first term as an undergraduate. Then I began to worry in case the intruder was armed. I seriously considered hiding under the bed, but the light was on and that would be a dead giveaway.

Then there was Lilian. What if the intruder was some sort of pervert? Someone had to protect her. I entertained thoughts of myself as a medieval knight, deftly fighting off the baddies, rescuing the damsel in distress who would, as a result, be mine forever.

It was in this rather infantile state of mind that, as soon as Lilian was decent, I signalled to her to hide behind the wardrobe, and myself tiptoed out of the room into the darkness.

I could feel G's presence. There was a chill in the air. It was the chill of the grave. I felt cold sweat all over my body. I had never been so scared. But the worst was yet to come.

All was still again. I went down a few more steps. There was nothing stirring. I was beginning to wish I had not had so much to drink. I held on to the hope that maybe I had imagined it all. I could tell from the look on her face that Lilian had heard the noise, but I began to take consolation from the fact that we had not talked about it. Maybe she had interpreted the sounds in a different way. Perhaps I was jumping to conclusions.

I hesitated between going back up to her and carrying on down the stairs. I remember becoming acutely aware of the candelabras on the landings and the wall-lamps, which reached out from the walls like human arms.

I took a deep breath and went down a few more steps. I hesitated. There was a face in one of the pictures on the wall, a Victorian painting of a knight and a maiden, and the face looked uncannily like G's.

Then it happened. It sent a chill right through my body, from the top of my head to my toes. I swear my hair stood on end. I was shot through with terror.

There was a laugh. Not loud, but loud enough. A high-pitched laugh, which might have sounded hysterical if it had not been so familiar. G's laugh. But mad, otherworldly. Yet the moment it stopped I could no longer believe it.

Then I heard footsteps. This time the source of sound seemed to be moving away from me, down the stairs. My reactions were more courageous than I would have expected of myself. I ran down the stairs, switching on every light as I went.

But I was too late. I did not catch sight of the intruder, who had reached the bottom of the stairs. Then nothing. I suppose I was making too much noise myself. On the first-floor landing I stopped to listen. Could whoever, whatever it was just have disappeared? Then there were more footsteps, this time coming from behind me. I looked round to see Lilian, now fully dressed.

'Who was it?' she said.

'I don't know.' Her presence near me prompted a further display of bravery. I told Lilian to go back to her room and I carried on down. In spite of what I said, Lilian followed me.

After the laughter, I strained my ears but heard no further sounds, no door being opened, no window catch being tampered with. I moved rapidly from room to room, window to window, switching on every light as I went.

There was no sign of anyone. Yet there was no way out of the house, none that I could find. I checked again. All the doors were locked and all the windows were closed. I went to the front door and looked out. If a car had drawn away we would almost certainly have heard it. But there was no movement in the street outside.

I gave up searching, found Lilian, and we went together to the kitchen. For me it was comforting to be with her, but she was afraid, though like me she did everything she could not to show it. I admired her for that.

The kitchen was the most familiar part of the house to us. It was ours, the part we had colonised, filled with our own atmospheres.

It was the secure territory from which we had struck out to explore the rest of the house. Now it was the place to which we retreated.

I doubt that either of us could have managed to return to the bedroom as if nothing had happened. We needed to regroup, take stock. If our intention to make love had been in some way an act of colonization, exploration, an attempt to come to terms with our new situation, then it had failed. We had been beaten back.

I made a cup of tea. We remained silent at first. When we started talking, it was to try to convince ourselves that we had bravely seen off burglars. We confessed to one another how much the laugh had been like G's. Then we tried to convince ourselves that we had imagined it all, we must have imagined it, since there was no way out of the house.

We got round to talking about ghosts. Neither of us really believed in them, yet it was G's funeral the next day. Both of us had heard stories about fuses blowing in houses of the deceased on the day before a funeral, about doors swinging open, furniture seeming to move, footsteps being heard and so on. We wondered if we had just been subjected to a similar experience. I knew there were some who believed that sex, especially the taking of virginity, could open doors to the spirit world, because of the nature of the energy it generated. I should not have mentioned that to Lilian, because she began to look very shaken, very pale.

## XVI The Stricken Tower

We decided that we could not bear to stay in G's house any longer that night, and that we would pack some things together and go to my bedsit, which was only a few streets away. Before we went, I decided that I wanted to make sure once and for all that there was no door by means of which an intruder could have escaped.

I left Lilian in the kitchen and started to check every door on the ground floor. All the doors leading to the outside were firmly locked. Not satisfied, I tried all the cupboards and all the internal doors.

There was one door, which led to a large walk-in cupboard under the stairs, easily large enough to contain the sink unit and rack of shelves filled with shoes and cleaning equipment and still leave room for two or three people to stand comfortably. I had been there before but not paid too much attention to it. Now I noticed for the first time that there was another door at the far end of the cupboard.

On it was a tile bearing the picture of a bearded saint: San Saturio.

I switched on the light and pushed. The door gave easily. It was on a spring action and closed quietly when I let go of it. Here, after all, was a possible means of escape.

I propped it open. Stairs led down directly from the door. I found the light switch. There was a vast cellar.

I decided to explore, but first I wanted to tell Lilian. I ran back to the kitchen and explained. I really wanted her to stay in the kitchen, but she insisted on coming with me, so, hand in hand, with me leading the way, we made our way back through the hall and tiptoed down the stairs into the cellar.

Halfway down, I put my finger to my lips so that Lilian would not be surprised. I called out, 'Is anybody there?'

No answer.

We carried on down. The wooden stairs were ill lit by a single light-bulb. The wood creaked, but there was little dust. There were strange doodles on the plaster, here a moon shape, there a Greek letter, zodiacal signs and so on. At the bottom of the stairs I found another light switch.

The light was not brilliant, but the scene that it illumined could not have surprised me more. The cellar was vast; it covered the whole area of the downstairs of the house. It was divided into three sections separated by bare brick walls. We switched on the lights and explored each in turn.

In the first we found a laboratory. The walls were lined with bottles containing chemicals, and there were large numbers of ancient manuscripts open on the desk. In the centre of the room there was a large glass retort, which looked like a great, ungainly bird. In it was some chemical that seemed to glow by its own light, shining now one colour, now another. Beneath the retort was an iron gate, in which there were cinders from a wooden fire. The fire was out and had been for some time, though being no expert I could not tell for how long.

We gazed round in amazement. It was as though we had been transported back in time and had walked into the den of a Renaissance alchemist. I wanted to explore more, to see what G had achieved down here. To think that all the time I had known him he had secretly been practising alchemy, or something like it, took my breath away. I went to look at the manuscripts. I wondered if they had come from the college libraries and reflected that, yes, Oxford was the ideal situation for such a pursuit. There was everything: the knowledge, the tradition, the money, the secrecy.

I could have spent the night there, just reading through the manuscripts, trying to retrace what G had achieved so far. Things that he had said about alchemy came to mind. Once I remember him saying, 'There is no alchemy in the world of things, only in the text.' I wondered what he meant by that. There were certainly enough texts down there.

But Lilian wanted to go round the rest of the cellar. There were more surprises in store.

The second room, the largest, was empty but for a wooden stairway leading to a trapdoor. There was no electric light in this room, so it was half dark. I went up the ladder and pushed gently at the trapdoor; it gave immediately. I raised it and saw a ground level view of the garden, which was bathed in moonlight, like something out of a Victorian fairy painting. This would have been the way our intruder, if he had been flesh and blood, would have escaped.

I decided not to go out into the garden because I was not sure whether I would be able to get the trapdoor open again from outside. Besides, if anyone had used this exit, they would have been long gone by now.

From the vantage point of the ladder, I looked back down at the bare room beneath me, which contrasted strongly with the alchemical laboratory I had seen in the other room. It was only then that I saw, chalked on the cement floor, a Star of David and a pentagram. As my eyes adjusted to the gloom, I saw that round the edge of each of these there were symbols. At first they looked like planetary signs, but, when I got down from the ladder and studied then, I realised that they were not. I did not recognise them. But they made me feel very uneasy.

As I stared into the middle of the space defined by the chalked star, it was almost as if I could see something glowing. For some reason I started thinking very strongly of words I had glimpsed in the Walter text. It was as though I could hear the hero speaking some of the words I had read. In my mind's eye I even had a strong impression of what Walter would have looked like. But when I blinked the impression faded. I was sure it was only a trick of the light, of tiredness - unless, as I had read in certain old texts, the spaces defined by those chalked lines provided a different sort of exit – but from what, and for what?

Lilian had seen the star and the pentagram too. In the meantime, whatever was in the third room was occupying her attention even more. She was beckoning to me to follow her.

Again she took my hand. We were both nervous and there was comfort in the physical closeness.

The third room could not have been more of a contrast with the other two. If the first had been Renaissance, and the second medieval, this was certainly from the twentieth century. Because of the way the separate areas were laid out, I had not glimpsed inside, and had not guessed what this room would contain. There were banks upon banks of computers, screens, printers and keyboards. In one corner there was video equipment, some cameras and tripods, as well as lights, like in a photographic studio.

I turned to Lilian. She had noticed too: some of the equipment seemed warm, as though it might have been in use very recently, in the last hour or so.

On the far side of the room was a door. I opened it. Beyond it there was only a brick wall, which was oddly warm. The warmth made me think of hell.

Lilian was pointing to the large ON-OFF switch on the wall above the banks of screens.

'Shall we try?' I said.

'Why not?' she answered.

I pulled the switch and immediately all the screens in front of us lit up.

Some of the screens contained texts of G's, some he was working on currently and some old ones that I knew. On one of the screens was the text of the poems we had found. I tried the next file. Sure enough, these contained poems labelled from XIII onwards to XVI. I decided to work out how to print them out. The print code was easy enough, and soon the high-tech printer was whirring into action.

While the machine was printing, we looked at the other screens. Apart from the texts of G's work, there were other displays showing sets of figures and symbols I failed to recognise. I decided not to tamper with them; we would have the rest of our lives for that.

I took the poems and was about to read them, hoping that I might find in them some clue to what was going on, when Lilian said, 'Look!'

I turned towards her. Something had upset her, really upset her this time. I stuffed the printout of the poems in my pocket to read later.

Lilian was staring at a set of smaller displays above the computer screens. I had not yet taken in what was on them. Then I realised that each showed the various rooms of the house. In each of the rooms there must be video cameras hidden. One showed the kitchen, and was directed exactly at the table where we had been sitting. Another showed the hallway, another the room where the painting hung that looked like Lilian. Then there was each of the guest-rooms, including the room where Lilian and I had prepared to go to bed. The camera was directed at exactly the spot where the two of us had undressed.

'They... they must have seen me naked,' said Lilian. Her voice was distant, hurt.

'Come on,' I said, and took her hand to lead her up the creaky stairs to the hall. I left Lilian by the door and went up to get some things from the bedroom - clothes, a copy of the manuscripts we wanted to look at. I was particularly keen to make sure we still had the Walter text – perhaps it would provide some clue.

By the time I found Lilian again, she had rallied a little. She made an effort to smile as I took her arm and led her out of the house to cross north Oxford into the less salubrious area where my bedsit would welcome us to relative, if squalid, normality.

On the way, she did not talk. Or rather, I made an effort to tell her how much I loved her and she made an effort to smile. But really, both our minds were occupied with the events of the previous hour and trying to come to terms with them.

On the doormat as we entered the house there were two letters. I picked them up and we made our way up the lino-covered stairs.

## XVII The Star

We entered the shabby, claustrophobic room that contained, until two days ago, everything that I called my own. Lilian turned and smiled faintly at me as we entered the room, as if to say that she understood, that she too knew what it was to live like this.

I offered her something to drink, but she refused. I tried to talk, but she said, kindly enough, that she was tired and shocked and wanted to sleep.

I gestured to my bed. She lay down. I lay down next to her. She did not object. I tried to touch her, to undress her but she said, 'Please, not now.'

She was right. This was hardly the appropriate occasion. I felt desire for her, but I am able to control myself. Besides, I respected her and wanted to care for her more than anything else.

I lay on my back next to her and stared at the ceiling. I was trying to think of the right thing to say. I can't remember what I did say, but there was no reply. Lilian must have been exhausted. She had fallen asleep.

I lay still for a while. The light was still on. I snuggled against her, gently so as not to wake her, but sleep would not come.

Then I remembered the two letters and went to open them.

The first was from Arott and Marcanu. It looked boring and official. I supposed that it was the usual solicitor's letter confirming in writing what we had discussed. But I opened it to find that there was a note of desperation in the letter from Miss Marcanu. She said that there had been a major reversal in circumstances concerning G's will, that I should take no further action regarding his property, and that we must meet as soon as possible to discuss matters. She said that she would be at the funeral and that we should meet there.

Putting two and two together, I assumed that the inheritance was not mine, that I was back to square one.

The other letter was from Rosemary. Normally I would have recognised the writing and wanted to open it straight away; but this one was typed on her new word processor, envelope and all. Hardly inviting.

In tone it was a sweet letter compared with the one I had received two days ago. But the content was the final straw. She said how sorry she was that we had split up, that she had really liked being with me and that she was sorry she had lied to me. Then she said the real reason she did not want us to carry on was that she had been seeing G and had been to bed with him. She said she knew things would be impossible between the two of us after that, and that she was very sorry.

She was right. I would never have forgiven her. And I would never forgive G. Of course I was foolish ever to have introduced her to G, knowing G's reputation when it came to pretty young women and knowing how intrigued Rosemary would be by G's theatrical manner, good looks (she often told me that she was quite 'into' older men) and, of course, his money. But I was not taking the blame. Rosemary had done this to me, and I was furious with her – which was stupid considering I was with Lilian now, and much happier than I had ever been with Rosemary.

Then there was a PS, which read:'By the way, if you run into a pretty girl called Lilian or Iris or something floral, don't be taken in. She is an impostor. G mentioned her a lot, though I could never get to the bottom of what they were up to.'

I could not believe it. I looked at the sleeping girl on the bed, her long blond hair swirling about the pillow like a vortex of honey. What was I supposed to do? Challenge her? It would have been cruel to wake her. Besides, I loved her and already trusted her more than I would ever have trusted Rosemary. What could Rosemary have meant? How could Lilian be an impostor? Was Rosemary being malicious, spiteful?

All that would have to wait until the morning. I stared at the badly painted magnolia plaster walls of my bedsit and at my cheap posters stuck on with Blu-Tack. No, I was not going to sleep, so I took out the printout of the poems and the Walter text. All the time I kept on thinking about the odd feeling I had had in G's cellar. Then my mind began to perceive bizarre coincidences, between what had happened to me over the course of the last couple of days, the imagery in the poems and the Walter novel.

Then I started chuckling to myself as I remembered a theory of G's he called COST (Chance Occurrences Systematisability Theory). This was a complex mathematical theory (the maths of which I am ashamed to say I did not understand), which calculated the probability of the discovery of systems in chance events.

The theory is best illustrated by a simple experiment. Means are dreamt up to make random dots on pieces of paper. This could entail anything from throwing darts to getting a monkey to splash ink. Then the paper is fed into a computer, which is designed to devise mathematical systems to describe the layouts of dots. The computer nearly always finds solutions. Many of them are uncannily elegant and make one doubt that random distributions are actually possible. Moreover, there is a distribution curve. Apparently non-random distributions are more likely to be found where there are small and large numbers of dots. Only in between does it become harder for the computer to perceive patterns that are not there.

G believed that this distribution could be transferred to events in the real world. If one looks at systems containing very large or very small numbers of events, it is easier to perceive a pattern than if one has a moderate number. Thus it is easier to see a pattern in a war than a battle, and it is easier to describe the relationship between two people than between six. COST can be used to explain why such things as horoscopes and sociology seem to work. It is because they describe such large and complex patterns of events that almost any systematization of them will probably turn out to be true in some way.

There were implications in this theory with regard to the reading and writing of texts. Hence G's random sonnets. He wrote these using a technique he referred to as the *flèche proximale*. This meant throwing a dart at his bookshelves in order randomly to select a book. Then he would throw the dart at the page to get a random word. This process would be repeated until at last he found a word that would fit into the rhythm and rhyme structure of a sonnet.

The result would always seem nonsensical on first reading, but then, after a while, it seemed to hit on all sorts of allusions to something deeply meaningful, even self-referentially so. Here is one we wrote together during a supervision one day. The book randomly selected happened to be Roget's Thesaurus. We ignored initial anacruses for speed.

*Satisfactory vernacular*
*Pool works laid unbeaten holocaust*
*History stirred multicellular*
*Post wideawake possessor soldier false*
*Speculate abbreviation lake*
*Pugilism bibliolatry*
*Aggravate domestic certain make*
*Influence fort unbelieving be*
*Storage decrease obstacle town heinous*
*Thermodynamics multiplicand reptile*
*Nobleman inalienable capricious*
*Adjective inelegant nouns servile*
*Unpopularity justiciable*
*Firewalker ambition metrical.*

All these thoughts whirred round in my mind. It is only now, in retrospect, that I can fit them into a definite shape. Still, they seem bound up with that endless night, the bleakness of the white walls, the single light-bulb, the aching fatigue... the beautiful night sky through the window. Was I really part of some pattern, involving the poems and the book? I tried to believe there was no pattern, that there had never been one, that any meanings I perceived were of my own invention, an inevitable result, not of the way things are, but of the way I inevitably end up having to see them.

I was still too nervous to feel like sleeping. I changed position to sit on the floor. Lilian was still asleep, breathing gently. I picked up a pen and paper, closed my eyes and dotted randomly for a few moments.

I stared for a while. Then I saw a way of joining up the dots. By the time I finished I had an almost perfect Star of David.

I looked at the beautiful sleeping young woman on my bed. I reflected that perhaps it did not matter what course of events had led here; the important thing was that she was there.

I looked out of the window. There was a massive full moon shining through the branches of the lime tree. That was the last thing I remember before sleep came.

## XVIII The Moon

By the time I woke, it was already light. The first thing I became aware of was the pain in my neck. I had been sleeping on the floor with my head twisted awkwardly. There was a lark singing.

Then there was a feeling of darkness and oppression. I wondered for a moment why I was sleeping on the floor. Yes, Lilian. She would be there. In my room. I felt a sudden surge of desire – and love. I stood up with the thought of jumping into bed next to her.

The scent was there. So were the crumpled sheets. But she had gone. I stared, Orpheus-like, too late.

I went to the door, ran down the corridor, looked down the stairs. There was no sign of her. I felt stunned, numb, as the events of the previous day came flooding back to me.

For a moment I wanted to kill G. Then I realised I was being stupid and decided instead to boycott his funeral. Then it occurred to me that it would be an infantile and futile protest.

I could hardly believe Lilian had even been there. Like some mooning adolescent, I went over to my bed, on which she had slept. I knelt down and sniffed. It was her scent all right, heady, voluptuous, yet fresh and pure like the forests after spring rain. I fought back an involuntary pang of desire. To think I could have had her. Just hours ago...

Then I noticed a page of writing to the left of the pillow. It was her handwriting, only cramped, almost illegible:

Dearest Ian,
You will hate me for this. I woke before you and I read Rosemary's letter. I know what you must think of me. Especially after what happened in the cellar. It is better for it to end this way.
Best Wishes,
Lilian

I read the letter over and over, and the more I read the less I understood what she really meant. I kept thinking about what had happened when we were in the cellar the previous evening. There was an odd sense that the two of us together created some kind of alchemy. Then there was that sense of the other presence. Walter. I shuddered.

But her letter was utterly opaque. What had she meant?

## XIX The Sun

I stood in silence for a while. I shall not try to describe my emotions at that point. I was beyond surprise, beyond shock. One way of putting it would be to say that I felt confronted with myself. So much had been stripped away that all there was left was me, and I realised how little I actually liked myself. But there was no time for that. I decided to put off feeling anything until later, when I was less busy. At least Lilian was giving me the push more kindly than Rosemary.

In the meantime I looked at my alarm clock and realised that if I did not hurry I would be late for the funeral.

I possessed only one halfway decent suit, and that was pinstriped rather than black, the one I had used, unsuccessfully, to try to impress merchant bankers during my final year that I really did want to join their ranks. I also realised that I had no black tie. Why had I not thought of that the previous day when I had all the money and time in the world to buy myself something?

I never thought I would be so grateful to discover the old college tie I had bought in an ill-placed fit of enthusiasm about Oxford during my first term as an undergraduate. I put that on and inspected myself in the mirror. The result was appalling, but it would have to do. I combed my hair and was just about to go downstairs.

There were still images in my mind. Something to do with the Tarot. Processes of individuation.

Then I looked at my watch. Now I was almost bound to be late for the funeral. I stuffed the Walter text into the old briefcase I use because it is the right shape to strap on the back of my bike, rushed down the stairs to the back garden, rescued the bike from the landlady's cluttered shed, and started riding.

There is something inappropriate about riding to a funeral on a bike, especially if one is wearing an ill-fitting pin-striped suit – maybe because the display of fitness entailed by cycling contrasts strongly and rather indecently with the state of the person one is mourning. As I mounted the bike I decided that maybe the figure of eight formed by the wheels represented a cosmic system. Was the bicycle the ultimate 'wheel of fortune'? If I got there on time it would certainly be fortunate enough.

I enjoy riding my bike. It is a good time to think. Maybe it is something to do with the rush of oxygen to the brain. These are the thoughts that ran through my mind as I rode:

Firstly, I realised that I did not resent Lilian for disappearing on me. Oddly enough, my reaction to her letter was that I wanted to be with her even more. Whatever had passed between her and G, I missed her. I did not feel angry, or slighted, or embittered by the events of the last couple of days. It is odd, but I felt more amused than anything else.

After all, nothing had really changed. I was still the same person as three days ago. I had lost nothing - nothing except G, and his death was the result of an inevitable process of nature. After the way he had treated me with regard to Rosemary, I could hardly say that I would miss him beyond measure.

In the meantime, I was well. There was still time for me to make something of my life. I had been the victim of a couple of petty betrayals, but I would survive.

As to the events of the previous evening, no doubt there was some rational explanation. And if there was not, I would just have to settle for an irrational one.

I looked around at the magnificent buildings of Oxford, so majestic, so geometrically splendid. I reflected just how much this city, like so many beautiful cities, was a tribute to the philosophy of Neoplatonism. I thought of the nobility of the medieval idea that, in our actions and in our art, we humans are capable of reflecting and incorporating the divine Order, and that it is possible for us to build cities, cathedrals, churches, colleges, using systems of geometry that reflect the divine geometry, and imitate the Heavenly City, providing a foretaste of paradise, the mineral city that is the apotheosis of the vegetable bliss of Eden. Though maybe such ideas would have been lost on the designers of Milton Keynes.

But then, since the collapse of the Neoplatonic world order, those who had tried to breathe life back into its ideals were few and far between. Perhaps G had been one. Yet there I was, on my bike, hurtling through dingy streets of cramped houses on my way to his funeral.

## XX Judgement

I had never been to a funeral at a crematorium before. In fact, I had never been to a crematorium. So the one I cycled up to on the outskirts of Oxford was a shock. The chimneys were visible, but they were oh so harmlessly modern. I supposed in these days of market forces the dead are seen as clients purchasing an appropriate Last Exit. I thought of Auschwitz and supposed that, if you crossed that appalling place with a hypermarket, this is what you would get.

There were flowers everywhere in the car park. Ironically, there was nowhere for bikes, so I had to lean mine up against a wall. There seemed to be miles of brand new, modern brick walls to negotiate before finding an entrance. I began to fear going in by a wrong door, a works entrance of some kind, in case I saw anything I was not supposed to see.

At last I found the main entrance. I had to fight my way past pallbearers and mourners to get to the reception desk, which was, for some reason, behind glass doors that swung open of their own accord as one approached them. Or were they propelled by the invisible hands of the dead?

A very kind young American woman behind the desk told me she was working here temporarily and, smiling a very inappropriate toothy smile, led me through to the chapel.

I was late, as I had feared. The congregation was making a very decent attempt at the hymn 'Jerusalem'. One of G's jokes, I supposed. They were just taking up their arrows of desire as I edged my way into the back row. I bowed my head and pretended to pray. My overall impression was of the whiteness of the walls and the varnish of the wood, and the clinical, churchy smell, too musty to be a hospital yet too hygienic to be a church. There were far more people there than I had imagined there would be.

I looked round at the pews in front of me. There were lots of G's old cronies from the Senior Common Room at the college, men and some women with whom he drank, ate and was convivial, but most of whom he unashamedly despised.

At the very front was the coffin. It was a thing, an object. I could not imagine there was a real corpse in it, something that was once a human being.

Then the college chaplain started reading the usual passage from St John about the New Jerusalem, the New Heaven and the New Earth. I wondered, idly, if one day God actually will return and sort everything out. I remembered something I once saw written on a pub wall: '*God is not dead. He is alive and well. Rumoured to be working on a less ambitious project.*'

The chaplain's voice and presence were comforting enough, but I could not help wondering what he would have said if I had told him about the goings-on of the previous evening, the ghouls and hauntings in G's house.

The moment of the service I remember best was when the chaplain leant lovingly over the coffin and, so as to reassure the congregation of the certainty of a blissful afterlife, he said, 'G...' (long pause for effect) 'G is all right!' Only a clergyman, I thought, or maybe an academic, would ever dream of getting away with that.

There in the front row was Rosemary. She was easily recognisable from her long, flowing black hair. She seemed to have had it specially curled for the occasion. A part of me was looking forward to getting a better view of her in black. I was sure it would suit her figure.

We would have some interesting things to say to one another over the wine and finger food. I wondered if she could keep her temper. I knew that I could keep mine. *La vengeance est un repas qui se mange froid*, I thought in my most sophisticated French accent.

I looked everywhere for Lilian. It took me ages to register that she was the girl with plaited hair next to Rosemary. She looked so different in that black funeral hat. At first I thought she was someone much older. Suddenly I felt nervous. Was it just chance that she was sitting next to Rosemary?

At last the time came for the chaplain to pull the lever and for the coffin to disappear behind the neatly embroidered curtains, just like in the films. To accompany this final vanishing G had selected a movement from a late Beethoven quartet. It was the one entitled

'*Sacred Song of Thanksgiving in the Lydian Mode of One who is Recovering*'. It was music I loved, and the joke seemed moving, deeply significant, rather than in bad taste. Less crass than the chaplain, anyhow. And it was more original than 'The Lord is my Shepherd'. At last the lever was pulled and the coffin went off on its final journey. Thank God it was all so unreal.

Then there was the grace, and then silence as everyone tried not to be the first to get up and look round. People looked at each other without really seeing.

That is how he must have got away with it. I do not know how long he must have been sitting there, just to my left. Had I seen him when I came in? If so, I could not have registered him. Maybe it was because his form was so familiar I just accepted his presence. Or maybe one is so self-conscious under such circumstances that one takes in nothing of other people. Anyway, there he was, just feet away, wearing an immaculate black suit, sober dark tie, deep blue pocket handkerchief...

The smile was typically ironic, but warm and oh so forgivably boyish.

'How are you, Ian?' he whispered, leaning over, just as other people began to talk. I smiled uneasily. My first thought was that I was seeing a ghost. But I was curious, uneasy, rather than frightened. Then I wondered if he was perhaps not a ghost in the traditional sense, but some kind of being that never really dies.

'What are you doing here? I thought you were... ?' I stopped myself before saying anything too stupid.

'Quickly, outside. I've got some things to tell you before everyone else notices.'

No one else had noticed. Everyone was too engrossed in their grief, in consoling themselves, or at least in being seen so to do.

We stepped outside into the courtyard. There were all the flowers for the day's cremations. 'For Daddy', 'To a beloved wife' - cards with all the platitudes of death, where the ink was running now that it was beginning to rain. The mourners had all gone, leaving the neat displays of flowers propped on iron stands with the messages to be read by... by whom?

G said, 'You know the one about the difference between a

wedding and a funeral?' He left a pause of just the right length. 'At a wedding you get to smell your own flowers.' He grinned.

I was slow to react. There were so many different emotions pulling in so many different directions. I was pleased to see him alive. I was furious at so cruel and macabre a trick. In a way I was relieved that maybe now I would be able to get back to my normal life. In a way, too, I admired him for the sheer grandiosity of the deceit. It was an amazing gesture. When I came to write his biography...Yet I realised that that had been taken out of my hands now. I began to feel cheated once more. Then again I had the odd feeling of a meeting-place between two worlds, of an intersection at which I was curiously, and uniquely, present.

'I've got some things to tell you, Ian. First of all, I am sorry about all the tricks – Lilian and the charade last night. There was a reason for it all, but you won't understand yet. Before we go on, I have a couple of questions to ask you. Would you have accepted the offer?'

I hesitated.

'Go on,' he said, 'we don't have much time. They will all be out in a moment.'

'Yes.' I said, 'I had decided to.'

'What about Lilian?'

'Yes. Only...' He did not let me finish. It was as if he knew.

'What did you think of her?' I saw no reason to lie.

'She's lovely,' I said.

'I'm pleased. I was no good for her. Or rather, she was too good for me. You're the sort of man she needs. You were models for the Walter story. You saw the pictures, didn't you?'

I looked down at the tattered briefcase in which I had been carrying the script about the place. 'You did write it?' I asked.

'Only in a manner of speaking. You and Lilian were the mediums. You are probably beginning to understand by now.'

I did not know what he meant, but I was in such a state that I did not dare admit to not knowing. Surely either you write something or you don't. I thought again of Lilian's letter. What had she meant?

Before I had a chance to press him, he went on. 'By the way, I saw what went on between you and her last night thanks to the video camera. Don't worry. There are no records. It was all very touching... very touching.'

There was something in his tone that stopped me from losing my temper with him. He really did seem to be communicating under time pressure, as though he needed to make every word count. Maybe I was talking to a ghost after all. Maybe the cock was about to crow.

'Why are you doing all this? How...?'

'The death? It's all simple, if you've got money. There are still such things as corrupt Spanish officials, and the coroner out there is a good friend of mine. Arott and Marcanu was easy enough to set up. Miss Marcanu is an ex-lover, I'm afraid. Her real name is Tracy Smith. You ought to think more about anagrams.'

'But why?'

'Theatre. Besides, I had something to say. You'll see. Listen, before they all come out, I must tell you this. The will. It still stands. There is an identical copy with my real solicitor. The address is in my papers. One more thing before they all come. You will need it for a biography. The relevant documents are in my safe. My father was not Jewish like I told everyone. He was not killed in the camps. He was SS. The Allies killed him.'

(I recall now a line in one of his lectures: 'This is true of the whole of the West. We identify with the Jews. But we are descended from the SS.').

'What about the pentagrams, the things in the cellar?' I asked.

'Ask Walter,' he said.

I stared at him. He stared at me. I wanted to laugh, to cry, to hit him. The mixture of fury and affection was, I suppose, intoxicating.

'By the way,' he said. 'Here are the rest: He thrust some papers into my hands: the remaining poems, numbers XVIII to XXI...

By then people had started coming out of the crematorium. I had to admire what followed. It was a hilarious, if tasteless, spectacle. The sense of irony I experienced as I looked on would have been delicious had it not been so outrageous. At first G mingled inconspicuously with the mourners, saying the sort of things one says at funerals. How long it lasted before anyone reacted I do not know – probably only minutes, seconds, though it seemed a lot longer.

Firstly there was disbelief tinged with fear. Then, funnily enough, there was resentment, almost as if, after all they had been through, the people were disappointed that G was not dead.

G laughed this off. I overheard G saying something about it not being every day that one comes across a resurrection in the modern world. If he had not said it with such charm, it would have sounded appallingly messianic.

Then, of course, they all saw the funny side, and began to savour the trick that had been played on them. Everyone vied to appreciate it better than the others. Already, profound and meaningful remarks were being made, complete with show-off references to G's works, quoting chapter, verse and date of publication in the competitive way only academics at a funeral can.

Then it was realised that the atmosphere of supercilious frivolity which was setting in amongst the party was hardly appropriate considering where we were. It was hardly fair on the groups of mourners coming out of the other, parallel chapels, who were mourning people who really had died. So we all got in our cars, or in my case on my bike, and headed back to the college. I looked everywhere for Lilian, but she had already got a lift.

At the Senior Common Room buffet, G was the star of the show. He was at his most ebullient, his most charming, his most witty. He was so delighted that so many nice people should have come to his funeral and they were charmed that he was charmed, and they all talked about old times. It was a great love feast. He was like an emperor holding court, the Emperor Lazarus, the One who comes before the Antichrist.

No one saw him slip away into the toilets after an hour or so. Everyone was slightly drunk and talking so much *about* him, it went unnoticed that no one was talking *to* him.

I was in the midst of some frivolous conversation about how

the image of the SCR had changed in the last few years, how it was not long since all the chairs had been leather and there had been hunting trophies over the medieval hearth, skulls and antlers that had outraged the now socially dominant vegetarians. Since the advent of women fellows, the sofas, chairs and wallpaper all looked like they had sprung out of a Laura Ashley catalogue...

Then two shots rang out in rapid succession. How he managed to pull the trigger twice is a mystery, though it is not the sort of question one likes to ask. There was silence. Then one or two uneasy chuckles. I heard someone say, 'Where is G?', but then the conversation began again, no one having quite realised yet that they were pistol shots.

In the meantime the college butler and one of the kitchen staff did go through to find out what the noise had been. In the men's toilets they found G's body. He had shot himself twice in the temple. Part of the head had been blown away and the brains were a pulpy red mass, visible for all to see.

## XXI The World

My memory of what happened next is not clear. Perhaps it was at this point that I began to lose control. Not that I went mad or cracked up. Only odd things began to happen.

There was a commotion of people pushing and shoving, dropping wine glasses, shouting, trying to reach telephones. Then there was the sound of sirens.

I was one of those who went to the toilets, to the place where they found G's body. I was surprised by the smell. Almost a sweet smell. I don't know what impelled me to go; I suppose I had to be certain that he was dead. There was no doubt about that. It was G's body and there was no way that anyone could survive what G had done to himself. If only the eyes had been closed, the sight of the spilt brains, blood and meat-like stuff behind the face might just have been bearable.

I stumbled to a basin and was sick. Then there were policemen milling about all over the place. Someone helped me out of the toilet and brought me water, then sweet tea. Then I remember seeing G's body being carted away, covered with a blanket.

I sat there with Lilian and, foolishly, drank wine. I realise now that I must have talked too much, about G, about what he meant to me, about my past and problems I had had with my father... things that were quite out of place. It was as if dam gates had been blasted open and all manner of thoughts and feelings that I normally keep to myself gushed out.

Eventually I realised that she was quite annoyed with me. When finally I shut up, she made an excuse to leave and strode out.

I sat and stared for a while. More than anything else I felt exhausted now. Dizzily, I stumbled down the steps to fetch my bicycle from the undercroft. I felt numb. My immediate reaction to the incident was not anger, nor wry amusement, nor intensified grief, nor anything one might properly expect. Rather, it was an extreme and gnawing sense of emptiness.

For a while my mind was capable only of two thoughts. One was a vague annoyance at having to organise another funeral. The other was something G had once said and which reverberated more and more: 'The answer is not in the answer but in the structure.'

At the same time, it was as though the whole appalling incident must *mean* something, that it *would* mean something, if only I could think what.

As I rode through Summertown and past all the normal, workaday shops, I was torn between going back to G's house and back to the bedsit.

The odd thing was, of course, that nothing had changed. I had thought G was dead, and now he was. Surely there was nothing to it really.

Looking back, I can still almost feel that numbness, which haunted me, engulfed me like a cocoon I ached to burst out of. Part of it was shock. Part of it was indecision. After all this, could I really face taking over G's inheritance?

There were still some things of mine back at G's house. I decided to go there first, to try to get my bearings, to see how I felt. Again it was all so still, and the blossoms on the lime and birch trees in the front garden were beautiful. Only now, the thought of walking through that black-painted Victorian wrought-iron gate chilled me. It was as though the house was surrounded by a force field of some kind.

I pushed my bike over the gravel and up to the front door. Then, I saw there was something moving in the porchway. First there was shuffling, then something that looked like hair at head height, then a hand reaching out. At the very moment and in the very place I had least expected to see anyone, suddenly there was a figure, wearing black, coming towards me. It was Lilian.

'Sorry,' she said. 'I did not mean to be rude - at the funeral.'

'We were all a bit stressed,' I said. 'Are you coming in?'

She nodded. I fumbled with the key and we stepped into the hallway. I tried to put an arm around her, but she pulled away.

'What's the matter?' I said.

'Nothing.' She said '*Nothing*' in that tone which really means 'of course something's the matter, but since you are part of the problem you are going to have to do a lot of the running to drag it out of me'.

I went to the kitchen and made tea for us both. I needed time to collect my thoughts. I had not reckoned on her being there. I did not know what to say. I tried to compose myself, but my mind kept returning to the previous night, to the realisation that G had been there all the time, spying on us. I kept thinking that he would turn up again at any moment, to tell us that it had all been a tremendous joke and burst into cackles of laughter.

But I had seen the body. I knew he was dead. If he came back now, it would not be in body. Or else...

I handed Lilian her cup of tea and we sat down in the front room, the room where the portraits hung that looked so much like me and Lilian.

'What are you going to do now?' I asked. 'G said that the offer was still open. In theory nothing has changed.'

'In theory.' She looked really depressed, defeated.

I decided not to press her. 'There's no rush,' I said.

'I don't know,' she said. 'I actually don't think I can cope.' I sat next to her and took her hand. She did not pull away this time.

Then the phone started ringing. The timing could not have been worse. It was the undertakers. Yes, I said, I would take charge of arranging the next funeral. Yes, I was glad there was to be no autopsy. Yes, I could see no reason why the next funeral should not take place the day after tomorrow. No, I did not want to view their selection of coffins and the oak one would do just fine. Of course they could send the bill to me at this address.

No sooner had I put the phone down than it started ringing again. It was the chaplain. This time arrangements would be simple: announcement in the national press and a small gathering at G's house. The college was to supply the wine and some finger food, but G's estate would have to pay for it this time. Just the job.

I heard movement from the sitting-room and, during the course of these conversations, I was forced to watch helplessly while Lilian fetched her coat, cleared away the tea things and waited at the door for me to finish.

The chaplain was in one of his talkative moods and made a show of trying to comfort me, when really he was just trying to comfort himself.

Lilian was looking impatient and making signs that she wanted to leave. I, meanwhile, tried desperately to communicate that she should not go yet. Unfortunately, the chaplain mistook the urgency in my voice for emotion and sermonised all the more.

At last I got away from him.

'The funeral is the day after tomorrow, then?' said Lilian.

'Yes.'

'I've got to go now, Ian. I need time to think.' I tried to kiss her goodbye, but she turned her face away, so I was left clumsily kissing a mixture of cheek, hair and ear. As she walked away she did not look back.

If I had had the energy, I might have run after her, tried to explain. But there was nothing to explain. I returned to the sitting room we had just left and collapsed into an armchair.

When, eventually, I stirred myself, it was to fetch the Walter text and the poems, which I had been carrying about all day in the squalid briefcase.

The next forty-eight hours were painful for me. Though now I see they formed part of a pattern, at the time it seemed to me that I might have been going out of my mind.

In short, I read the text over and over again. I kept getting the impression that I had actually been present at a lot of the events described. I saw them so vividly, it was as though Walter's voice was coming, not from the written page, but from inside my own head.

There were so many things in the text that mirrored my own past. The passages about Walter's early years made me think of my own childhood, my mother's death, my father's remarriage, holidays I used to spend away with an aunt and uncle. The descriptions of Walter's school-days made me think of how I felt when I started at grammar school. Katrin was like my first girlfriend, and Walter's thirst for knowledge was just like my own when I was young. The monastery made me think of my early days at Oxford... and so it went on. Most striking were the sections about the dreams and visions, which were similar to experiences I have had, but never dared to talk about to anyone.

I became obsessed too by the way the sequence of events in the Walter text tied in perfectly with the development of ideas in the poems G had left for me. The poems seemed to be the clue, the key to everything. I stared and stared at them, until they became real, living things, inner landscapes that reflected and explained the Walter text, my own life, and even the events of the past few days. Hence the present chapter headings.

At the time, this was not just idle speculation. Each realisation came like a stabbing in the back of my head. It was as though I was losing myself. Sometimes I wondered if I actually was Walter. I would pace round the house, stamping, shouting, calling, singing Walter's songs. I would imagine I was Walter on Crusade, and I would throw myself on the floor, sobbing, digging my nails into my flesh. It was as though I was losing myself, losing my place in the present. The slightest stimulus would send me off into a different place and different time. I remember at one point turning on the radio, hearing a snippet of a Mozart string quartet, and *knowing* what the room was like where Mozart had composed it.

It makes me shudder to think of it now, but I would even go down to the cellar to try to call on Walter's spirit from within the pentagram. It was during one of these visits that I found the chalice.

I know that I drank quite a lot of G's wine over the next two days, and I helped myself to some food from the fridge. But I did not eat or sleep properly. And I did not wash or change my clothes.

By the third day I had forgotten about G's funeral, which was to take place in the afternoon. Fortunately, Lilian telephoned early in the morning to say that she was coming. I tried to explain what had happened to me, but she cut me short.

When she arrived a couple of hours later, she was very kind, helped me to get myself together and get some breakfast inside me, and encouraged me to wash and change. I tried to explain to her what had happened, about my past, about odd experiences I have had from time to time. I thought she would understand, given the conversations we had had, and which I have recorded above. But no. She tried to suggest that I was overwrought because of the strain of the suicide and all the other events of the past few days.

I admitted that I was overwrought, but I insisted that these experiences were real, more real than anything else that had ever happened to me. She just cut me - became merely efficient, distant, in retrospect probably scared.

She did most of the setting-up of food and drink, which was delivered by the college kitchen staff, and tidied up the kitchen, which I had left in an appalling state.

Just thirteen people turned out for the funeral, including the chaplain. I suppose that we all had the same feeling. Just as it had been unthinkable, three days before, that G would ever return from the dead, now it was impossible to stop looking over one's shoulder, just in case he turned up again.

I was grateful to see Rosemary. In many ways she was more sensitive than Lilian. She saw that I had been in a state and made a real attempt to be kind to me. She looked pale and haggard herself, and was not sarcastic once.

After the funeral a number of mourners said their excuses and made off. Rosemary and Lilian came back to the house with me, and five others, all close friends of G's from the university. It was a difficult occasion. There was Father Anthony, the college chaplain, Professor Fabrizzio, the politics don from Trinity, Professor Dreigross, a fellow medievalist from Worcester, Doctor Quentin, who was attached to the Psychology Department, and the American business tycoon James F. Franks, who had worked together with G on a number of fund-raising projects for the university.

We stood in an awkward half-circle in the room where the Saracen shield hung, and chatted stiltedly. I was embarrassed, for some reason, by the fact that I was in the same room as a girl I loved and a girl I had loved. Matters were made worse by the fact that the older men were obviously charmed by the two young women and found it hard not to pay too much attention to them. James F. Franks was particularly shameless in flirting. Now, in retrospect, it all seems quite amusing.

Hardly any wine was touched and the mourners were, thankfully, quick to depart. Rosemary went first, then the chaplain, then the others – but only after insisting that they would call in the next day or so to see how I was getting on.

Lilian stayed to help clear up. She was calm, kind and efficient.

After everything was in order, she said, 'I'm sorry, Ian. I know you want me to stay. But there are two things you have got to understand. The first is that I am not what you think I am. I was acting on orders from G all the time. He wanted me to lead you on and I did. Even when we were in the restaurant, all the stuff he got me to learn by heart. It was all a set-up – for your benefit. Though I never expected him to kill himself. Now I've got enough troubles of my own. I like you, Ian, and I hope we can stay friends. But I don't love you and I'm certainly not going to hang around to be your mental nurse.'

I thanked her quietly. What else was there to say? I said I was sorry too and went with her to the door. I did not try to kiss her and I did not watch her walk away.

That afternoon I started looked at the Walter text again. I was calm now. The experiences I had had were all with me still, but I knew now that I could control them. I was in charge.

I went to the music room, looked through the CDs and found one of Walter's music. I put it on at top volume, then sat alone in the kitchen, chomping my way through the finger food and emptying the bottles of wine that had been opened but not finished. I did not feel self-pity, for a change; rather, I was engulfed by the reassuring sense that I did not matter.

I kept thinking of the Cathars who had marched so willingly into the flames after they had been tried for heresy. Then I thought about the suicide of Walter's father, Uqhart's burning. I thought I saw a pattern, though nothing I could put into words.

I took a recorder from the music room and played through the melodies from some of Walter's songs. I decided to go for a walk, and put the recorder in my pocket.

It was wonderful. Oxford in the spring. I walked through the colleges, through the Meadows, down by Magdalen Bridge. Then I realised it was Saint John's Day. Of course it had to be. So I walked back up to north Oxford again and out on to Port Meadow to watch the sun go down. It was lovely. And I had never enjoyed being on my own so much in all my life.

When the sun had set, I sat by the river and watched the mists swirl. I took out my recorder and once again played through all the Walter songs I could remember. As I did so, I allowed all the events, thoughts and ideas of the last few days to form patterns before my eyes.

By midnight it had turned quite cold, although it was summertime, and the grass and buttercups were wet with dew. There was an odd, otherworldly warmth, all the same. I remembered the various legends about Saint John's Day; how if a virgin culled Saint John's wort and placed in under her pillow she would dream of her future lover. I thought too about all the legends involving mistleberry and the ritual slaying of kings and priests. It occurred to me that this scene would have been identical for hundreds, thousands of years. These stars, this grass, the buttercups, the swirling mists, the river flowing past, motionless and moving, like time.

The mists became quite thick; eventually it was not possible to see far at ground level. Yet the stars were visible, dotted here and there behind the wispy clouds.

Still I played, and the sounds of Walter's songs on the recorder soothed my shattered nerves.

I thought continually about the Walter text, how he had stared into just such a river when he heard of his father's death, how he had looked up at the stars and dreamt of Aristotle's crystal spheres that first night he made love to Hildegunde, and then, that night before he set off for Venice, how he had gazed up at Aldebaran, the eye of Taurus... All that idealism leading to the historical calamity of Constantinople in 1204, one of the sickest jokes in history.

I thought of the irony, that for all he thought he was resisting the Brotherhood, he was really part of them.

G's poems were constantly in my mind, the figure of eight of Walter's chart. Then there were G's words: *the answer is not in the answer but in the structure*. Maybe that was it. The figure of eight, the eternal return, the self-referentiality of the two nothings which formed the sign for sterile stability and also the sign of eternity.

Over to my right there was a clump of trees. The mist curled round it like a giant spiral. For a moment there seemed to be a silver glow. Then there was darkness again. Then, just in front of the trees, I saw a figure, with a mop of dark brown hair, wearing a dark red tunic and russet red breeches, carrying what looked like a lute. And there, just a few yards further, there was a girl, with long blond hair, wearing a blue dress. When I looked back, the male figure was the same but older, now with grey hair and smiling, wearing an Augustinian habit. The girl had gone.

It was not a ghostly haunting. There was no chill but rather a feeling of peace, of warmth.

They could only have been there for a moment. Or rather, their presence was vivid in the way that a memory is vivid.

That was the moment when I really understood what it meant to move through time, when I decided to carry on working at G's papers, to accept his offer, to become his successor. In short, that is how I came to accept the chalice, and to become a member of the Brotherhood of Prayer of Charlemagne.

# APPENDIX II

## The Poems

✟

### The Fool

High on the cliff the Fool will stand,
A White Rose clutched in his Left hand:
And in his Right, the Net – he'll try
To catch the Golden Butterfly:
Nearby the Black Dogs bark – with joy
They start to chase the hapless boy,
Whilst down below in the Abyss
Sirens are waiting with their Kiss.

### I The Magus

At Once he is the Magus, clutching Fire
Stolen in Fennel stalks from Heaven. Fear
Of Retribution drives the youthful Seer
To seek the Chalice, which will never tire
Of yielding Blood; the Lance which pierced Christ's side,
The Sword that never fails in mortal fight,
The Sacred Salver, which tells wrong from right...
He seeks such powers as can only hide
The Truth – and yet Eternity hangs low

Above his head; he thinks he has grasped Life,
Claiming Jove for Father, Myrto for Wife.
Yet round his feet the Rose and Lily grow.
He grasps the Tree where power and beauty flow –
Yet all it bears is pain, deceit and strife.


## II High Priestess

He sees, translucent in his lunar sight,
Between the cloudy pillars of the sky,
The Queen of Ancient Days, Princess of Night,
Forgetfulness breathed in her starry sigh,
Enthralling, wooing with her sad half-smile,
In gold-red angel garments brightly clad,
Enthroned above the Earth's deep Peristyle,
Queen of the Wise, Protectress of the Mad,
She who could not have touched his heart too soon:
More bright than fading magic of this World,
Queen of the Silver Star, the dark New Moon,
Bearing the sacred rune-scroll half unfurled.


## III The Empress

Next he confronts the Empress, Queen of Life,
With flowing robes, with sceptre, angel throne…
The One subtracted, Three returns as Wife;
The young man knows her, yet remains alone.
Her world is the beguiling crescent moon:
He senses, yet cannot obey her law.
The shield she holds bears the unyielding rune:
The Yellow Eagle, Ancient Bird of War.
And yet her absence holds a harmony,
A kinder music drifting from above,

THE RESURRECTION OF G

Which hints that it will be his destiny
One day to become worthy of her love.
Then he'll no longer wander fruitlessly:
The Eagle will have turned into a Dove.


## IV The Emperor

When dreams yielded him all their power,
When every sheaf had bowed its head,
There emanated from his Tower
Involuntary influence and dread.
His was the pit, the prisoners' cries,
And yet he feared vengeance from blood
His sword had shed; he feared the sighs
Of lonely spirits, those which brood
At dusk; all that was not his own
He feared. Sternly, sceptre in hand,
With eagle-shield and heart of stone,
He ruled for ruling's sake. His land
Grew barren round his Ram's head throne:
Once fertile lands all turned to sand.


## V Hierophant

Therefore, beyond the Four he sought the Five,
Yearning for Keys to Laws above his own:
He sought the binding Powers to bring alive
His empty loves, the futile seeds he'd sown.
He found the Hierophant with Triple Crown,
Cloak of red blood, the Two kneeling before,
Hermes thrice great, the Master, eyes cast down,
His Triple Cross spelling the Ancient Law
Of Spirit, Ether, Earth. His words were Fire.

As quintessential Teller of the All,
He named, yet could not contradict the Liar:
He understood, yet could not fight the Fall.
To know the Phoenix leaves us wanting more:
To turn to Love, to resurrect the Lore.


## VI The Lovers

Beneath cruel Antares, the Lover stands
Between two women – one, hair saturnine,
Dark as Desire, wears a red cloak, her hands
Reach down towards Illusion's sensual sign:
The other woman, golden haired and bright
With love for him, her hand upon his heart,
Has learnt to bind Desire to Good and Right:
Her gold crown is the token of her art.
Above the three, blindfolded Eros flies,
A messenger of Love, of the Ideal.
Between the golden crown and carnal sighs,
Freedom and Sense, Appearance and the Real,
The Lover cannot choose just as he likes –
All will depend on how the Arrow strikes.


## VII The Chariot

He cannot lose: he thinks himself triumphant,
And like a Dionysian charioteer
Fresh from a victory feast, or Jove exultant,
He forges on his self-obsessed career,
Pleasing no man or woman but himself,
Master, not of true Nature but of Dice,
Not of true Light, only of empty wealth,
Success no virtue, but a hollow vice.

Despite his white hair, sceptre, blue cuirass,
The Nature, which he thinks he dominates,
In fact drives him. He thinks he's served by Mars,
Yet he is Mars' sublunar puppet.
Fates strike him down, for Triumph cannot last.
He seeks beyond the world where dice are cast.

## VIII Justice

He turns to Themis with her golden Scales,
The Titaness who dethroned Mother Earth
At Delphi, tries to glimpse beneath her veils,
To see her face, its radiance, her worth.
He sees nothing. He tries to grasp her sword,
Serve her through force, yet then she disappears.
He speaks. She flees before the spoken word.
The more he seeks her out, the more he fears
He's lost her. She is nowhere in the din
Of this world. All that he can do is wait
And try to find her by looking within
For new Dimensions of the Cubic Eight.

## IX Hermit

The Hermit with his staff and starry light,
Which shines like gold against the deep blue sky,
Treads on across the white wheat, through the night,
Not heeding serpents, or the wild dogs' cry.
His face glows, lily-like. He turns away
From daytime things, from money, power and love;
He seeks in silence, darkness, for a way
To distil spirit powers, below, above.
Yet Saturn is the first god to be seen,

His glass guarding the world with time and sands –
Yet soon the gods of Triumph and of Spleen
Drag his poor soul across their vast, dark lands:
Outside him peace and harmony both breathe,
And yet within, lusts, pains and sorrows seethe.

## X The Wheel Of Fortune

A lying girl now leads the King
To sit high on a massive wheel:
She says the whole world, everything,
Is his, and subject to his will.
He looks around: all that he sees,
Woods, lakes and forests, far and wide,
Are subject to his royal decrees –
There is no limit to his pride.
A rosebush grows beneath the wheel.
A monkey climbs behind the King.
The King's royal sight begins to reel:
Something has caused the Wheel to spin.
More apes now climb in front; behind,
A fish-dog monster creeps with stealth:
Now Terror strikes the poor King blind
And down he plunges with his wealth –
He falls into the vast abyss
Losing more than he ever won.
A gold light flickers like a kiss,
Like light reflecting from the Sun.

## XI Fortitude

The first beast that he meets looks like the Lion
Whose jaws are held apart by Fortitude,

The daughter of the flaming sword, who's union
With the appalling beast he misconstrued,
Perceiving in it tension, discord, strife.
Had he been rash enough to kill the Beast,
He would have had to bring her back to life,
Or be excluded from the Lover's Feast.
At first the Beast looks like the Evil One,
And yet her mane might be the burning Sun.

## XII The Hanged Man

The lover hangs above the old abyss
Whilst weeping moon obliterates the sun,
The dead will moan and meteors will run
A wild ungoverned course with fateful hiss;
And he will groan for death's most sacred kiss
Before his fear-struck agony is done,
And horrifying emptiness will stun
His being into pain-racked lifelessness -
And then the old Ash Tree will hang with frost
Until the wakening of the Shepherd King,
Whose ancient soul was torn, whose lifeblood lost,
Whose pipe will play, whose gentle voice will sing,
That he has learned the runes and paid the cost
Of turning lifelong Winter into Spring.

## XIII Death

The bodies cease to writhe.
Death's Angel with his scythe
Rakes in their bones,
Bleached white as stones.
All men are One in death

As they await new flesh:
That Day they'll be
Still One, but free.


## XIV Temperance

To save him from the Eagle and the Lion,
From Cup to Cup and back the angel pours
The Water, which she transforms into Wine,
Distilling Excess and distempered Laws
Into a Harmony where all things sing
With the true balance of the natural world;
And she will help him bear the suffering
And fear of the next rune to be unfurled:
The yellow-blue clad Angel looks from heaven:
About her feet grow yellow irides –
On Earth her sign is Fourteen, two times Seven.
Her flowers shake in the frigid, evil breeze.


## XV Devil

The grimace now is of the Evil One,
Baphomet, half goat, half hermaphrodite,
Bat-winged and horned, whose drug, Satyrion,
Obscenely distorts Knowledge, the True Light,
All that is good. He is the false black Sun.
Two howling demons are chained to the plinth
On which he stands triumphant, their ropes spun
From Hemp, binding as Deceit's dark absinth.
Lord of the Gates of Matter, winged shaman
Or fraud, is he the Dragon of the Threshold,
Of hopeless Hell? Or is he, more like Pan,
Like Lucifer, the bearer of the old

Light, the old Energy, which must be known
Before its source, the True Light, can be shown?

## XVI The Stricken Tower

The Lightning strikes the Tower, men hurtle down,
Amidst the flaming rocks spinning to Earth;
The top of the Tower tumbles like a crown.
No Knowledge he possessed had any worth:
All was deceit. If the Millennium comes
It will be thus, a firebrand in the night,
Which burns to chaff all familiar wisdoms –
Then what we learn anew, we'll learn aright.

## XVII The Star

Beyond the Stricken Tower shines the Star.
She heralds spring rain like the Pleiades;
Like Aldebaran, eye of Taurus, far
Beyond the darkness of the Earth, she sees
The virgin lover pouring fresh blue streams
Of water, and sheds light into the void
Of Consciousness, where that which merely seems
Has finally, forever, been destroyed.
The water mingles with the lush green earth.
Desire and Knowledge now at last are one:
Amor, the Nightingale, sings of rebirth.
And Ideal flowers grow where pure waters run.
She is the Reborn Priestess, lover, Queen,
The One with Sixteen rays, the Seventeen.

## XIII The Moon

Within the drugged blue waters of the soul,
The Scarab stretches red claws to the Moon:
Dogs of fleshly desire begin to howl –
Sickly the minstrel's lute plays out of tune.
The moon weeps silent rays over the towers
Where loved ones waited for deceits to pass,
Hoping for realignments of the powers
To be dreamt of in Signs beyond the Stars.
Yet no true source of true Light shines in the skies:
The Moon sheds watery, reflected light
Of Melancholy – last, greatest of lies.
As Cancer, brilliant in the summer night,
Greets the sweet harvest home, it is Earth's Green
The Scarab yearns for: twice nine, the Eighteen.


## XIX The Sun

Beneath the Sun dance a young girl and boy,
Wearing blue scarves, desire in innocence:
Their hair is white with purity, no sense
Of age or guilt can undermine their joy.
Now the Eclipse is over, the pure light
Of God, the Intellect, shines on the pair:
Only as children can these Ancients bear
The brilliance, power of the Seers' Sight –
Nineteen, two sevens balanced, and the five,
The energy that hitherto was sealed
Within all things becoming and alive,
At last to living vision is revealed.
And yet some fear, who do not know Him well –
This fiery Sun will burn like fires of Hell.

## XX The Judgement

The Angel blows his Trump. The dead arise
Out of green tombs, once more to breathe the air.
They are not judged. Their glory is the prize
Of being. All they ever *were*, is there.

## XXI The World

The perfect nought obscured by Fortune's Wheel
Is wreathed in laurel, both funereal
And glorious, forming a bond and seal:
Outside are four Signs, the ethereal
Eagle, the Bull, which signifies the Earth,
The Lion, whose element is Fire, the Angel
Of spiritual waters: each a Gospel.
Within the wreath, the mirror of rebirth,
He is Lover and Loved, Hermaphrodite,
The Seeker and the Sought, the soul and Christ
The Union of the lowest and the highest,
Where Light is Harmony, and Music Light,
And in this harmony, where all powers rule,
He finds again the Chalice of the Fool.